O9-BTO-211

Praise for
Without a Trace

"Suspense, action, mystery, spiritual victory—Colleen Coble has woven them all into a compelling novel that will keep you flipping pages until the very end. I highly recommend *Without a Trace*."

—JAMES SCOTT BELL,
Author of *Deadlock* and *A Higher Justice*

"Colleen Coble hooked me on page one, then reeled me into her story with a cast of characters I can't wait to meet again, a plot so intricately woven that I marveled at its construction, and a mystery that kept me guessing till the final pages. *Without a Trace* is a page-turning, eye-misting, don't-miss-it masterpiece!"

—DEBORAH RANEY,
Author of *A Scarlet Cord* and *Beneath a Southern Sky*

"*Without a Trace* is a tautly plotted who-dun-it with a wide-ranging cast of characters that captures the essence of small-town America. Colleen Coble brings Michigan's Upper Peninsula to life and gives you a whiff of what it's like to own a Search and Rescue dog."

—RANDALL INGERMANSON,
Christy award-winning author of *Oxygen* and *Premonition*

"*Without a Trace* offers an intriguing mystery about a disappearance and a murder. But the story is much more than a simple who-done-it as it delves deep into the emotional mysteries of loss, betrayal and guilt, and the redemptive power of God's love. A powerful beginning for a new mystery series."

—LORENA MCCOURTNEY,
Author of *Whirlpool, Riptide* and *Undertow* (The Julesburg Mysteries)

"Colleen Coble spins a story of unsettled relationships, deceit, and the frustrations of seeking the lost into a warm tale of the hope of healing."
—JANET CHESTER BLY
Author of *Hope Lives Here*

"I couldn't turn the pages of *Without A Trace* fast enough. The suspense built with each new chapter, right up to the breathless conclusion. This is a series readers won't want to miss!"
—ROBIN LEE HATCHER,
Best-selling author of *Firstborn* and *Speak to Me of Love*

"Colleen Coble draws such rich characters, you have to force yourself not to pray for them! Her descriptions of the frigid Michigan UP made me shiver. This page-turner kept me up at night, and anxious for book two in the series."
—KRISTIN BILLERBECK,
Author of *What a Girl Wants*

"*Without a Trace* is an absorbing, page turning read with well defined characters and all the excitement and apprehension surrounding Canine Search and Rescue. A great read!"
—LORI COPELAND,
Author of Brides of the West and Morning Shade series,
Co-author of the Heavenly Daze series

Without a Trace

Other Books in the
Rock Harbor Series:

Beyond a Doubt
Into the Deep (available October 2004)

Without a Trace

COLLEEN COBLE

WESTBOW
PRESS
A Division of Thomas Nelson Publishers
Since 1798

visit us at www.westbowpress.com

©2003 Colleen Coble. All rights reserved. No portion of this book may be repro-
duced, stored in a retrieval system, or transmitted in any form or by any means—
electronic, mechanical, photocopy, recording, or any other—except for brief quotation
in printed reviews, without the prior permission of the publisher.

Published by WestBow Press, a Division of Thomas Nelson, Inc., P.O. Box 141000,
Nashville, Tennessee 37214. Published in association with Karen Solem, Spencerhill
Assoc., P.O. Box 374, Chatham, NY 12037.

Scripture quotations are from the Holy Bible, New International Version (NIV).
Copyright ©1973, 1978, 1984, International Bible Society. Used by permission of
Zondervan Bible Publishers.

Library of Congress Cataloging-in-Publication Data

Coble, Colleen.
    Without a trace / by Coleen Coble.
        p. cm.
    ISBN 0-8499-4429-5
    1. Upper Peninsula (Mich.)—Fiction. 2. Missing Children—Fiction. I. Title.
    PS3553.02285W57
    813'.6—dc21

                                                                            200301

    0150

Printed in the United States of America

05 06 07 08 RRD 11 10 9

For my wonderful, supportive family:
my husband, David, my son, David Jr., and my daughter, Kara.
I love you all very much!

Acknowledgments

The joy of working with Ami McConnell, my editor at W Publishing Group, has been a dream come true. Thanks for believing in me, Ami! Her fabulous eye for character and my editor Erin Healy's plot suggestions helped mold the story in many ways. Thanks, gals!

Every writer ought to have an agent like mine. Karen Solem sent me back to the drawing board when it was needed and encouraged me when I wanted to crawl into bed and pull the covers over my head. Karen, thanks for the handholding and the equally necessary swift kicks! I thank God for bringing you into my life.

Kristin Billerbeck and Denise Hunter read and reread every word I write. Thanks, friends, for all the hours you put into helping to make my writing better.

My husband of thirty-two years, David Coble, helps keep me straight on time lines and other necessary things. Thanks, honey, for your faith inand constant prayer for me.

My "grandpup" Harley was the inspiration for Samson. His constant love and happy smile for all of us exemplify the very best of canine friendship.

A special thanks to Harry E. Oakes Jr. Harry founded the International K-9 Search & Rescue Services & Consulting Firm. He and his team are often called in when amateur teams fail to find missing persons. Harry sent me all kinds of training materials and sample cases. His information was invaluable. Harry's dog Ranger was the first of Harry's SAR dogs to hold an International SAR Dog Record of 370 missions with 157 documented finds. Ranger was the only SAR dog to win the Higgens and Langley Swift Water Rescue Award. He jumped into the Pacific Ocean and saved a drowning child while Harry jumped in and rescued her brother. Ranger died in 1994, and Harry's current award-winning dog, Valorie, is an eight-and-a-half-year-old Border collie–schipperke-mutt mix. Valorie was saved from the dog pound at age five months and trained for SAR. She has documented 2,348 missions with 924 documented finds and assisted finds of people, pets, suspect identifications, and evidence. This is a world record. Thanks, Harry! I owe you!

And, finally, my thanks to Pete Connor, Yankee Aviation Services in Plymouth, Massachusetts, for answering my questions about small planes. Thanks for your patient answers, Pete!

I fled Him, down the nights and down the days;
I fled Him, down the arches of the years;
I fled Him, down the labyrinthine ways
Of my own mind; and in the mist of tears.

—"The Hound of Heaven"
(FRANCIS THOMPSON, 1859–1907)

1

It was days like this, when the sun bounced off Lake Superior with an eye-squinting brilliance, that Bree Nicholls forgot all her qualms about living where the Snow King ruled nine months of the year. There was no other place on earth like the U.P.—Michigan's Upper Peninsula. With Keweenaw Peninsula to the north and Ottawa National Forest to the south, there could be no more beautiful spot in the world. The cold, crystal-clear waters of the northernmost Great Lakes stretched to the horizon as far as she could see.

But she'd never find those kids by focusing on the seascape. Pressing her foot to the accelerator, she left the lake behind as she urged her old Jeep Cherokee forward along the rutted dirt track. Bree's best friend, Naomi Heinonen, steadied herself against the door's armrest and looked over her shoulder at the two dogs still safely confined in their kennels. The Kitchigami Wilderness Preserve lay to the east, past Miser, a drive of only fifteen miles or so, but on this washboard road, it took longer than Bree liked.

"Don't kill us getting there," Naomi shouted above the road noise.

Bree didn't reply. These lost children weren't some vacationers without ties; they were residents of Rock Harbor, two of their own. And night would be here soon. If Naomi were driving, her foot would be heavy on the accelerator too. The preserve was a formidable tract that could swallow up two kids without a trace.

The wind churned autumn's red and gold leaves in eddies and blew them across the road like brightly colored tumbleweeds. Equally colorful trees crowded the hills like giant banks of mums. The U.P. in autumn was Bree's favorite time, except when ever-shorter days put strangleholds on their search efforts.

M-18 headed on east, but Bree made a sharp turn onto Pakkala Road, which would take them into a heavily forested area. In the spring, motor homes and SUVs pulling campers plied the road on their way to experience some of the last wilderness left in the Midwest. Today the road was practically empty.

"Fill me in on what we know," Bree said.

"Donovan O'Reilly reported Emily and Timmy missing three hours ago. They were on some outdoor nature thing with their school," Naomi said.

Bree knew Donovan O'Reilly—he owned the local Ace Hardware store. His wife had left him and the kids nearly two years ago, and now his eyes had a haunted look, as though he wondered what fate would hand him next. Bree often stopped by Ace to pick up supplies for the ongoing renovation of her lighthouse home, and a friendship of sorts had developed between them.

"One of the students said she heard Emily talk about seeing a raccoon," Naomi continued, "so that might be what caused the kids to wander off. It's not much to go on, but they've started searching." She chewed on her lip. "You remember Timmy has diabetes? I wonder when his shot is due."

"I was thinking about that." Bree imagined Donovan was out of his mind with worry. "Donovan asked me out last week; did I tell you that?" she asked. She'd been tempted to tell him yes. Her lighthouse echoed with silence, but she had realized it wasn't fair to use someone like Donovan to ward off her loneliness. "I said no, of course."

Naomi didn't reply, and Bree looked at her curiously. "What? You don't like him? Didn't he used to be your brother's best friend? You probably know him and the kids pretty well."

A flush moved to Naomi's cheeks, and she looked out the window. "That was a long time ago. I only see him at the hardware store now, and I like him fine. Why did you say no?"

"I'm not ready. Maybe I never will be." Bree tapped the steering wheel with impatient fingers, wishing the Jeep could go faster over the bumpy, rutted road. Instead, she slowed and turned onto the access road that would take her back to the campground parking lot.

As she pulled in, Bree saw people fanning out in a search grid. There was an assortment of searchers, ranging from teenagers like Tommy Lempinen to professional types like Inetta Harris, who was still dressed in her business suit. When one of their own was threatened, Rock Harbor residents pulled together.

Bree and Naomi got out, attached leashes to the dogs, and shrugged their arms into their ready-kit backpacks, fully outfitted with first-aid kit, small plastic tarp, energy bars, flashlight, flares, bug repellant, towelettes, compass, Swiss pocketknife, radio, topographic map of the area, canteen, sunglasses, sunscreen, and every other item one was likely to need on a search. A young woman in a brown National Park Service uniform was Bree's first target.

"We're the Kitchigami K-9 Search and Rescue team," Bree told her, though that much was printed on the bright orange vests that both the women and the dogs wore. "I'm Bree Nicholls. Who's in charge?"

The young woman pointed toward a group of people nearly hidden by a stand of sycamore. "The lead ranger is over there." Bree looked and recognized Donovan's ink-dark hair among them.

Bree and Naomi headed toward the group. Donovan saw Bree and broke away. Pain contorted his handsome features. With his black hair and dark blue eyes, Bree had always thought he looked a bit like Pierce Brosnan, though today he was too upset and pale to carry off the James Bond sang-froid.

"Please, you've got to find the kids!" His hands trembled as he thrust two small jackets toward her. "They don't even have their jackets on, and it's supposed to get to near freezing tonight." The torment in his eyes spoke of his fear of loss more clearly than his words. "Timmy's shot is overdue now."

His voice quavered, and Bree put a comforting hand on his arm. She knew the anxiety he felt. "We'll find them, Donovan. The dogs are well trained, and Samson has a special radar for children."

His head snapped up as if mounted on a spring. A dawning hope filled his face. "I'll come with you."

How well Bree remembered that overwhelming desire to help. The waiting was the hard part. When her husband's plane went down, taking their son and all her hopes for their future with it, she had felt a crushing need to *do something*. In her case, there had been nothing to do but try to move on. With any luck, Donovan probably would not be in that situation.

She shook her head as she took the jackets from his hand. "You have to stay close to base, Donovan. The kids will be scared when we find them, and you'll need to be in a position to get to them quickly when they're found. Try to stay calm. We still have several hours before sunset. We'll find them."

Donovan nodded, but his gaze flickered from Bree to Naomi with a naked appeal in his eyes. "I want to do something."

"Pray," Naomi advised.

His eyes squeezed shut. "I started that as soon as I learned they were gone," he whispered.

Naomi's answer to everything was prayer. Prayer had done little for Bree's own desperate pleas. What use was a God like that?

"Let's go," Bree said.

As they approached the tree line, a slim, feminine figure stepped out of a stand of jack pine and came toward them. Bree lifted a hand in greeting. She should have known her sister-in-law wouldn't be far from the action. She craved media attention the way the mine owners craved cheap workers.

Hilary Kaleva pushed aside the branches barring her way into the clearing as though they were a personal affront. Hilary, Rock Harbor's mayor, was having the mother of all bad-hair days. Her hair, blond like her brother Rob's, was swept up in a formerly elegant French roll, but strands loosened by tree branches now clung damply to her neck. Streaks of mud marred her navy suit, and bits of pine needles clung to the fabric.

"It's the poodle," Naomi muttered to Bree. "I'm out of here. I'll wait with the rangers."

"Coward," Bree murmured. She wished she could laugh. Rob used to call Hilary his "poodle sister," which Hilary found less than amusing, but Bree and Naomi had always thought the description apt. Hilary could be sweet and loving one moment then turn and bite without provocation. And she talked until Bree grew weary of listening. But she could be just as endearing as a poodle when she wanted to be. From the expression on her face, today wasn't one of those days.

Samson woofed at Hilary in greeting and strained at the leash to meet her. The mayor flinched at the sniffing dog, pulling away with a moue of distaste. As if sensing Hilary's animosity, Samson lurched toward Hilary then came alongside Bree and rubbed his nose against her knee. Bree tugged him farther away from her sister-in-law. No sense in upsetting her.

Hilary's scowl eased when Bree pulled the dog a safe distance away. "What are you doing here? I thought you were searching the northeast quadrant today."

Bree's smile faltered. Hilary always managed to drain her confidence with a relentless determination to bend her to her will. "I was home when the call came in. The brick is crumbling on the tower, and it seemed like a good day to repoint it. I was just about to mix the mortar when Mason called." Bree stopped and chided herself for babbling like a kid caught playing hooky. Maybe it was time they both realized

Rob's plane might never be found. Not in the northeast quadrant or any other. The forest had swallowed the Bonanza Beechcraft like Superior could swallow a sinking ship.

Hilary's eyes flashed. "You have more important things to do than to repoint the brick on your lighthouse. Let a professional do it."

"The last time I checked, my bank balance was screaming for mercy, Hilary."

Hilary sighed, and she gave a smile that seemed forced. "I'll pay for it. You promised you'd find them, Bree. It's been nearly a year. Rob's birthday is the day after Thanksgiving. I'm counting on giving him a decent burial by then."

Bree wanted to run away from the admonishment. The graves at Rock Harbor Cemetery were as empty as her heart. Even if she found the bodies to fill those graves, it wouldn't change things, but at least maybe then she could bring herself to go there to mourn. Besides, Bree was tiring of Hilary's constant harping on her failure to find them.

"Samson and I are doing the best we can, Hilary. But they could be anywhere. Here in the Kitchigami or maybe even down in Ottawa."

"My patience is running out."

Bree had trained her temper to stay on its leash when she was around Hilary, but some days were harder than others. "I want to find them just as much as you do, Hilary. But I'm not Superwoman." A muscle in Bree's jaw jerked. Hilary didn't understand how hard a task Bree had set up for herself. At least there was still a chance for Donovan's kids. "Look," she finally said, "I need to get on with the search for the O'Reilly children."

She turned and rushed into the woods then hurried along the pine-needle path toward Naomi and the group of rangers under the trees. The rush of cool air soothed her hot cheeks. Would she never find them? *Never, never,* her footsteps answered.

A dark-haired man was giving directions. About six feet tall and stocky, he gestured with broad hands that looked tanned and capable.

When Bree approached, he stopped talking, and his gaze settled on her. Bree smiled and nodded a hello as she stepped forward with an outstretched hand.

"You look like the man I need to see," she said. He looked vaguely familiar, and she wondered if she'd seen him around town. His brown park service uniform matched his hair, and his blue eyes were as keen and intelligent as an Australian shepherd's. She guessed him to be in his early thirties. "I'm Bree Nicholls with my dog, Samson, and this is Naomi Heinonen and her dog, Charley."

The blue eyes narrowed when they saw the dogs. "Who called in the SAR?"

"The sheriff did," one of the men said.

The man pressed his lips together then nodded with obvious reluctance. "I'm Ranger Kade Matthews. I wouldn't have called you in yet, but since you're here we'll try to use you."

Kade Matthews. Bree had heard talk of him at the coffee shop. Rumor said he'd given up a promotion that would have taken him to California when his mother died and left him as guardian of his sixteen-year-old sister. It was to his credit that he'd followed his mother's wishes to have his sister finish school here, though Bree pitied the poor girl. Who would want him as a guardian? She'd run into his kind before, law-enforcer types who wanted to run the show their way even if it cost lives.

"Has anyone found a trail yet?" Bree's gaze wandered toward the gloom of the thickly wooded forest, and she shuffled her feet. The setup always took too long, in her opinion. While people stood around discussing where to start and how to begin, Samson could be homing in on the scent. She knew organization was important, but there was a limit.

Ranger Matthews shook his head. "Not a hint of one. But we're down to the wire here. The little boy's diabetes is a bad case. I've divided the search area into quadrants. The board is over there." He pointed to the trailer set up as a command post. "You and your team can take quadrant two."

"We find our dogs more effective if they're allowed to scent on an article of the victim's then follow where the scent leads. Donovan already gave us—"

The ranger interrupted with another shake of his head. "It's not an efficient way to search. I need to know who's where."

Bree hunched her shoulders and gave Naomi a helpless look. Why did she find it so impossible anymore to speak her mind? When she had first met Rob, her nickname at school was "Brassy Bree" because she had the nerve to do anything she was dared to do. Now she wavered when asked what she wanted to drink. She wanted to argue, but her mouth refused to open.

"We've only got a few more hours of daylight left," Ranger Matthews said. "The sheriff is in the camper briefing the searchers. Please join them."

Thank goodness Mason was here. Bree left the arrogant ranger and went to find her brother-in-law in the camp. Naomi trailed behind her, pausing to say something to Donovan, and Bree wondered at her friend's reluctance to leave him.

The camper sat along the side of the parking lot. It hadn't been leveled and tilted heavily to the right. The silver siding bore scratches and gouges from its many brushes with tree branches and thorny shrubs. The door to the camper opened as Bree approached and Mason stepped out.

"Oh good, you're here," Mason said. Sheriff of Kitchigami County, Mason was thickly built and good-natured, a mellow, golden retriever sort of man instead of the pit bull some in Kitchigami County thought a sheriff ought to be.

"Who's Attila the Hun?" Bree asked.

Mason frowned. "Who?"

"The ranger honcho. Kade Matthews."

"He's a good man. You have a problem with him?"

"He's insisting on a grid search. That will take forever," Bree said. Naomi joined her finally, and Bree thought she looked a little flushed.

Mason shook his head. "I'll handle Kade. You two take this insulin for the boy and find those kids." He handed Bree a syringe.

Bree took the insulin and tucked it into her ready-pack. The hormone was a stark reminder of the urgency of the search. Tomorrow wouldn't be good enough—they had to find those kids tonight. She knelt beside Samson and Charley and held the jackets Donovan had given her under their noses. The jackets had been contaminated with other scents, but Samson had worked under these kinds of adverse circumstances before, and she had confidence in her dog. To help the dogs, she had them sniff the insides of the jackets where there was a greater likelihood of strong scent untainted by handling.

Samson whined and strained at the leash. Bree released his lead and dropped her arm. "Search!" she commanded.

Samson bounded toward the trees. Charley plunged his nose into the jacket again then raised his muzzle and whined. Naomi unclipped Charley's leash, and he raced after Samson. Both dogs ran back and forth, their muzzles in the air. The dogs weren't bloodhounds but air scenters. They worked in a "Z" pattern, scenting the air until they could catch a hint of the one scent they sought. Samson's tail stiffened, and he turned and raced toward the creek.

"He's caught it!" Bree said, running after her dog. Naomi followed Charley. Bree heard the ranger shout as he realized they were disobeying his instructions, but then the sounds of people and cars fell away as though they had slipped into another world. The forest engulfed them, and the rustling of the wind through the trees, the muffled sounds of insects and small animals, and the whispering scent of wet mud and leaf mold all welcomed Bree as though she'd never been away. In spite of their familiarity, Bree knew the welcome was just a facade. The North Woods still guarded its secrets from her.

⁕

After nearly two hours, Bree was hot and itchy. She started to sit on a fallen log, then the drone of honeybees inside alerted her, and she avoided it, choosing instead to rest on a tree stump to catch her breath. Though the bees were sluggish this time of year, she didn't want to take any chances. Naomi thrashed her way through the vegetation as she rushed to catch up with Bree and the dogs.

Samson had lost the scent about ten minutes ago, and he criss-crossed the clearing, searching for the lost trail with his muzzle in the air. Bree unfastened a canteen from her belt and took a gulp of water. Though warm, the water washed the bitter taste of insect repellant from her tongue. She dropped her backpack onto the ground and pulled out a small bag of pistachios. Cracking the nuts, she tossed the shells onto the ground. She munched the salty nutmeats and took another swig of water.

Naomi came up behind her, short of breath. "Anything?" She pushed away a lock of hair that had escaped her braid. Naomi was like a cocker spaniel with her soft brown hair and compassionate eyes—and like a spaniel, just as persistent. Her spirit never flagged, and she always managed to transfer her optimism to Bree.

Bree shook her head and held out the bag of nuts to Naomi. "Want some?"

Naomi wrinkled her nose. "I don't know how you can stand to eat those things. Give me walnuts or pecans, not those funny green things. You eat so many of them, we'd never need search dogs to find you; we'd just follow the shell trails."

Bree grinned and put the bag of nuts back in her bag. She screwed the lid back onto the canteen and fastened it to the belt around her waist. "Time to get moving again."

"Charley's lost the trail," Naomi said. Charley nosed aimlessly among a patch of wildflowers while Samson thrust his head into the stream running to their right.

"Maybe the other searchers are having better luck." Bree snapped her fingers, and Samson came to her. He shook himself, and droplets of water sprayed her jeans. She knelt and took his shaggy head in her hands and stared into his dark eyes. "I know you're trying, buddy," she whispered. "But can you try just a little harder?" Samson's curly tail swished the air, and he licked her chin as if to say he'd do what he could. And Bree knew he would. As a search dog, Samson was in a class by himself.

Bree knew dogs. From the time she could barely toddle, she'd had a dog. When she and Rob had lived in Oregon, she'd been introduced to K-9 Search and Rescue, and she knew it was what she was meant to do. Margie, her first dog, had been a pro too, but she'd had a stroke three years ago, about six months after Samson had come along.

She'd never seen a dog with as much heart as Samson. His markings and size betrayed his German shepherd lineage, but his curly coat was all chow. Since the day she'd found him in a box by the river, barely alive and not yet four weeks old, his gaze had spoken to her more clearly than any human words could. When he'd turned his head that day and tried to lick her hand, she lost her heart. There was a special bond between her and Samson, and he loved search and rescue as much as she did. Together they'd been on search missions all over the country as part of the FEMA team.

He whined and sniffed the air as if determined not to let her down.

"If Samson can't find the kids, we might as well all go home," Naomi muttered. "He could find a flea in a hay field."

Bree grinned. "The fleas seem to find him." But she knew Naomi was right. Samson was special. She wanted him to prove it today.

Up ahead, Samson began to bark and then raced away. Bree's adrenaline kicked into overdrive. "He's found the scent again." Her fatigue forgotten, she followed the dogs.

2

*T*wilight cast deep shadows in the little clearing in the woods, but Rachel Marks had no trouble picking out the shack with the stack of split logs beside it. She could find everything in this meadow with her eyes closed. As she shuffled through the thick carpet of leaves and pine needles toward the woodpile, her feet kicked up the sharp scent of pine. Sam limped along beside her, and she slowed her pace to match his.

She frowned. His thin arms stuck out from the sleeves of his blue jacket, and his pants didn't even come to the top of his socks. He could barely squeeze into them anymore. Thank goodness he was almost well enough to take to town. Otherwise, she'd have to buy him some new clothes. His pinched white face beneath the blue stocking cap he wore showed a tinge more color than it had last month. Day by day he grew stronger.

He was quiet, as always. Too quiet. Of course, there was no one for him to talk to but her and his pet squirrel, Marcus. She couldn't put off the inevitable much longer.

But not yet. He'd only been walking for twenty minutes, yet his limp had grown more pronounced over the past few yards. He needed to rest. She beckoned to him, and he followed her toward the cabin.

Just outside the door, he stopped and tilted his head to one side. "I hear something." Sam's hushed voice seemed unnaturally loud in the still night.

Rachel stopped, her booted feet settling into the soggy leaves on the ground. Had they been found out? Her adrenaline surged and she tipped up her head and listened. "It sounds like a little kid crying," Rachel said.

Sam turned his face up to hers, his eyes glowing. "A kid like me?"

"You stay here, Sam. Let me check it out." She'd heard of cougars sounding like a child, but this sounded like no painter she'd ever heard. Just to be safe, she grabbed the ax as she passed the woodshed. Stepping cautiously toward the sound, she hefted the ax to her shoulder.

She caught her breath as the sound came again. That was no wild animal; it was a child. A crying child. She pushed aside the brush and peered into the tangle of shrubs then stepped into the fir grove. It was darker here than in her clearing but still bright enough to see the two children who sat on the ground. The little girl was weeping, her arms around a smaller child, a boy. Her woebegone face was streaked with mud, and she rocked back and forth, shudders wracking her small frame.

"I'm sorry, Timmy. It was my fault," the girl sobbed. "Now you're sick, and it's all my fault."

Rachel looked around warily until she was sure there was no danger of discovery. Could these children possibly be alone this far from town? "Hello," she said, stepping near the children. "What's your name, little girl?"

At the sound of her voice, the little girl whipped her head around and stared up at Rachel through saucer eyes. Twigs and debris matted her dark curls. She looked about seven or eight.

Rachel saw the fear in the child's face and realized how frightening she must seem to the children, a fifty-year-old woman with braided gray hair topped with an old leather fedora.

"It's all right; I'm not as mean as I look." Rachel stepped closer. "Is this your brother?"

The little girl wiped her face and nodded. "His name is Timmy, and he needs his shot. I'm Emily. Daddy is going to be awfully mad at me." Her voice was doleful. "We just wanted to see the raccoons."

"I'm sure your daddy will be too glad to be angry when he gets you home safe and sound." Rachel surveyed the little boy and frowned. He looked about Sam's age, maybe four or five. She needed to get him inside where she could see him better.

She slid her bony arms under the little boy and lifted him up. Heat radiated off him like hot coals, and he shook like the few leaves still clinging to the trees above her head. She hoped he was as tenacious. His sister had mentioned a shot. Could he be diabetic? Rachel's nurse's training kicked in, and she leaned forward and sniffed. A fruity scent issued from his open mouth, and she winced. Yep. Poor kid. She had no insulin here, and town was miles away.

"Come with me," she told Emily. "We'll get you something to eat and drink." Then she had to get them out of here. Without drawing attention to herself. The last thing she needed was the law on her tail.

Emily followed her into the clearing. "Is that your house? It's sure little."

"It suits us," Rachel said shortly.

Sam was still standing where she'd left him. Motionless, he watched her come toward him. His gaze darted from her and the child she carried to the little girl who followed them.

"Sammy, open the door for me," she said. He limped to the cabin and fumbled at the latch then swung the door open. He held it wide while Rachel carried the little boy inside.

The cabin wasn't much, but it had been home for over a year. Only one room, but they made do. Sam's cot was pushed up against one wall, the colorful log cabin quilt she'd made for him now faded but still serviceable. A battered table, four chairs, and a braided rug, faded and worn, completed the furnishings.

It was all scrupulously clean. She might live in the back of beyond, but that was no reason for slovenliness. Laying the little boy on the bed, she studied him. His face was flushed beneath the numerous scratches, and his breathing was labored. This little guy needed his insulin, now. Looking at the sunken areas under his eyes, Rachel saw he was dehydrated as well. A saline IV would come in handy, but that wasn't something Rachel kept on hand.

"There's a pitcher of water on the table," she told Emily. "Pour some water for you and the lad. I'll fix you a peanut butter sandwich, and we'll get you back to that daddy of yours."

Emily looked weary, but she stepped to the table and poured two cups of water. She drank thirstily from her cup, but Timmy turned his head and closed his eyes when Rachel offered him a drink.

As quickly as she could, Rachel slathered some peanut butter on slices of homemade bread. The law would be searching for these kids, and she had to get them out of here before the rangers found her cabin. Timmy refused to eat, and Rachel waited until Emily finished her sandwich. "You ready to go back to town?"

The little girl didn't answer. She was too busy inspecting Sam. The food and drink had calmed her, and her eyes were inquisitive. "Are you his grandma?" Emily gave Sam a tentative smile.

Rachel searched for an answer. "I'm his mother," she said, struggling against the irritation she felt at the girl's assumption. It wasn't only twenty-year-olds who were blessed to be mothers. She'd seen plenty of women who'd waited until later in life to have children. Her own grandmother had given birth to her last child at fifty-two. Thank goodness Sam wasn't as inquisitive as this child.

Emily sidled closer to Sam. "What's your name?"

Sam ducked his head and didn't answer.

"He's shy," Rachel said. She fought the panic clawing at her belly. All these questions! She could only hope the kids would remember little of what they saw here. Luckily the stocking cap still covered Sam's hair. The children wouldn't have much of a description.

"Sammy, you hop into your pajamas, and I'll be back soon."

"I want to go too." Sam stared up at her, his green eyes pleading.

"You're not strong enough, Sam. I'll have to carry Timmy—I can't carry you too." He knew to stay inside and keep the door latched until she came back. She'd had to leave him often over the past months.

Sam's lower lip trembled, but he didn't argue with her. It was no wonder the poor little guy wanted to go along. These children were the first contact he'd had with other people in months. Rachel gnawed her lip. She wished she could do better by him. But sometimes you just had to play the hand you were dealt. He would learn soon enough how life threw you punches and you had to stiffen your backbone and fight back, just as she did.

Giving Sam a little push, she went toward the little boy. "I'll be back soon. You rest."

Sam nodded and watched with wistful eyes as she picked up Timmy then took Emily's hand and led her out the door. "Wait!" he cried suddenly. He limped toward them and thrust his beloved stuffed koala bear in the little boy's hand.

Rachel frowned. "You don't want to do that, Sam." The kid had few enough toys. He didn't need to be giving them away to strangers. From the looks of these two, they were middle-class and probably had bedrooms full of toys.

Sam's lip protruded farther. "I want to give it to him," he said.

Rachel shrugged. "Just don't come crying to me tonight when you miss it."

"His name is Pooky," Sam said, ducking his head.

The little girl took the bear from her brother's unresponsive hand and cradled it in her arm. She gave Sam a brilliant smile. "Thanks. I'll give it to Timmy when we get home." She fumbled in her jeans pocket and pulled out a yo-yo. "Here, you can have this."

Sam stared at the yo-yo then back up at Emily.

"You play with it like this." Emily took the toy back, slipped the string over her finger, and threw it. Sam's eyes grew wider as the yo-yo returned to her hand. "Here, you try it." She thrust it back into his hand and showed him how to put the string on his finger. He awkwardly tried to throw it, but it only came partway back.

"You'll get the hang of it," she told him. "Just practice. Thanks for the bear." She leaned over and kissed Sam on the cheek. With Pooky in her hand, she scampered out the door behind Rachel.

Carrying Timmy, Rachel led Emily across the yard and entered the forest. Stumbling over branches and brambles, they wound their way through the thick trees. Rachel's back ached from the little boy's weight.

❧

Over an hour later, Rachel set Timmy down to rest her arms then stood and stretched. The road wasn't far now, another fifteen minutes maybe. It was still light enough to see. She could park them by the side of the road, and someone would be along shortly. It was the best she could do.

Leaning down to retrieve her burden, she froze at the sound of voices. People—more than one. And dogs. That could be trouble. She set Timmy back on the forest floor.

"You're safe now, kids," she said hastily. "I've gotta go."

"Don't leave us!" Emily scrabbled for her hand, but Rachel evaded her, cursing herself for ever getting involved. She hoped she didn't regret this day, but she was a sucker for kids.

Flipping her braid over one shoulder, Rachel took off at a run. "You'll be okay," she called behind her. "There are people coming. They're probably looking for you." The safety of the forest beckoned her, and she plunged into its sheltering depths. Emily's wails followed her.

❧

Kade's temper was short as he organized the teams and finally got them on their way. The K-9 team he'd worked with before in Yellowstone had represented the height of ineptitude, scattering evidence and leading searchers in the wrong direction. He knew all teams were not that bad—the media reported plenty of success stories—but this search was his responsibility, and those kids were depending on him. Bree Nicholls had deliberately disobeyed his orders. Worse, the sheriff had made it clear his sister-in-law was to be allowed to have her own way. Typical of the nepotism in a small town like Rock Harbor.

He saw the mayor talking on a walkie-talkie and stalked her way. "Anything?"

Hilary clicked off the device. "None of the dogs has picked up the scent yet," she said.

Kade leaned against the truck. "I thought this was a hotshot K-9 team."

"Samson has been written up in more magazines than you can count," Hilary said. "But even he isn't perfect. They still haven't found the plane that went down with my brother and their son."

An awkward silence passed between them. "Your family issues are none of my business," Kade said. "But I don't like the way Bree Nicholls disobeyed my orders and put those kids in jeopardy."

"She knows what she's doing," Hilary said. "You haven't been here long, but she and Samson have found quite a few lost campers since she and Rob moved here."

Before Kade could reply, a familiar red car slid to a halt in a cloud of dust. The door on the battered Plymouth spilled open, and his sister, Lauri, got out, her face its usual mask of petulance. He'd often thought of taking her picture and showing her that expression. Would she want her face to take on those lines for the rest of her life? He hadn't done it, because he knew it would just make her mad. Everything was his fault these days.

"We've already missed the movies," she said with her hands on her hips. Her gaze traveled to the two young rangers standing near the path to the pavilion. Straightening at their looks of interest, she preened and gave them a sultry smile.

Kade gritted his teeth. She was way too young to be flirting like that. At sixteen, his sister was a budding Lolita, using the power of her beauty in ways he probably didn't want to know about. "What are you doing here?" he asked abruptly.

Lauri turned from her silent flirtation with the rangers and gave her brother a smoldering glare. "You didn't even phone. If I hadn't called headquarters, I'd still be wondering where you were."

"I should have called, but things developed too fast for me to remember. There are two children lost in the woods, and one of them is sick. I forgot all about the movies. Sorry, kid."

"Don't call me 'kid'!" Lauri tossed her head again. "I'm sick and tired of always taking second place to your job. If you don't want me around, just say so. I could go stay with Grandma and Grandpa."

Kade sighed, weariness settling over him like a suffocating wave from Lake Superior. "We've been over all that, Lauri. You are not going to our grandparents. You'd run over them inside a week. Besides, I promised Mom you'd finish school here, and I intend to keep my promise."

Lauri gave him a calculated look far too mature for a sixteen-year-old. Where did she get that manner? He wanted her to enjoy her remaining years of school, to be a normal teenager, but he didn't know how to ensure that, how to reach the vulnerable child he still sometimes glimpsed in her eyes. She refused to go to youth group at church. It was all he could do to get her to go to church at all.

"Fine," she said through gritted teeth. "I'll see you later." She slung her long legs under the wheel and slammed the car door shut.

"Lauri, come back here!" he yelled. Her face set as though she didn't hear, she tore off down the road, dust spitting from the tires. He clenched his jaw.

"Why don't we drive along the access road?" Hilary asked. "It would be better than sitting around here doing nothing."

Kade nodded, thankful the mayor had the tact to ignore Lauri's little scene. He felt the need to be doing something. Otherwise, he might go find his sister and strangle her. He opened the truck door for the mayor then slammed it shut and got in on his side. He started the truck and drove into the dark forest.

Hilary cleared her throat. "Kids can be a trial, can't they? I was a lot like Lauri at that age. It was an admirable thing to take on her care."

"I'm regretting it daily," he said grimly. The mayor's sympathy surprised Kade. In their few encounters, he'd always thought her all business. "You have any kids?"

She turned to look out the window. "Not yet."

That was a stupid question and clearly none of his business. When would he learn to keep his mouth shut? The radio attached to his belt crackled to life.

"Ranger station, come in." Bree's voice cut out then surged stronger. "We've found them, and I'm sending up a flare. We're in sector four."

Kade grabbed the radio. "Ten-four. What kind of shape are they in?" Only a crackle of the radio answered his question, then a light shot from the forest and illuminated an area to their left. He gunned the truck down the rutted track. Hilary clung to the door as the truck pitched from side to side. He tossed the radio to her.

"Call an ambulance!" When the truck finished grinding to a halt beneath the spreading light, he jumped from the vehicle, grabbed his first-aid kit from the back, and ran toward the cluster of people huddled at the base of a giant sycamore.

Bree and Naomi were kneeling beside the two children. The little girl's face was streaked with mud, and tears had left blotches on her face. She held her younger brother's hand. Kade's gaze dropped to the little boy cradled in Bree's arms, and his heart sank at his condition. Even in the fading twilight, Kade could see him shaking. The sour smell of vomit lingered in the air, which didn't bode well.

"Timmy is sick," Emily sobbed. "Is he going to die?"

"We just gave him his shot," Bree said. She pulled the little boy closer to her and wrapped her coat around him. Timmy visibly relaxed at her tender touch. He turned his face into her chest and sighed.

Bree appeared oblivious to everything but Timmy, and Kade wondered if holding the little boy brought back memories of her own loss.

Kade opened his canteen and knelt beside the children. He poured a few drops of water into Timmy's open mouth. The little boy coughed but managed to swallow it, then Kade gave Emily a drink too. Running his hands over their arms and legs, he was relieved to find nothing broken.

"Just insect bites," he said. "They seem to be all right. But we need to get them to a hospital. The mayor is calling the ambulance."

"I already did," Naomi said. "It should be here any minute."

Kade whipped off the jacket of his uniform and knelt beside Bree. He wrapped the jacket around Emily like a blanket. "The ambulance won't get here any too soon. I think we'd better run them to the hospital in my truck. Some of you will have to ride in the back of the pickup or wait for the ambulance." He took Timmy from Bree and moved toward the road without waiting for an answer. Timmy's head lolled against Kade's chest, and his small feet dangled from the folds of the coat. Kade didn't like the boy's limpness.

Bree took Emily's hand, and they started toward the dirt access road. As they reached the road, Kade heard the shrill wail of the ambulance in the distance. Relief left him almost lightheaded. Timmy and Emily would soon be under medical care. Moments later the flashing lights came into sight, followed by the headlamps of two other vehicles.

Putting her radio away, the mayor came toward them. She reached out a hand and touched Timmy's hair. "You're safe now, sweetheart." She stroked his face then reached down and touched Emily's head. "You're both going to be just fine."

Emily took her hand, and Hilary's face softened. Kade turned away from the naked longing in Hilary's face. He felt he was intruding on something private. His eyes connected with Bree's, and he saw sorrow in them. All this motherly angst made him put his hackles up, and he tensed.

Kade signaled with his flashlight in case the driver had trouble seeing them in the twilight. Crunching gravel under the tires, the ambulance came to a stop and two paramedics leaped out. One of the men took Timmy from Kade and rushed him to the back of the ambulance. The second paramedic led Emily to the back as well. The other two vehicles stopped, and two men got out of the battered Dodge truck, its paint a dull orange-red in the light of the full moon.

"Daddy!" Emily dropped the paramedic's hand and ran to Donovan. He dropped to his knees and folded Emily in his arms.

"Thank God you're safe. Where's your brother?" He gave her a little shake. "What have I told you about wandering off by yourself?"

Emily gave a little hiccup. "That I was never supposed to leave without an adult. I'm sorry, Daddy."

The man looked around wildly. "Where's your brother?" he repeated. Hilary reached out her hand but let it drop when the distraught father made no move to take it. "Your children are going to be fine, Donovan. Timmy is in the ambulance."

Donovan let go of Emily and ran to the ambulance, where he stood watching the paramedics work on his son. An occasional groan issued from Donovan's mouth. Kade could only imagine how he felt.

"Daddy's mad at me," Emily said, tears making her voice tremble.

Bree held out her hand. "He's just worried, sweetheart. Come with me, and let's see if I can find you a candy bar or something to eat."

"I'm not hungry. The witch in the woods gave us some peanut butter sandwiches."

Kade frowned. "Who's that, Emily?" No one had been with the children. His gaze met Bree's, and he saw the same confusion in her face.

"The witch in the woods. I was afraid she was going to eat us like the witch in the woods in the Hansel and Gretel story, but she gave us a peanut butter sandwich. Timmy wouldn't eat his though."

"There was no one with you," Bree said.

"She ran away when she heard you and the dogs," Emily said.

The little girl may be more stressed than they thought. Either that or she had quite an imagination. "Better get her checked out," Kade mouthed softly to Bree.

She nodded. "That's fine, but let's get you back to town," Bree said. "You'll get to ride in the ambulance. Won't that be fun?"

Emily's lip trembled, but she nodded. "Is Timmy going to die?"

"No, he'll be okay in a few days. But the doctors are going to want to look at him, and at you, just to make sure you're okay," Kade said. He took her other hand, and they led her toward the ambulance.

Her head haloed by the light from the ambulance, Emily stopped and looked up at Bree. "What's your dog's name? Will you bring him to see me?"

Bree smiled at Emily and touched her head. Kade dropped his gaze and wondered how old her son would be now. As young as she was, he couldn't have been very old. Sometimes Kade had to admit he wondered how the Almighty chose who to save and who to take.

Bree nodded at Emily. "This is Samson. Samson, say hello to Emily." The dog thrust his nose into the little girl's hand. Emily giggled as the dog licked her face. "We'll check on you tomorrow," Bree told her.

Kade had trouble keeping his eyes off Bree. Though not really beautiful, she was arresting. The cut of her short red hair emphasized the delicate column of her neck and the fine bone structure of her face. Large green eyes that seemed a bit sad tilted up at the corners. It was no wonder, considering what she'd been through, what she was still going through. Though she looked fragile, Kade had seen her heft a heavy backpack with ease and knew she was stronger than she appeared. He guessed her to be a little younger than him, maybe late twenties.

Within minutes the ambulance, trailed by the kids' father in the pickup, tore back the way it had come, leaving only dust and the fast-fading echo of the siren in its wake. "I'll run you home," Kade told Bree and Naomi. He could see both women visibly wilting. The day had been grueling, even for him, so they had to be exhausted. The dogs lay panting on the side of road, spent as well.

"My Jeep is at the parking lot," Bree said.

"I've already arranged for your vehicle to be left at your home," Kade said. "I'll take you straight there."

Bree stared at him. "Without asking me?"

He shrugged. "You left the keys in it. I figured you'd be too tired to drive."

Bree motioned for Samson to jump into the back of Kade's pickup. The dog moved slowly on sore feet. Charley followed him. "You were wrong," she said. Her gaze dropped. "I had things I needed to attend to before going home," she said softly. She bit her lip like there was more she wanted to say then headed toward the passenger door.

His lips tightened. She had been no saint today in spite of her success. "And you disobeyed orders!" Kade snapped. Bree just looked at him, and the calm confidence in her face irritated him even more.

Naomi jumped into the fray. "You have no idea who you're talking to, do you? Bree and Samson are one of the top search teams in the country—in the world! Those kids would still be out there if we'd followed your orders."

"I've worked with some bad teams in my time," he snapped.

"Well, we aren't one of them!" Naomi said hotly.

Kade compressed his lips. This was getting them nowhere. "How about we call a truce? I made a mistake and so did you. Sorry, Miss Nicholls, Miss Heinonen."

Naomi opened her mouth, and from the fire in her eyes, Kade expected a scathing reply, but Bree shot her a quelling look and held out her hand. "Truce," she said. "But it's Mrs. Nicholls. And the only mistake was yours."

He gritted his teeth but held his tongue. "Let's get you home." Naomi opened the door and slid in first, then Bree scrunched in beside her. Suddenly anxious to be free of the whole prickly mess, Kade slammed the door behind them and crawled behind the wheel.

They rode in silence to town. As they rounded the last curve, the twinkling lights of Rock Harbor came into view. Part of the town's special flavor came from the setting. Surrounded by forests on three sides, it had all the natural beauty anyone could want. Old-growth forests, sparkling lakes where fish thronged, and the brilliant blue of that Big Sea Water called Superior along the west side.

They drove through town, down Whisper Pike to Houghton Street and past the businesses that comprised Rock Harbor's downtown. "You'll have to direct me," Kade said.

Bree pointed toward the far light. "The lighthouse is mine. Naomi lives in the Blue Bonnet Bed and Breakfast right beside me—the house that used to belong to Captain Sarasin."

Kade knew the house. Built by a famous captain of the area so his wife could watch for his return, it was the last house on Houghton Street before it curved into Negaunee, the road out to the lighthouse. He hadn't realized it was a bed-and-breakfast until now. He rarely drove to that side of town. The lighthouse was perched just behind it at the end of Negaunee on a sliver of land that bravely faced Superior's fury.

"You live in the lighthouse?" he asked. "I haven't been to town much since I returned two months ago. When I was a kid, I used to prowl around that deserted lighthouse. I figured someone had turned it into a museum by now."

"It's not a lighthouse anymore. The Coast Guard replaced it with the offshore automated light years ago," Bree said. "I'm in the process of restoring it. I'm on the last room now."

"How long have you owned it? I figured someone from out of state bought it—someone with more money than sense." He grinned to take the sting out of the slur.

"That might have described me and Rob at one time." Bree laughed. "When we bought it, the chimney had fallen through the roof, and the porch boards were all decayed. Rob had inherited some money from his grandmother and a plane from his uncle. The lighthouse was just another piece of Rob's dream. Our dream," she amended.

"You've done most of it yourself," Naomi said. "I don't know how you've managed all alone."

Bree smiled. "I plan to reinstall the Fresnel lens and light the tower, someday." Her gaze softened and took on a faraway look. "I'd like to think my light might save a ship someday."

Kade wondered what had triggered her obsession with rescuing people. It was admirable, but surely something had caused it. Did it start with the deaths of her husband and son, or had she always been that way?

Kade stopped in front of the bed-and-breakfast and let Naomi and Charley off. Naomi waved at them from the front porch then went inside. Kade drove on down Negaunee to the lighthouse.

Gravel crunched beneath the pickup's tires, and Kade stopped the vehicle in front of the lighthouse. The brick building's pink paint gleamed in the glare of the porch light, but the light tower was dark. Bree opened the tailgate for Samson and followed him to the front door. Kade lowered the windows. The smell of boat exhaust hung heavy in the moist air blowing in from Lake Superior. A ship's horn bellowed a lonely note in the middle of the bay. The Ojibwa called the lake *Kitchigami,* which meant "giver of life," though right now he felt that meaning was erroneous. It was more a taker of the life he wanted. At one time he thought he'd left this place for good, only to find he was trapped in it as easily as a rabbit in a hunter's snare.

The slap of the water against the pier carried across the water. "Thanks again for all your help. I'll call again if we need assistance."

"You're welcome," Bree said. "Let's hope you don't have more lost campers anytime soon."

"We both know that's not likely," he said with a wry grin. "People are pretty foolish when it comes to the wilderness. They think diving into the forest is no more dangerous than taking a stroll in the city park."

Bree grinned. "I guess I'll see you around then, Ranger Matthews."

"Call me Kade," he called through the window as he pulled away. The few businesses open in Rock Harbor's three-block business center spilled enough light onto the sidewalk to make it appear quasi-welcoming. The neon still shimmered above The Coffee Place. He pulled into the café parking lot.

The rich aroma of espresso took the edge off the day's frustrations. He'd been as surprised as everyone else in town when The Coffee Place got a newfangled espresso machine. It had proven surprisingly popular with more than just tourists. Milt Granger's boy, Brad, was behind the counter, but he was too busy talking to a sweet young thing with three studs up each ear lobe to pay much attention to Kade. Kade coughed several times before Brad took his order. Kade finally succeeded in getting his latte and a turkey club sandwich with a piece of chocolate pie.

"Mind if I join you?"

Startled, he nearly spilled coffee down the front of his shirt. "Hello, Fay," he said. Just what he didn't need. Fay Asters stood behind him with one hand on a slim hip. He pushed out the chair opposite him with his foot. "Have a seat."

"You seen Eric around?" she asked, sliding into the chair. Her slim fingers played with her hair then slid down to fidget with the chain around her neck.

"I've told you to stay away from him. He's trying to straighten his life out. You'll just muck it up again." It was hard to keep his gaze from the quick movements of her hands.

"You're not his keeper."

"No, but thanks to you, he had one of those for three years." He'd never understood what Eric saw in Fay. Slim to the point that she had none of the womanly curves most men admired, she didn't even wear makeup unless she was in her femme fatale mode. It must be that innocent, little-girl way she had about her, a facade that hid the truth of her real nature.

She laughed, a silvery, tinkling sound that drew his gaze to her mouth. Okay, so that was attractive too.

"If you see Eric, tell him I have important news," she said.

She slid away from the table with a grace that reminded Kade of a sleek cat. He drummed his fingers on the tabletop and wondered what he could do to keep her away from Eric. Whatever her news was, it would likely bring trouble.

3

The Blue Bonnet Bed and Breakfast might not have been the most popular lodging spot in the Keweenaw Peninsula, but Naomi and her mother were beginning to get some repeat visitors. Naomi closed the register with a sense of satisfaction then stretched out the kinks in her back. The scent of lemon polish and the faint aroma of pine cleaner in the air were worth the soreness in her muscles. Six thousand square feet of house, and every inch of it polished and shining. The new crop of weekend visitors would arrive later in the morning.

The registration desk stood at the end of the entry hall. They'd opened the wall between the office and the foyer, and now an antique marble counter separated the two. Naomi sneaked a book from under the counter. Maybe she could get in a few pages before her mother came down. She flexed the spine, and, as if on cue, her mother floated down the curved walnut staircase. She disappeared momentarily into the parlor before hurrying toward the office in the room behind the entry.

Though fifty-eight, Martha Heinonen's skin glowed a pink, healthy hue of fresh air and hard work. Strands of silver were just beginning to highlight her hair, and her consistent exuberance made her even more attractive. Dressed in a pink-flowered dress with a soft skirt that swirled around her still-shapely calves, she looked every inch the lady. Someone had once told her she looked like England's reigning monarch, Queen Elizabeth, and since then she'd played up any resemblance to the hilt, a fact Naomi found amusing.

Naomi guiltily tucked away the book before her mother could see it and level her usual litanies about ruining her eyes and how men weren't interested in a bookworm. Maybe her mother had a point. The men weren't exactly beating a path to the door.

"There you are, darling. I peeked in the parlor on the way down. It looks lovely. I see you managed to get that stain out of the piano scarf. You are such a treasure!" She disappeared again, this time in the direction of the kitchen, and emerged a few moments later carrying a heavy tea-and-cookie-laden tray as though it weighed nothing.

"Come along before the tea gets cold," Martha said.

Naomi followed her to the parlor. Martha set the tray on the coffee table and sank into the plush armchair upholstered in pink cabbage-rose chintz. "It's nearly time for our guests to arrive. Are you going to greet them dressed like that?" She wrinkled her nose at Naomi's faded jeans and oversized T-shirt.

Naomi often wondered how she had been born to such a woman. She preferred denim while her mother craved silk. Her mother teetered daily on two-inch polished pumps, while the footwear on Naomi's shoe rack looked like castoffs from the Salvation Army: scuffed boots, flats with eroded heels, and ragged tennis shoes. Still, Naomi and her mother got along well. Naomi did the heavy cleaning; her mother prepared the elegant teas and made small talk with the New York businessmen and the bored Connecticut housewives. Her mother's pies were famous throughout the peninsula.

Naomi had been gearing up to deal with the subtle guilt her mom would try to impose. "I'll change my top to something nicer." It was as great a compromise as she was willing to make today. Some days she wished she could let the real Naomi come out in full view, but it just took too much energy to confront her mother. Compromise had led her to a placid state of living with her mother at nearly thirty-two. She found small victories like this one hollow, knowing the battle had been lost long ago.

The doorbell pealed. "I'll get it." Naomi made her escape and stepped into the long entry hall. She opened the door and found Bree standing on the front porch.

Naomi grabbed Bree's arm and drew her inside. "You're just in time to save me from strangling my mother."

Bree chuckled and followed Naomi into the parlor. "You may not be so thrilled when you hear what I've come to tell you."

"Mom just put out some tea and cookies. Come tell us all about it."

Bree followed Naomi into the parlor.

"Bree, dear, I was just thinking about you." Martha smoothed her flowered skirt and leaned over to pour the tea. "You look like you could use something to drink."

Bree plopped onto the sofa and curled one denim-clad leg under the other. "You two are my sanity. Oops." She fished around under her and pulled out a book. "This has to be yours." She handed it to Naomi.

"I was wondering where I put that one," Naomi said with a surreptitious glance at her mother. She'd managed to hide the book she'd been reading in the office from her mother, but not this one.

"I don't know why you tote a book everywhere you go; you're always losing them. I could stock a library with the books you've lost." Bree took the cup of tea with a smile of thanks. "I have a summons from the mayor," she said with a dramatic flourish of her hand.

Naomi wrinkled her nose. "The poodle has issued a decree?"

"Girls, that isn't respectful," Martha murmured.

Naomi felt a shaft of shame. But Hilary got under her skin in the worst way. She bossed Bree around, and Bree let her. Naomi didn't understand the hold Hilary seemed to have on her friend. She pushed away her unspoken censure of Bree, who had been through so much. It was no wonder she craved peace at any cost.

"What for?" Naomi asked.

"Hilary's reelection campaign kickoff dinner is tonight. Mason's too, of course, but since he coasts on Hilary's coattails, his campaign is immaterial as far as she's concerned. I thought maybe I could evade an order to appear, but my luck ran out. So did yours." She looked over her teacup at Naomi and raised an eyebrow for effect. "She wants *us* to come so she can show off yesterday's successful search like her latest trophy." Bree took another cookie and bit into it.

Naomi groaned. "Not a dinner party! Anything but that!"

Martha smiled, her eyes lighting with pleasure. "That means a fancy dress, Naomi dear."

Bree grinned. "I'm afraid your mom is right, Naomi. It's pull-out-all-the-stops, knock-'em-dead time."

Naomi fell back against the couch in an exaggerated posture of despair. "And here I thought you were my friend."

"Hey, that's what friends are for," Bree said with a trace of smugness. "For that and chocolate-chip cookies." She took another bite of cookie and grinned.

⸎

Bree studied the large topographic map that decorated the wall in the lighthouse's spare room. She needed to get an updated copy. This one had some inaccuracies. She was almost done with sector fifteen, which was smack in the middle of the southern half of the Kitchigami Wilderness. Should she move east or west? Or keep pushing north? The Rock River Gorge wilderness lay east of sector fifteen. She hadn't even begun to search there. The monumental size of her task felt almost suffocating.

Saturday was not normally her preference for a search day. Hunters and fishermen were out in force on weekends, and they tended to try to engage her in conversation when their paths crossed hers. But October's Indian summer wouldn't last long, and she needed to take advantage of every hour.

Though she knew she should spend the day preparing for Hilary's party, she decided to finish sector fifteen, on the west side of the gorge.

She pulled her backpack and rescue vest out of the spare room's closet, found her cell phone, and headed for the woods.

⊰⊱

Six hours later, the only thing she'd accomplished was closing the door on sector fifteen. No sign of a crash anywhere.

Weariness gripped her as she drove home. A party was the last thing she felt like attending. Driving up Negaunee Street, the light tower of her lighthouse seemed illuminated from within by the last shafts of clear sunlight, and she was reminded again of the repair that needed to be done. Yet one more thing to attend to. Suppressing a sigh, she parked the Jeep, let Samson into the backyard through the gate, then went inside to get ready.

She took a quick shower and washed her hair then cinched her robe around her waist. The thick terry cloth felt warm and comforting after schlepping through the cold forest mist all day. She sat at the dressing table with her makeup bag in hand. Dark circles marred the pale skin under her eyes. It would take some major paint to pass Hilary's critical inspection. Bree made a face at herself in the mirror. If Hilary didn't like the way she looked, she'd be glad to go home. She finished dressing and drove to Naomi's.

Bree pulled up outside the Blue Bonnet and honked the horn. Naomi came out the front door almost immediately. Dressed in a classic black dress with pearls and heels, she looked every inch a lady. A gold lamé shawl reflected light into her elegant upswept hairstyle.

"Looks like your mom got hold of you," Bree said with a grin. "You look great though."

Naomi rolled her eyes. "I wanted to wear my red dress, but Mom said it made me look cheap. *Cheap.*"

"You couldn't look cheap no matter what you wore," Bree said comfortingly. "Hop in and let's go wow them all."

Naomi managed a faint smile. "You always know how to make me feel better," she told Bree.

Naomi fastened her seat belt then leaned forward to fiddle with the radio. "How do you listen to this stuff?" she complained. "No one listens to Elvis anymore." She punched the search button until Houghton's country station came on. Singing at the top of her lungs, Naomi belted out the lyrics to a Reba song.

Bree grinned. "You've missed your calling."

Naomi smiled back. "You have any idea who all will be there?" Her bejeweled fingers played idly with the fringes of her gold shawl.

"Everyone who can help Hilary. Business owners, other politicians, ordinary people with a tad of influence. The guest list will read like a *Who's Who of the Upper Peninsula.*"

"Do you suppose Donovan will be there? That's pretty cool he asked you out. He'd make a good husband," Naomi said.

The diffidence in Naomi's voice struck a wrong chord with Bree, who glanced at her friend sharply and said, "I'm not interested in Donovan, but it sounds like you are. I hope you know what you're letting yourself in for. He'll find it hard to trust another woman after his wife ran off like that. And two small children can be a handful, especially when they aren't your own."

"It's getting to where a girl can't ask a question without risking her ring finger," Naomi complained. "I didn't say I was interested. I was just wondering if he would leave the children for something like this. That must be the worst thing about being a single parent."

A chuckle bubbled out of Bree's throat. "Cut the outraged spinster act, Naomi. This is me, remember? I know the difference between casual interest and something more, and this is something more."

Naomi compressed her lips and looked away. "Mom will have me married by the end of the month if she finds out. I'm sure there's no hope anyway. If you're his type, I'm obviously not. Besides, you've got an advantage: Emily likes you. Did you notice she tagged after you right up to the time the ambulance took her away?"

Bree would allow no man to come between her and Naomi. Men were as plentiful as salmon, but a best friend was a freshwater pearl. "She's just a kid enamored with Samson. Give her time. I have no intention of dating him. When did this interest of yours start?"

"When I was fifteen." She chuckled, but it was only halfhearted. "I was just a pesky little twerp back when he was my brother's best friend."

"Bat those big brown eyes at him, and he'll be a goner."

"I'm not very good at flirting." Naomi sighed and twisted her bracelet around and around on her wrist.

"What is it about Donovan that's kept you hooked all this time?" Bree turned into the parking lot of the community center.

"He's real," Naomi said. "And he loves God as much as I do. I don't know how to explain it, but it's like God is telling me he and the children belong with me, that I need to take care of them. They need me."

Bree hunched her shoulders at the God talk. Fortunately, they'd arrived. Any conversations about God and his expectations would have to wait.

Built by Rock Harbor's early residents during the heyday of the Copper Queen mining era, no expense had been spared in the construction of the beautiful community center. It stood in stark contrast to the rough wooden buildings in other parts of town.

Inside, the patina of age and old money gave an elegance to the central hall that newer, more expensive buildings couldn't match. Crystal chandeliers glittered with prismatic color and light while men and women arrayed in every imaginable style of dress milled around the floor. Some wore suits and brightly colored dresses, while others came dressed in jeans and flannel shirts. Hilary wouldn't turn away anyone who could cast a vote. Glassware tinkled while laughter and conversation formed a constant background hum.

Bree felt as out of place as a starling in the ocean. "We should let Hilary know we're here." What she really wanted to do was find a corner to hide in until she could slip back to the lighthouse. Though she called Rock Harbor home, many in town still regarded her as a newcomer, even after nearly five years as a resident.

"You go ahead," Naomi said, looking past Bree. "I want to talk to Donovan."

So he was here. Bree watched Naomi move to Donovan's side and smile up at him. If that man hurt sweet Naomi, she'd make him regret it. How Bree intended to protect her friend, she wasn't sure, but she'd lay down her life for Naomi. First, though, she needed to let her presence be known to her sister-in-law.

Hilary and Mason were talking with Jacob Zinn, an older man who ran a fishing resort on the edge of town. Mason gave Bree a smile.

"Bree, how nice you look," Hilary said. She leaned forward and touched her lips to Bree's cheek. "You know Jacob Zinn, don't you?"

Bree nodded and shook hands with Jacob.

"Mrs. Nicholls." He pressed her fingers briefly. "I had thought you would have headed back to Oregon by now. There's not much in Rock Harbor to interest an outsider, eh?" His dark eyes flickered over her then just as quickly dismissed her. He spoke with the familiar Yooper cadence, punctuating his sentence with an "eh" and ending with an upward lilt that made the statement almost a question.

How long would she have to live here before people like Jacob accepted her? Twenty years, fifty? If she took out an ad in the newspaper and proclaimed her intention never to leave, he still wouldn't believe it. "This is my home, Mr. Zinn. My family is here."

He snorted and waved his hand in a dismissive gesture. "They will never be found, Mrs. Nicholls. The North Woods guards her secrets well. I suggest you pick up your life and get on with it." Without waiting for a reply, he nodded to Hilary and strode away.

"That man is so rude," Hilary said. She linked arms with Bree. "We're your family, not just Rob and Davy. Come with me. The Asterses just arrived, and I want to say hello."

Though Jacob Zinn's invective had made Bree reel, Hilary's words made her heart sing. Words of approval from her were as rare as a Michigan monkey flower. If she could freeze this moment, the next time Hilary bit her head off she could remember this and savor it. She walked arm in arm with Hilary to greet Fay and Steve Asters, with Mason trailing at a distance.

Hilary dropped Bree's arm and held out a hand to Fay. "I'm so glad you could make it," she said, her gaze on Steve.

Bree knew Fay and Steve Asters fairly well. As manager of the Rock Harbor Savings and Loan, Steve had been forced to handle the mortgage paperwork on the lighthouse when the loan officer quit. Rob had trusted Steve, and Bree found him quite charming. She and Fay met for coffee once in a while, though Bree found the other woman's intense need for attention somewhat off-putting. An hour at a time was the most she could usually stomach being with her.

Hilary launched into easy conversation with Steve. Bree sometimes wondered if there was more history between Hilary and Steve than a simple high-school romance that ended when Steve fell for Fay.

"How goes the search?" Fay asked with a flip of her palm while Steve chatted with Mason and Hilary. Fay's fingers fluttered in the air to punctuate every word. Her dark blue eyes glittered with avid interest in everything around her.

"Nowhere," Bree said. Just once, she wished people would talk to her about something else. But the search was always the first topic. Did they ever stop to think she might be interested in the weather or politics?

"Maybe I could join you one day," Fay said, twisting the gold hoops in her ears. "I saw something the other day that needed checking out. There was a woman outside a cabin. In the ravine beside it, I thought I saw an old airplane seat."

Bree had learned to take everything Fay said as the bid for attention it usually was. Six months ago, Fay had told everyone in Anu Nicholls's shop that she'd seen a jacket like Davy's along the river near Ontonagon. Bree had rushed there only to find a man's red parka rather than a child's blue jacket. "An airplane seat?" she asked, measuring her interest. "Are you sure?"

"Not totally sure, but it looked odd sitting there. I just can't remember what sector I was in. I'll try to remember."

"Can you think of any identifying landmarks?" That would be one way to see how much truth was in Fay.

"Oh, let's talk about this later," Fay said, waving away her earlier comments. "It's probably nothing."

Almost certainly it was nothing. Still, what did she have to lose by looking? There were no other clues clamoring for attention. She just needed to know where to look. "Why don't we meet at the Suomi for coffee in the morning?"

"Fine." Fay stretched with ferretlike grace then tugged on her husband's arm. "As long as I don't have to eat anything."

Fay normally ate like Samson. Bree lifted an eyebrow. "Dieting?"

"Hardly." Fay gave a little laugh. "I'm going to look like a tub by the time the next seven months are up. Steve and I are going to have a baby!"

Bree didn't miss the triumphant smile Fay tossed at Hilary. Hilary's face froze for several long moments, then she managed a brittle smile that didn't include her eyes.

"Congratulations. When is the . . . the baby due?" Hilary asked.

Bree heard the pain underneath the lighthearted voice, though she didn't understand it. Did Hilary still really care for Steve? Poor Mason. Her gaze lingered on the sheriff's face, but he seemed unperturbed.

"Not until May. I'm just barely knocked up." Fay's tinkling laugh came again.

"How . . . how wonderful," Hilary managed. "You must excuse me."

Bree watched her rush away then excused herself and followed her to the rest room.

The ladies' room was a luxurious space with marble floors and counters, gold-plated fixtures, and mauve wallpaper in a subtle acanthus pattern. Hilary stood at a counter in front of the mirror, her eyes too bright in her white face.

"I couldn't stay another minute," Hilary said. Her chest heaved in small pants. Her fingers darted into the picture-perfect coiffure of curls piled atop her head.

"What's wrong, Hilary?" Bree went to her and touched her shoulder.

"Why, nothing, of course. What could be wrong? My reelection is a shoo-in, Mason's job is going well, and he'll certainly be reelected too." She stopped, and chagrin spread over her face. "I didn't mean that the way it sounded. But really, I need to count my blessings."

"What's wrong? Is it Fay's announcement? Did something happen today? You can tell me." Bree's unease grew. Whatever ailed her sister-in-law, it was something major.

Hilary's lips twisted, and she began to tremble. She leaned forward and gripped the edge of the marble counter with both hands.

"I'm never going to have a baby, Bree." She sobbed. "You can't imagine the money we've poured into the fertility clinic in Marquette the past weeks as they've run all those tests. But today another disappointment. I was sure I was pregnant," she whispered. "I was nearly two weeks late, my stomach was bloated, nausea—all the symptoms. I'd hoped to announce it tonight. I finally got up the courage to buy a pregnancy test. It was negative. Then the doctor called with all my test results, and . . . and . . ." Hilary leaned against the wall for support. "He says Mason has a low sperm count. We may never have a baby. Now Fay flaunts her pregnancy in front of me like a war trophy. I could have had Steve, you know. He was mine before she moved to town. I hate her; I hate her! That baby should have been mine."

"You don't hate her. Come sit down." Bree embraced Hilary and led her to a wingback chair positioned against the wall. "Sit here. I'll get you some water." The marble counter held crystal glasses with cardboard covers in a neat pile on a mirrored tray. Bree's hand shook as she held a glass under the faucet and filled it with water.

Hilary took the glass Bree offered and gulped it down. "I haven't told Mason yet. I can't bear to disappoint him again; he'll blame himself. We intended to have at least four, you know. And here we are ten years later with just the two of us rattling around in that great mausoleum that was built for a family."

"What about adoption?" Bree said tentatively. She'd thought of adopting a child herself. None could ever replace Davy, but maybe another child, one who needed a home as desperately as she needed a reason for living, would fill the empty void in her heart.

Hilary shook her head. "I want a child of my own, a baby I carry in my body."

"I see." Words of advice rose in her throat and died there like a cake gone flat in the oven. Rob's family was all she had left, the only safe haven left to her. Hilary's rage could rise like Vesuvius, and Bree didn't want to be caught in the lava flow. Not now.

As Bree predicted, anger quickly replaced the sorrow on Hilary's face. She rose and grabbed a tissue from the counter. "I should have known you wouldn't understand! Everyone would know it wasn't my baby. I don't want their pity! Oh, why am I even talking to you about it? You never say anything that matters. I don't know what's wrong with you lately."

Bree couldn't explain it to her sister-in-law any more than she could explain it to herself. Hilary brushed past Bree and began to repair the damage to her makeup. Dabbing at her face, she tested a smile, then her face crumpled again. She dabbed at the tears until she finally succeeded in putting on a serene face.

"It will be all I can do to even speak to that cat Fay. I hate her!" She swept out the door without looking back.

Bree followed at a distance. Hilary melted into the festive crowd with a laugh that seemed to fool her friends but pierced Bree with dregs of sorrow as bitter as old tea. Hilary was right. Since Rob and Davy had died, she'd lost hold of who she was, and she didn't know how to find herself again.

"Bree, *kulta,* I have looked everywhere for you."

The soft sound of her mother-in-law's voice was enough to ease Bree's tension. Anu Nicholls always knew what to do. Bree turned to greet her with a smile. "How lovely you look!" Bree told her.

Dressed in a creamy gown overlaid with exquisite Finnish lace, Anu Nicholls wore her fair hair high on her head in a coronet of braids. Though nearly sixty, Anu boasted shining hair that held no trace of gray, and her face was as unlined as Bree's. From the moment Bree had married Rob and became a Nicholls, Anu had claimed her as one of her own, though the same couldn't be said for the rest of the family.

As Anu embraced Bree, her mother-in-law's subtle perfume slipped over Bree like a caress.

"So *kumoon* you look. Slim and so beautiful." Anu linked a graceful arm through Bree's and strolled toward the pastry table. "Come with me. You know how wonderful Hilary's thimbleberry tarts are. Even when I know my hips will pay, never can I resist."

"Like you have to worry about your figure!" Bree eyed Anu's lithe, long limbs with envy. She hated being short. If she could pick someone to look like, it would be Anu Nicholls. In fact, Bree wished she were like Anu in all ways. They had a lot in common even now, especially in love. They both had loved and lost. Anu's husband had run out on her after five years of marriage, leaving her to raise Rob and Hilary alone. He'd never so much as written to let her know he was still alive. The abandoned woman had never remarried, though not for lack of admirers.

Rob's father never knew the way the town looked up to Rob. The night he was appointed fire chief, Bree and Rob had lain in bed and talked far into the night. Rob confessed he'd always worked hard in his profession so that maybe someday he could make his dad proud enough of him to come back. Bree had held him as he cried that night, and it made her hate Rob's father for more than just abandoning Anu.

Anu had bounced back though. She'd opened Nicholls's Finnish Imports nearly twenty years ago, and it had grown into one of the finest Finnish shops in the country. Bree loved to touch the shop's beautiful items, treasures like Arabia china and colorful Marimekko linens. Working there was a joy, not a chore.

"Something has caused that long face, eh?"

Bree came back to earth and managed a smile. "Did you find anything new in Finland for the shop?" Bree said, knowing shop news should distract her.

Anu brightened. "Some lovely wool sweaters. And a new line of saunas I will carry." She wagged her finger under Bree's nose. "Do not change the subject. You were about to tell me what hides that lovely smile. And do not tell me 'nothing.' I know you too well."

Hilary would be livid if she revealed something she didn't want her mother to know. "I was with Hilary," she began, trying to think of a way to deflect the question.

Anu held up a slim hand. "That is enough of an explanation. I suppose she was badgering you again. I'm sorry, my Bree. I have tried to talk with her, but she refuses to listen to reason."

Bree took the invitation to drop the topic and switched to another. "I'm still having no luck finding any trace of the plane crash," she admitted.

Anu was silent for a long moment, her gaze pensive, then her eyes grew luminous with tears. "I spent much time thinking at the Puulan Lake cottage," Anu said. "The time has come to let it go, Bree." Anu's blue-eyed gaze gently traveled over Bree's face. "When Abe left me, I clung to the hope he would return. At holidays, the children's birth-days, I was sure he would call or write, or show up at the door. I spent my life imagining how I would act, what I would say. Then one day I woke up and knew he wasn't coming back. He was as dead to me as if he were buried in Rock Harbor Cemetery." She rubbed her forehead.

"It is time we all faced facts. Rob and Davy are gone. It is time for you to move on with your life. We must cease asking the impossible of you. They are gone. Let them rest in peace."

Bree's throat clenched, and she felt the beginning flutters of a panic attack, an experience she hadn't had in nearly six months. She couldn't let go of Rob and Davy, not quite yet.

"Soon," she whispered. "But not yet, Anu. Not yet."

Anu laid a hand on Bree's cheek. "I know it is hard, *kulta*. But you will grow stronger when you let go."

Bree shook her head. "I'm giving myself until the first of the year. It seems appropriate, don't you think?" Anu shrugged in acquiescence, and Bree wondered if she would give it up even then. The search was the only connection she had with her son and her husband, faithless though he was. Without that search to give her life meaning, what else was there?

4

$\mathcal{B}$ree dutifully made the rounds through the room, shaking hands, smiling until her face hurt, and garnering all the goodwill and votes she could manage for her sister-in-law. Most folks had heard of the latest rescue and congratulated her. In spite of such kindness, events like this emphasized her presence as an outsider even as she slogged on in her quest to be accepted.

One family, however, loved Bree in the way she craved. She spotted Palmer and Lily Chambers from across the room and went to join them. Their friendship was birthed in the context of misery loving company, since they were outsiders to Rock Harbor themselves. Lily and Palmer had opened a fitness center after Palmer's stint as an airplane mechanic in the military was over. Today, two years later, the fitness center still barely limped along, a fact not too surprising, considering most of Rock Harbor's residents believed true exercise could only be had outdoors. Fishing, swimming, hiking, hunting—all these were acceptable forms. The Chamberses' high-tech machines were viewed with suspicion that was lifting only little by little.

Lily turned as Bree approached. Her round, homely face was wreathed in smiles of welcome. "Bree, I've been meaning to call and invite you to dinner. What are you doing tomorrow night? Or is that too late of a notice?"

"Let's see, dinner at your home or macaroni and cheese from a box? That's a no-brainer, I think." Bree laughed. "What time, girlfriend?"

Lily turned to Palmer. "Six sound good?"

Palmer nodded. "I should be done with my meeting by five." He hugged Bree with one arm around her shoulders. "You've been too much a stranger lately. Bring Samson; the girls have been yammering to see him."

Slender with fine blond hair and green eyes, Palmer's good looks seemed incongruous next to Lily's plain features. The fact he'd seen beyond Lily's plain exterior to her beautiful spirit endeared him to Bree. And she adored their two-year-old twins, Paige and Penelope.

"There are some darling puppies at the shelter," Bree said. "Why don't I pick up the girls one night next week and take them over to pick one out?"

Palmer wagged his finger at her. "I haven't decided to get one yet."

"Oh, Palmer, you know perfectly well you'll give in sooner or later. You might as well do it gracefully now," Lily put in.

"We'll see," Palmer said, smiling. "Now we'd better go. The sitter will need to get home."

"We'll see you tomorrow at six," Lily reminded Bree.

Bree watched a moment as Palmer and Lily wove their way back through the crowd. A warm contentment settled in her bones. It was nice to have friends like that, friends who cared about her in tangible ways.

Around nine o'clock, her feet throbbing, Bree slipped into a corner and found a chair by the curtains that formed a small hallway between the main hall and a smaller room. Scooting her chair partially into the other room and away from the crowd, she eased out of her shoes and rubbed her feet. Another half an hour and she could go home. She'd look for Naomi next.

Moments later Fay joined her. She sat in the chair beside Bree then opened her purse and took out a cigarette. She lit it and blew a circle of smoke in the air.

"Smoking isn't good for the baby," Bree said, knowing Fay wouldn't care if she spoke her mind.

"I'm not about to give up my life for this baby," Fay said. Her gaze roamed the room.

Such disregard for her baby's well-being made Bree want to get up and walk away. "Aren't you happy about it?" she asked.

Fay shrugged. "I'm not sure yet. Ask me again after it's here and I can tell whether the changes are good or bad."

A movement across the empty room caught Bree's attention. The side door opened, and a man stepped in. Bree had never seen him, though he reminded her of someone. Then she realized he looked like a younger version of the pictures she'd seen of Elvis before booze and drugs had marred his good looks. Though "the King" had died when Bree was a child, she'd been fascinated by articles she had read about him in old *Modern Screen* and *Photoplay* magazines she'd found in the back of her mother's closet.

The same petulant expression crossed this man's face as he scanned the room from his partially hidden position in the curtains. When his gaze settled on Fay, the smoldering look deepened, and he swaggered across the room toward Fay as though adoring fans screamed along the sidelines. Fay saw him approach and scowled. He stopped in front of her and stood with his hands on his hips, looking down at her.

"You said you'd meet me at nine." The man made no attempt to lower his voice.

"What are you doing here, Eric?" Fay hissed. "Get out before Steve sees you. He's already asking questions."

"Then tell him the truth!"

"Don't tell me what to do. We're playing this my way." Fay ground out her cigarette on the floor and stood to walk away.

Eric grabbed her arm. "You think you can snap your fingers and I'll follow at your heels. Don't make that mistake. I'm not a lap dog like your husband."

"Take your hands off me." She jerked her arm away, but he grabbed it again.

Bree rose, and Eric glared at her. An older man materialized from the main hall. Bree recognized him as Fay's uncle, Lawrence Kukkari.

"This man bothering you, Fay?" he asked.

"No, he's just leaving," Fay said. "I'll meet you later," she said softly to Eric. "Now please leave before Steve comes looking for me." She smiled prettily, but Eric's scowl just deepened.

"I won't wait forever, Fay."

"I'll meet you later," Fay whispered. "Please, don't make a scene."

"One hour. Then I come looking for you again." With a muttered oath, Eric spun on his heels and stalked away.

Bree's gaze followed him as he made his way through the crowd. Kade Matthews put out a hand to intercept him, and Eric stopped to talk to him. Bree frowned as she saw them talking. Kade appeared to be as angry as Eric. At one point he stabbed his finger in Eric's chest for emphasis. How did he know this guy?

Lawrence's voice drew her attention back to Fay. "You know better than to get mixed up with him again."

"Don't start, Uncle." Fay's voice was soft with weariness. "I don't meddle in your private life, and I don't want you meddling in mine."

The scowl on Lawrence's face eased. "Very well. Have you thought any more about the new offer for the mine? Mr. Simpkins wants an answer."

"I told you, I've already agreed to sell the mine to Palmer Chambers."

"You're throwing away a hundred thousand dollars!" Lawrence's voice rose.

Bree looked around for a place to slink away. Being in the middle of someone else's argument felt awkward. Unfortunately, Lawrence blocked her path to escape.

Lawrence glanced at Bree and lowered his voice as he continued to argue his case with his niece. "Take this offer, and you'll have enough money to leave Steve and this hick town and start fresh."

"I think you're more concerned with your share than with my happiness," Fay said. "Let's not talk about this anymore. I don't want to be mixed up with mobsters from New York, and I sure don't want them traipsing around my mine. I don't trust them, and I *do* trust Palmer."

"If you force my hand, I'll tell Steve everything."

Fay laughed, but the tinkle was gone. "What will you tell him, Uncle Lawrence? That I married him for his money and now that it's gone I'm splitting? He already knows why I married him. But in spite of your high opinion of me, I'm not leaving him. Not now. Things have changed. I've got a baby to think about." She slung her purse over one shoulder and moved away.

"You can't do this!" Lawrence shouted after her.

Fay just waved a hand over her head and kept going. Lawrence shook himself, his face a mask of bewilderment. He saw Bree staring at him and scowled then stalked off. "She's going to get me killed," he muttered.

Fay's covert exchanges were too complicated for Bree to think about. She would find Naomi and head for home. Fay could work out her own problems.

The next morning Bree woke in time to watch the sun break free of the horizon. In Bree's mind, Sunday morning should be time spent leisurely over a plate of eggs and bacon, but as she surveyed the contents of her refrigerator, she knew her kitchen couldn't produce such a repast: a near-empty tub of margarine, half a bottle of water, a plate of week-old salmon patties covered in a suspicious moldy tint that could be seen even through the pink plastic wrap. The lone apple in the produce drawer looked more like a prune.

"Nothing fit to eat here, Samson. You want to go out for breakfast?" He barked and ran to the door. "I guess that's a yes." She slipped into her jacket and hooked the leash to his collar. By the time she finished breakfast, Fay should be along for coffee.

Stepping outside into the cool morning air, she and Samson set off at an energetic clip toward Suomi Café, four blocks down Houghton Street. Two blocks in, she tugged on Samson's leash and slowed their pace to enjoy the walk. No one was stirring this early, but Bree thought everyone should see the radiant blue of the sky. The fog bell out in the harbor was tolling, and the blue that was Lake Superior glinted briefly between the houses lining the water. Another altogether glorious day in paradise.

Some would laugh at her for describing snow country as paradise, but then they likely had never smelled the cold freshness of pollution-free air or watched a white blanket of snow cloak everything in clean, pristine beauty. Bree couldn't imagine a better place on earth. A colorful autumn day like this offered a glimpse of perfection.

Rock Harbor, population twenty-five hundred if you counted Anu's chickens, couldn't be more picturesque. From the first moment Bree set foot on the volcanic soil of Michigan's western Upper Peninsula, she knew she'd come home. The Victorian storefronts looked the same as they did in century-old photographs. That fact had always been a comfort to Bree, but especially in the previous year. She'd had too many changes in her life.

Nestled at the base of Quincy Hill, Rock Harbor's three-block downtown area could have come straight from a child's storybook. The town's major businesses lined Houghton Street, which was intersected by Jack Pine Lane and Pepin Street. To stroll the village streets was to step back in time. Even the corner butcher showed a marked resemblance to Barney Fife. With the recent influx of tourists, many store owners were busy sprucing up and painting the storefronts with cheerful schemes that reminded Bree of San Francisco row houses. From her lighthouse tower, she could look down on the town and marvel at its perfection.

Suomi Café overlooked Lake Superior from its perch on the steep slope of Kitchigami Street. Named for the Finnish word for Finland, the humble café offered no exterior hint of the culinary delights inside. Just thinking of the possible menu choices made Bree's mouth water.

She quickened her step and had almost reached the café entrance when a squawk came from overhead. Bree looked up as a starling flew down at her. She ducked, suppressing a scream and barely avoiding the dive-bombing bird. The bird peeled around and came at her again.

"What's the matter with you, stupid bird?" Bree waved her arms, trying to frighten it away. She liked birds fine as long as they stayed in the trees. This one must be psychotic. It dived at her a third time, and she turned quickly for the door. Samson whined then barked at the bird before following Bree inside the restaurant.

She tousled her hair to make sure there were no feathers in it. The head waitress, Molly, a full tray in her skinny arms, nodded to her. In her forties, Molly was a whirlwind of activity every time Bree came in. It was no wonder she carried not an ounce of spare flesh on her thin frame.

Molly set the steamy plates before her customers then stopped beside Bree. "You look wild-eyed, kid. Why's your tail in a knot this morning, eh?" she quipped as she patted Samson's head. Having received his welcome, Samson went to lie down at the door.

"Some stupid bird was after my hair. It's hanging around outside your café."

Molly grinned. "Other customers have been complaining too. I think it's someone's pet. It landed on my shoulder this morning and took some crumbs right from my hand."

"Well, they ought to keep it home then!" Bree glanced around the restaurant. "The place looks packed this morning."

Every booth and table was taken. Bree looked over the pastry case. Suomi's specialty was *pulla,* a Finnish sweet roll made with sourdough bread that Bree was particularly fond of. But she didn't really want to take it back home. She'd spent too much time alone lately.

"It's usually not this busy until later. You might see if there's anyone willing to share a table," Molly said before hurrying off to the kitchen.

Bree glanced around the restaurant again. Fay sat in a corner booth with her elbows on the table. She caught Bree's eye and motioned to her. Today Fay looked like a fifteen-year-old on her way to school, her hair casually windblown and her pale complexion devoid of makeup. A backpack even lay at her feet. An ashtray holding two cigarette butts sat next to a cup of coffee between Fay's elbows.

Molly scurried by with a cup of coffee for Bree and a plate of half-eaten eggs for Samson. "For our hero," she said.

"You look a little green," Bree told Fay. "Try eating some toast or crackers."

"How long does this last?" Fay moaned. "I don't have time to be sick."

"Going climbing again today?" Bree asked, pointing toward the backpack. Though the U.P. didn't offer world-class mountains, there were some pretty good cliffs in the area.

"I might as well, if I can muster the energy. Steve is working, and I'm bored." Fay fiddled with one of the distinctive gold hoops that adorned her ears. Then she dropped her hand and sighed.

"Are you sure it's safe for you to climb?"

Fay grimaced. "I told you last night, I'm not going to change my life for this baby. I'm still me. The doctor said I could do whatever I'm used to doing."

Bree felt a twinge of guilt for the judgment in her question. No need to dig her hole any deeper. "Have you remembered anything more about the cabin and the airplane seat?"

Fay scowled. "No. Steve and I had another fight last night, and I didn't get a chance to think about it. Give me a few days. If there's anything worth remembering, it will come to me."

So the story about the woman and the airplane seat *was* just a bid for attention. Bree doubted the same could be said of Fay's encounter with Eric the night before. Bree had a feeling she should know something about Eric, something she'd read or heard. She wanted to ask Fay about him, though it was none of her business. She decided against it.

They drank their coffee and talked about last night's party, carefully skirting the arguments Bree had overheard. Fay kept glancing at her watch and fidgeting. Finally, she stubbed out her fourth cigarette and rose. "I'd better get going. I hope you find something."

Fay's diffidence made Bree second-guess whether she really did know something about Rob's plane. Her usual mode was high drama, and this understated comment seemed out of character.

Fay stepped into the aisle and right into Palmer's path. He stopped abruptly. "Just who I was looking for. I have the papers ready for you to sign. Is it okay if I drop by tomorrow night?"

Fay nodded. "I suppose so. We'll be around." Her voice seemed lackluster, and Bree wondered if it was just her morning sickness or if she wished she wasn't selling the mine. Did Fay and Steve need the money?

She moved past him. "Now, if you'll excuse me, I've got a cliff calling my name."

Palmer winked at Bree then joined two men at the back table.

"I'll come with you," Bree told Fay impulsively as she started to walk away. "We can talk while we hike." Though climbing was out of the question for Bree, they could talk on the way.

Fay shook her head. "I'm sorry, but I really need some alone time this morning."

Fay could be as immovable as a thirty-foot jack pine, and her obstinate expression warned Bree to let it go. The thought crossed Bree's mind that Fay was adamant because she was meeting someone, maybe Eric.

"Sorry to be a pest," Bree said. "I'll talk to you later."

Fay gave her a distracted smile before she hurried out the door.

Molly appeared at Bree's table. "Fay is upset, eh? She looked like she'd been crying when she came in." Molly's speech was typical of a Yooper. A blend of Finnish and Canadian cadence and an accent that Bree found charming.

Bree picked up a menu. "You know Fay. No one understands her moods."

Molly sniffed and nodded. "What will you have, eh? The *panukakkua* just came out of the oven."

Panukakkua. The thought of the custard pancake dripping with hot raspberry sauce brought a Pavlovian response from Bree. The *pulla* would wait. "You know my weakness," Bree said, nodding. "And more coffee."

"You got it." Molly tucked the order pad in a pocket of her apron and went to the kitchen.

Moments later Hilary rushed up to Bree's table with Mason in tow. Her eyes sparkled with excitement. "I knew I'd find you here. You're as predictable as an atomic clock." She dropped a newspaper onto the table. A picture of Bree and Samson stared back at Bree from the front page of the *Kitchigami Journal*. "Just the publicity my office can use!" she crowed. "It even mentions you're the mayor's sister-in-law."

Bree looked at the paper but didn't pick it up. Newspaper articles were nothing new to her and Samson. Something of a nuisance, actually.

Hilary and Mason sat down. "Where are you searching next?" Hilary asked.

"I'm starting a new sector, west of the gorge."

Mason cleared his throat. "We need to attend to the debriefing for yesterday's search as well. I thought you might come by yesterday. What can you tell me?"

She'd meant to but had forgotten all about it. Glad to get Hilary off the search topic, Bree told Mason of the clues they'd followed, the areas they'd searched, and how they had found the children. Molly brought Bree's breakfast and coffee. Mason took notes in backward looping letters simple enough for a grade-school kid to read.

Ten minutes later Hilary tapped her fingernails on the table. "Are we about done? We're going to be late for church if we don't get going." Gathering her purse, she slid from the seat and waited for her husband.

Mason shrugged. "I reckon we are now. Call me if you think of anything else, Bree, eh?" He nodded to Bree and followed his wife out of the café.

Bree lifted her cup and took a gulp. Hilary was happy with her now, but it wouldn't last long. Nothing would satisfy her but for Bree to find little Davy and Rob so they could all move on. Sometimes she felt stuck in an old black-and-white episode of *Twilight Zone,* facing a life that had been twisted by her own hands into something unrecognizable.

She shivered and looked at the *panukakkua.* It was cold.

5

utside, the autumn sunshine lifted Bree's spirits. She'd better enjoy it while she could. Once winter hit, days of sunshine would be replaced by gray clouds. On her way to the hospital, she passed folks raking leaves and mulching flower beds. Rock Harbor Hospital, catty-corner from Siltanen Piano Repair, was an unimaginative square brick building that didn't do justice to its setting. Manicured grounds at the rear of the facility swooped down to a peaceful beach. Bree pointed to a blazing red-leafed tree close to the rear entrance and told Samson to stay. He sat obediently while she went inside.

Emily was flipping through TV channels when Bree poked her head into the room. "Hi, sweetheart. Remember me?"

Emily's face brightened. "Bree! I was just thinking about you. Where's Samson?"

"He's waiting for you in the garden." Bree turned off the TV and glanced at the other bed. Timmy's small face was turned into the pillow, and a slight snore issued from his nose. "How's your brother?"

"Okay. I get to go home when Daddy gets off work." The little girl bit her lip. "I asked Daddy to stay with us today, but he said he didn't get inventory finished yesterday because of my sen . . . sh . . . shenanigans. I think he's still mad at me."

The plaintive note in Emily's voice touched Bree's heart. "He's just glad to get you home," she said. "But I'll keep you company for a while. The nurse says it would be okay for me to take you down to the garden to visit with Samson. Would you like to do that?"

"Sure!" Emily hopped from the bed.

Bree found Emily's fuzzy raccoon slippers under the bed. "Let's hope these raccoons don't lead you into trouble like the last ones."

Emily's cheeks flushed. "I won't do that again," she said. She tiptoed to Timmy's bed and touched his head. "I'll be back in a little while, Timmy," she whispered.

Her brother just muttered in his sleep. Though his lashes fluttered on his cheeks a bit, he didn't awaken.

"Do you think we should leave him?" Emily asked. "He's my 'sponsibility."

Bree put her hand on Emily's head. "The nurses will take good care of him, sweetie. We'll only be gone a few minutes." Emily carried a heavy burden, and Bree wished she could ease it.

Emily leaned her head into Bree's hand. "That feels so good," she said. "Mommy used to braid my hair before she went away. I miss her."

Bree swallowed hard. Did Davy miss her combing his hair, or were there angels to do it for him in heaven?

Emily smiled up at Bree. "Do you think Samson will remember me?"

"I'm sure he will. He was very excited when we got to the hospital. I think he smelled your scent here." Bree took Emily's hand. "I have a wheelchair right outside the door. The nurse said you had to ride down to the garden in it."

"Cool!" Emily raced to the door and climbed into the wheelchair. Her feet stuck out in front of her, and she wiggled her raccoon slippers.

Bree wheeled her past the nurses' station and into the elevator.

"Have you ever been to Florida?" Emily asked Bree as the elevator jerked into motion.

The look on Davy's face when he saw Mickey at Disney World flashed into Bree's mind. "Yes," she said.

"Did you go to Disney World? Daddy says he's going to take us someday, and we can see our grandma."

Bree nodded slowly. "W—we took our son to Disney World for his first birthday."

"Oh, you have a little boy! I wish you could have brought him along for me to play with," Emily said. "How old is he?"

"He's in heaven now, but he would be four." She was quite proud of herself for holding her voice steady.

Emily contemplated this news. "Timmy's four."

The elevator door opened, and Bree wheeled Emily into the lobby and down a hall. Through the glass doors, Samson watched them come, and he stretched as he stood.

"What kind of dog is he? He has a curly tail."

"What we call a 'Heinz fifty-seven.' He's a mixture of several things, some German shepherd, some chow, maybe a bit of Border collie."

Bree wheeled Emily through the doors and into the sunshine of the hospital's garden area.

"Samson!" Emily cried. The dog trotted to her and licked her chin. Emily laughed and rubbed his head.

"You want to sit under the tree?" Bree asked. Emily nodded, and Bree rolled the wheelchair along the brick walk to a huge tree whose trunk was covered with ivy.

"Can I sit at the picnic table?" Emily asked.

"How about we play ball with Samson?" Bree produced a ball from her jacket pocket. Samson barked excitedly. "Samson, quiet!" Bree commanded. The dog instantly stopped barking.

"I bet you're a good mommy," Emily said. She took the ball and threw it as hard as she could into the yard.

Bree swallowed. What could she say to that? If she were a good mother, wouldn't she have thought of Davy before she called Rob? If only she hadn't upset him before he got into the plane, wouldn't they both still be here?

Samson raced across the grass, snatched up the ball, then carried it back to Emily, his tail waving proudly. He dropped it in her lap. Emily picked it up. "Oh, gross!" she said. "Dog slobber."

Bree laughed. "But it's full of love." She took off her jacket. "That sun is getting hot."

"I was cold in the woods. I didn't want to leave the cabin," Emily said.

Bree stared at her. "What cabin?"

"The witch in the woods took us to her cabin. I told you." Emily's lip trembled. "You don't believe me either!"

"You keep talking about the witch in the woods. There is no witch, Emily. You must have dreamed it." Bree was beginning to wonder if she should talk to the doctor about Emily's peculiar obsession. There was no way the story could be true. No one would have fed the children just to abandon them in the forest again, especially with Timmy so sick.

Emily's stormy expression vanished. "I like to tell stories," she said. "Maybe I'll write books someday. But I did see a lady there."

Bree sighed, but she smiled and took Emily's hand. "I think we'd better go check on your brother." Davy had had an active imagination too. Children were such a joy that way. It was better not to argue with them over their imaginary friends.

By the time Bree got home, it was one o'clock, so she fixed herself a peanut butter sandwich. The day could not be more perfect. The repair on the brick wouldn't take long, if she could just convince herself to try it. This should be an easy fear to face. Little by little over the past year, she'd overcome the terrors that woke her in the night. Her fear of heights could be overcome too. But not if she didn't try, if she didn't get up and do something about it.

Bree forced herself to stand, then moved on leaden legs to the back patio where the mortar still waited. She mixed it then carried the bucket up the curving iron steps of the light tower. She fastened the leather work belt around her waist and stepped out onto the metal catwalk that circled the tower of her lighthouse home like a tiara on the head of an aging beauty queen.

The wind freshened, bringing the scent of Lake Superior to her nose. The waves along the lake made a booming sound as they struck the buoy out in the cove. Her lighthouse home had stood for over a century on a thin slice of land that thrust itself into Superior's waves with all the arrogance of a scepter extended to a penitent. But it would soon crumble around her if she didn't marshal the courage to get this job done.

Looking over the railing, a wave of dizziness swept over her, and the ground tilted. Gripping the railing with tight fingers, she whispered, "I can do this."

Fay had loaned her a rappelling harness weeks ago. Bree fastened it to the railing. Her heart raced. She knew the sturdy rope should hold her, but she couldn't help imagining spiraling down the side of the tower and slamming against the grassy knoll far below. She squeezed her eyes shut. Had there been time enough for Rob and Davy to feel this fear that dried her mouth like the Sonoran desert?

Bree swallowed and tightly gripped the catwalk post and rail. She wedged the toe of her boot against the lower rail and swung around so her back was to Superior's cold spray. Standing with one foot on the lower rail, she silently castigated herself. All she had to do was swing that other leg over the railing, and she'd be standing outside the catwalk. Why couldn't she perform such a simple action?

With blood roaring in her ears like some Superior squall, Bree gripped the railing and told herself she could do it. The bag of mortar bumped against her thigh and startled her. She closed her eyes again and shuddered. *Just get it over with.* Still straddling the railing, she tested the strength of the rope again, more to delay the inevitable than anything else.

She was going to do this. Swinging her other leg over, she stood poised on the edge of the balcony. *Now* all she had to do was step into space. The rope would hold her. The lead in her legs had turned to jelly, but she forced herself to go on. She could conquer this fear. She stepped away, and then she was walking along the vertical side of the lighthouse, rappelling down the tower. This was easier than she'd thought it would be.

Squinting against the harsh sun, she glanced up at the hook that snapped around the railing. Her eyes widened in spite of the glare. The railing was beginning to bend. Her stomach lurched. She had to get back up before it came loose.

She was going to die. Her breath came in short gasps. The railing wouldn't hold long, and she would plummet to her death. She tried to shout for help, but only a squeak slipped past her tight throat.

"What are you doing?" Naomi poked her head over the edge of the balcony. "This is not a job for you. You get back inside right now."

"I would if I could," Bree whispered.

Naomi stepped onto the metal catwalk, and it shook a bit with her steps. Bree shuddered.

"Hold on." Naomi grabbed the rope and began to wind it around her waist. In jerky movements, Bree began to rise to the balcony. She was afraid to move, afraid she would take Naomi down with her.

Naomi grunted with the exertion. "Almost there," she panted.

Then Bree was at the top, and Naomi was helping her over the railing. Both women tumbled to the shaky deck and lay gasping.

Bree's breathing began to return to normal, and she sat up. "I would have died if you hadn't come. The railing was giving way."

"I saw." Naomi's eyes were bright with tears. "Something inside, almost like a voice, told me you needed me. It had to be God," she whispered.

Irritation flared up in place of Bree's relief. Of course Naomi would give God the credit. Her gaze traveled to the misshapen railing. She felt her annoyance wane. Could it be possible Naomi was right?

Naomi touched Bree's shoulder in a comforting gesture. "You're all right. Let's get you inside."

On wobbly legs, Bree managed to walk to the door and step through into the light tower. "That wasn't pretty," she said. "Thanks." She attempted a smile. "I guess I'll have to sell this and buy one of those new tract homes going up on Cottage Avenue. Look at all the money I'd make. People would be lining up at the door to buy a dilapidated lighthouse with a crumbling tower and mold in the basement."

"Don't joke. I know what it cost you to go out there. I think you're very brave," Naomi said.

Bree looked away. If Naomi only knew. "I need a cup of coffee," she said.

Naomi nodded. "Want to join us for dinner?"

Bree didn't want to face the pity in Naomi's expression. She couldn't face her own failure again. "I'm supposed to go to Lily and Palmer's for dinner." She squeezed her friend's hand. "But thanks, Naomi."

As Bree left the lighthouse, a hint of rain freshened the air. The wind began to blow across Lake Superior, kicking up scuds of white foam and flotsam onto the beach. What had happened to her perfect day? Bree tightened her jacket around her chest and bent against the wind. The rich aroma of espresso wafted through the door of The Coffee Place. Bree followed the fragrance like it was the Pied Piper. Caffeine was what she needed.

The bell on the door jingled, and she shut the door against the wind. "I'll have a double espresso with whipped cream on top. Lots of whipped cream."

The young woman behind the counter nodded. Bree didn't recognize her. Probably new. Bree waved to her hairdresser, Sally Wilson, and nodded to Steve Asters. He got up when he saw her and moved to join her at the counter.

"I'm glad to see you," he said. A faint scratch ran across his right cheek.

"New at this shaving stuff, Steve?" Bree asked, teasing.

His hand went to his cheek and he flushed. "New razor," he said. "Can I talk to you for a minute?" He gestured to a table in the corner.

The new girl put Bree's espresso on the counter. "Sure." Bree picked up her coffee and followed Steve.

He sat in the seat opposite her. "Fay hasn't come home," he whispered, glancing around to make sure they weren't being overheard. "At first I didn't think anything about it. She went climbing this morning. But we're supposed to go to a dinner with the bank's board of directors at six-thirty, and she still isn't home." Bree glanced at her watch. Nearly three. "She promised to be home by one."

"I saw her this morning," she admitted. "About eight. She was heading out to climb."

Steve nodded. "I'm getting worried. It's not like Fay. I tried calling her cell phone, but she never answered. I'd like you to look for her."

"First things first. Have you contacted the sheriff?"

He shook his head. "That wouldn't do me any good. It hasn't been twenty-four hours yet."

"Let's call Mason. Since Fay is pregnant, he might bend the rules. I could meet him out there and take a look around."

Steve's eyes brightened and he nodded, taking his small fliptop cell phone from the inside pocket of his jacket. Bree sipped her espresso while Steve explained the situation to Mason.

"He's on his way," he said after closing the phone. "He's in Houghton. Said he'd meet you at Rock River Gorge. I think that's where she was going." Steve put away his phone. "Can you take Samson up to the ridge to look around before he gets there? Just to see if maybe

she's twisted her ankle or something? I could get you an article of clothing for the dog to scent from."

An evening at Rock River Gorge was not nearly as appealing as her
plans for dinner with the Chambers family, but she was needed. "I
have to make a call," she said. She took her own cell phone from her
pocket and dialed Lily's number. Her friend promised to keep dinner
warm for her.

"I need to get Samson," she told Steve.

Steve stood. "I'll run by my place and get something of Fay's for
the dog. Maybe a sock?"

Bree nodded. "Pick up the item with your hand inside a paper bag,
then turn the bag inside out so you don't touch the scent article," she
instructed. "Then drop that bag into another paper bag before putting
it all inside a plastic bag."

He blinked and his mouth dropped open. "Can't I just put it in a
plastic bag?"

"Nope. Do it my way so we can keep the scent uncontaminated."

Steve sighed and nodded then hurried out. Bree stayed a moment
longer to make one more call. Maybe Naomi could join her.

By the time she got home and put Samson's vest on him, the sky
had darkened to pewter. The wind shrieked through the eaves and rat-
tled the windows of her old lighthouse. The sound always made Bree
think of Ojibwa Windigos, legendary Indian spirits who prowled for
human flesh. The delightful autumn day had morphed to early winter
without notice. Bree climbed into her insulated nylon jumpsuit and
pulled the hood over her head. She grabbed a bag of pistachios and her
ready-pack and went down the steps.

Samson followed her to the door, and they stepped outside as Steve
pulled into the drive in his new Lexus. He was dressed in a suit and tie.

Bree frowned. "Aren't you going with us?"

He shook his head. "Wish I could, but I'm expected at the dinner," he shouted above the wind. "Here's my cell phone number. Oh,

and one of Fay's socks." He handed Bree a slip of paper with his number written on it through the window, along with a plastic bag containing a sock encased in two paper bags. He began to back out.

Bree stuffed the paper in her pocket and tucked the bag under her arm. "Steve," she began.

He braked and looked at her, and she shook her head. "Nothing," she said. "I'll let you know what I find." He nodded and then sped away.

Bree couldn't believe he would go to a bank dinner rather than help search for his pregnant wife. No wonder Fay had a brittle edge about her. It also explained Eric's presence in her life.

Samson whined, and Bree waved at Naomi and Charley as they hurried across the yard toward the Jeep. Naomi wore her orange jumpsuit, and Charley had on his orange vest. Samson jumped into his kennel at the back of the Jeep then barked a welcome to Charley as Naomi steered her dog into the back also.

"Was that Steve leaving?" Naomi slid into the passenger seat and fastened her seat belt. She raked her fingers through her hair and quickly braided it. Her cheeks were pink from the wind.

"Yes. He had a fancy dinner to attend." Bree didn't bother to hide the disgust in her voice.

"He calls us out on a night like this then goes to a party?" Naomi's voice lifted with indignation.

"Yep. If I were Fay, I'd be giving him a dose of his own medicine too."

"You think that's what this is?"

"I wouldn't be surprised. She didn't seem to be her usual barracuda self this morning. I almost felt sorry for her." Bree started the Jeep and drove down Houghton Street. Leaving the town behind them, she drove out to the gorge.

Bree loved the Rock River Gorge, with its rugged falls and rapids in beautiful forests of pine and hemlock. But tonight, the thick trees deepened the gloom that had blown in with the clouds. Watching the wind whipping the trees and bending the shrubs and bushes over double brought a sense of unease to Bree's throat. Why would Fay stay out in weather like this? Maybe something really was wrong.

She drove slowly through the area looking for Fay's car and found it under the sweep of a blue spruce. Bree parked the Jeep, and she and Naomi got out. Rock River Gorge was just over the hill, It was a favorite place of Fay's; they would check there first. Naomi released the dogs while Bree fetched their gear from the backseat.

Her ears ached from the cold, and she tugged the hood of her jacket a little tighter. She heard a rustling in the thicket. Peering through the vegetation, she tried to see if anything was there. Maybe it was just the wind. She hunched her chin into her jacket then jerked her head around again. There it was again.

"Is anyone there?" For a moment she thought about Emily's witch in the woods. Then a tall figure encased in a tan uniform and a matching jacket stepped through the tangle of brush. Samson and Charley bounded to meet him. Naomi raised her hand in greeting.

"I thought that sounded like Samson and Charley." Kade scratched the dogs on the head before walking toward Bree. "What are you doing here? Weather's turning nasty."

"Fay Asters is missing," Bree said.

He processed this information in silence. "Anyone seen her today?"

Bree nodded. "I saw her this morning before she went climbing. She didn't come home. I can't imagine she's still out here, but I promised Steve I'd look around."

"Was she alone?"

The question seemed casual, but a muscle in Kade's jaw twitched, and Bree remembered his argument with Eric at Hilary's campaign party. She assumed Fay had been seeing Eric, but what was Kade's connection to him?

She forced her inquisitive thoughts away. "As far as we know."

Glancing around, she wondered where Mason was. She'd rather he got there before they started in case something really was wrong.

"Sounds like a wild-goose chase to me," Kade said. He shifted his weight from one foot to the other and pulled his coat around him. "I hear you went to see the O'Reilly youngsters today in the hospital."

"Great kids," Bree said. She opened the hatch and grabbed her backpack then slung it on. "Emily about talked my leg off."

"Mine, too. I stopped by the hospital first, but the doctor had released her so I went by the house. Have you been there?"

She shook her head. "I thought I'd stop over later in the week."

He grimaced. "It's a mess. I think young Emily has tried to be caretaker for the whole family since her mother ran off. She was trying to fix supper when I got there. Donovan invited me to eat with them. Lukewarm hot dogs and potato chips. There was a mountain of laundry on the back porch."

"I've known Donovan a long time," Naomi added. "He seems overwhelmed."

"Poor kids," Bree said. "Hey, maybe Naomi and I could stop over and get the place in order."

"I've got a day off tomorrow. Could you use some help?"

Bree's eyes widened. A man who wasn't too proud to do housework? Now that was an unusual fellow. She took another look at Kade. Broad-shouldered with a face weathered by the sun and wind, he seemed the type to be more at home in the garage than the kitchen. There must be more to the man than met the eye.

"What time?"

"How about we meet at the house after school, say, three o'clock? I don't want to go in while Donovan is home. He seems to be as proud as Midas, though hardly as rich. I hear the hardware store is ailing. That's probably why he hasn't hired someone to help out."

"He's doing the best he can," Naomi put in.

Naomi's voice was a bit truculent, and Bree hid a grin. Her friend had it bad. She turned back to Kade. "Donovan seems pretty harried at the store." Bree felt an unexpected wave of protectiveness toward Emily come over her. Bree remembered only too well the defeat she'd felt as a child trying to keep up with the housework when her mother was gone to the bars all night, and the shame she'd felt when someone from school would stop by.

"We'll meet you at three then," she told him. "Ready to find her, boys?" she asked the dogs. Twilight was coming, and she couldn't wait any longer for Mason. Besides, Kade was here.

Samson barked at Bree as if to ask whom he was looking for. "Here, boys." She opened the sack and held it under the dogs' noses so they could sniff it. "Search!" she told them. The dogs bounded off toward a steep hill covered with vines and the small trunks of new-growth pine and birch.

Bree, Naomi, and Kade followed, trying to keep the dogs in sight. Bree loved to watch the dogs work. Samson paused in the meadow at the top of the hill and worked by zigzagging in a circle with his nose held high as he tried to catch the scent cone. He was focused and intent. Charley raced back and forth across the area in straight lines with his tail wagging, pausing occasionally to sniff out a rabbit. She could tell the moment they both caught the scent, and her heart sank.

Samson gave a little stiff-legged jump before tucking his tail between his legs. He raised his muzzle to the sky and howled, a mournful sound that raised the hair on the back of Bree's neck. Charley hung his head and whimpered then urinated on the leaves. Both dogs trotted toward the scent, but their reluctance was obvious.

Bree looked at Naomi, whose eyes were wide with shock. "They're wrong this time," Bree said. "There's always a first time."

"What's wrong?" Kade asked.

Bree didn't answer. Adrenaline surging through her body, she followed the dogs through the tangle of overgrowth and brambles, the wind driving the thorns against her legs. Eagle Rock was that direction. Even from here she could see the dark walls of the cliff jutting against the leaden sky. A creek ran through a thicket, and Bree splashed across the water. As she reached the other side, she heard Samson's whimper turn into a howl. Then Charley's howl joined Samson's, and the mournful chorus confirmed what Bree and Naomi already knew. They wouldn't find Fay Asters alive.

Stepping into the clearing at the foot of the cliff, Bree's gaze swept the scene then reluctantly came to rest on the crumpled body at the cliff base. Her head twisted at an odd angle, Fay Asters lay on the ground, her purple jacket a bright splash of color on the drab rocks.

6

$\mathcal{M}$ason and his deputy arrived minutes after Fay's body was discovered, and they immediately secured the scene. Kade left to report to headquarters. Bree studied the rocky ground as high up the side of the cliff as she could see. From here there didn't seem to be any pitons in the rock face, but it was getting too dark to see. Moving closer caused bile to rise in her throat. No matter how many times she came face-to-face with death, it never failed to shock her. The strobe of the searchers' lights cast a strange glow over the tragic picture. Something about Fay's posture struck a wrong chord in Bree, but it was probably just the surreal experience of seeing Fay lying there when she'd been so alive this morning.

Bree kept her eyes downcast. What had Kade Matthews been doing out here? She told herself not to be ridiculous. This wasn't murder; Fay had just slipped. And even if there were more to it than that, Kade wouldn't have had anything to do with it. The sight of Fay's sprawled body was enough to bring gruesome thoughts to anyone's mind.

"Anything?" Naomi came up behind her. Both dogs trotted at her side.

"Not that I can see. I'm sure Mason will come back in the morning and look around when there's more light. Not that I expect him to find anything. Fay evidently just slipped. I don't see her backpack though."

"Maybe wild animals dragged it off."

Bree nodded then laid a hand on Samson's head. "We should play with the dogs for a few minutes before we go back. They seem a little depressed."

Naomi nodded. "You want to hide, or you want me to?"

"I will." Bree gave Samson a final pat and hurried away to the path that led through the woods to the road. She hadn't always played hide-and-seek with her dogs after a tragic ending to a search, but she found that Samson grew depressed if he lacked the feeling that he had succeeded. Now she or Naomi would hide a few times and let the dogs think they had found and rescued a live victim. Too bad such tricks couldn't help Bree's own growing sense of failure.

There were never guarantees at the end of any search, only hope. And too often that hope became twisted like a ship in the grip of a nor'easter until it broke apart in the waves of self-incriminating failure. But Bree determinedly clung to the hope of finding Davy's body, having the peace of knowing he was not alone in the wilderness.

Spying a clump of thick brush near the road, she hurried over to hide in it. The dogs would find her soon, but that was the point. Once they were happy again, they could go home. Maybe she could watch some TV or read a book—something to forget the failure that mentally flogged her.

She heard the dogs scramble along the path, and only a few minutes later, both dogs began to bark and lick her face. Bree laughed and threw her arms around Samson's neck.

"Good dog! You saved me." But who would save her from herself? Anu and Naomi would say God, but that was a vain hope.

Naomi reached her and held out a hand to help Bree to her feet. Bree stood and brushed away the bits of twigs and mud clinging to her pants' leg. "I'm beat. Let's head for home. The dogs seem fine, and the sheriff can take care of everything else."

Naomi nodded. "Popcorn and TV in front of the fire sound good to me. I'm freezing. You want to come over?"

Bree shook her head. "I wouldn't be fit company. Besides, Lily and Palmer are keeping dinner warm for me."

Naomi studied her face. "This isn't your fault or responsibility, Bree. God will carry Steve through this."

There it was, Naomi's answer to every problem—a too-simple answer for Bree. If He cared so much, why was there war and death and deadly disease? Why did children like Davy die?

Bree hunched her shoulders and turned away. "Let's go. I'm freezing."

"Bree—" Naomi began.

Both dogs began to howl, then they slunk toward the road. Bree's head came up, and she wheeled to look. This didn't sound good. She ran after her dog. Samson neared the pavement then veered to the right. Giving a stiff-legged jump, he began to howl then crouched in the leaves. Bree's breath came fast. The full moon illuminated the clearing a bit, and she hurried to join her dog. Charley was piddling on the leaves again too, his head down.

"What is it, boy?" Bree put a calming hand on the dog's head, but Samson continued to howl, a mournful sound in the cold air. There was a death scent here too, but Fay lay clear over by the cliffs. How was this possible? The moon glimmered around her, and she noticed the dim light reflected on a large rock. Was that something wet? Kneeling beside Samson, she touched the patch of moisture. It was sticky. Raising her fingers closer to her face, she peered at the substance clinging to her fingertips. The coppery odor told her it was blood.

"What is it?" Naomi knelt beside her.

Bree wordlessly held out her hand. Naomi stared then sucked in her breath. She stood and went to the bottom of the cliff. "Sheriff! Over here!"

Bree frowned. Opening her ready-pack, she dug out a flashlight and flicked it on. The powerful beam probed the darkness, and she focused the light on the rock. Her frown deepened. Was that hair? She started to touch it but drew back. The sheriff would have her hide if she mucked up the investigation.

"You find something?" Huffing from his run, Mason hurried toward them.

Bree pointed to the rock. "Looks like hair and blood. And both dogs gave a death response."

Mason's mouth gaped, then he shut it with a snap. "A death response? What's that mean?"

"This is Fay's hair and blood. Her dead body lay here at some time."

The sheriff's professionalism slipped into place. "Back away from the site." He turned and cupped his hand to his mouth. "Montgomery, come here. And bring Rollo with you." He shone his flashlight on the rock. "Focus your beam here too, Bree. I want to get a good look at this. We can't be going off half-cocked. Let's think about this a minute, eh?"

She aimed her flashlight beam at the rock. Naomi did the same. It sure looked like hair and blood to her. She looked away. Samson was still distressed, whining and fidgeting to get away. He had begun to eat grass as well, and Bree knew he was nauseated.

Doug Montgomery, one of Rock Harbor's deputies, came lumbering up the trail. He was a big man, though he wore his weight well, and most people stepped out of the way when he approached. Rollo Wilson, the county coroner, followed him. About forty, Rollo always wore an expression of perpetual surprise, as though life was not what he'd expected. But he was good at his job.

Rollo grunted. "Looks like hair and blood," he said.

"Bree says the dogs gave a death response here."

Rollo's eyebrows went even higher. "What's that mean?"

"The dogs say this evidence was left by Fay's dead body."

A ghost of a grin crossed Rollo's face. "I didn't know they could talk."

Bree didn't laugh. "They can talk, all right. Just look at them."

She gestured toward Samson and Charley. The muzzles of both dogs drooped nearly to the ground, and they were still whimpering with their tails tucked between their hind legs.

Rollo snorted. "I think we'll see what science has to say before we accept such nonsense." He took a plastic bag from his coat pocket and tweezed off some hair then applied the blood to glass slides. "My lab will tell the real story."

Bree gritted her teeth. Rollo was just ignorant of how sensitive these dogs were. She turned to Mason. "This makes no sense."

"Something sure doesn't smell right," Mason admitted.

The silence between them stretched out. There was only one answer, but Bree didn't want to be the first to voice it. She shuddered.

Rollo sat back then stood. "Explain this to me, Bree. Tell me how these dogs work."

Bree's gaze wandered to the dark woods. "Every human scent is different. The skin gives off dead skin cells called rafts. We each shed about forty thousand of them per minute. Every tiny raft has its own bacteria and releases its own vapor that makes up the unique scent each of us carries. When the body is dead, the scent is the same, but it has the scent of decay mixed in. That's what the dogs smell. They can't lie; they just report what they smell. Fay lay here dead at some point."

Rollo snorted again. "This hair and blood could very well be that of a deer or some other animal." He gathered up the evidence and walked toward the parking lot. "I'll have some results in a few days. In the meantime, I would suggest you don't go running around town talking about some murderer loose on the streets of Rock Harbor. We don't want a panic."

He was right about that, even if he was wrong about the hair and blood. The dogs wouldn't react like this to an animal's remains. Samson didn't know how to lie, and Bree trusted her dog's nose. He was reacting to the search scent, not a dead animal.

They all trooped single-file down the path. Fay's body had been removed, and the parking lot held only their cars—and Fay's. The sher-iff's bubble-gum lights were still flashing, and Bree was glad for that bit of light. There was a murderer out there, no matter what the coroner said. *What was Kade doing out here?* Bree wondered again. He was a ranger, after all. What was so suspicious about him being in the woods? Still, it seemed too coincidental for him to appear just before they found the body.

She put her hand on Mason's arm. "Um, just so you know, Kade Matthews was here poking around in the bush when we arrived. He is a ranger and all, so that shouldn't make him an automatic suspect, but I thought you should know."

Mason's gaze grew thoughtful. "I see. I've known Kade a long time. I can't see him doing something like this. Besides, let's not jump to conclusions. It's probably a climbing accident."

Bree knew it was hard for others to trust the dogs as she did. She didn't try to argue with him. Dropping her arm, she started to get in her Jeep.

Mason stopped her. "I could use some help telling the family," he said.

Bree put up a hand and leaned against the Cherokee. "I'm no good at that, Mason. I know what it's like to be on the receiving end. Take Naomi."

"That's exactly why I'm asking you. You know what it's like."

He wasn't giving her any options. Bree pressed her lips together to stop their quivering then nodded grudgingly and tossed her car keys to Naomi. "Can you feed Samson?"

"Sure." Naomi's brown eyes were wide with sympathy.

"I still say Naomi would be a better helper. She has the words to say to comfort him. I don't have any answers."

"There are no answers for a tragedy like this," Naomi said. "Mason is right. You've been there and know what it feels like. You go ahead. I'll take care of the dogs."

Bree hunched her shoulders and followed Mason. He instructed Montgomery to finish helping Rollo with the investigation then headed toward his car. Now that Fay's body had been discovered, it struck her as even odder that Steve had refused to come with them.

"Do you know where Steve is?" the sheriff asked, opening the squad car door for Bree.

"He told me he'd be at a dinner party at his boss's. I think they live on Mulberry Drive." She slid into the car and fastened her seat belt. "Like I told you, he asked me to look for her because she was late getting home for an important party."

"Seems odd he didn't go with you to search."

"I thought the same thing. Do you suppose he could have killed her?"

"Let's not be so quick to talk about murder. Fay was pregnant, and it might have affected her balance. She could have gotten dizzy."

"That doesn't explain her blood by the road."

He sighed. "We don't know for sure it *is* her blood, Bree."

"I'm sure."

Mason just shook his head. Bree wondered how her brother-in-law really felt about Hilary's inability to conceive. Hilary's words the night of the party came on the heels of that thought. *I hate her.* No, Hilary was no murderer. She was hotheaded and self-willed, but Fay's death was not Hilary's handiwork.

No matter how hard Bree tried to convince herself, the echo of Hilary's words wouldn't fade.

"I'd better call Lily and Palmer and tell them I won't be able to stop by tonight." Bree made the call then turned to stare out the window. As they drove to town, she struggled to think of what she could say to Steve. She couldn't even remember exactly what Hilary and Mason had said to her when they had come to tell her Rob's plane was missing. It was all a blur, a merciful blur.

But the hours leading up to that moment were burned into her memory.

~~~~~

The phone's ring jarred Bree awake as she lay napping on the couch. Rubbing her eyes, she glanced at her watch. Rob and Davy would be heading home in a few hours.

She grabbed for the phone and punched the talk button. "Hello?"

"Bree Nicholls?" a woman's husky voice asked.

Probably a sales call, Bree thought. The voice wasn't familiar. "Yes?"

"You don't know me, but my name is Lanna March, and I'm in love with your husband."

Bree held the phone away from her ear and stared at it as though it had just grown fangs. She put it back to her ear. "What did you say?"

"I think you heard me. Rob and I are in love. If you want him to be happy, you'll let him have a divorce."

The line clicked, and Bree was left listening to a dead line, then the dial tone. Her thoughts spiraled, and she tried to make sense of what the woman had said. Rob, an affair? Impossible. But even as her heart frantically denied it, memories of late nights at work and his recent detachment flooded her mind.

Her hands shook as she dialed Rob's cell phone. After what seemed an eternity, Rob answered.

"I know, you miss us." There was a smile in his voice. "I suppose you want to talk to Davy."

"Is he close by?" Bree managed to ask.

"He's outside. I can call him."

"No, wait! I wanted to talk to you." Bree swallowed. "Who is Lanna?"

"Who?"

Rob's voice sounded strained, Bree thought. "Lanna. Lanna March. She just called here and told me the two of you are in love."

"What?" Rob's voice sharpened. "What are you talking about? Are you accusing me of having an affair?"

"Are you?"

"You seem pretty certain of it. You've found me guilty and pronounced my sentence, all without a trial." His voice was tight and clipped.

Bree ran a hand through her newly cut hair. Rob was going to have a fit when he saw how she'd hacked off her long tresses. She gave an exasperated sigh. "The woman called here, Rob. Do you hear me? She actually called here and told me if I loved you, I would give you a divorce."

"That's ludicrous! Are you making this up?"

Bree's temper flared to an even higher pitch. "You can't twist this and blame me. I'm not the one having an affair."

"I'm not having an affair!"

"Well, you can have your divorce! But I'm not going to be the one to tell Davy his father is a faithless, conniving philanderer." She slammed the phone into its cradle and burst into tears.

The phone rang, and she paced back and forth, refusing to give in to the urge to answer it. She knew it was Rob, and she couldn't listen to his lies.

The afternoon inched by at a glacial speed. The phone rang periodically, and she finally took it off the hook.

Rob was due home by six. When he still wasn't there by eight, she told herself she didn't care. He was probably with his lover. The thought made her burst into tears again. At 8:15 the doorbell rang. She went to the door and found Mason and Hilary standing there, both of them in tears. Rob's plane had gone down somewhere between Iron River and home.

"Can I help you?"

Bree was jolted out of her painful memories by the harsh light spilling from the front door of the palatial home. Music echoed from the house as well. Bree recognized the blond woman who stood framed by the light from the room as Barbara McGovern, wife of the man who owned Rock Harbor Savings and Loan.

"We'd like to see Steve Asters," Mason said.

Behind Barbara, Steve Asters stood talking to a curvaceous redhead who wore a tight black dress, slit up the side practically to her waist. He glanced up, and his gaze met Bree's. His smile faded.

Barbara motioned to Steve, and he came slowly toward them. The fear in his expression heightened when he saw Mason standing behind her.

"Did you find Fay?" Steve directed his question to Bree. The color leached from his face, leaving him as pale as sand.

Bree gave an almost imperceptible nod. Suddenly, she wanted to be anywhere but in this stuffy room full of cigarette smoke and the scent of booze and perfume. The stress of the day bore down on her in an overwhelming rush of weariness.

Mason cleared his throat. "Is there somewhere we can speak in private?"

Steve glanced at Barbara with a question in his eyes. Barbara's frown deepened, but she nodded. "Follow me." She led them down the hall to a study lined with bookshelves. "I'll be with my guests if you need me." Closing the door behind her, she left them alone with Steve.

Steve ran a finger over the oak bookshelf nearest to him then thrust his hands in his pockets. "Is Fay all right?" Gazing at Mason, he seemed to be avoiding Bree's eyes.

"No, sir, I'm afraid she's not," Mason said gravely.

Steve blanched. "Is she injured?"

Mason cleared his throat. "I'm afraid she's dead, Steve. We found her at the base of Eagle Rock. Or I should say, the dogs found her."

Steve's gaze finally shifted to Bree, and she saw the shock and pain in his eyes. And something else as well. Was it guilt? She'd always heard murder was usually committed by someone close to the victim. Steve's contact with the red-headed bombshell made him more suspicious.

Steve swayed on his feet, and Bree reached out a hand to steady him. He jerked away from her grasp and walked to the window. The blinds were open, but the window reflected the light, and it was impossible to look out. Still, Steve stood staring at the window. Was he trying to gain time to think? Bree exchanged a glance with Mason. The sheriff seemed as puzzled as she felt.

Steve turned around. His eyes were dry, and he nodded to them. "I appreciate you both coming to tell me in person. Where is her body? Do I need to identify her or anything?"

Mason nodded. "The ambulance took her to the coroner's office. They'll do an autopsy."

Steve's eyes widened. "Why? You said she fell. I told her a thousand times she was going to fall and break her neck one of these days."

He was babbling. It sounded like guilt to her. She mentally shook her head. She'd watched too many episodes of *Murder, She Wrote.* This was Steve Asters, the man who had loaned her the money to buy her lighthouse, the respected manager of the bank, not some heartless murderer. Grief caused people to say and do strange things. She resolved to give him the benefit of the doubt.

"Actually, there is some question as to the cause of death. Once we get some tests back from the lab, we'll know if we're dealing with an accident . . . or something else," Mason said.

Steve's face paled even more. "I don't understand." He swiped a shaking hand through his hair.

"It's possible someone killed her and then put her body at the cliff base to make it look like an accident."

"Murder?" Steve's lips barely moved, and he swayed where he stood. He held his hands out in front of him, and Bree noticed the tremble in them. "Next you'll be saying I did it! But I've been here all evening. Ask anyone."

Mason nodded. "Shall we drive you to the morgue?"

Steve's face flushed, and he raised his voice. "I know what you're thinking! It's always the husband. Well, I loved Fay!" He paced in front of the window as his voice rose.

"Steve, no one is accusing you of anything." Mason followed him and touched his arm, but he jerked away.

Steve turned and stomped to the door. "If you want to talk to me, you can contact my attorney." He slammed the door behind him, and an oil painting of the Porcupine Mountains fell to the floor with a crash.

Bree picked it up. One corner of the frame was chipped. She felt rather battered herself. This night had brought back too many memories.

7

Nicholls's Finnish Imports was already buzzing with the news of Fay's death by the time Bree arrived Monday morning at nine. She worked as a salesclerk in the store three days a week, and though the money supplemented the insurance Rob had left, the real reason she enjoyed her job was that it awarded her time with Anu.

The aroma of Anu's famous cardamom rolls filled the store from the bakery at the back. As well as Finnish imports, the store sold Finnish pastries and desserts. Eino Kantola, forty and as round as a snowman, rushed to greet Bree. "The radio said you found Fay's body!" She tsk-tsked, a habit that set Bree's teeth on edge. Eino's hazel eyes were bright with curiosity. Several customers turned eager faces their direction.

Bree blinked at the bombardment then nodded. "Yes, I found her."

"I thought she would come to a bad end." Sheba McDonald sniffed. Sheba made everything in town her business. With a husband who had been the county court judge for going on forty years, she knew secrets that should never be told, though she was never reticent to reveal many of them.

Sheba's hands stilled their rummaging through the sweaters, and she moved closer. "I'd seen her with that old boyfriend. If you ask me, that baby of hers probably wasn't even Steve's."

She turned to her friend Janelle Calumet, and they both began to discuss Fay's shortcomings. Bree heard mention of Steve's money troubles. So that was common knowledge as well. Surely Mason had heard the rumors too.

Eino looked at Bree. "They're saying Steve needed money in a bad way these days. I wonder if Fay had insurance."

Anu wiped her floury hands on the red chef's apron she wore. "Eino, it is unseemly to display such nosiness," she said softly. "Please return to working on the display for the Arabia china."

Eino's face fell in a comical expression of chagrin and disappointed petulance. "I'm almost done with that. Aren't you even curious about Fay's death, eh?" She turned away and went back to arranging plates on display shelves.

Bree took off her coat and went to hang it in the back room. "Thanks," she whispered as she passed Anu.

Anu followed her. "Don't thank me, *kulta*. I must admit to curiosity myself, but Hilary filled me in this morning. Did you sleep?"

"Not much," Bree admitted.

Anu nodded. "Come, have some coffee with me. Eino can handle the store for a bit." A battered table painted white with mismatched chairs sat in the middle of the break room at the back. Bree sat at the table while Anu poured them both a cup of coffee then joined her. "So, I think there is something more on your mind this morning than finding Fay's body. I'm here if you wish to talk."

"You always are," Bree said with a fond smile. "Mason told you it might be murder, right?"

Anu's blue eyes saddened. "Yes, he told me this grim news, though he tried to downplay it."

"You realize it has to be someone we know."

Anu nodded, and a shadow crossed her face. "I cannot imagine any of our friends committing such a crime."

"Everyone wears a mask, Anu. Everyone but you, that is. Sometimes I look at my friends and wonder what they really think and whether they're hiding something important from me."

"What has caused this cynicism, eh?" Anu shook her head. "It saddens me, *kulta*. Do you have suspects yet? Hilary mentioned no one."

"Several come to my mind. I haven't discussed it with Mason yet, but I couldn't sleep last night for worrying about which of my friends could have done something like this." It was after two the last time she'd looked at the clock.

"Maybe it was an outsider, someone she met while climbing."

"It's a possibility," Bree said softly. "I hope that's the case."

"You have someone in mind, I can see this." Anu wore a troubled frown.

"We ran into Kade Matthews just before we found her body. He seemed on edge." As soon as the words were out of her mouth, she wished she could snatch them back.

"Kade is like a rock. I cannot believe this of him," Anu said slowly. "He could have taken his sister to live with him in Yellowstone or on to his new post in California, but he honored his mother's request to let Lauri graduate here. A man like that does not murder."

Bree wished she could be so certain. "I'm supposed to meet him and Naomi at Donovan's house after school to help out a bit. I'll see if I can find out anything from him. I hope you're right."

"Read Psalm 112 when you can, my Bree. From the Scriptures we can learn discernment. We must pray and ask God to open our eyes to truth."

Somehow when Anu spoke of God, Bree did not bristle the way she did when Naomi mentioned him. "You are my rock," she said. "I couldn't have made it through the last year without you."

Anu leaned forward and touched Bree's cheek. "This worries me, *kulta.* Always you fear to break away from me, to face life by yourself. I see the way you hold your tongue when you wish to say what you really think to Hilary. I see how you barricade yourself in your home and fear to make new friends. If you speak your mind, you won't lose the love of your family and friends. But even if you do, loss is part of life."

"But—" Bree started to protest, but Anu shook her head gently.

"You hold so tightly because you have lost so much, but day by day I see the Bree who first came to us—the one who was not afraid to experience life—shrink into this small, driven mouse who lives only to search for a family who will never return to her. You must go on, Bree. You must let go of your fear of the future." Anu leaned forward, her voice urgent.

"How?" Bree whispered. "Hilary—"

"You must tell Hilary it is over, that you will no longer cater to her demands. I have some money to invest. I want you to start a search-and-rescue training facility. You love dogs and helping others. Reach out and take charge of your future, *kulta*. Find a reason to go forward and no longer look back. You are young, Bree, too young to sit and mourn over a life that is gone."

Something broke within her, and Bree put her hands over her face and wept. Vaguely aware of Anu kneeling beside her, she turned to her comforting arms and wept for the life that would never be. Yet when her cry was over, she felt different, less fragmented.

She pulled away from Anu and stared into her eyes. "You're right," she said. "I must let go and go on. A training facility!" A huge grin stretched across her face. "That's a dream come true, Anu. Do you know how much I love you? You're the mother I wish I'd had growing up."

Anu, tears in her eyes, stood and touched Bree's hair. "I could not love you more if you were a child born from my own body. Now this is enough emotion for one day. We have work to do. Come."

Bree's day rushed by. As she worked, her mind evaluated then rejected most of the suspects in Fay's death. It was a puzzle too hard for her.

Just before three, she hung up her work smock, said good-bye to Anu, and drove to the Blue Bonnet.

"Ready for some cleaning?" Bree asked as Naomi climbed into Bree's Jeep.

"Sure thing," Naomi said, setting a bucket of cleansers and rags on the floor. "You look happy today."

"It's been a good day. Busy but good." She paused then pushed on. "Anu wants me to give up the search, to start a training center for search-and-rescue dogs."

The dazed expression on Naomi's face made Bree laugh. "I'm thinking about it, but I don't know if I can yet."

"The day will have to come, Bree. I'm not trying to push you, but you have to face facts sooner or later."

"You sound like Anu. Are the two of you conspiring?"

"She's smarter than I am," Naomi said with a light laugh. "But this is something even I can see. You're still young. Someday you might want to remarry and have more children."

Bree began to shake her head, but Naomi cut her off. "I know you're not ready for that yet, but you have a future, Bree. All it takes is for you to recognize that fact and step out to meet it."

Bree didn't know what to say. "This must be the right house," she said, relieved to hear that her voice was calm and steady. "Emily and Timmy are in the front yard. Looks like Kade and his sister are here too." She swung the Jeep into the driveway behind Kade's truck and killed the engine.

Naomi sighed but said no more. They got out and opened the door for the dogs. The children bounded toward them. Timmy was pale beneath the red blotches left by the insect bites. Emily's hair looked as though it hadn't been combed yet this morning. Poor motherless lambs. Bree had been right to come today. Kade and his sister followed the kids.

Bree hugged Timmy and Emily then put her hand out to greet Kade's sister. "You must be Lauri," she said as the teenage girl came toward her with an eager smile. Bree would have known she was the ranger's sister even if she hadn't been told. Lauri was the feminine version of Kade, right down to the confident way she walked.

His tail wagging, Samson came to Lauri and sniffed her hand. "Hi," Lauri said.

Bree shook her hand. "I'm Bree Nicholls, and this is Naomi Heinonen."

Lauri glanced at Naomi but quickly turned her attention back to Bree. "I read about you in the paper." Lauri ran her fingers through Samson's curly coat. "He's beautiful. This is Samson, right? Can search dogs really follow a person's scent through the air? How long does it take to train them? Do you think I could do it?" The last was said in a breathless rush with a sidelong glance at her brother.

Bree held up her hands. "Whoa. One question at a time."

Lauri flushed. "Sorry. I've just been interested in search dogs forever."

Charley nosed against her for his share of attention, and Lauri obliged. "You boys are heroes," she crooned.

"Don't encourage them," Bree told her lightly.

"It's so cool how you found these kids," Lauri said. "I wish I could do something like that."

"Do you have a dog?"

"No. Kade is afraid a dog will chase his precious wildlife," Lauri said with a glance of resentment at her brother.

Bree smiled. "They can be trained not to chase animals."

"I like your sweatshirt," Kade said.

Bree glanced down. The sweatshirt said JUST TRY TO HIDE on the front and KITCHIGAMI K-9 SAR on the back. "Thanks." She turned. "Let me get our stuff from the Jeep. Can you kids watch the dogs while we work inside?" she asked Emily.

Emily nodded vigorously. "Our backyard is fenced. We can play there. Daddy brought us home a Frisbee to play with. Do Samson and Charley like Frisbees?"

"They'll chase you down and take it from you," Naomi told her. She reached into the car for a beat-up disk and held it out to Timmy.

"Here, use their Frisbee. Your new one would get chewed up by their teeth." Timmy grabbed it, and Samson rushed up to him and began to lick him on the face. The little boy giggled and threw his arms around the dog's neck.

"Keep them in the yard," Naomi called as Lauri, Emily, and Timmy led the dogs away. She turned and grabbed her bucket of cleaning supplies.

Bree watched them go then turned to smile at Kade. "Lauri seems to be a sweet girl."

He returned her smile, but it seemed forced. "You haven't seen her other side yet. Sometimes I think the Windigos came in the night and left this other girl in my sister's place."

Bree grimaced. "The Windigos wouldn't dare try to consume a teenage girl! Even they would find her tasteless."

Kade didn't smile. His gaze followed Lauri. "I wish I knew what to do with her."

Bree handed him the vacuum. "As another female, I can tell you there's nothing you can do but love her and be patient. What is she— sixteen or so?"

Kade nodded. "Sixteen going on thirty."

"It's a hard age," Naomi said.

"You're telling me!" Kade hefted the vacuum and followed the two women across the front yard. "When will Donovan be home?"

"About five forty-five." Bree pushed open the door and stepped inside. She blinked at the chaos. Clothes were strewn around the furniture and floor like gaily colored confetti. Her sneakers stuck to some substance on the entry linoleum. A tower of newspapers leaned precariously against the side of a recliner, and a toy train lay like a miniature wreck at the foot of the burgundy sofa. The carpet looked as if it hadn't been vacuumed in weeks.

"Holy cow," Kade whispered behind her. He set the vacuum on the floor. "Where do we start?"

"Do we even want to start?" Naomi asked.

"I've seen worse," Bree said. She set her pail of cleaners on the floor. "Raccoons had been living in the lighthouse when Rob and I bought it. Believe me, we can do this."

"Speak for yourself," Kade muttered.

Bree sent him a challenging look. "You a quitter?"

His answering scowl reminded her of a little boy who had been dared to jump from the top of the monkey bars, and she had to remind herself he was a possible suspect in Fay's murder.

"Just tell me what to do," he snapped.

"I brought some laundry baskets. Get them out of the Jeep and pile everything on the floor into them. We can sort the stuff by the rooms they go in. Then, Kade, you can dust and vacuum while I tackle the kitchen. Naomi, you take the baskets and start the laundry then try to find where the toys and other things go when you clean the bedrooms. I'd guess the bedsheets haven't been changed in weeks, so let's do that too."

Kade nodded. "This is going to take all night."

"It doesn't have to be perfect. We won't clean drawers or kitchen cupboards. You'll be surprised at how fast it goes." Naomi pulled yellow plastic gloves from her bucket.

Bree carried her supplies into the kitchen. Dishes covered every surface in the kitchen. Cheerios crunched underfoot, and ants congregated over a pile of sugar on the floor. How could Donovan allow the children to live like this?

Even as the condemnation crossed her mind, she gave a slight shake of her head. She well remembered the days and weeks she'd been sunk in despair herself. Dishes had piled in the sink, and she'd only washed them when the cupboards were empty of clean ones. It would have been an overwhelming job for a father. Two children, a business to run—no wonder Donovan hadn't been able to face it all.

Ant spray first. Rummaging in the cabinet above the sink, she pulled out a can of insecticide and sprayed the ants. Once they were dead, she cleaned them up and tossed the soiled paper towel in the trash. After loading the dishwasher, she washed the dishes that wouldn't fit. By the time she'd mopped the floor, Bree's spirits had lifted with the sheer joy of restoring calm to chaos. She tackled the bathrooms next, and the satisfaction she felt when that job was finished had nothing to do with pride in her job. And it all had taken only two hours.

She found Naomi folding clean clothes in the laundry room. "I got the bedrooms in some semblance of order," she said. "There's not a trace of Donovan's ex-wife in the bedroom."

Bree grinned at the triumph in her voice. "Don't go thinking you'll just move your stuff right in. You've got to convince him you're not like other women first. Oh—and *marry* him, of course."

"I'm working on it," Naomi said.

"Oh?"

"I said I'm working on it. When I have something to report, you'll be the first to know."

Bree laughed. "I think I'll order supper from the Suomi."

"Anything to get out of cooking," Naomi said.

Bree laughed again and went to find Kade while Naomi went upstairs for another load of laundry. She walked into the hall and found Kade holding a skateboard over his shoulder as he surveyed the closet—a jumble of boots, gloves, bent wire hangers, a skateboard with two wheels, and winter coats in disarray. Dust balls like billowing clouds stood guard over the strange assortment of items.

"What a mess," Bree said.

A wire hanger caught on Kade's jeans when he turned toward her, and he grimaced. "I figured I'd better do it, or you'd think you had to. After that bathroom, I thought you needed a break."

Bree gave a mock shudder. "Little boys don't have the best aim, do they?"

"I wouldn't know," Kade said, deadpan.

Bree laughed, the tension she felt around him easing. "What's with the skateboard? You're holding it like you want to bean someone." She wasn't entirely certain she was joking. Though she admired him for his fortitude today, she still regarded him with some suspicion. Everyone said it was impossible to suspect him, and she wanted to believe in his innocence, but the ugly picture of Fay's dead body haunted her.

He glanced at the battered skateboard in his hand. "I think someone already used it for that. Too bad Fay didn't have it with her."

Bree's merriment faded. "Sorry," Kade said. "I guess we joke about things we don't understand."

"I always thought things like that didn't happen in Rock Harbor," Bree said. Chilled, she wrapped her arms around herself. "When Rob and I were deciding where we wanted to raise our family, that was the determining factor. We wanted Davy to have what we had—the safety to play along the sidewalk with his bike and the freedom to toss a Frisbee to Samson in the front yard without one of us standing guard. How sad something like this had to happen here." She bit her lip at all she'd revealed. He had a way of getting past her suspicions.

Kade shrugged. "Maybe it's not what it seems. The blood could be a deer or something."

Was he trying to redirect her line of thinking? She shook her head. "Samson alerted on the blood. It's Fay's. He's as good as any DNA test."

"Maybe it was an accident, and the person didn't want to admit what they'd done." Kade knelt to reach the back of the closet.

Bree watched him a moment. He liked her now; did she want to run the risk of losing that by asking hard questions? Anu had said she needed to let go of that fear, that it was what kept her isolated. Be yourself, Anu had said. But Bree wasn't sure who she was anymore. She took a deep breath.

"You were there; did you see anything?" That came out wrong, full of accusation.

"You suspect me?" His eyebrows shot up.

She'd gone this far, she might as well finish. "Should I? You were there that night. I saw you. And you seemed ill at ease."

His lips compressed to a thin line, and his nostrils flared. "If you mistrust me, what am I doing here?"

"I thought you were helping out the kids." Anu was right—it felt great to speak up instead of holding back her thoughts. "Who is Eric? I saw you talking to him at Hilary's party."

His shoulders stiff, Kade turned away and grabbed the vacuum. "My cousin. Now, if you'll excuse me, I need to get back to work so I can leave. I wouldn't want you to think you were in danger."

His cousin. All the more reason to try to help him. They'd argued at the party, possibly about Fay. Did their confrontation have anything to do with her death? "Was your cousin having an affair with Fay?"

Kade turned back around, his eyes dark with anger. "I still think you're jumping to conclusions," he said coldly. "At least wait until the coroner's report comes back."

Bree shook her head. "I don't need the coroner's report to know the truth that there's a killer in our town."

"Killer. You seem set on using that term. You can't know that, Bree."

"I know it," she said firmly. "I trust Samson. Someone killed her, either deliberately or accidentally." She didn't want it to be Kade, she realized. In spite of her suspicions, she liked him.

Naomi came down the stairs, and they both turned. "I'm bushed," she said. "But Donovan will be happy when he sees the house." Pride gave a lilt to her words.

Bree grinned. "This doesn't look like the same place, does it?" Every surface shone with cleanliness. "I was going to cook dinner," she explained to Kade, "but I just ordered it from the café instead. You want to go pick it up for us?"

"I suppose."

She could tell he was still miffed. Well, he could just live with it.

Maybe it had been a small step for her today to actually question him, but it sure felt good. Anu would be proud.

"We done here?" he asked.

"I think so," Bree said.

"I'll go get the food." He grabbed his coat from the sofa, but before he opened the front door, the back door slammed, and Emily raced in with Timmy on her heels. Lauri followed with both dogs. Her face was red with exertion, and she looked happy and carefree.

"We're starved," Emily announced.

Naomi went to Emily and put her arms around her, but the little girl jerked away and went to Bree. Bree's gaze took in Naomi's agonized expression. She patted Emily and stepped away.

"Kade is going to pick up supper at the café. When your daddy gets home, you can all eat together. How about a cookie to tide you over until then?" She went to the cookie jar.

Emily's wide eyes began to turn pink at the edges, and her lower lip trembled. "I want you to be my mommy," she said.

Bree swallowed and tried to maintain her composure. She attempted to smile, but her lips just trembled. Blinking furiously, she managed a smile. "You're a sweet girl, Emily."

Kade moved between them, and Bree was grateful for the interruption. Scooping up Emily, he hugged her then perched her on his shoulders.

"You can go with me to get the food, then you can watch for your daddy. I bet he'll think you did all this work by yourself." He carried her through the door.

Timmy began to wail to go along, but Bree couldn't force herself to go to him. One step forward and two steps back.

8

The autumn days were lengthening. Rachel stood at the door on the moist October day and watched a ruffled grouse run through the aspens. She had trouble keeping track of the days, but she thought this was a Tuesday. Her larder proclaimed the necessity of a trip to town.

"You stay here." Rachel tousled Sam's unruly hair. Choppy from her inexpert use of the scissors, his red hair stood up like a rooster's comb. She smiled, but there was no answering grin on his pale face, just a solemn nod. Her smile faded.

Rachel knew he was used to the drill by now, though she worried every time she had to leave him. This would be the last time though. When these supplies were gone, she would take Sam to town, find out who he was. It was time. No one could blame her; after all, she'd saved his life. His limp was evidence of that. They would all applaud her for saving him.

For a moment she allowed herself to imagine the acclaim, the way the papers would laud her as a hero. A smile tugged at her lips. Maybe the news story would reach those who had accused her so unjustly. They would see how wrong they were. All her life people had said she didn't have good judgment, that she didn't think things through. She'd finally prove them wrong.

But what if this new story brought out all the hounds onto her trail again? She'd been cleared of all wrongdoing, but that hadn't stopped the nursing home from firing her and her neighbors from snubbing her. Her surfacing would be fresh fodder for the news mill.

Maybe they would bring charges against her because she hadn't returned him before now. You couldn't trust law enforcement. Look what they'd done to her. Hounding her out of a job she loved.

Her face tightened at the memories. One false story, and a career of thirty years had been swept away like tumbled debris in a flood. It wasn't fair; life had never been fair. But no, not this time. This time she would be rewarded with praise and honor. Sammy's mother would lavish attention on her son's savior.

She chewed on her lip. Maybe there was no mother to go back to. His father had been dead when she'd found the plane, and it had been a year. They'd just take him and put him in foster care, and if anyone knew the hell that could be, it was Rachel. She and her brother had been shunted from one home to another throughout their troubled childhood.

Her gaze traveled to Sam. He was always frightened. Rachel despaired of ever hearing him squeal and play like a normal child. The most animated she'd seen him had been when those children shadhowed up. She frowned. She'd had entirely too much contact with the outside world this week. First that snoopy woman climber, then those children. And that man at the mine had seen her too. What if he came looking for her?

She'd found a haven here, a place of peace and rest for her and Sammy both. But it looked like they would be driven from their safe harbor, just as she'd been driven from Detroit. What if someone came before they were ready to leave? Would they suspect her of kidnapping the boy?

"Sammy, what's my name?" she asked slowly, an idea beginning to take shape. If busybodies believed he was her son, they would be less suspicious.

His forehead wrinkled, then he shook his head, and she realized he'd had no need to call her anything before now. "It's Mother. Can you say 'Mother'?"

"Mother," Sam repeated. "Is that like mommy? I had a mommy once."

A shaft of jealousy surprised her with its intensity. She was the one who had taken care of Sam. Where was his mother? She hadn't come looking for him. "It's kind of like that," Rachel told him. "I take care of you like a mommy, don't I? I feed you and bring you treats from town."

Sam nodded.

"Can you remember to call me Mother? That's my name. Mother."

He nodded. "Mother," he repeated again.

"I'll be back by lunchtime. Don't open the door to anyone." She waited until he nodded again before she left the cabin, pulling the door tight behind her.

Dry leaves crunched underfoot, and a blue jay chattered angrily at her from the tall pine over her head. She would miss these woods. But it was time to take up her life again. Hers and Sam's. The furor had died down enough, and she could surely find another nursing job. But how did she go about finding Sam's family?

It took Rachel nearly two hours to walk to Rock Harbor. She knew she was close when she began to hear the sound of the waves and the gong of the fog bell out in Lake Superior. She quickened her step. As she entered town, she kept her floppy leather hat pulled down low over her face and avoided looking anyone in the eye.

The bell tinkled on the door as she pushed into Rock Harbor General Store. Lars Thorensen wiped his hands on his massive white apron and nodded to her. Rachel avoided his inquisitive gaze. The last thing she needed was to get into a conversation with the loquacious Lars. He could talk until her eyes glazed.

The shop had changed little since its inception in 1868 and still resembled a general store straight out of *Mayberry RFD,* Rachel's favorite show of all time. Narrow rows of basic food items stood in the center of the store. The counters and shelves that lined the walls were filled with fabric and notions, a few toiletry items such as toothpaste and deodorant, and glass jars of candy. The floor was made of wide boards of unfinished native timber. Rachel almost expected to see Sheriff Andy Taylor come strolling through the doors that led to the storeroom. Being here always made her nervous for that very reason. After her one and only brush with the law, the thought of even talking with the sheriff made her throat close up.

"I was beginning to think you lit out for other parts, ma'am," Lars said. His blond mustache quivered, and his pale blue eyes roamed over Rachel's face with an avid curiosity.

Rachel ducked her head and turned away to find what she needed. The last thing she wanted was to deal with a nosy Parker like Lars digging into her business. In a frenzy to be done with the owner's prying eyes, she hurried along, depositing items in her basket. She knocked a tin of cocoa to the floor near the checkout counter and Lars bent to retrieve it, but she snatched it up before he could touch it.

"Where'bouts in the North Woods you come from, ma'am? You don't seem to get to town much."

Rachel compressed her lips. She wasn't about to indulge in chatter. She'd learned the hard way not to trust anyone. Maybe if she refused to speak to him at all, he'd get the picture.

The bell on the door tinkled again, and two men entered the store. Rachel's eyes widened at the shiny star on the man's shirt. Blood thundered in her ears. She couldn't let the sheriff see her. She only hoped those lost kids hadn't told the authorities about her. She turned and went down an aisle then stooped to look at cake mixes.

"Howdy, Sheriff," Lars said. "I was hoping you'd stop by today— I just got in some thimbleberry jam Hilary was asking me about last week. It's from this year's berries."

"That's why I'm here. Hilary used all hers up on the campaign dinner, and she wanted to make some thimbleberry tarts for Thanksgiving. How many jars do you have?"

"Five right now, with more promised from one of my distributors by the end of the week."

"I'd better take all of it. At ten dollars a jar, I hope she appreciates it."

Her fingers tightly clamped on the basket, Rachel gauged the distance to the door. If she could just slip out unseen. But no, that wouldn't work. Lars would likely accuse her of stealing. He knew she had come in to get supplies. Maybe the sheriff would just finish his business and leave. Rachel pressed a hand against the galloping beat of her heart.

The old cash register clanged as Lars rang up the sheriff's purchase. "Any news on Fay's death? I hear tell you're thinking it might be murder."

The sheriff cleared his throat. When he spoke, his voice was sharp with dismay. "Where'd you hear that, Lars? We haven't even got autopsy results yet, let alone DNA testing. Don't go starting any rumors. I get enough of that on a daily basis."

"DNA on the blood by the road?"

"You know I can't discuss the case," the sheriff said. "And I don't know where you're getting your information, but I'd appreciate it if you zipped your lip about this until we know more."

"Is Steve a suspect?" Lars seemed undeterred by the sheriff's rebuke.

The sheriff gave a heavy sigh. "I'm not going to discuss it with you, Lars. I just remembered something else Hilary needed." His footsteps echoed against the wood floor as he approached Rachel's aisle.

She was trapped and she knew it. The best she could do was to face him and not let him see her fear. She rose with a box of devil's food cake mix in her hand.

His gaze touched her face, skittered on, then jerked back to look at her again. "Sheriff Mason Kaleva, ma'am. You look familiar. You just move to town?"

"No, no, just a summer visitor," she babbled. "I have a cabin in the woods."

"Whereabouts?"

She could see the suspicion on his face. He probably had old wanted posters plastered all over his office. Panic froze her.

"Sheriff, we got a call," the deputy said.

The sheriff's frown deepened. He gave her a final stare and turned to exit with the deputy.

Rachel let out the breath she'd been holding. Reprieved, but for how long? Now, more than ever, she had to get out of the area.

The bell on the door clanged, and she breathed a sigh of relief.

Murder. She shivered. They'd already figured out that much. How much longer before they knew all of it? She needed to get away before the trail led right to her cabin door. She had been wrong to think she could bring Sam back to a small town like this. No, she needed to stay invisible. Maybe she could turn him over to authorities in a large city like Chicago. They could track down his mother and reunite him from there. At least Rachel herself would be out of the limelight. The thought of having her face plastered on the front page again was enough to give her hives.

She finished filling her basket then carried it to the counter. The store carried an assortment of Michigan newspapers plus the *Chicago Tribune*. She grabbed one as Lars began to ring up her purchases. Lars seemed to sense her agitation, for he stared at her as he packed her supplies in the knapsack she gave him. She ducked her head so all he could see was the top of her hat. Nosy old man. Why couldn't he mind his own business? That was the trouble with a small town like Rock Harbor. People felt they had the right to pry.

Rachel knew people thought her a strange hermit of a woman, but why couldn't they see beneath her old clothes? She had the same hopes and desires they had. A place to call home, a family, peace, contentment. She thought she'd found all that here in these North Woods, but she could already feel it sliding from her grip. Seizing true peace was like trying to catch the morning mist over Lake Superior.

Her revised plans racing through her head, she nodded her thanks at Lars, took her knapsack, then rushed toward the door.

What a change to have something to look forward to. Bree sat on the couch with her legs under her and pored over a real estate book. Where could she buy land for her training center? For the first time, she saw how the publicity that came Samson's way could benefit her. An old schoolhouse was for sale about five miles out of town. It came with ten acres that ranged from meadow to forest. That might work. She'd have to call the agent and take a look.

In spite of her enthusiasm for the project, Bree couldn't seem to settle tonight. Staying home with a frozen pizza didn't sound at all appealing. Anu would be glad to have her come by for supper, or she could go to Naomi's, but neither prospect felt right. Her thoughts drifted to Fay's death. The information Fay might have had about the cabin in the woods was gone with her. But if she could track Fay's movements for the past few weeks, maybe she could get a feel for what quadrant to search. She couldn't imagine there really was a plane seat outside that cabin, but she had no other direction to look right now. At least it was a goal.

Samson needed to be fed, then she could go to town and see if she could find out anything. She fed the dog then got her coat. "Want to go out, Samson?"

His ears pricked at the word "out." He barked and ran to the back door. "No, we're going to town," she told him. She could stop by the sheriff's office to see if he'd heard anything. The blood test might be back by now. At work today, she'd hoped Mason might stop by with news, but there had been no sign of him.

The air held a hint of moisture that promised rain or snow. October was not too soon to get major snow, but they'd been lucky this year. The stars were like ship lights bouncing off the black waves of the lake. The wind had picked up, and the crash of the waves on Lake Superior was oddly soothing. Rock Harbor's streets were deserted, a pleasant state of affairs after summer's high traffic.

Visitors loved the quaintness of the town with its Victorian buildings and community activities. But for a time, the residents owned the town again. Rock Harbor had "nine months of winter and three months of company," the saying went, and that was pretty accurate. Tourists came for the fishing and hunting, for the natural beauty of this land of waterfalls, and for the festivals with their Finnish or Cornish food and fun.

Many people in the Midwest never seemed to realize the enormity of the North Woods. And it wasn't just the miles and miles of pristine forest, it was the heavy snow and frigid temperatures that hindered Bree's efforts to find her family.

Rock Harbor County Jail sat stolidly in the center of downtown, across the street from the Copper Club Tavern. Built five years ago, its white stone edifice seemed out of place amid the gracious brick buildings that lined downtown. She opened the door, and Doug Montgomery looked up from his perusal of a fishing magazine. The desk was battered with gouges made by countless deputies over the past fifty years. Montgomery eased his bulk back into the worn leather chair and gazed at her over the top of his spectacles.

His oversized head sported a great thatch of thick blond hair like some Nordic warrior of long ago, though the resemblance stopped there. The blue eyes peering at her were too dulled with apathy to ever envision sailing across the ocean in an ancient longboat. Bree had to wonder what criteria the sheriff used to hire his deputies. But maybe in a town the size of Rock Harbor, Doug was one of the best he could find.

"What can I do for you, Mrs. Nicholls?" he said.

"I don't suppose the sheriff is around?" she asked.

Doug shifted in his seat. "Nope. He left about an hour ago."

"Any news on the blood we found by the road?"

He scratched his head. "I don't know if I'm supposed to let out that information or not."

"Come on, Deputy, I'm the sheriff's sister-in-law. I found the blood." Bree took a step closer to the desk and tried to peer over the deputy's arm at the papers lying scattered under his meaty hand.

He covered the papers with an arm then slowly lifted it again. "Well, I guess that's all right then. The blood seems to be hers, all right. At least it's the same blood type. We don't have the DNA back yet."

Samson had been right. Bree's initial elation faded, and her stomach roiled. Murder in Rock Harbor, or manslaughter at the very least. "That means Fay didn't die of a climbing accident," she said slowly.

"Looks that way," the deputy said. "The sheriff called in the state police forensic experts. They're coming over tomorrow."

"What time?" She intended to tag along and see what they had to say.

"About eight."

"Thanks, Deputy." Snapping her fingers at Samson, Bree turned and went to the door. Outside, the evening winds had picked up, and she pulled the hood of her sweater up over her head. Her hunger faded in light of this more pressing news. If it hadn't been so dark, she would have been tempted to go out to the site and poke around. Instead, she settled for a pensive walk around the quiet streets.

By the time she'd crossed the courthouse square for the fifth time, her head was clearer. The neon light above the Suomi Café glared through the gathering mist along Kitchigami Street like a lighthouse guiding the ships to port. The aroma of fish stew and cabbage rolls wafted into the street, and her hunger raged to the fore again.

Across the street she saw Steve Asters exit the bank. Bree glanced at her watch. Seven o'clock. He was working late. Steve locked the door behind him then came toward her. Even from here, she could see the way his shoulders slumped.

Bree watched him for a moment before walking toward him. "Hi, Steve," she said softly.

His head jerked up as if pulled by an invisible rope. The pallor on his face deepened when he saw her, then color flooded into his skin. "What do you want?" he muttered, his gaze wandering back to the ground.

"Want to join me for a sandwich and coffee?"

"No thanks. I couldn't eat anything." He looked at the ground. "Everyone looked at me today like they think if I really loved her, I would be home grieving. Well, I can't stand the empty house. Is that so hard to understand? I don't know how I'll get through the funeral tomorrow."

"Have you talked to the sheriff?"

"He stopped in to see me about an hour ago." His gaze probed her face. "He said it looks like the blood you found by the road is Fay's. That means someone killed her, doesn't it?"

"It still could have been accidental, a hit-and-run driver maybe."

"You don't believe that," he said.

His shoulders slumped even lower, until Bree wasn't sure he wouldn't simply slide to the ground. In spite of herself, she couldn't help the niggle of sympathy she felt for him. But maybe it was all an act. She, of all people, knew how convincingly a man could lie.

She narrowed her eyes. "No, I don't believe she was hit by a car. And even if it did happen that way, it's still manslaughter, especially since whoever killed her arranged her body at the foot of the cliff." That's what had bothered her, she suddenly realized. Fay had been arranged like a mannequin. Her body had been staged, even to the arm flung out as if to try to catch herself.

"Well, it wasn't me!" Steve finally seemed to recover some life and straightened his back to stare her squarely in the face.

She'd always liked Steve, but then, whoever said she was a good judge of men? She'd laugh if it weren't such serious business.

The wind blew tendrils of hair across Bree's eyes, and she brushed them away. "Let's get out of this wind. You can at least drink some coffee."

He shrugged then followed her into the café, where she led him to a back table.

Molly came to the table. "What'll it be, Bree?" She barely looked at Steve.

"I'll have some cabbage rolls and fish stew," Bree said. "And maybe some lingonberries for dessert. Oh, and a coffee—for Steve too."

Molly wrote down the order then nodded and hurried away, returning moments later with the coffee pot. She filled their cups without comment.

"See what I mean?" Steve said. "Everyone looks at me like they think I'll pull a knife on them any second. I'll probably have to move away."

Bree dug a handful of pistachio nuts out of her pocket. "Want some?" she asked. He shook his head, and she split a shell with her thumbnail and popped the nut into her mouth. "The sheriff will find out who did it," she told him.

Steve gave a bitter laugh. "Mason's too wrapped up in the election campaign to care. As long as he has a suspect—namely, me—that's all he'll care about. I've always laughed about small-town gossip. But now the finger is pointed at me, and it's not fair! I loved Fay. We had our problems, including money. I'm not denying that. But that doesn't mean I killed her." He wrapped his fingers around his coffee cup and stared at the liquid.

Bree stared at him. Could he know something about the location of the cabin? He was her only source of information. "Do you know where she'd been hiking recently? She mentioned seeing a cabin with an old airplane seat in a ravine near it. It's probably nothing, but I'd like to check it out. I just don't have any idea of where to look."

Lost in his own thoughts, Steve didn't answer for a long moment. He finally blinked and looked up. "She never talked much about her hiking."

"Think," Bree urged.

He took a gulp of coffee. "I think maybe she mentioned hiking out near Ten Mile Peak. But she was all over the place. I can't even remember when she said something about it. Sorry."

At least it was a start. She wouldn't be searching totally blind.

Steve stared at her for a long moment, then his face grew thoughtful. "You could figure it out, Bree. Fay always said you were smarter than the rest of the town rolled together." He leaned across the table, and his voice grew excited. "Will you poke around for me?"

Committing herself to Steve—who she still wasn't convinced had nothing to do with Fay's death—was more than she was prepared to do. "I'm just a search-and-rescue worker," Bree protested. "The sheriff has called in forensic help. They'll figure it out."

Anger flashed across his face. He stood slowly, as if he wasn't sure his legs would support him. "So you won't help me either," he said dully. "I might as well have the sheriff lock me up." He turned and rushed from the restaurant.

Bree watched him go. There seemed to be a desperation about him—a desperation that could be caused by guilt.

9

The macadam road narrowed until it was little more than a track through the thick forest. The moist scent of leaves and mold drifted to Bree's nose as she and Samson walked along the side of the road behind the state police forensic experts. She'd been surprised to find that the lead was a woman. Somehow she'd expected a thin man with spectacles and an attitude. Too much TV, she guessed.

The reality was Janna Kievari, a woman of about forty with soft brown hair styled in a becoming chin-length bob. With steel-blue eyes set above a sharp nose, her fine bone structure proclaimed Finnish heritage more loudly than did her name. Dressed in tan wool slacks and a black-and-tan wool blazer with sensible hiking shoes, her no-nonsense manner appealed to Bree. This woman emanated a fearlessness Bree intended to emulate. Janna wouldn't be afraid to ask questions, to stir the pot even if it angered someone. And neither would Bree.

Mason hadn't objected to her request to tag along, but Bree suspected it was because the sheriff was relieved to have any kind of help. Rock Harbor was not a metropolis of criminal activity, and she knew Mason felt out of his element at the nature of this crime committed under his watch.

But by the time Janna's team had collected samples and departed for Houghton, Bree knew no more than she did before they arrived. She'd hoped for some riveting piece of evidence that would indicate what had really happened. The only thing Janna said was that it didn't appear to be a hit-and-run accident. There were no impressions left by skidding tires, and the spot where they'd found the blood and hair was too far from the road.

Bree had hoped it would turn out to be just that. Someone covering up an accident would have been better than the alternative. She shivered. It was the sheriff's problem though, not hers. Her job was to trace Fay's path the last few weeks and find the woman in the cabin. Useless as it was probably going to be, it was becoming an obsession.

She glanced at her watch. If she hurried, she could get in a couple of hours of searching before the funeral. Samson nudged her hand with his nose, and she absently patted his head. "Ready to search, boy?"

He hunkered down and barked. She opened the Jeep door, and he jumped in. Bree drove out to quadrant sixteen and took Hegg Road to Rock River. Some of the most dramatic scenery in the U.P. could be found here. Volcanic rock outcroppings framed the falls and created a breathtaking 325-foot-deep gorge.

She and Rob used to come here a lot. Staring up at the last traces of fall foliage, the memories washed over her. It was so hard to reconcile the man she loved with what she knew now about his unfaithfulness. In spite of his angry denials, she'd had to face the truth. If he'd come back from the fatal trip, what other excuses would he have offered? She sometimes wondered if she would have forgiven him for Davy's sake and tried to patch up their marriage. Infidelity would be hard to live with. Besides, he might have wanted to marry that Lanna, whoever she was.

Opening the bag, she held it under Samson's nose. Davy's blue shirt, the one with the Superman emblem on the back, had been his favorite piece of apparel. Now it was merely the search article of choice. Sometimes Bree wanted to take it out of its protective bags and bury her face in it, breathe in the scent that had been her son, that aroma of mud pies, Play-Doh, and candy.

She grimaced. This was her new life now—no more dwelling on the past. Samson's great plume of a tail wagged, and he barked as if to tell her he was ready to find Davy. Though she always came out here with fresh hope, it was getting harder and harder to sustain that hope in the face of constant defeat. She would probably always search once in a while as she trained dogs in the woods, but this quadrant would be the last for a formal search. Bree closed the bag and tossed it back in the car.

"Search, Samson," she told the dog. He leaped away in a bound and raced toward the woods with his nose held high.

For a moment Bree thought he really had a scent. Her heart gave a great leap of joy, and she ran after him. Maybe today was the day. Samson seemed driven as he headed for a stand of white pine. The towering trees blocked out the sunshine, and the two raced over a thick carpet of pine needles. The softness underfoot reminded Bree of a plush carpet. Her focus was sharpened by the scent of pine.

On the other side of the pines, the forest changed to oak and hickory. Samson paused and seemed to peer through the gloom of deep woods. His tail drooped, and Bree's spirits plummeted with it. He didn't have a clue where to go next.

"Go on, boy," she urged. "Find Davy."

Samson wagged his tail and started off again, but she could tell he was wandering aimlessly, just as he'd done every time they'd searched for the past year.

She and Samson thrashed their way through thickets of brambles and vines for nearly two hours before calling it a day. In the clearing by the Jeep, Bree played fetch with the dog for a few minutes to encourage him before heading to town. She would be expected at Fay's funeral.

Would Fay's murderer be there too? She ran through the possible suspects in her mind. Eric was at the top of her list. Then Steve. And what about Fay's uncle Lawrence? It had sounded like he was involved with the mob or something sinister. Could he have been so desperate to get his hands on the mine that he killed her? Kade was still a possibility, and Hilary too, though Bree didn't want to consider either of them as candidates.

She stopped at the lighthouse to drop off Samson and change her clothes before driving to the church. Rock Harbor Community Church stood on Quincy Hill overlooking downtown. Built in 1886, it stood guard like a sentinel over Rock Harbor. The church was already filled with people when Bree walked in. Scanning the rows of pews, she saw Anu's fair hair. Bree walked over and slipped between Anu and Mason. She craned her neck to look around. Naomi and her mother sat on the left in the third pew from the front, and Bree wondered if that was their regular pew. Many of the people crowding the pews attended regularly. The last time Bree had been here was for Rob and Davy's memorial service. The need to escape made her tug at her skirt self-consciously.

Fay's casket sat at the front of the sanctuary. The lid was closed, and Bree was thankful for that. The minister droned on, and she began to fidget. She hoped something would happen that might reveal who had killed Fay, but the service progressed without incident.

Kade's cousin Eric, dressed in a T-shirt and black leather jacket, wept openly in the pew in front of Bree. His grief seemed almost too overwhelming to be real, and she wondered again if all the gossip in town was true and Fay had been having an affair with him. Maybe she should ask him.

Palmer and Lily Chambers were on the other side of the church, and Lily gave Bree a small wave. Bree smiled back, then her gaze roamed the room again. She glanced at Hilary and found her sister-in-law's gaze fastened on the back of Steve's head. The last person Bree wanted to suspect was Hilary, but the questions wouldn't go away. Did she dare ignore them?

Fay's uncle sat on the front row with Steve. Bree thought again of the argument she'd been witness to the night of Hilary's party. Fay's uncle had been afraid Fay's stubbornness would get him killed. Maybe it had gotten Fay killed instead.

Anu pressed her hand against the knee Bree jiggled. "Patience, *kulta.* Soon we will leave and have some food."

Bree stilled her knee. She wanted out of here. Mercifully, the service ended and the people began to file out. Since they were seated near the front, the church was nearly empty by the time Bree and the rest of the Nicholls family reached the door. His eyes bloodshot, Steve stood at the door, accepting condolences. Eric pushed past them and stood with his hands on his hips in front of Steve.

Steve's face twisted into a snarl when he saw Eric. "You've got some nerve coming here," he spit out.

Eric pushed his face in front of Steve's. "Look, I'm the only one here who really loved her for who she was. You make me sick, standing there pretending to mourn her. She never loved you; she just loved your money."

Eric's voice was slurred. Drunk.

Steve's face grew redder and more outraged. He grabbed Eric by his jacket lapels and shook him. Though Eric was smaller, he put his hands up and broke Steve's hold on him with ease.

"The truth is hard to take, isn't it? That was my baby, Steve. How does that make you feel? You aren't man enough to give her a baby."

Mason reached the fracas and grabbed Eric's arm. "I think it's time you left. This is no place for a fight."

Eric tried to jerk his arm out of Mason's grasp, but the burly sheriff was too strong for him. "Whacha hassling me for, Sheriff? There's your man." He pointed an unsteady finger at Steve. "He killed her when he found out she was pregnant with my baby."

"That was *my* baby," Steve shouted. "She told me about you, how you were obsessed and wouldn't leave her alone, that you wanted her to leave me. You probably killed her when she told you she was staying with me."

"I would've convinced her," Eric muttered. "She didn't mean it, and I knew she didn't."

Mason propelled Eric through the door. "Go home and sleep it off," he ordered.

Eric stumbled down the steps, and Bree watched him stagger across the street to the corner of Quincy and Jack Pine Lane. She saw Kade's truck and watched him get out. He reached out to steady Eric then took his arm and propelled him to the truck. Bree hadn't seen Kade at the funeral. She thought again of him emerging from the trees just before Samson found Fay.

She had to find out the truth about Kade, but how? The beautiful Indian summer day seemed dull even in the sunshine. She normally worked at Nicholls's on Wednesdays, but she felt a need to be outside, away from everything. Maybe Naomi would have time to look for the woman at the cabin with her.

"It's such a beautiful day, Anu. Do you mind if I slip out and do a bit of searching? Can you get along without me today?"

"I think it will be a slow day because of the funeral. Go ahead. I will see you tomorrow, *kulta.*"

Bree hugged her, then found Naomi to see if she wanted to come. She did, so they both rushed home to get the dogs. Naomi promised to bring sandwiches and meet her outside in fifteen minutes. Bree put Samson's search vest on him and grabbed her ready-pack. By 2:30 they were in the forest, heading toward Ten Mile Peak.

October possessed a special quality of light, Rachel decided. There was a sadness to it too, a knowledge that winter was coming. The deep woods sounds had a frenzy about them, as though all nature realized time was short and it must make the best of the remaining clear, warm days.

She intended to be gone before the worst of the snow fell. The question was where to go. The only family she had in the world was her brother, Frank. He was in Chicago, and Rachel hadn't seen or heard from him in over ten years. It was unlikely he would welcome his long-lost sister, especially after what she'd done.

Rachel glanced out the cabin's kitchen window and saw Sam sitting under a tree. He held out bits of bread in his hand as he tried to coax a chipmunk to come closer. She needed to do better by him. A little boy needed playmates beyond the forest's denizens.

What was she thinking? "That's not my problem unless I keep him," she muttered aloud. Speaking the words seemed to make them take on a life of their own. Her mouth still hung open, and she shut it with a snap. She could keep him. He was young, and he'd soon forget he had any other life before the accident.

A jolt of joy quickened her pulse. Sam would be her own boy. She would finally have a real family. Did she dare do it? She squeezed her eyes shut. One month, that's all she had money for. By Thanksgiving they would have to get out. She turned and shuffled over to the scarred pine table at the other end of the kitchen.

Rachel sat at the table and opened the paper. Turning to the medical jobs section, she began to scan the possible positions. She had her RN license. It needed to be renewed every two years, so it was good for another eight months, and that's what she loved to do. Surely many retirement homes were in desperate need of help. By the time she finished, she had a list of ten possible jobs. There was no time like the present to get started.

She went to her bed and stooped, pulling out a battered manual typewriter from under the rickety cot. A grimy layer of dust coated the keys, but the old workhorse still typed like a champ. She'd done all her homework on it from the time she was in high school. Rachel plunked it on the table then went back for a box of paper. If she could find a job, they could be gone from this place within the month.

Part of her dreaded leaving. The cabin had been her haven, and the thought of facing the world's derision for a woman past her prime made her shudder. But another part of her rejoiced at the knowledge that once she faded into the obscurity of big-city Chicago, no one would ever find Sam. She could quit looking over her shoulder. He would be hers and hers alone.

Closing her eyes, she imagined watching him graduate magna cum laude from some elite college. He would tell the world how he owed everything to his mother, Rachel. Sharing his appreciation for all she'd done for him, he would let her know she'd been the best mother in the world.

She opened her eyes and smiled. Why not? She deserved a son after all she'd been through. And Sam deserved a chance in a big city. This small cabin and the heartache of the first few weeks would fade from his memory, as the pain of childbirth faded once a mother held her newborn child. She and Sam would be reborn in Chicago. And nothing would ever come between them.

After she typed the letters, she stuffed the envelopes. Tomorrow she would take them to town, buy stamps, and send them off. Setting them aside, she rose to prepare lunch for Sam. He loved peanut butter and jelly. She spread it thinly so her supply would last longer and called him in to eat.

Dirt marred his right cheek. Bits of twigs and grass stuck in his hair. "Who was the man?"

Her hand paused in midair, and her pulse fluttered in her throat. She turned to stare at him. "What man?"

"He was here just now. He talked to me."

"I've told you never to speak to strangers!" She gripped his shoulders, and he began to cry and squirm.

"I didn't—he talked to me."

"What did he say?" Her mind reeled feverishly. Was it the man at the mine? They would have to leave *now*.

"He was a hunter, he said. He asked if I'd seen any deer."

"Did you talk to him?" she whispered, though she could read the answer in the way Sam cast his gaze to the floor and shuffled his feet.

"He surprised me," he said. "I couldn't help it."

"Maybe it will be all right," she muttered. "As long as he doesn't shoot his mouth off to everyone in town." Her gaze sharpened, and she looked Sam over closely. His bright red hair would be a giveaway to someone of his true identity. But that was easily fixed. She let her breath out slowly.

"Did the chipmunk come for his supper?"

Sam shook his head. "Marcus still won't come either." He'd been trying to coax his "pet" squirrel to eat from his hand all summer.

She scooped him into her arms. "I know what's wrong, Sammy. They're afraid of your hair."

He touched his hand to his head. "What's wrong with my hair?"

"Nothing's wrong with it. But it's a bright color, and it probably scares them. If we color it, I bet they'll come right to you."

"Can we do it today?" A smile broke across his face.

"I have to go to town, so I'll get some dye for it. We'll just color it brown, and Marcus won't be afraid anymore."

A noise outside drew her attention. "Is that hunter still out there?"

Sam shrugged his small shoulders. "I guess so. He has a red-and-black hat on." She put Sam on the floor and went to the door.

Rachel grabbed her hat and sweater, a shapeless gray garment so full of pills and snags it looked as though it needed to be combed. Slinging it around her shoulders, she threw open the door and hurried into the yard.

A blue jay chattered a warning over her head, and she stared around the yard and into the shadows of the large trees that swallowed up the bright autumn sunshine. A movement caught her eyes, and she stepped hastily in that direction. A red-and-black plaid hat bobbed in the shadows as the man hurried away from the clearing. She followed at a discreet distance. Maybe she could find out who he was.

The leaves overhead blotted out the sunshine. It was colder among the trees, and she was glad she'd thought to grab her sweater. Stepping carefully through the forest, she kept the man's hat in sight. He never turned or looked to the left or the right, which struck her as strange for a hunter, but maybe he had given up for the day.

His stride was quick and confident as though he knew exactly where he was going. Finally, he paused at a large rock near the Kirin Brook. Stooping, he rinsed a handkerchief in the rushing water and mopped his face. As he turned his head to run the hanky over his neck, Rachel saw his face for the first time, and her stomach plunged to her toes.

He'd found her! Rachel didn't see how that was possible. But why else would he be here in her part of the forest? It seemed more than mere coincidence. Now more than ever, it was imperative she get out of these woods before someone else died.

10

Autumn was Kade's favorite season. Fighting black flies in summer, he always longed for the fabulous display of red and gold, the crisp, cool nights, and the rich, earthy odors. Glistening droplets of water brightened the rich hues of fall foliage.

He turned up his jacket collar against the cool dampness and settled more securely in the saddle as his gelding made his way along the path to Eagle Cliff where Fay Asters had been found. The funeral had been two days ago, but the yellow crime-scene tape still fluttered from the trees.

A hawk swooped overhead then dived. Kade heard a squeak as the bird snatched a field mouse in its talons and wheeled away with its prey. Nature could be harsh, but there was a simplicity and rightness to death in this environment.

He heard the leaves rustle ahead of him and urged his horse to break into a trot. Rounding a curve in the path, he found Bree and Samson wandering off the path in a bramble patch. "Finding anything?" he asked.

Bree shook her head and snapped her fingers at Samson. The dog came right to her. A wary look came into her face. "Nothing so far. Fay said she'd seen what looked like an airplane seat near a cabin, but Naomi and I have looked for days and haven't found anything. Fay has exaggerated things like this before, but I have to at least look. Have you seen anything in your treks around?"

Kade shook his head. "Sorry. So if you're looking for the cabin, what are you doing here?" He knew she'd scoured this area already.

"Naomi and I searched the only place Steve knew she'd been and found nothing. Her backpack was never found. I thought maybe Samson could find it. There might be something in there to lead me to the cabin and the person she talked to."

"But if it was usual for her to exaggerate things . . ."

"You never know. Maybe she really did see something."

Kade wasn't sure he wanted her poking around. She might get hurt. "Want some help?"

"I'm not sure where to start. Maybe if I begin where we found Fay's body and work backward, we could find where she was killed. Naomi and Charley are checking down the road."

"I heard forensics confirmed your initial hunches. Pretty impressive. Why were you so sure it wasn't a hit-and-run?" Kade dismounted and tied his horse's reins to a tree.

Bree picked her way through the leaves and brambles to the path where Kade waited. Samson followed. "I don't know; it was just a gut feeling. Besides, why not just leave her? Why run the risk of having someone see Fay being dragged to the cliff? What would she have been doing walking along the road when her car was in the parking lot and the cliff was the opposite direction?"

She had a point.

"Hello up there!"

They both turned to see Naomi and Charley making their way up the slope to join them. Naomi's dark braid hung over one shoulder. Her orange-and-black plaid wool jacket appeared then disappeared through the thick foliage as she scrambled up the slope. Charley gave an excited bark, and Samson scrambled toward him. Nose to nose and tails wagging, the dogs greeted each other.

"Let's check out the cliff face again," Kade suggested. "The pack could be stuck in a crevice or something." He swept aside arching bramble branches and headed that direction without waiting for an answer.

The misty fog began to lighten, and the cliff face rose from the grayness like a blue whale breaching from the sea mist. Sunshine began to filter through the rich hues of orange and gold, and the forest appeared to have gilded edges. The women tramped behind him.

Kade paused a moment to appreciate the beauty. "God sure knows how to create, doesn't he?"

Bree stopped behind him, and he heard her soft intake of breath. "Nature can be awe-inspiring."

"When you look at scenery like this, you know the creation of it had to be a conscious act. The Bible says creation was finger play for God. Did you know that? It makes me wonder what other marvels he's created in the universe."

"He destroys too," Bree said.

Kade swiveled his head at her clipped tone and caught the look of dismay on Naomi's face. So Bree blamed God for the loss of her son and husband. Who was he to judge her though? Maybe he'd react the same way if he ever faced a similar tragedy.

"I'll check out the top of the cliff," Kade said. "Why don't you and Naomi take the dogs and scour the riverbank? A wild animal might have dragged off her backpack. If she brought any food along, it could have tempted a bear or raccoon."

"You're not going to climb the cliff, are you?" Bree's voice rose with dismay.

Her concern warmed Kade. "Do I look that stupid?" He grinned to soften the words. "No, I'll go around to the backside and take the path."

Bree's stance relaxed, and she called Samson. The dog bounded toward her, then she and Naomi headed over the rocks toward the glimmering river.

Kade's breath came hard by the time he'd made his way around the hill and followed the steep but passable path to the top of Eagle Rock.

From his vantage point, he could see the sweep of the river and the rounded masses of the trees like great banks of colorful mums.

Bree's suspicion of him bothered him more than he liked to admit, but maybe she had good reason. His thoughts turned to Eric, and he sighed. Things could get ugly.

⋯⋯

"Why are you walking so fast?"

Naomi's plaintive voice brought Bree up short. She stopped and turned with an apologetic smile. "Sorry. There has to be some clue out here we're missing." She dug a handful of pistachios out of her backpack. "I'd offer you some, but I know you'd just turn them down." Biting reflectively into a nut, she nodded toward the forest. "Time to get back to work." She tossed the nutshells to the ground and dusted her hands on her jeans.

"You seem positively . . . driven about this, Bree." Naomi's chest heaved from exertion. "What's up with that? Mason can handle the investigation." She finally caught up with Bree. "That's his job."

Bree chewed on a nut. "I know the story about the woman and the airplane seat is probably nothing, but what if it's not? The only way to find out what Fay knew is to retrace her steps, and if that involves finding out who killed her, so be it."

"Are you sure you're not just trying to find a reason not to give up the search?"

Bree swallowed and turned away. Naomi's words had hit a little too close for comfort. "That's not it at all," she said. "I should be done with the quadrant by the new year. I'm done then if I don't find them. I told you, Anu is helping me get started with training search-and-rescue dogs. I've even started looking for a place. But I have to give it my best shot until then."

"Just so you don't go overboard," Naomi said.

Bree scanned the landscape. Both dogs began to bark then ran toward an object along the riverbank. A flash of red drew her attention, and she squinted. "What's that, Naomi?"

"I think it's her backpack!" Bree ran after the dogs. As she drew nearer, the red object came more into focus, and she smiled in triumph. Samson picked up a stick, his signal of a find, and brought it to her. She paused long enough to praise her dog then followed him to the backpack.

"Don't touch anything," Naomi warned. "Mason will want to run forensics on it."

Bree drew back her hand. Naomi was right, but she longed to open the backpack and see if it held any clues to Fay's death. "You got the cell phone with you?"

Naomi nodded. "I'll call it in."

Bree was thankful Kade waited with them for the hour it took the sheriff to arrive, though she knew she needed to get back to work. The dark shadows in the woods spooked her. Mason and his deputies arrived and Kade left to find his horse.

It was another hour before Janna and her forensics team arrived. Bree and Naomi stood out of the way and watched as they went over the backpack and combed the surrounding area for clues. Bree shifted her feet restlessly, wishing she could peer inside the pack herself. She knew Fay, and these strangers didn't.

"I think we can wrap it up now," Janna finally said. Mason stood and nodded to his officers. He joined Bree and Naomi at the edge of the action. "Good work," he told them.

His praise warmed Bree. "Any idea how the pack got down here?" she asked. "It's at least a mile from the cliff."

Mason shook his head. "No teeth marks from animals, which would have been my first assumption. My gut feeling is that the killer dumped it. But maybe the lab can come up with something."

"What was in her backpack?"

"The usual. Climbing gear like pitons, rope, a compass, that kind of thing. A bottle of water. No food, which would explain why the animals left it alone. Oh, and a notebook of some kind." He grimaced. "The backpack seems to be a dead end." His penetrating gaze lingered on her face. "This has really gotten to you, hasn't it?"

Bree nodded. "Not much I can do to fix it."

Mason shook his head at her dejected tone. "You're a crusader, Bree. If you'd been a man during the Middle Ages, you would have been the first to vie for a seat at King Arthur's Round Table. But you can't right every wrong. Sometimes bad things happen to good people." His voice held kindness, and he clasped her shoulder. "Innocent people like little Davy. You can't stop it from happening, and you can't fix it. The sooner you realize that, the easier time you'll have."

Bree didn't know what to say. "Could I take a look at the notebook when forensics is done?"

Mason released her shoulder then put his hand to his face and pinched the bridge of his nose. "We'll see," he said with heavy resignation. "Steve will want to see it first, and it will be up to him whether to let you look at it. Now I've got to get back to town." He joined his deputies and they began to wrap up.

Bree, Naomi, and the dogs went back the way they'd come, clambering over huge boulders and picking their way over slick stones along the water. Bree pulled an unopened bag of pistachios from her pocket. Before she could open them, the back of Bree's neck began to prickle. She whirled around, expecting to find someone standing behind her, but there was no one there. Samson whined, and she gave a shaky laugh. "Sorry, boy, I must be going wacko."

"What is it?" Naomi asked.

"Nothing." Bree said.

The dog didn't seem to sense anything, but then he often ignored scents he hadn't been told to search for. Bree started off toward the Jeep again. The tingling feeling returned in a rush, and she glanced around uneasily as her breath became sharp in her chest. Another panic attack? She fought the encroaching terror.

Her gaze scanned the shrubs around her, but she saw nothing. Still, the feeling of being watched persisted. If she told Naomi, she'd likely say it was God pursuing her. She shook her head nervously. More likely it was her imagination; Samson and Charley remained unconcerned. But all her self-reassurances failed to quell her panic.

Her pace quickened, and the bag of nuts slipped from her hand. She and Naomi were practically running by the time they got to her Jeep. She opened the back door and let Samson in then slid quickly into the driver's seat. Starting the Jeep, she slammed it into reverse and floored the accelerator. Bits of gravel spit from under her tires, and the vehicle roared toward town.

Her breath fogged in front of her in plumes. Rachel rushed from tree to tree and watched until the red Jeep disappeared from view. She bent over at the waist, panting with exertion. A bag of nuts lay at her feet. Sam loved nuts. She picked up the bag and stuffed it into her pack.

Her breathing finally relaxed. She wasn't as young as she used to be. There had once been a time when crowds cheered as her long legs ate up the fifty yards to the finish line. Now those same legs were layered with more fat than muscle, and the last crowds she'd heard had been howling for her conviction.

People were too quick to judge others. Just because she lived alone and worked with old folks, the public had been quick to believe she would kill to put them out of their misery. They didn't understand that the love of her work came from the friendships she'd formed with these elderly folks. She'd been innocent.

Rachel worried her lower lip between her teeth. Those women and their dogs had been too close. Could the one woman be Sam's mother? Same red hair. Rachel set her jaw. No. It was ridiculous. Besides, he belonged to her now. With his hair dyed brown, he didn't even look like the same boy. She had to find some way to get that red-haired woman's focus away from here. At least until Rachel found a job somewhere. Maybe she would hear soon from the applications she'd mailed out yesterday.

She could feel the blood pumping through her veins as she walked toward the cabin. Sam would want his lunch. "Such a good boy, so obedient, a boy any mother would be proud of." She said it aloud now, and the pride she felt calmed her anxiousness.

Nearly an hour and a half later, Rachel located the path she'd marked in such subtle ways only an expert would be able to follow it. Her gaze scanned the clearing. Sam had stacked the wood she'd chopped before heading to town. Some of it had fallen over, but for such a young child, his efforts were praiseworthy. Her lips curved in approval.

She cocked her head and listened, but the only sound in the clearing was the rasp of her own breathing. Sam must be inside, where she'd told him to stay once he finished his chores. Rachel pushed up the sleeve of her wool jacket and glanced at the watch on her wrist. Nearly two. Sam was probably starved. Though she always fixed him a peanut butter sandwich before she went on her excursions, he rarely ate it until she walked in the door.

She didn't know whether that was because he didn't like to eat alone or because his fear of being abandoned killed his appetite. Her own stomach rumbled like an avalanche coming down Squaw Peak, and her pace quickened.

Sam was sitting on a chair at the table. His peanut butter sandwich lay before him, unwrapped and drying. Jerking his head around at her entrance, he stared at her through frightened green eyes. A tremulous smile touched his lips as Rachel went quickly toward him.

"You still haven't eaten, son. Were you waiting for Mother?"

Sam nodded. "My tummy's hungry."

"You don't always have to wait for me, darling. That's why Mother fixed you a sandwich before I went to town. I don't want your tummy to complain. You go ahead and eat, and I'll fix me something and join you."

Sam looked down at his sandwich with obvious reluctance then picked it up and bit into it. He chewed slowly, his gaze fixed on Rachel. She hurriedly tossed her knapsack on the floor and went to the old table that served as her counter. She slathered peanut butter on bread then mixed Carnation milk powder into a glass of water and gave it to Sam.

"Drink up, son. Milk gives you strong bones." She eased herself onto the other chair.

Sam drank it down with gusto, his upper lip coated with white by the time he set the glass back on the table. "Can we have reading lessons after we eat?"

"Maybe. I saw you got the wood stacked."

He nodded, his face bright from the approval in her tone. "And I made my bed. Yours too." His small chest swelled with pride as he said the last.

"What a good boy you are! I brought you a surprise."

"You did? Can I have it now?" He gulped the last bite of his sandwich. "I'm all done with lunch."

"Bring me my knapsack." Rachel's heart felt as though it might burst with love for the boy—her son, she reminded herself—as he jumped to his feet and limped across the floor to her discarded bag. It was too heavy for him to pick up, but that didn't stop Sam. He grabbed it by one strap and tugged it across the rough floor until it lay at Rachel's feet.

"Can I look inside?" he asked.

"I'll get it. I might have another surprise for later," she said with a wink. She'd picked up a surprise for him after she mailed her letters. She drew the knapsack onto her lap and opened the flap. Sam's eyes widened when he saw the bag of nuts in her hand. "'Stachios," he squealed. He clapped his hands together. "Can I shell them?"

"If you think you're big enough."

"I'm big now. See how big my hands are now?" He held out his small hands for her inspection.

"I had no idea," she said solemnly. "Okay, you are now the official sheller of nuts. Do you need the nutcracker?"

"Oh yes, *please*," he breathed.

Rachel kept the nutcracker in a chest beside the supply cabinet. She didn't need the nutcracker for pistachios, but it helped Sam manage the task, and he got such pleasure out of using it. "You can get it out," she told him.

He raced to the chest and threw open the lid. His small face shone when he pulled out the nutcracker soldier. Running his fingers lovingly over the chipped and worn paint, he brought it back to the table and climbed back onto his chair.

"It might be easier for you to use it on the rug," Rachel suggested. She helped him get started shelling the nuts then settled back on her chair and watched him.

His lower lip was caught between small white teeth, a frown of concentration furrowing the spot between his eyes. An aching wave of love washed over her as she watched the boy. Her son. Hers alone. And no one would ever take him from her.

11

$\mathcal{T}$he puppies tumbled over one another in the large metal cage and barked in high yips. Rock Harbor's Humane Society reeked of animals, but the doggie smell was as fine as the most expensive Paris perfume to Bree. Between fruitless searches on her days off and a busy sale going on at the store since Monday, she'd looked forward to this ever since Lauri called on Wednesday and asked her to help her pick out a puppy. Bree had called Palmer and coaxed him into meeting them here. Saturday wasn't a busy day at his fitness center, and he'd finally agreed.

Now Lauri sat on the floor surrounded by puppies, and the sound of her laughter warmed Bree's heart. Lily and Palmer had brought the twins as well, and their squeals of delight brightened the scene even more.

"I want this one," Lauri announced. She picked up a black-and-white puppy and rubbed his fat belly. "His name is Zorro."

"You've made a good choice," Bree said, nodding in approval. "His eyes are clear and intelligent, and from his coloring, I'd say he has some Border collie in him. Borders are good search dogs." She scratched the pup's head, and he wiggled all over with joy. "You realize your brother is going to kill me? He didn't want a dog. Did you even tell him you asked me to help you today?"

Lauri dropped her gaze guiltily and shook her head. "But he'll get over it when he sees how darling Zorro is," Lauri said.

Bree wasn't so sure. She'd noticed the tension between Lauri and

Kade at the O'Reilly house and could sense the rebellion in Lauri. She hated to make things worse.

"I'll be your training center's first customer." Lauri nestled the dog against her, and Zorro nibbled on her chin. Bree laughed and patted the puppy's head.

"And we'll be the second," Palmer said. "What about this pup, Bree?" He held a yellow Lab in his cupped hands.

"Oh, he's darling," Bree said. "He's a good choice too. He'll make a loving, loyal pet. Are you getting one for each of the girls?"

"I think we'd better start off with just one," Palmer said.

"He's afraid he'll be the one stuck taking the dog for walks until the girls are old enough to do it," Lily said.

"I already *know* that will be my job." The playful whine in Palmer's voice made them all laugh.

"Now these pups have all had their shots," Mathilda Worrell said. The older woman shuffled across the floor to her desk.

For as long as Bree could remember, Mathilda had run the animal shelter, though she must be nearly seventy by now. With hair as white and springy as fresh baby's-breath, her faded blue eyes peered through gold spectacles with such genuine love and interest that no one ever took offense at her meddling. Everyone from the mayor to the children called her Aunt Mathilda. She'd always seemed indomitable, but today Bree noticed a bit of grayness in her normally pink skin as the woman lowered herself into a desk chair and gave an uncharacteristic sigh.

"Are you all right, Aunt Mathilda?" Bree hurried to the desk when the older woman put a hand to her forehead.

"Fine, fine." Aunt Mathilda waved a hand in Bree's direction. "This dratted murder has just been wearing on my mind. I've spoken to the Lord about it nearly every night, but he is silent on the subject. For the life of me, I can't imagine who would want to hurt that sweet child."

"Sweet child" was not how Bree would have described Fay. Self-centered forest sprite maybe. But Aunt Mathilda never saw bad in anyone.

"Folks are saying it was her husband. You don't think Steve would do something like that, do you? You know I don't like to gossip, but folks are scared. With Fay dead, we have to watch out for one another. It worries me so to wonder who in town could be capable of such an act," Aunt Mathilda said.

"It could have been anyone." Bree was barely listening as her thoughts drifted back to Fay's death. It did seem odd that Steve had asked her to look for Fay but refused to go along. Fay had often complained about his obsession with his work, but maybe he used work as an excuse to stay away from a wife he didn't love. The line between love and hate could be blurry.

Aunt Mathilda finished writing the receipt for Lauri's dog. "He'll make you a good pet, dear."

Lauri threw her arms around Bree. "Thanks so much for helping me get a puppy," she said, her face shining. "When can we start training him?"

"First, we'll just work on obedience and establishing yourself as the alpha dog."

Lauri grinned. "I'm the alpha dog? What's that?"

"Sounds like science fiction," Palmer said.

"There's a pecking order in a household, and puppies need to discover the place doesn't revolve around them. Since they're so young, it shouldn't be too hard for them to figure that out. You're the boss of his pack, the alpha dog." Bree scratched Zorro's ears, and the dog squirmed with delight then peed on Lauri.

"Oh no!" Lauri held him away from her wet sweatshirt. "Bad Zorro!"

She started to swat him, but Bree stopped her. "You only want to punish him for disobedience. He's just a puppy. He'll learn to control his bladder just like children learn to use the toilet." She smiled to soften the sting. "Give him some time."

Lauri nodded and, still holding the puppy away from her shirt, started toward the door.

"We'll run Lauri home," Lily said.

"Thanks," Bree said. "Work on bonding with your dogs for the next few days. This weekend, concentrate on calling him to you then rewarding him when he comes. He has to learn he's *your* dog. And when he comes to greet you after school or work, walk in and don't make a fuss over him. If you make a huge fuss, he'll think he's the alpha dog. That will cause him stress when you leave and he can't protect you. Start off right, and it will make things a lot easier. Palmer, you figure out a name for yours yet?"

"Jasper," Lily offered.

"He looks like a Jasper." Bree scratched the dog's ears.

Palmer shrugged acquiescence. He and Lily managed to corral the girls and the dog and get them all into the van for the drive home.

"Hey, why don't you come to church with us tomorrow?" Lily asked.

"The roof would fall in if I ever came to a church service." Bree tried to deflect her refusal with a laugh, but a part of her wanted to accept.

Aunt Mathilda turned her penetrating blue eyes on Bree. "That's no laughing matter, Bree. The Hound of Heaven is searching for you. Can't you hear his baying, Bree? Don't ignore him, child."

"The Hound of Heaven? Sounds ominous." Bree would indulge her. Besides, she was curious.

Aunt Mathilda smiled. "Jesus, child. Jesus is looking for you, searching for you. He'll follow you wherever you go. You can't run from him or hide where he can't find you. All this searching for your boy and your husband is just another way of running from his call and blocking out his voice. If you want to run, run *to* him, not away."

Bree raised her eyebrows. She didn't like where this conversation was headed. Hound of Heaven, indeed. Her mind flitted to Naomi's showing up just when she was about to fall to her death. She pushed the thought away. "I didn't know you thought I was such a sinner, Aunt Mathilda."

"We're all sinners, child. Every last one of us. I've seen you this past year, trying to atone for yourself with good deeds, turning all meek and mild, afraid to make a peep that Hilary doesn't approve of. It won't work, Bree. You've got courage, child. Use it to do yourself some eternal good. Take a good, hard look into your heart. Turn to God for forgiveness, then forgive yourself too."

Bree hadn't come in here for a sermon. "See you later, Aunt Mathilda. Call me if you hear anything important." Shivering in the wind, she tried to put the image that Aunt Mathilda's words had conjured out of her mind. Visions of some slathering dog howling as he chased her was too scary to think about. Though everyone told her God was a God of love, all she'd seen was his hand of judgment. If he'd judged Rob's sin, he'd taken innocent Davy as well. She wanted nothing to do with a God like that.

Rock Harbor Savings and Loan was across the street and two doors down from the animal shelter. The bank windows glinted in the late October sunshine. Bree glanced at her watch. Eleven. The bank was open on Saturday mornings; maybe Steve would be working. She pushed open the ornate door and stepped onto the tile floor. Steve was walking toward his office. Bree hurried to catch up with him.

"Steve, you got a minute?"

"I guess." He held the door open for her.

She followed him into the office with Samson close on their heels. The dark mahogany desk gleamed, and the plush chairs matched the desk and the bookcases that lined one wall.

Bree sat in one of the guest chairs. "How are you doing?" she asked.

"Why do you care? You're so suspicious of me you won't even help me try to find Fay's real killer."

"I . . . I want to help. But I don't know exactly what I can do."

He leaned forward eagerly. "You'll help? I just want you to take the dog and poke around, see if you turn up any clues, maybe trace where she was the last few days before she was killed."

Which was precisely what Bree had been doing. She suppressed a sigh. "All right. Now, how are you doing?"

He looked away. "I'm getting by. The house is sure quiet. You know how Fay was, always yammering about something. You know, I'm the first to admit we had our troubles. I knew her old boyfriend had been calling her, but to find out the baby might . . ." His voice trailed off.

"You don't know that for sure," Bree said. "Eric might have just wanted to hurt you."

"He did a good job of it. I guess I could have the baby's DNA tested to see for sure, but I don't think I want to know. Sometimes ignorance is easier to take."

And sometimes it plays you for a fool. Bree had been the ostrich type too often in her marriage. If she'd been more in tune with things, maybe Rob wouldn't have strayed. She had chalked up his distraction to work. Now she knew better.

Steve swiveled his chair around to the coffeepot on the credenza behind him. "You take your coffee with cream?"

"And a little sugar," she said. He stirred the coffee and handed it to her. Smiling her thanks, she wrapped her cold hands around the warm cup.

Steve took a gulp of his black coffee. "I'm sure you didn't come by just to see how I'm doing."

"I just thought we ought to team up . . . see what we can find out. I need to find out where that cabin she mentioned is too. I'm not having much luck finding it," Bree explained.

"You know how Fay was—she always had to be center stage. I wouldn't put too much stock in what she said about the cabin and the airplane seat. It sounds pretty far-out."

Bree nodded. "That's what I thought too, but since she died, I can't seem to get it out of my head. I just want to find it and make sure."

"Sorry I can't help you more there." Steve picked up a pen and twirled it around in his fingers. "I just hope the sheriff is checking out Eric thoroughly. His temper has gotten him into trouble before."

"Could I poke around in her things at home, see if she wrote down anything, left any clues about this?"

"I guess, but I don't think you'll find anything. Give me a few days though. The house is a mess, and I've got a maid coming to clean it up in a couple of days. Give me a call next week."

Bree didn't doubt it was a mess. She remembered her own state of confusion and disarray, and the memory stirred her sympathy. "Another thing . . . Mason has a notebook that was in Fay's backpack. You mind if I take a look and see if it mentions the cabin?"

"Sure, that's fine. He showed it to me. I don't think there was much in there except for ramblings about different trails."

Which might be exactly what she needed.

He eased back against his seat again. "Please don't stop believing in me, Bree," he said softly. "I loved Fay. Keep poking around, and you'll discover I didn't kill her."

She nodded, although she couldn't shake her doubts. "I'll call you next week." Bree moved past him to leave, and he shut the door behind her. Glancing at her watch, she saw she only had fifteen minutes before she'd promised to be at Nicholls's. Saturday wasn't her usual day to work, but Anu had an appointment and needed her help.

Nicholls's Finnish Imports was bustling with shoppers sorting through the new treasures. Anu had just stocked the new merchandise she'd brought back from Finland two weeks ago. Bree paused to glance through a stack of wool sweaters and grabbed one for herself, a bright green one with navy trim. She stashed it behind the cash register then went to find her mother-in-law.

"There you are," Anu said. "I was beginning to wonder if you would make it."

"Looks like you need all the help you can get. This place is packed!" Indeed, even more shoppers had crammed into the small store until there was barely room to walk around.

Anu smiled. "They could smell the *pulla* from down the street. I made a fresh batch, and every shopper must get one." She untied her apron. "My thanks for taking over for me, *kulta*."

When Anu was gone, Bree wandered through the store, answering questions as best she could and chatting with the customers about everything from children's homework to the latest news. Being part of the woof and weave of Rock Harbor never failed to bring a sense of grateful joy to her life. This was her home, and these folks were her family in all the ways that really mattered.

Just after five, she escorted the last of the customers out and shut the door. Folding sweaters at the table by the front window, she glanced out into the street and saw Fay's uncle Lawrence talking to Steve. Lawrence had his fists clenched and his face thrust into Steve's. Both men were red-faced, and their shouts carried indistinctly through the window. Bree opened the door and stepped out to the sidewalk.

"It's stupid to go through with that sale now!" Lawrence was yelling. "We can get twice that from my contact in New York."

"It's my copper mine," Steve said tightly. "You might have browbeaten my wife, but don't try it with me. I'm a man of my word. The matter is closed."

The man doubled up his fist as though he might punch Steve in the nose, but instead he wheeled and rushed away. Bree knew they had to have been talking about the old Copper Queen.

Lawrence Kukkari had been a bit eccentric and difficult ever since he'd returned from Vietnam. If he could cause a problem, it seemed to make him happy. His letters to the editor of the newspaper were legendary in Rock Harbor. It seemed every time Bree saw him, he was angry. Could he have been angry enough to kill Fay over the mine, believing he could get Steve to see things his way about backing out on the sale to Palmer and taking the higher offer instead?

His hands clenched at his sides, Steve watched Lawrence walk away, then his gaze settled on Bree. "There's another suspect for you, Bree," he called. "Why don't you investigate why he practically forced Fay to agree to sell that useless copper mine? I've half a mind to cancel the sale altogether just to spite him. I'd do it too if I didn't like Palmer so much." He gave a disgusted snort and turned to walk away.

Bree ran down the sidewalk. "Wait, Steve." She ran to catch up with him. "Did Fay ever say anything about that other buyer of Lawrence's being with the mob? I overheard an argument she had with him. She told her uncle she wanted nothing to do with his buyers, that they were mobsters."

Steve frowned. "We didn't talk about the mine much. It belonged to her and Lawrence, and I tried not to get involved."

He turned and walked away. Bree stared after him thoughtfully. Maybe she'd just make a visit out to the mine next week and see if anything was stirring around the old place.

12

Rachel smoothed the three letters flat against the table. A future. She and Sam might have a future. The first two letters were the standard "Thank you for applying, but we've already filled the position" type, but the last one had brought a smile to her face. She'd read it over and over, and the words were still the same after two days.

The director of a facility called Golden Years Nursing Home, a Mary Bristol, had invited her to come for a job interview. Rachel hadn't thought that far ahead. What could she do with Sam? She would have to take the bus to Chicago, and her funds would barely cover the cost for herself. There was no way she could take Sam. Besides, she'd have to spend the night on a park bench, and she couldn't endanger her son that way.

She glanced at him, playing with his toys by the stove. Surely he could stay overnight by himself. Though she figured he couldn't be more than four years old, he was smart and resourceful. And even more important, he was obedient. If she told him to stay inside and not to go out for any reason, he would do just that.

Frowning, she decided to worry about it later. In the letter, the director had asked her to call and schedule an appointment, which meant she'd have to go back to town. She'd tried to call before she left town two days ago when she first received the letter, but the woman had been out of the office. According to her secretary, Rachel was supposed to call her today, Friday.

She hurriedly dressed and put on her boots. "I have to go to town, Sam," she told him. "I'll get the wood chopped before I head out."

Sam stared at her for a moment then pushed his bowl of cereal away. "Can I go?" he asked.

From the hopelessness in his voice, she knew he already expected the answer. She hesitated. Why not allow it this once? He could stay in the trees while she used the pay phone. No one would see him. And even if someone did, the color on his hair was fresh. No one would ever recognize him.

The thought of the red-haired woman and her dog flashed through her mind. She lived in Rock Harbor. But Rachel couldn't stand the helpless, lost look on Sam's face any longer. It was unlikely that the woman would be anywhere near the pay phones. They wouldn't be in town more than five minutes.

"Okay," she said finally.

An expression of disbelief crossed Sam's face, followed by incredulous joy. He bounded to his feet. "I'll help you chop wood," he said eagerly.

"I'll do it. You need to rest for the trip to town."

Rachel chopped wood all morning. After lunch she told Sam it was time to go. They would get to town about three. Taking his wool jacket from the hook by the door, she held it out for him to slip into. "We'd better get going."

For nearly two hours they walked through brambles and over hills, past streams and thick forest. At times Rachel carried Sam when his small legs got too tired.

When they crossed the road, he cried out, "It's Pooky!" He limped to the ditch where the koala bear lay partially covered by leaves. "Didn't Timmy and Emily want him?" he asked. He cradled the stuffed bear in his arms.

"I bet they dropped it by accident," Rachel said.

"I need to find them to give it back," he said.

"Come along," she told him. No use in upsetting him by telling him he'd never see those kids again. They trudged toward town. The sounds of vehicles and people reached her ears as they paused on a hill overlooking Rock Harbor.

Curls of smoke rose from the houses and cottages below them. Rachel scanned the streets close to the line of phone booths that was her destination. No sign of the red Jeep. Sam gripped her hand and started to walk forward with her, but she gently disentangled his small fingers.

"You have to stay here," she told him.

"You said I could come!" He sat on the ground and began to sob, his wails growing louder and more pronounced.

Rachel hardly knew what to do. Never had she heard him cry like that. His usual reaction of disappointment was a silent tear or two. But he must be very tired—they'd never traveled such a long distance before. She knelt beside him and pulled him onto her lap.

"Hush, Sammy. I won't be gone five minutes."

"But I wanted to see Emily and Timmy," he sobbed. "They need Pooky."

"Timmy and Emily are home with their mommy and daddy," she said. "We don't even know where they live."

"But I want to see them!" He wailed louder, and Rachel looked around nervously. If someone heard his cries and came to investigate, they might be in big trouble.

"Tell you what," she said. "You stay here real quiet like a mouse, and when I get back, we'll walk around the perimeter of town and see if we can find Timmy and Emily. If they're outside by themselves, we'll stop and say hello. Will that do?"

Sam's tears dried, and he nodded.

Rachel stood with him in her arms then set him on the ground. "Now remember, be very quiet."

Sam nodded. "I 'member."

Clutching her letter with the woman's phone number, Rachel took off at a dead run down the hill. Her legs wobbled, and her head spun with fatigue. Entering the phone booth, she pulled the bifold door shut behind her and opened the letter with shaking hands.

Her palms slick with sweat, she dialed the phone and waited.

A woman's voice answered. "Mary Bristol."

"Hi, Ms. Bristol, this is Rachel Marks. I received your letter about setting up an interview?" Rachel hoped her voice didn't betray her nervousness. Confidence, that's what sold an employer.

"Ah, yes, Rachel."

She heard the woman shuffle pages, then her voice came back over the line. "Can you come Monday at nine?"

"Um, that's a bit soon. Would next Wednesday work for you?"

In a voice heavy with disappointment, Mary Bristol told her they were in desperate need of someone but finally agreed that Wednesday would be acceptable. As she hung up the phone, Rachel wondered what she could wear. Somehow she had to overcome the bad impression she'd made by not agreeing to come when the woman wanted. It needed to be something professional and attractive, both traits that Rachel wondered if she even possessed anymore. Maybe if she stopped at Goodwill, she could find something she could afford.

She yanked open the phone booth door and trudged up the hill to where she'd left Sam. She didn't see him. "Sam," she called softly.

The only answer was the call of a gull from overhead. "Sam!" She raised her voice and turned to stare around her at the thick phalanx of forest crowding close.

The trees seemed to press in on her. She couldn't lose him, not now. He couldn't have gone far. Rachel began to run from tree to tree. Perspiration poured down her face and clung to her back. "Sam!" Tree branches reached for her, and she fought her way through them.

Think, Rachel. Where could he have gone? An instant later, she heard children laughing and whirled to see where the sound had come from. Leaning against a massive oak tree for support, she stared down the hill into a yard enclosed with a white picket fence. Three children were swinging on a swing set.

Her frantic gaze raced from face to face. Emily, Timmy—and Sam. Relief flooded through her in a rush of sweetness that left her nearly sinking to her knees. No one had taken him. He was still hers and hers alone.

The children turned at her approach. Emily's eyes grew wide with fear, and Timmy's feet thumped on the hard dirt, stopping the movement of his swing. He looked at his sister uncertainly.

"Hi," Emily said. Her voice trembled, but she raised her gaze to meet Rachel's hard stare.

Rachel was too distraught to care if she frightened the children. She opened the gate and rushed into the yard. Sam hadn't seen her yet. His eyes were closed as he swung his legs and pumped the swing higher into the air.

Watching him for a moment, Rachel felt a shaft of pain so strong she wondered if she might be having a heart attack. His carefree abandonment was a new sight to her. A child was supposed to be like this, wasn't he? Had she deprived the child she loved from the happy existence he deserved?

Squeezing her eyes shut, Rachel rubbed them with her fists. When she opened her eyes, Sam's gaze was boring into hers. His features froze in a blanket of guilt. One toe dug into the dirt until the swing was merely rocking side to side.

His frantic gaze jittered to his friends. "I found Emily and Timmy. Timmy missed Pooky."

Struggling to control herself, Rachel rushed forward to grab him by the arm. She'd never mishandled him before, but now she found herself shaking him by the shoulders.

"You know better than to wander off," she hissed. Her breath came in ragged gasps. "What if someone had seen you?"

Sam whimpered, and his face went white. Too late, Rachel remembered his injuries. Stupid, that's what her brother always said.

"Don't hurt him," Emily said in a small voice. "It was my fault. Mine and Timmy's. We saw him on the hill and called to him."

Rachel whirled to face them. "Leave him alone from now on, do you hear me? You could have lost him to me." Aware she was babbling but unable to control herself, she whipped back around to Sam and turned him to face the hillside. "Go, Sam. Run to the top of the hill. I'll follow you."

Sam took off like a deer with a dog at his heels, though with his limp his progress was slower than she would have liked. As Rachel followed, she could feel the stares of the children boring into her back. All she could do was hope they had enough sense to keep their mouths shut.

She stopped at the gate and turned to face them again. "You tell anyone about us, and I'll come to you in the middle of the night and take you away. You hear me?" She saw the stuffed bear clutched in Timmy's hand. "And don't tell anyone about the bear. Not anyone, do you understand?"

Timmy's face screwed up with tears and he nodded. Emily gulped but held her head high. "We won't tell anyone," she said.

"You'd better not," Rachel warned. As she ran through the gate, she passed the kitchen window and saw a teenager talking on the phone. The girl's mouth dropped open and she came closer to the window. She just prayed the girl hadn't seen Sam. Her lungs burning in her chest and her eyes hot with unshed tears, she raced up the hill.

What had she become that she would frighten children? And even her own Sam had looked at her through terror-filled eyes. Rachel felt such self-loathing, she wished she could die. But all she could do was get them both home and out of these woods before those children finally told someone about her.

✦

Noiselessly, Naomi pulled the door shut behind her then breathed a sigh of relief that her mother hadn't awakened from her afternoon nap.

The last thing she wanted was to be peppered with questions about what she was doing. Naomi wasn't even sure herself what she was doing.

She'd hung out at the hardware store for two weeks, and while Donovan seemed to enjoy her company, he had yet to extend an invitation to dinner or a movie or otherwise indicate he saw her as anything more than a friend. Naomi grimaced. Maybe she was fooling herself. What made her think an attractive man like Donovan O'Reilly would be interested in her? He could have his pick of women in Rock Harbor.

Naomi shifted the offering she held in her hands, and the aroma of cheesy potatoes baked with thick chunks of ham drifted to her nose. The warmth of the dish contrasted sharply with the cold thud of her heart. What would he think when she showed up at the door? She gulped and headed toward her Honda CR-V.

Charley pressed his nose against the living room window and stared after her with a mournful expression. Naomi opened the truck door and set the casserole inside then wiggled her fingers at her dog. Charley disappeared from the window, and she knew he would ignore her as punishment when she returned. He hated to be left behind.

Maybe she should have brought him. Charley might have helped break the ice with the children, especially Emily. The little girl made no effort to hide her disdain of Naomi. Naomi didn't understand it. At church the children flocked around her, and she was the baby-sitter of choice for half the town.

Naomi glanced at her reflection in the rearview mirror. Her own anxious brown eyes peered back at her, and she nearly groaned aloud. Add a pinafore and she'd look like a little girl. Her cheeks were too round, and those ridiculous curls just added to the immature effect. Maybe she should have straightened her hair and worn something besides jeans, but she'd wanted her arrival to appear casual.

Keeping an eye on the traffic, which in Rock Harbor was no chore, she dug through the paraphernalia in her purse and pulled out a red lipstick. Maybe that would add a sheen of sophistication. But the slash of red across her lips merely made her look like a little girl playing dress up. She blotted it with a tissue and sighed. You'd think a woman of nearly thirty-two wouldn't look like such an ingénue.

She parked in front of the house, taking a deep breath before she climbed out with the casserole in hand. Donovan's car, a blue Ford sedan, sprawled across the driveway like he'd been in too much of a hurry to park in a straight line.

Naomi's legs wobbled as she walked to the door. She pinned what she hoped was an impersonal smile on her face as she pressed the doorbell firmly. When Donovan opened the door and she found herself staring into his dark blue eyes, she lost the carefully rehearsed speech.

"Oh, um, hi, Donovan. I had some . . . some casserole. I mean, I made too much casserole for supper and thought of . . . um, have you eaten yet?" Heat rose up her neck and settled in her cheeks, and she knew she looked like a rosy-cheeked child. Donovan, bless his heart, didn't seem to notice her agitation, and Naomi felt a wave of gratitude come over her.

"Naomi, hello. Come on in. You're a godsend. I was just staring in the refrigerator, wondering what I could fix. The kids are nattering about that witch of the woods again and her little boy. I swear, I don't know where they get their imaginations." He stepped aside to allow her entry then followed her to the kitchen.

The children were seated at the kitchen table. Emily's eyes darkened with hostility when she saw Naomi, but Timmy ran to her and threw his arms around her legs. Naomi's grip on the casserole dish loosened, but she managed to hang on to it. Setting it on the table, she scooped Timmy into her arms. He wrapped himself around her like a monkey, and she enjoyed the feel of his small body nestled against her.

"I'll get the plates out," Donovan said. "You'll join us, won't you?" The earnestness of his expression warmed Naomi like soup on a snowy afternoon.

"I'd like that." She ignored Emily's glare and settled onto a chair with Timmy still on her lap. Glancing around, she noticed smears of mud on the kitchen floor and piles of dirty dishes in the sink. Their top-to-bottom housecleaning hadn't lasted long, but then it wouldn't with two children around.

Timmy wound one of Naomi's curls around his finger and gazed into her face with rapt attention. Naomi smoothed the hair back from his face. "How about we get you washed up for supper?" she told him. "Come on, Emily, you could use a wash too."

Emily put her small hands on her hips and scowled. "I can do it myself. I don't need *your* help."

"Emily, mind your manners," her father said sharply. "Go along with Naomi."

Emily's scowl deepened, and she stomped after Naomi and Timmy. In the bathroom she refused to look at Naomi. Naomi put Timmy down, and he went to the sink.

Naomi glanced around the cluttered bathroom. Towels lay on the floor in crumpled heaps. Two boats lay upside down in the bathtub, and a rubber duck sat motionless in a shallow puddle of water on the floor. She picked up the towels and hung them on the side of the tub to dry, taking time to mop up the standing water as well.

"Are you a maid or something?" Emily's upper lip curled.

"No, but there's nothing wrong with doing housework. Don't you like an orderly home? I always find it soothes me to have everything in its place."

"I like my house just fine," Emily proclaimed. She flounced to the sink and washed her hands with gusto, flinging water onto the already spotted wall and floor.

Naomi bit her lip. How could she reach this little girl? She cleared her throat. "You have such pretty hair, Emily. Is your mother's hair that color?"

Emily's noisy splashing grew still. "Don't talk about my mother," she said in a muffled voice. "I don't need another one."

What a stupid comment! She'd forgotten Donovan's ex-wife hadn't been back to see the kids since she left. Town rumor had it that she'd moved to California and was modeling. The woman was beautiful, but Naomi couldn't see how any fame or fortune could replace her two darling children.

"Is that why you don't like me? You think I'd try to take her place?" Naomi touched Emily's shoulder, and the little girl flinched away.

Lifting her chin, Emily glared at Naomi. "You want to be my friend so Daddy will like you. But I don't want you for a friend. I want Bree to be my friend and for Daddy to like her."

Naomi gulped. Were her feelings for Donovan so apparent? Looking into Emily's sneering face, she saw a loneliness there that broke her heart. "Bree is my friend too," she said quietly. "Can you and I just be friends without involving your daddy?"

Emily stared at her suspiciously. "I'll have to think about it." But the set of her chin told Naomi her mind was made up and she wanted nothing to do with any grown woman except Bree.

Naomi stood. "We'd better eat before our supper gets cold." It had been a mistake to come. Donovan probably saw right through her as well. Her face burned as she dried her hands and followed the children back to the kitchen.

Donovan had made an attempt to clear some of the clutter while they were gone. He turned a tired but eager smile toward them that soothed Naomi's bruised ego.

They sat at the table, and Timmy said grace. Naomi spooned the casserole onto plates while Donovan poured milk for the children.

"I'm afraid all I have is milk or water," he said.

"Water is fine," she told him.

He poured water for both of them and sat beside her. Naomi caught a whiff of his cologne, a warm, spicy scent. His warmth radiated into her arm, and her throat grew so tight she wasn't sure she could eat.

She cleared her throat. "What was this about the witch of the woods?" she asked.

"Ask the kids," Donovan said with a heavy sigh.

Naomi lifted an eyebrow as she looked at Emily. "Is this the same person you saw in the woods when you were lost?"

"Yes, but she didn't have her hat on today," Timmy put in eagerly. "Sam came to play, and she was mad."

"Sam?"

"Her son, I guess. He's not supposed to go anywhere unless she says it's okay," Emily said with a warning look at her brother. "We're not supposed to talk about it. She said she'd get us in the middle of the night if we told. But it's okay to tell you, Daddy, right? We can tell you without getting into trouble?"

"You can tell me anything," Donovan said. "But there is no witch of the woods, Emily. You know that."

She thrust out a chin that looked like a small version of Donovan's own. "There *is*, Daddy. We saw her, right, Timmy? We were swinging after school, and there she was."

Her brother nodded. "And Sam."

"That's enough, kids," Donovan said. "Lauri was here with you, and she didn't say a word about a woman and her son. Imagination is fine, but lying is not, and you both know it."

"Lauri was in the house talking to her boyfriend," Emily said. "Sam was only here a few minutes."

"Just like William, the talking tiger who came for a visit last summer, right?"

Emily flushed. "That was just pretend, Daddy; this is real."

"Emily, that's enough. I won't tolerate lying, and you know it. Now eat your supper and don't say another word about it."

Emily evidently recognized her father's warning tone, for she picked up her fork and lapsed into a sullen silence. "They were here," she muttered under her breath, too softly for anyone except Naomi to hear. Emily flashed a glare at Naomi, as if daring her to tattle.

Naomi gave her a tiny smile of sympathy. Emily must be very lonely to hold to her story that way. "After supper, I'll push you in the swing," she offered.

A tiny flicker of interest lit Emily's eyes but quickly died. She picked at her food listlessly. Timmy began cramming the food into his mouth until he looked like a chipmunk.

Naomi smiled in amusement then turned to catch Donovan's gaze. Was it her imagination, or was there an awareness in Donovan's eyes she'd never seen before? Her cheeks grew hot, and she looked down at her plate.

"Um, I'm glad you stopped by," Donovan said. "I'd been meaning to call you."

Naomi was afraid to breathe. "Oh?"

He cleared his throat. "Yes, I wondered if you'd be willing to go shopping with me and the kids Sunday after church. They need some new clothes, and I'm hopeless at stuff like that."

Her warm glow faded. Was he interested only in free help? She risked a glance at him and found him still staring at her. Her gaze probed his, and what she found there eased her worries. There was something between them. It might not lead anywhere, but she had to find out what their relationship could be.

"I'd like that," she said softly.

Donovan's gaze held Naomi's for a long moment. Emily threw her fork to the table and pushed her chair across the tile with a screech, breaking their exchange. Naomi winced. The little girl flung her napkin to the floor and ran from the room. The back door slammed.

Donovan rose. "I don't want her outside alone. Bears were raiding the restaurant's garbage last week, and though they should be in their winter dens by now, I don't want to take any chances."

Naomi touched his forearm. "Let me go," she said.

He hesitated but then nodded and sank back onto his seat. "Don't take her attitude personally. She's been difficult since Marika left."

"I remember how I felt when my dad died. She's just lost and afraid of the future." Naomi stood. "Have you tried to contact Marika—see if she could come visit them? That would help."

"She didn't leave a forwarding address. All correspondence was through her lawyer, and once the divorce was final, even that stopped. I don't even know where she is."

Naomi gave him a sympathetic smile then went to find Emily. Glancing out the window of the back door, Naomi saw her sitting in a swing, her elbows on her knees and her chin cupped in her hands.

The remembered pain of loss brought tears to Naomi's eyes. She had been about Emily's age when her father had died, and some days she still missed him with a fresh intensity that resurrected the horrible day in vivid Technicolor. She hurried to join Emily.

November had arrived this week. Snow was late this year, but it couldn't be far off. A cutting wind blew from the woods, and Naomi wrapped her sweater more tightly around her chest. Emily wasn't wearing a jacket either.

"Hi," Naomi said softly.

Emily swiveled in the swing and stared at her with eyes so miserable Naomi wanted to cry with her.

"I'm in trouble, aren't I?" she said. "I always get in trouble. I bet Daddy wishes you and Bree never found me in the woods."

"Oh, sweetheart, your daddy loves you so much. He would never wish that." Naomi stepped closer. "Here, put my sweater on, and I'll push you."

Naomi shrugged her arms out of the sweater and helped Emily into it. The cold wind punched through her thin turtleneck and chilled her whole body. Emily settled back onto the swing, and Naomi grabbed the cold steel of the chain and gave a gentle push.

"My daddy died when I was about your age," Naomi said after a long minute.

"He did?" Emily said. "Was he killed in a climbing accident like Mrs. Asters or did he get cancer like Anika's mommy?"

Naomi hid a smile. Children related everything to their own experiences. But then, she guessed everyone did the same. "No, he was the captain of a ship that sank in Lake Superior."

"That's sad," Emily said. "I would go to Bree's lighthouse and watch for him to come back."

"He's in heaven though. I wouldn't want him to leave a nice place where he's happy."

"I want Mommy to come back." Emily thrust out her chin. She turned, gave an uncertain look in Naomi's direction, and asked in a small voice, "Are you going to be my new mommy?"

"I'd like to be your friend," Naomi said. "Can we start there?"

Emily dug the toe of her sneaker into the ground and stopped the swing. "Okay," she said, getting out of the swing. "I'm cold. Can we go inside now?"

"Sure." Naomi was glad to. Her bones hurt with the cold.

"Oh look!" Emily ran forward and stooped in front of the sandbox. "See, I told you Sam was here." She held up a small glove. "This is Sam's."

Naomi frowned and took the glove. Something inside her stomach twisted, and she was glad Bree wasn't here. The glove looked similar to ones Davy had once worn.

She handed it back to Emily. "We'll have to give it back to Timmy."

"It's Sam's," Emily insisted. "Timmy doesn't have gloves like this."

She certainly was sticking to her story. Naomi wanted to chuckle, but she knew the child would be offended. As a child, Naomi had had an imaginary friend, Wendy, and she'd been highly offended when her mother refused to believe Wendy existed. Emily would grow out of it soon enough. At least Sam was there for Emily when her mommy wasn't.

She ruffled the top of Emily's hair. "If you beat me inside, I'll make some fudge and we can play a game."

"You don't believe me." Emily pouted. "Call Lauri and ask her. Maybe she saw Sam and the witch."

Looking into the child's confident eyes, Naomi couldn't bear to shatter her trust. "All right, let's do that."

Emily's huge smile was Naomi's reward. She followed the little girl back inside. Donovan had stacked the dishes around the sink, and Naomi made a mental note to wash them after calling Lauri. She left Donovan in the kitchen and went to the living room. Emily showed her Lauri's number in the back of the phone book.

Lauri answered in a breathless voice rife with expectation. She probably hoped it was her boyfriend.

"It's Naomi Heinonen, Lauri. I have a question about this afternoon. Did you see a woman in the backyard with the O'Reilly children?"

Lauri's answer flipped Naomi's heart right over. Her hand shook as she hung up the phone. "Let me see that glove again," she told Emily. She took the glove and turned back the cuff. Her eyes grew wide at the initials she saw there.

She rushed to the kitchen. "I have to go see Bree," she told Donovan.

13

Some Friday nights at the store were boring, and this was one of them. No one had entered for the past hour, and Bree was ready to close the place down and head for home.

"Bree?"

The door to Nicholls's slammed, and Bree heard Naomi rushing through the aisles.

"Bree, come quick!"

Naomi sounded . . . well, Bree wasn't sure she'd ever heard the note of incredulity resonating in her friend's voice, a kind of breathless hope and wonder. She came from behind the counter at the back of the store.

"Back here. Don't have a coronary. What's wrong?"

Naomi rushed to her and grabbed her by the arms. "You're not going to believe this!" She took Bree by the hand and pulled her toward the break room. "Where's Anu? She should hear this too."

Anu poked her head out from the break room. "What has happened? Perhaps the clock on the courthouse has begun to chime again after fifty years of silence? Or the Coast Guard has spotted the Loch Ness monster?"

"Better. Sit down, both of you."

Her eyes sparkling, Naomi waited. Bree and Anu looked at each other.

"Perhaps we'd better humor her," Anu said. She pulled out a chair and sat down, folding her hands in her lap.

Bree did the same. "Tell us now, or you'll never get another of Anu's sweet rolls," she threatened.

"Okay, here's the story: I took a casserole over to Donovan's." She frowned at Bree. "Don't look so surprised. I told you I was going to see if there could be anything between us. Anyway, the kids were talking about the woman they saw the day they were lost in the woods. The witch in the woods, remember?"

"I'd forgotten."

"It's not a fantasy. I called Lauri, and she saw her too—today. And look here." With a flourish, Naomi pulled a glove from her pocket. "Doesn't this look like Davy's?"

Beside her, Bree heard Anu's soft inhalation. Her own lungs seemed to constrict. She reached out and took the glove in her hand. "Yes," she whispered. "He had a pair just like this."

"Look at the tag." Naomi's brown eyes sparkled with tears.

Her hand shaking, Bree rolled the cuff. On the label, printed in black marker, were the letters DRN. David Robert Nicholls. Her fingers went numb, and her vision blurred. "It's his; it's Davy's," she whispered. "Why would she have Davy's glove?"

"She must have found it," Naomi said. "This woman must know where the downed plane is. If we can find her, she can tell us where the plane is. You'll finally have closure."

Just when she was ready to move on, the door she was about to shut had swung wide open again. Bree clutched the glove in her fist and brought it to her nose. "It doesn't smell like him anymore."

"The woman's son was probably wearing it. This has to be the woman Fay was talking about—the one with an airplane seat in a ravine near the cabin."

"The backpack!" Bree said.

"What is this?" Anu asked.

"In Fay's backpack there was a book, a log or notebook of some kind. Mason said I could look at it when he was done, but he hasn't called to tell me to come get it." Bree stood.

Anu caught her hand. "Please, *kulta,* do not let this drag you back to the past. I've seen your efforts to move forward. While I want to bury our loved ones, you must not find a new obsession in locating this woman. You still have no idea where to look."

Bree's exhilaration ebbed. "Just until the first of the year," she promised. "But surely you agree that we should follow this lead."

Anu nodded. "But if it dead-ends, you must let it go, Bree. If God ordains the forest must keep Rob and Davy, we must accept his decision."

Everything in Bree's heart shouted that she would not, could not let it go. For the first time, the realization of her quest seemed possible. Anu couldn't ask her to turn her back on this. Her free hand curled around Davy's glove so tightly that her nails cut into her palm.

Anu sighed. "Go see Mason. I'll close the store," Anu said as she released her hand.

Bree bent to kiss her mother-in-law's forehead. "I love you, Anu," she whispered. "I'll call you."

Anu patted her cheek, and Bree grabbed her coat from the rack against the wall. "Let's go," she told Naomi. Now more than ever, it was imperative that she trace Fay's whereabouts. The key to finding her family rested in her ability to find out what had happened to Fay.

Bree and Naomi ran down the street toward the Rock Harbor County Jail. A cold rain drizzled, stinging Bree's face as she loped along just ahead of Naomi. She burst through the doors to find Mason behind his desk, a roast-beef sandwich halfway to his mouth.

"Mason, I need to see Fay's notebook—the one in her backpack." Bree shook the cold water from her hair.

Mason put down his sandwich. "What's this all about?"

Bree hadn't let loose of Davy's glove for a moment. The texture of the wool kept her from thinking it had all been a dream. She held it out wordlessly.

Mason's eyebrows shot up as he took the glove from her. "Davy's?"

The door crashed open, and Hilary rushed into the room. "I stopped by the store and Mother told me the news." She hurried to her husband's side and snatched the glove from his hand. "It *is* Davy's."

"Would someone please tell me what's going on?" Mason demanded.

Naomi quickly explained. Hilary danced around the room, waving the glove like a trophy, then spun around to Bree and hugged her. Bree clung to her tightly. Apparently Hilary had forgiven her for their tiff the night of the campaign party.

Mason stroked his chin. "I reckon we could take a look at that notebook. It doesn't say much though. I didn't see anything about a woman and a cabin." He went to the back room.

"You have to find this woman, Bree," Hilary commanded. "Drop everything you're doing and find her."

Hilary usually ordered her around, so why did this particular command cause something within her to rise up and rebel at the demand? She had intended to drop everything anyway, but all at once she'd had enough of meekly obeying to keep the peace. She wasn't an extension of Hilary's brother; she was Bree Nicholls, a woman in her own right with hopes, dreams, and desires. Somehow she had to make sure her efforts to resurrect the old Bree didn't fizzle like green wood in a fire.

She lifted her chin, but the words of independence died on her tongue when she stared into Hilary's face. "I will," she said. "I'll do everything in my power to find the woman."

Mason came in with the notebook in his hand. "Here it is, but like I said, I don't think you'll find anything in it." He held it out to Bree, but Hilary made a grab for it.

"Let me see. I'm a fast reader. I'll take it home and read it tonight." Hilary held the book to her chest. "I'll call you in the morning, and we'll decide what to do next."

Bree's hand dropped. She saw the look of censure on Naomi's face and hunched her shoulders. "Let's go, Naomi," she said.

Back outside, the cold wind stung her cheeks. Naomi walked silently at her side toward the lighthouse.

"Why do you let her do that to you?" Naomi burst out when they finally reached the gate to Bree's home. "I thought you were developing some backbone lately. You curl up like a pill bug when it comes to Hilary."

"You don't understand," Bree said.

"You're right, I don't understand. I remember what you were like when you first came here. Bright, interested in everything, open about your feelings. Now you never talk about how you feel. It's 'Yes, Hilary,' and 'I'll take care of that right away, Hilary.' You never say no to her. You poke fun at her and laugh when I call her the poodle, but the minute she arrives on the scene, you crumple. What gives?"

Bree wasn't sure she could explain it. "I never had a sister before," she began. "When we moved here, I was desperate for Hilary to like me, for everyone to accept me. I don't know how it happened, but little by little, as I tried to fit into the Nicholls family, I left pieces of myself strewn along the way. I'd always felt like a misfit. My mom is an alcoholic, and I never knew my dad. What did I know about how a real family acted? So I tried to emulate Hilary, to become someone she would approve of."

The wind teased tendrils from Naomi's long braid and blew them out around her head in a halo. Her eyes softened. "Bree, that must have been awful. But God loves you just as you are. His opinion is the only one that matters. We all have things we wish we could change about ourselves. You admire Hilary's self-assurance, the way she fits in. But she's not perfect, and you know it."

Bree nodded.

"So be yourself, speak your mind, be your own person. God created you for a purpose."

"You sound like Anu," Bree said softly.

"Anu is a wise lady. Listen to her." Naomi gave her a little shove. "Now go feed your dog. Tomorrow we'll figure out what to do next."

"I'm going to Palmer and Lily's for a late supper. We've been trying to get together for nearly two weeks. Can you and Charley get away tomorrow? We'll take the dogs to Donovan's and see if they can pick up the scent."

"Sure. What time?"

"Early. Maybe seven-thirty? I'd like to start tonight, but it's already dark. Daylight would be better."

"See you then." Naomi squeezed her hand then jogged toward the Blue Bonnet.

Bree hurried inside and fed Samson, then she and the dog climbed into the Jeep. It was already later than she'd planned. The Chamberses would be wondering what had happened to her.

When Bree arrived, after the warm greetings and the cries of delight from the twins at Samson's appearance, they went right to the dining room table. Lily had fixed a big pot of vegetable soup with warm, crusty rolls made from her grandmother's recipe.

After supper, Palmer lit a fire. Paige and Penelope giggled and climbed on Samson's back as if he were a pony while he panted on a rug in front of the great stone fireplace. Their new puppy yipped and tugged on Samson's fur with a ferocity the adults found comical.

Lily brought Bree a mug of hot spiced cider. Wrapping her cold fingers around the hot cup, Bree settled back against the plump sofa cushions. "I love this room," she told her host and hostess. "It reminds me of a ski lodge, with the exposed wooden beams and that wonderful fireplace."

"That's why we bought it," Lily said. She sat beside Bree and offered her a cookie. "It reminded us of the ski lodge in Lake Tahoe we go to so often. Palmer did such a great job on the fireplace, but I thought we might end up in divorce court before it was over. You know how anal he is about his tools, and when he couldn't find that one screwdriver, he accused me of using it."

Palmer gave her a wounded look. "I never loan my tools, so I thought you or the twins had taken it."

"Where was it?"

Lily shrugged. "He never did find it."

Bree chuckled at the sight of another family's minor tiffs. She missed that camaraderie. She took the plate of cookies and passed them to Palmer. "Those look great, but I'm stuffed. I haven't had a meal like that since the last time you had me to supper. My meals usually consist of peanut butter sandwiches or a cup of soup."

"No wonder you're so slim," Lily scolded. "I'll have to invite you over more often and fatten you up."

"I hope that's not the only reason you invite me over," Bree said with a laugh. She felt a real kinship with Lily and Palmer. Lily had rushed to be with her the minute she heard about Rob's plane going down. For months, Palmer had blamed himself. Rob had asked him to give the plane a once-over before the trip, but Palmer had gotten held up on a business trip to Milwaukee. Palmer had cried with Bree the minute he got back to town. Their support and encouragement had been vital to her. They still were.

"You know better," Lily said.

"How's the investigation going?" Palmer asked. He sat in a brown leather armchair with his feet propped on a matching ottoman. "Sad business."

"It's not going anywhere fast," Bree told him. "There are no real leads I know of. Samson and I found Fay's backpack, but Mason said there wasn't much of anything extraordinary in it. Hilary took Fay's notebook home tonight to see if there are any clues in it."

"You should let Mason handle it. Why are you getting involved? It might be dangerous," Lily said.

"You're not going to believe this," Bree said. She told them of the woman and the discovery of Davy's glove. "So you see, this woman could be my link to the plane."

Lily clapped her hands. "Oh, Bree, how wonderful! I know finding them means everything to you. You've kept so much of yourself bottled up this past year. I do pray for closure for you."

Bree took a sip of her hot cider. "You had some business dealings with Fay, didn't you, Palmer? Had you finalized the deal to buy that old mine?"

He nodded. "Pretty much. The papers were ready to be signed. Steve is dragging his feet now, but I think we've got all the kinks ironed out and are ready to close the deal."

"I still don't understand what you want with that old place," Lily sighed.

"Our town will die if we don't get some tourism," Palmer said. "That old mine will make a great living museum. I could buy another mine, but I'm glad this deal is going through. It might help Steve out a bit. Besides, I'm doing my part to save a slice of Yooper history."

Bree leaned forward. "Did Fay ever mention the plane crash to you?"

Palmer's brow furrowed. "Not that I recall. Oh, she was sorry about it when it happened, of course. Why?"

"I need a clue for where to look for that cabin. Fay was all over the U.P., and it's as hard to know where to look for the woman's cabin as it is to know where to look for the plane. I'm going to Donovan's tomorrow to see if the dogs can pick up her scent, but if that fails, I'll have to figure out where to look next."

"You don't suspect a link between Fay's death and the plane crash, do you?" Palmer asked.

Bree considered his question then slowly shook her head. "Not really a link. How could there be? The crash was nearly a year ago, and it was an accident. But maybe retracing her steps could lead me to the woman. Besides, Steve has asked me to help."

Lily moved the fire screen back into place and returned to sit beside Bree. "You do what you have to do," she told her. "Though Palmer wants to help Steve by taking this mine off his hands, I'm still not convinced he didn't kill her himself. He had plenty of motive."

Palmer frowned. "Steve is too strait-laced for murder. He's not dangerous, but the real murderer sure is. I don't want you to get hurt, Bree. Whoever killed Fay is dangerous. He may not want to hurt you, but if you keep poking around, he may have no choice."

"I'll be careful," Bree said. "I have Samson, after all."

At the sound of his name, Samson pricked his ears forward and got up. The girls protested and called to him when he came to stand at Bree's knees. He pressed his cold nose against her hand, and she rubbed his thick fur. "You'll protect me, boy, won't you?" He whined, his dark eyes full of love, and she petted his back.

Palmer snorted. "Samson is a great dog, but I'm afraid the only danger a prowler would face would be getting licked to death."

Samson seemed to understand this slur on his integrity, for the fur on his neck stood up, and he gave Palmer a long stare. They all laughed.

"Better watch out, Palmer, or Samson will show you just how protective he can be," Bree said.

Palmer leaned forward and patted the dog's back. "He doesn't scare me any."

Samson gave him another long stare then turned back to Bree.

"I think you've offended him," Lily laughed. "Maybe a doggie treat will sweeten his mood."

"I happen to have one in my backpack." Bree dug into her pack and pulled out a box of doggie treats. Palmer took one and offered it to Samson. The dog sniffed it but turned away and laid his head on Bree's knee.

"He's never done that before." Bree rubbed her hands over her dog. "I wonder if he's getting sick."

She grasped Samson's chin and raised his head so she could look into his eyes. The dog's dark and alert gaze reassured her. He pressed his nose against her hand again. Frowning, she rubbed his head. "He seems to be all right. I don't know what's up with him. Maybe he's tired. I'm beat myself."

"Let me put some of these cookies in a plastic bag for you to take home," Lily said hastily when Bree rose to say her good-byes.

"I wouldn't turn them down." Bree scooped up Paige and hugged her. The feel of the little girl's warm body, round and innocent, brought back so many memories, both good and painful. She set her down and grabbed up Penelope.

"How much do you love me?" she asked the child.

Penelope wrapped her arms around Bree's neck and squeezed.

"Wow, that much?" Bree hugged her close and kissed the petal-soft cheek.

The little girl nodded, and Bree kissed her again before setting her down. "I'd better get going. Samson and I are going to get back on the search trail again tomorrow."

"Good luck," Lily said. "I'll be praying."

"Thanks." She wanted to say it wouldn't do any good, but maybe her heart was changing about that. Someone seemed to be watching out for her.

"And watch your back," Palmer advised.

"I'll be careful," Bree promised. "Nothing is going to happen to me." Lightning didn't strike twice in the same place. Fate had tapped Rob and Davy on the shoulder and left her alone. She had a feeling that state of affairs wasn't going to change.

She drove home and parked the Jeep. Walking to the door in the cold night air, she heard wolves howling in the distance. Samson growled low in answer and sounded much like a wolf himself. The sound brought back Aunt Mathilda's words about the Hound of Heaven, and Bree shivered. Such nonsense was just that—nonsense. Wasn't it? Bree didn't know anymore.

14

$\mathscr{S}$aturday dawned with more cold rain drizzling from a glowering sky. Everything was gray, from the sky to the wind-whipped waves on Lake Superior. Not a good day for a search, but Bree didn't have time to wait for good weather. With a yellow rain slicker and hat covering her orange jumpsuit, Bree would stay mostly dry, but the dogs would be wet and muddy by the time the morning was done.

Hilary had called first thing in the morning to report she'd found nothing in the notebook. She agreed to meet for coffee at two and give Bree the notebook then. Bree loaded the gear in the Jeep then drove to Naomi's and honked the horn. Naomi dashed through the rain and hopped into the car.

Shaking the water from her hair, she slammed the door. "Wouldn't you think it'd be snowing by now? I'd rather have snow than this heavy rain."

"Me too. Though the dogs should have no trouble getting the scent. The problem is the glove has been handled so much."

Naomi seemed lost in thought as they drove to Donovan's. Bree thought about asking her what was happening with her quest to get closer to Donovan, but she held her tongue. There was nothing more annoying than being questioned about your love life when nothing was going on.

The O'Reilly house was dark when Bree parked the Jeep. A dim blue glow brightened one window. "The kids must be watching cartoons," she said.

The women got the dogs out of the vehicle, then Bree let them sniff Davy's glove. She wasn't too hopeful for the day's search. Too many people had handled the glove. The scent they needed would be overlaid with the entire O'Reilly household, her own scent, Hilary's, Mason's, and Naomi's.

Sure enough, the dogs nosed aimlessly through the brush and grew more dispirited as the rain continued to pelt them. They found no clear scent cone to follow. "This is getting us nowhere," Bree said after an hour. "It's nine o'clock. I'm ready to pack it in and head home. It was a long shot anyway."

"You go ahead. I'll walk back. I'm going shopping for clothes for the kids with Donovan today." Her color high, Naomi winked at Bree and took Charley toward the front door of the O'Reilly house. "I bet there are two kids ready for some breakfast."

"Good hunting," Bree called with a chuckle. She put Samson in the Jeep and drove home.

Her lighthouse seemed warm and welcoming. The rain had finally stopped, and the clouds were breaking up. A fire would be welcome after the wet search. She toweled off Samson then lit the gas log in the fireplace. After a hot shower, she'd feel almost human again. A half-hour later, dressed in jeans and a warm fleece top, she took the wool throw from the back of the couch and curled up in front of the fire.

Though the morning's search had been fruitless, Bree felt a sense of hope and purpose. At least she had a clue now.

Rob's Bible still sat on the end table by the window. Bree's gaze lingered on it. How could it hurt? She reached for it hesitantly. Anu had said to read Psalm 112 for words of wisdom on discerning true motives. She held the Bible to her nose and smelled the aroma of leather and print. Rob had read this book every morning, yet he'd still betrayed her. She almost put it aside, but she bit her lip and flipped open the cover to the table of contents. She found the page number for

Psalms and flipped through the thin pages almost to the middle of the book. She turned to number 112.

> *Praise the LORD.*
> *Blessed is the man who fears the LORD,*
> *who finds great delight in his commands.*
> *His children will be mighty in the land;*
> *the generation of the upright will be blessed.*

These verses reminded Bree of Anu. Hilary was respected and had married well, and even Rob had been someone the town looked to for leadership as fire chief.

> *Wealth and riches are in his house,*
> *and his righteousness endures forever.*
> *Even in darkness light dawns for the upright,*
> *for the gracious and compassionate and righteous man.*
> *Good will come to him who is generous and lends freely,*
> *who conducts his affairs with justice.*

She frowned as she thought of Steve. He loaned money generously, though it wasn't his own money. Did that apply? This was harder than it looked.

> *Surely he will never be shaken;*
> *a righteous man will be remembered forever.*
> *He will have no fear of bad news;*
> *his heart is steadfast, trusting in the LORD.*
> *His heart is secure, he will have no fear;*
> *in the end he will look in triumph on his foes.*
> *He has scattered abroad his gifts to the poor;*
> *his righteousness endures forever;*
> *his horn will be lifted high in honor.*

The wicked man will see and be vexed,
he will gnash his teeth and waste away;
the longings of the wicked will come to nothing.

The wicked man was the one she was after. But she still didn't know how to pick him out. She ran through the suspects. Steve, Eric, Lawrence, Kade. And Hilary, though Bree didn't even want to think about that. But she couldn't rule her out yet.

Her gaze wandered back to the verses. *Wealth and riches are in his house.* Did that mean every person as rich and respected as Hilary was righteous? Surely not. She would have to ask Anu.

The words she'd read were strangely comforting. She'd been taught religion was a crutch for weak people, and she'd been appalled when Rob began to attend church and take Davy with him. They'd fought long and hard about it, but he'd refused to budge. If a Christian could do what Rob had done to her, what good was being a Christian? She wished she could talk to Anu about it, but she'd never told Rob's family of his infidelity. Let them keep the perfect image they had of him.

Samson put his cold nose against her bare ankle, and the wet sensation jolted her out of her reverie. She put the Bible aside. The sun had finally come out, and she could get her chores done, though the mud outside wouldn't make it easy. "Ready to get going, Samson?" Those flower beds wouldn't get mulched by themselves.

The dog woofed, practically dancing with excitement. What she should do was get that brick repointed, but there was no way she would ever climb out on the tower again. Handyman work had never been her forte. Before Rob's death, her expertise had started and stopped with wallpaper and paint, but little by little she was learning. She would have to pay someone to do it, though her bank balance might complain. After she mulched, she would make some calls. Snow would arrive any day, and the tower would never make it through another Upper Peninsula winter.

Samson followed her as she went downstairs and out the kitchen door to the backyard. She grabbed the pitchfork and began to layer straw onto her strawberry beds. The straw was soggy and heavy, and soon she was perspiring. After a few minutes, Samson turned his head and barked.

"What is it, boy?" Probably something as simple as the black squirrels raiding the bird feeders. As far as Samson was concerned, the neighborhood answered to him.

"I heard there was a tower around here somewhere about to fall down." Kade's deep voice startled her.

Bree jerked at the sound, and the straw on her pitchfork flipped onto Samson's head. He gave her a wounded look and shook himself. She laughed, and Kade's deep chuckle joined hers. Dressed in jeans and work boots with a rope slung over his shoulder, he grinned at the dog's outrage. A Chicago Cubs cap, marred with flecks of paint and dirt, was pulled low over his eyes. A leather apron hung from his right hand.

She set down the pitchfork and wiped her fingers on her jeans. "You look like you're ready for work." A surprising warmth spread through her belly at the sight of him. Anxiousness too. Was he angry about the puppy? Maybe he'd been too mad to call her on the phone and wanted to confront her in person.

He opened the gate and stepped inside the backyard. Samson rushed to him and rubbed his head against Kade's hand. Kade grabbed the dog's head in both hands and worried it back and forth. Samson growled playfully, pleasure in every line of his posture.

Kade released the dog and turned to Bree. "I bet you didn't know brickwork was the way I put myself through college."

Bree's eyes widened as the reason for his attire penetrated. "How did you know it needed doing?"

"I ran into Naomi and Donovan at the coffee shop this morning, and she mentioned it. I wasn't sure I should even help after the way you sandbagged me with that pup." His eyes narrowed. "You knew I didn't want her to have a dog."

Uh-oh, she'd known it was coming. "She needed one, Kade."

His mouth twisted. "If you could hear that puppy cry at night." He shook his head. "But the worst of it is she isn't taking responsibility for him."

Now Bree did feel guilty. "She's only had him a week. Give them time to adjust."

"I don't have much choice." He grinned, but it was feeble. He moved forward and grabbed her bucket. "Okay if I use this?"

"Sure. Naomi was with Donovan? Were the kids with them?"

"Yep. Looked like one big happy family."

Bree couldn't help the delighted grin that spread across her face. "She must be making headway."

"Looked that way to me, if by making headway you mean her and Donovan becoming an item." He took the hose and sprayed water in the bucket then began adding dry mortar mix from a bag.

Bree watched until she realized she was admiring the muscles in his back as they rippled under his shirt. Her cheeks heated and she looked away.

Kade gave the mortar a final stir. "It looks about ready. Show me how to get to the tower, and we'll have this job done in no time." He stood and hefted the bucket in one hand.

Much as she hated to accept charity, right now Bree felt like hugging him in gratitude. "This way," she told him. He followed her as she led him through the kitchen and up the steps to the second floor.

"I like your house," he told her. "You've done a great job on the floors. Naomi told me you and Rob did most of this yourselves."

High praise indeed, since he seemed to know something about house restoration. Bree's spirits lifted. "I'll just be glad when it's all done." His compliment gave her an inordinate amount of pleasure.

She paused outside the door to the catwalk. Her mouth went dry as her hand reached for the door handle. She didn't want to go back out there, but with Kade's attention on her, she had no choice. The handle resisted her, but she managed to thrust open the door and step outside. Thankfully, there was little wind, but the metal walkway shuddered under their weight. Her stomach plummeting, Bree gripped the railing tightly.

Kade moved past her and set down the bucket. He strapped on the leather apron and pulled a trowel from its pocket. Unwinding the rope from his shoulder, he tied it to the bucket, which he tied to the railing. He then opened a window and attached a harness to a post inside the tower. Within two minutes he was rappelling down the side of the tower.

Bree watched him and wished she could be so nonchalant about dangling forty feet from the ground. Gingerly moving to the railing, she peered over the edge and watched as he began to repair the mortar.

"It's not as bad as I was expecting," he called up to her. "The way Naomi talked, I thought the tower was about to crumble away. It just needs a little shoring up. I should be done in about an hour. There's no sense in you keeping a death grip on that railing. Go back inside, and I'll tell you about my fee when I'm done."

His fee? Her bank balance left much to be desired. Still, at least she hadn't had to do the job, and if she had to, she could borrow some funds from Anu. Her gratitude overwhelmed her disgruntlement at having to pay Kade for the job. He surely wouldn't charge her as much as a brick mason would.

He didn't seem to notice her surprise. He paused to swipe a hand across his forehead as a bird squawked from the power lines in front of the house.

Kade lifted his head. "Mazzy!"

A starling lifted from the lines and came swooping toward him.

"Watch out!" Bree shouted. She ducked as the bird tried to land on her head. Picking up a trowel, she tried to swipe at it.

"Don't hurt her, Bree! Mazzy, come," Kade called. The bird squawked again then flew down and perched on Kade's shoulder.

"You know this bird?" Bree blinked. How had he trained a wild bird to come when he called? Though he had a compelling personality, she found it hard to believe his charisma extended to wild animals.

"She thinks I'm her mother," Kade said, shooting an impudent grin up at her.

Bree covered her mouth and chuckled. "I can't imagine anyone less like a mother."

Kade's grin faded. "Or a father, according to Lauri." When he reached around and held out his hand, Mazzy stepped onto it. "I found this one on the ground, barely hatched and without feathers. I fed her until she was ready to scavenge for food then turned her loose in June, but she's hung around all this time."

"I didn't think it was possible to feed baby birds. Did you chew up the worms and regurgitate them for her?" Bree laughed again at the incongruous thought.

"She liked cat food mixed with water just fine, didn't you, girl?" He leaned back in the harness and stroked the bird's head. "I would get some on my finger then poke it down her beak. She gobbled it right up."

"You're a man of many talents," Bree said.

"Yeah, well, don't think you're getting something for nothing," he warned. "You'll have to pay for it with your time." Her smile faded as she realized his fee did not likely involve monetary payment. If he asked her out, what could she say? Her heart told her she wasn't ready for any new relationship. Not now, maybe never.

"I'll make some coffee," she said abruptly. "Come inside when you're done."

He nodded. "I'll rappel on down to the ground and come in the back door."

As Bree backed away from the rail, Mazzy came squawking toward

her. Bree ducked inside and shut the door, barely avoiding the bird's
demented attempt to perch on her head.

She found a tin of chicken downstairs in the pantry and decided
to make chicken salad. It felt strange to be preparing a meal for a man
again. Strange but good. She hummed as she chopped celery and
walnuts then stirred in mayonnaise.

By the time she'd prepared lunch, she heard Kade in the backyard
cleaning up his tools. Bree's palms prickled. How stupid to react like
that. She'd been out of contact with everyone but family for too long.

One of the verses she'd read in the psalm came to her. *His heart is
secure, he will have no fear.* That certainly applied to Kade. Giving of
himself and dangling fearlessly from the tower to help a friend. Did
that mean she could cross him off the suspect list? She wished she knew
for sure.

A few minutes later, Kade opened the back door and stepped into
the kitchen. He took off his cap and apron and hung them on a peg
by the door. "The coffee smells good."

"You don't even have any mortar on you." She was usually covered
from head to toe with paint or any other material she worked with.

He winked at her. "What can I say—I'm neat. I take my coffee
black."

Bree poured him a cup of coffee then made the chicken salad sandwiches and placed them on plates. She set them on the table and pulled
out her checkbook.

"How much do I owe you?" she asked.

"Whoa, I never said you would have to pay in money." He took
the checkbook out of her hand and tossed it on the table.

Here it comes. She crossed her arms over her chest. The last thing
she wanted to do was offend him, but anything more than friendship
between them was impossible. She couldn't deny the thought brought
her a mixture of elation and terror; however, it was a dizzying proposi-
tion she'd rather not face.

When she didn't respond or even laugh, Kade frowned. "You didn't really think I would charge a friend for something like this, did you?"

"Are we friends? I thought we were just acquaintances."

His frown turned to a scowl. "You sure keep that wall high around yourself, don't you? I don't have any designs on you. The good Lord knows I already have my hands full with Lauri. I don't need another difficult relationship." He pointed a finger at her. "You owe me. Thanks to you, I'm saddled with a pup I expressly told Lauri she couldn't have. Now you have to fix it."

"What's he doing?"

He sighed and took a bite of his sandwich then broke off a piece and tossed it to Samson. "Lauri's dog is driving us both crazy. He doesn't do anything he's supposed to do. Could you come out and give us some more pointers? You owe me."

"I'm sorry, Kade, I'd forgotten all about the puppy." How could she have been so self-centered? She'd promised Lauri to get started on the training right away, but the days had slipped past too quickly. Some trainer she was. "I'll be glad to do that. I have about an hour and a half before I have to meet Hilary for coffee. How about I come out now?"

A grin of relief spread across his face. "Great. If Lauri concentrates on something else, maybe those moods of hers will get better." He spread his hands. "What am I doing wrong with her?" he asked.

"You're asking the wrong person," she said. "I'm no good at sibling relationships. I'm an only child, and I don't even know where my mother is. I waffle like a kite without a tail when it comes to standing up to Hilary, and when it comes to speaking my mind I'm a sphinx."

"Sounds to me like you just did pretty good with speaking your mind." His gaze caught and held hers. His grin broke the tension between them. "What you're describing is exactly how I feel with Lauri. I can't seem to talk to her. I used to be the perfect older brother.

She would brag about me to her friends, and she never missed calling me every Saturday night. When I moved in, everything changed."

"Could it be because you've quit being her brother and are trying to parent her?" Bree offered the advice tentatively, aware she didn't have the right to judge anyone else's actions. Not when her own had been so faulty.

Kade didn't seem to take offense at her criticism. "I've wondered about that. But she's as wild as the porcupine under my front porch and just as prickly. She needs *some* guidance. If I didn't parent her, she'd be out every night with only God knows what kind of riffraff."

"Are you sure?" Bree asked quietly. "Maybe if her brother was there to run around with and show off to her friends, she'd want to stay home more."

"You don't understand, Bree." Kade rose and grabbed his hat from the peg. "I'd better get going. I need to pick up some dog food on the way."

She was an idiot. Advice had a tendency to turn into a rabid dog and bite the one who offered it. She followed Kade and Samson out the door.

They were both silent as Kade drove out past the city limit sign. He stopped at Konkala Service Station and ran in to buy dog food while the women waited in the truck. Once he was back in the vehicle, he turned onto Whisper Pike and entered the forest.

When the silence threatened to grow uncomfortable, Bree cleared her throat. "I'm sorry," she said. "You know your sister better than I do."

Kade made a noncommittal sound. Bree tried again to break the silence. "I haven't seen Naomi all morning. Did she say what she was going to do after lunch with the O'Reillys?"

"Something about going shopping with them."

Bree raised an eyebrow. "Sounds like she's making definite progress. She's meeting me this afternoon to see what we can find out about . . . ." She let her voice trail off. Maybe she shouldn't talk about it with him. There was still the issue of his being at the scene the night Fay died.

"Find out about what?"

He might know something about the woman. She didn't have to tell him everything she knew. "Have you seen a woman around in the woods? Shapeless clothes, old fedora on her head, maybe a little kid with her?"

Kade frowned. "Not that I can remember. Who is she?"

"I guess that woman the O'Reilly kids saw was real. I thought she might have seen the plane's wreckage."

"Why would she feed the kids then abandon them in the forest?" Kade's voice rose. "If Timmy had died when she could have helped him—" He broke off and shook his head. "I'll keep an eye out for her, but it sounds like a slim chance, if you don't mind my saying so."

She *did* mind. Terribly. But once again, she swallowed how she really felt and settled back against the seat with a shrug. He didn't know the full story, and it was just as well.

❧

A woodpecker, no doubt after beetles and other insects, pounded on the wall of the old cabin. Rachel had tried to shoo him away on numerous occasions, but he always came back, and now she was too distraught to care.

Sam's disobedience in town yesterday had given her pause over what to do with him while she went to Chicago. What if he disobeyed again and wandered off into the woods? With travel time, she'd be gone two days. Maybe she should take him with her. But even as the thought crossed her mind, she rejected it. Sam was too fragile to sleep on a park bench. Thanksgiving wasn't far off, and the autumn nights dropped to freezing and sometimes even lower.

There was no help for it. She would have to leave him home alone. Her gaze lingered lovingly on the boy. He sat coloring quietly on the rug in front of the wood stove. The wood stove! She gave a small gasp. Sam had never put wood in the fire. This was a different wrinkle in the problem. Rachel rubbed her forehead.

Could she find some discreet person in town to watch him? But she knew no one. She'd been careful to keep her distance, to meld into the background like a neutral wall color. People talked in small towns, and she knew a few people had noticed her on her infrequent excursions, but the rumor mill would rev up if she brought a small boy to town. That was out of the question.

Her gaze sought the wood stove again. "Sam, you're a big boy. Would you like to learn to help Mother by putting wood in the stove?" No one knew the danger of fire better than Rachel. But surely he was big enough to do a simple task like keeping the fire going.

Sam's head jerked up, and his green eyes widened. He scrambled to his feet. "I can do it!"

Rachel joined him in front of the stove. "This is very important, Sam. If you make a mistake, you could burn the house down. I want you to pay close attention."

He nodded, anticipation gleaming in his small face as if she'd offered him candy.

"Okay. First, you open the damper. See this thing? You move it so it's straight up and down. Can you reach it?"

Sam came around to the side of the stove and reached up. "Like that?"

"Exactly right," she said. "Then open the door to the stove. Take the poker and move the logs around until they are lying tightly against the coals."

Gingerly, Sam took the poker in both hands and managed to prod the logs a bit. It wasn't perfect, but it would have to do. Rachel nodded. "Good. Now grab a log and put it on top of the others, laying it the same way. Do three of them that way."

Sam laid down the poker and grabbed the first log. Puffing, he shoved it into the stove. He wasn't strong enough to push it where it needed to go, and it rolled out onto the floor along with hot coals. Rachel grabbed the bucket of water she kept near the stove for that purpose and doused the coals.

"Sorry." Sam looked as though he might cry.

"It's okay, Sam. It's my fault. You're not quite big enough yet." Rachel felt near tears herself as she finished loading the stove. Chewing on her lip, she knew she had no choice. She'd leave plenty of blankets. Sam would be warmer inside the cabin with blankets than he would be sleeping out in the open air with only his coat. And during the day, the temperature shouldn't be too bad.

"I have to leave in the morning, Sam. I'll be gone two days. I want you to stay in the cabin except to use the privy."

Sam's lips trembled. "Two whole days? Why can't I come?"

"I have to find us a new place to live, a better place. You can come with me next time. But I don't want you to bother the stove. I know it's a little chilly, but just stay bundled in the bed with the blankets. I got you a new book to read too." Sam liked nothing better than a new book, which was a good thing, for she knew he would need good reading skills to make it through med school. He would make her proud someday.

But her bribe did little to calm his agitation. "Who will take care of me?" He thrust out his lower lip, and tears pooled in his eyes.

"You're a big boy, Sam. You can help Mother by feeding yourself, can't you? I'll leave you some nice boiled eggs, a few peanut butter sandwiches, and cereal. I even got you some cookies. See?" She opened the cookie jar and was gratified to see his eyes go round. Cookies were a rare treat.

Then his lips trembled again, and tears spilled down his small face. "I'm scared. I don't like to be alone. What if the wolves come back?"

"They can't get inside the cabin," she said. "Besides, they won't bother you. Winter hasn't come yet, and they have plenty to eat."

"A bear could get in."

Rachel hid a smile. "You'll be fine, Sam. When was the last time we saw a bear?"

His forehead wrinkled, and he bit his lip. "I don't know."

"Exactly. The bears will leave you alone. You can practice printing your letters all you want. There's plenty of paper. I know it will be lonely, but I have to go, son."

"Take me with you." He began to cry in earnest, and Rachel wavered. She'd worry about him every minute anyway. If he were with her, at least she wouldn't have that anxiety.

Then she shook her head. "I have to talk to a lady about a job, and you would just be in the way. It might make me lose the job, and I must have it."

Sam threw himself against her and began to wail. Rachel gathered him against her and sat in the rocker with him in her lap. "Hush, Sam. I thought you were a big boy. These two days will fly by, you'll see. Now be Mother's big boy. We only have each other to depend on. I'm counting on you to be strong for me."

He hiccuped and buried his face against her chest. Rachel began to sing all the nursery rhymes she could think of, from "Farmer in the Dell" to "Three Blind Mice." Her gravelly voice would win no awards, but Sam seemed to like it. Soon his sobs changed to deep breathing. As he slept nestled against her, Rachel knew there was nothing like motherhood. Her life was so different with this little person in it. She cuddled him closer and dozed off herself.

Shadows darkened the room when she awoke. Though the fire had gone out, the warmth of Sam's small body kept the chill away. She laid him on his cot then began to prepare the food he would need while she was away. If only there were some other way. But there was no use wailing over what couldn't be changed.

Soon things would be different. It was only two days, she told herself. Two short days. She deserved to be happy after everything that had happened. And Sam too. Though he never talked about it, the nightmares in the beginning had been horrific. He'd hung in the seat belt beside his dead father for at least an hour before she rescued him. But those days were over, and the memories had already faded. His nightmare came less and less, and soon he'd have no memories of any life but the one he shared with her.

15

$\mathcal{B}$ree's enthusiasm was subdued when she entered The Coffee Place. Playing with Zorro had been a real treat, though Kade hadn't said much as she gave him tips on training the puppy, and she knew he was still annoyed with her observations of how he was treating his sister.

Hilary was already seated in a booth by the window overlooking the water. She'd ordered two mochas and pushed one toward Bree. "I've talked to Mason," Hilary said without preliminaries as soon as Bree sat down. "He saw that woman."

"What? Where?" Bree half rose from her chair.

"At Lars's store. She was getting groceries. He said she looked vaguely familiar, but he got busy and didn't follow up on it until this morning. She was on a wanted poster."

"She's a criminal?"

"The police were looking for her in connection with the murders of twelve nursing home residents in Detroit. But when Mason called, the Detroit police said she'd been exonerated. The poster was an old one. Mason is over at Lars's to see if she mentioned in what direction her cabin was located."

That must be why she'd abandoned Emily and Timmy by the road. She wanted to avoid being seen. "So at least we know Rock Harbor is the closest town to the cabin," Bree said slowly. "That narrows the search down some."

"Not necessarily. Mason has no idea how she got here. She could be driving considerably out of her way just to stay hidden."

Bree's elation died, and she nodded. "Then we wait to hear what Mason has to say."

"There he is now," Hilary said.

Mason's face was grim. He sat next to Hilary and nodded to Bree. "Well?" Hilary demanded.

"Lars has seen her several times. She comes in with a knapsack and hiking shoes, so he thinks she walks in. But he has no idea where she comes from. She just shows up at the store, gets her provisions, and hurries out. He says he's tried to engage her in conversation, but she never responds much. She comes in every couple of weeks, though she's been in a little more frequently lately. She might be due to come in next week. We could stake out the store and watch for her."

"I don't want to wait that long." Bree gave a heavy sigh. "She could be anywhere then—north, south, east."

Mason nodded. "That about sums it up."

"Then we're back to Fay. I need to go through her things at her home and see if there are any clues there. Any new leads in your office?" Bree asked.

"We're looking into the boyfriend, Eric Matthews."

"Matthews?" Hilary questioned.

"He's Kade's cousin. Been in jail for three years for assault and battery and just got out on work release. As an interesting note, Fay was the one who pressed charges. He beat her up pretty badly. I'm surprised she had anything to do with him once he got out."

"I saw them quarrel the night before Fay died," Bree said.

Mason frowned. "And you're just now telling me this?"

Bree hunched her shoulders. "It didn't amount to much. I knew you'd be looking into him."

"Good grief, Bree, you know better than to keep information like that to yourself." Mason's voice rose, and his glare grew more pronounced.

"Sorry, Mason; you're right. He was just ticked she didn't show up when she was supposed to. She told him she'd be along and to go back and wait. That's it."

His frown faded. "Not much, like you said, but with his history, it's likely he's our killer."

"He was angry that night. I gathered he thought she was stringing him along. He said something about not letting her call the shots this time."

"You holding any other tidbits to yourself?" he asked.

Bree glanced at Hilary from the corner of her eye. There was no way she was going to tell Mason she suspected Hilary. "What about Steve and her uncle?"

"We're looking at both of them. Lawrence had an argument with her over selling the mine, we know that much. And Steve could have killed her in a jealous rage when he found out the baby might not be his."

"He didn't seem to think the baby could be Eric's," Hilary put in.

"Yes, well, he'd say that now, wouldn't he?" Mason said.

Was it her imagination, or was there some tension between Mason and Hilary? Bree studied them covertly. Hilary would barely look at her husband, and Mason didn't have his arm around her as he usually did. Could Mason suspect his own wife?

"And Kade?" she asked in a small voice.

"He was out there on a call about poaching. I confirmed it with his office. The call came in about an hour before you saw him. That's not to say he couldn't have done it. He is Eric's cousin, and there could be some connection. I'm checking into it."

"I think I'll stop by the bank and ask Steve if I can look through the house today," Bree said, rising to her feet.

"Oh, I almost forgot . . ." Hilary dug in her briefcase. "Here's the notebook. Not much in it though."

Bree nodded her thanks and headed out to see Steve. He was in his office, and after some reluctance he gave Bree permission to check out the house. Within minutes she was on her way out of town.

The Asters home was about two miles out of town down Lamppa Lane. After parking at the end of the long driveway, she and Samson walked to the front door of the gracious two-story brick home. Steve had told her the door was unlocked, and the knob turned easily. She stepped inside onto a ceramic tile floor. The entry opened into the dining room to the left. Steve had spared no expense to turn his home into a showplace, according to Fay, and the Aubusson rug under the mahogany dining room table was ample testament to that. All the furnishings had the feel of elegant simplicity that costs the earth.

Where to start? "Let me know if you hear anything," she told Samson. "Stay." She left the dog in the dining room and went past a china cupboard filled with charming crystal figurines of every animal imaginable. Peeking into the kitchen, she saw cherry cabinets and a tumbled marble countertop. A kitchen desk ended the row of cabinets.

She froze. Was that a sound? The sound of her heart pounded in her ears, and she couldn't tell. Then it came again, and her breath eased out. It was just Samson coughing. Why was she so on edge? Steve knew she was here.

She went to the desk and opened it. A hanging file folder held bills; another file held things like insurance policies. She opened the one marked "Life Insurance" and scanned it. Bree blinked at the figure, not sure if she was seeing all the zeros correctly. One million dollars. Steve would have a very good reason to kill Fay. She put the policy back in its folder and continued to look. Rent receipts on several properties they owned in town, old correspondence, Christmas cards.

Bree flipped through the contents of another folder. A letter from a firm called Brannon, Metz & Associates caught her eye. It threatened legal action if the past-due amount of two hundred fifty thousand dollars wasn't repaid within thirty days. Fay had said Steve was out of money, and this proved it. But was that motive enough to kill his wife?

Besides, maybe selling the mine would have eased their financial woes. The money might be a good enough reason if he hated her for having an affair as well.

She closed the desk drawers and made sure everything looked in order before going down the hall to the bedrooms. The master bedroom was at the end of the corridor. It looked like something out of *Arabian Nights*. Opulent silk bed coverings in gold and purple and ornately carved furnishings dazzled Bree. She blinked then moved toward the walnut dresser. She opened a drawer.

Running her hands over Fay's things made her ashamed. She should have waited for Steve; then she wouldn't feel so intrusive. She started to close the drawer, but it wedged in the track. She yanked at it and heard a clunk as something fell out the back. Frowning, she knelt and reached a hand under the dresser. A leather-bound book lay on the floor. Bree took it and sat on her heels. The leather cover was embossed in gold: Fay Asters. She laid it on the bed and continued her search. An hour later, the leather diary was the only possible clue she'd uncovered. That and the insurance policy. She'd have to mention it to Mason, though he probably already knew.

She started toward the front of the house. Samson whined then growled low in his throat.

"Someone's coming, boy?" She heard a noise from the front yard, the muffled sound of a car door slamming. Bree stepped out of the bedroom and glanced out the entry windows. A white van bearing the words MERRY MAIDS on the side sat in the driveway.

She was done here anyway. Taking the diary with her, she opened the door and told Samson to go to the Jeep. Waving at the maids, she got in the Jeep and drove toward town.

The red light on the answering machine was blinking when she walked in the door. Dropping her coat on the chair, she punched the play button and heard Steve's voice: "Bree, this is Steve Asters. I got the autopsy report. Could you meet me at the Suomi at four? I'll be there. I hope you get this message and can join me."

The message ended. Bree glanced at her watch. Nearly 3:30. She would have to get moving if she was going to meet him. She looked at Fay's diary longingly then perched on the edge of a chair in the hall and opened the book.

Fay's distinctive writing slashed across the first page. *January 1.* Nearly eleven months ago. Bree flipped through the pages. They were all diary entries. It would take her awhile to read all of it. Fay's writing was tiny and difficult to decipher. Bree closed the book and went to the living room, where she slipped the diary into the top drawer of the desk. She locked the drawer, something she never did, then pocketed the key.

"Come along, Samson," she told the dog. He obediently followed at her heels.

Suomi Café bustled with customers, and Bree saw no spare tables when she stepped through the door.

"Bree!"

She turned at the sound of her name and saw Steve waving to her from a booth along the right side of the room. Jostling past Molly with a quick greeting, she slid into the seat opposite Steve.

"I wasn't sure if you'd be home to check messages," he said. "I'm buying today. What would you like?"

"Just coffee," she said. "I've eaten lunch." She folded her hands together in front of her and stared at him. "You said you had something to tell me."

He motioned to Molly. "Let me get our order in, then we'll talk."

While he gave Molly their order, Bree studied him. He seemed to have aged since Fay's death. He needed a haircut, his tie was askew, and there was dust on his suit jacket. This was not the put-together man she was used to seeing.

Finished with the waitress, Steve turned back to Bree with a smile she thought was supposed to be ingratiating, but she found it merely sad. Something was missing in Steve now, a vital something that had abandoned him. Maybe Fay had been the spark that gave his life meaning.

Molly brought their coffee. Bree thanked her and took a sip while she waited for Steve to gather his thoughts. His hands shook as he poured sugar from the dispenser into his coffee and stirred it.

"How are things going for you?" she asked.

"Terrible." He stared into his coffee cup then sighed. "The official autopsy report came back late yesterday. The coroner says the injuries aren't consistent with a fall from the cliff. A blow to the back of the head killed her. The other abrasions were postmortem. She was likely arranged at the cliff bottom, not killed there."

Barely daring to breathe, Bree sat back in the booth. Though the news didn't surprise her, she shuddered.

"None of her injuries is consistent with being struck by a car." He stirred his coffee absently. "I'm glad you're helping me, because I'm scared—scared the sheriff will think I murdered her. I wasn't the perfect husband, but I always intended to stay married to her."

For some reason, Bree believed him. Maybe she was gullible, but his grief seemed genuine. She didn't know what to think. This could all be a ploy to get her on his side. Steve might want her to argue his case with Mason. She would agree to help him only so she could find out what Fay might have known about Rob's plane crash.

"I found a diary in the bedroom," she said.

Steve blinked as though awakening from a trance, and Bree realized he'd been lost in his own thoughts. He shook his head. "Fay was always writing things down in her leather diary or that notebook she carried. I hadn't found her diary. Where was it?"

Bree told him. "I took it with me. I hope that's all right."

He nodded. "I'd like it back when you're done though."

"Of course."

Steve shifted restlessly and ran a hand through his hair. "On second thought, my lawyer says the authorities will try to pin this on me. I don't want to give them any more opportunity to do that than they have already. Maybe I'd better take a look at that diary first." A wall seemed to go up around him, and he pushed away his coffee.

"I'm only interested in seeing what she might have said about that woman. I won't pass along anything to Mason."

He stared at her doubtfully then nodded. "Can I trust you, Bree? I don't seem to know who my friends are anymore."

Bree nodded slowly. "I won't tell Mason anything incriminating. I'm only looking for something to lead me to the cabin in the woods."

"I'd still like to see it first. Please bring it to me tomorrow."

"I will." She'd just take a quick peek tonight.

Molly brought Steve's food. The aroma of the chicken pasty made Bree's mouth water, even though she wasn't hungry. "I haven't had a pasty in ages," she said. "These are the best in town. They have rutabaga in them," she added in an attempt to diffuse the tension.

"Those old Welsh miners knew what was good stuff," Steve said, taking a bite.

He ate in silence for a few minutes then cleared his throat.

"She left me with a zillion things to clear up," he said. "The sale of the mine should be done by next week, and I'm dealing with her uncle and all his demands as well as the final details."

"You're still selling it to Palmer then?"

"It's what Fay wanted, and I just don't have the energy to renegotiate with anyone else, so yeah, that's what I'm doing."

Bree had to wonder if that million-dollar insurance policy had anything to do with his decision not to pursue another buyer. It would also account for his desperation to find out who killed Fay. The insurance company would be unlikely to pay until they were sure Steve had nothing to do with it.

Everything about Fay's death seemed to go back to the mine. The mine was only about five miles from Eagle Rock. Could the mine have been where Fay's murder took place? Bree shuddered. Maybe she was clutching at straws, but it wouldn't hurt to check it out. Soon there would be a lot of activity going on out there. Palmer's grand plans to turn it into a mining museum called for quite a bit of construction and massive cleanup efforts. If there were any clues to be found, she'd have to find them right away. Maybe she could get out there tomorrow.

Steve pushed away his half-eaten pasty. "I have some things I want to clear off my desk before I go home. I'd better go. Thanks for believing me, Bree."

Bree watched him leave and wished she could give him the trust he needed.

What about Eric? Fay had been just a girl when she fell for his lines the first time. She'd thought Fay was too savvy to fall for him a second time, but Bree knew there was no guarantee of that. Some mistakes were easy to repeat. She thought of her marriage to Rob, which led to thoughts of Kade Matthews. She longed to put the past behind her and move into a relationship with someone like him, but she didn't know how. Her marriage had lasted eight years. The last time she'd dated, she had been a freshman in college, and she and Rob had married the following summer. Here she was, with her thirtieth birthday looming in four months. What did one do on a date these days? The thought of finding out left her as frightened as hanging from the side of the light tower.

16

Kade groaned and threw his arm over his eyes. That dratted puppy of Lauri's had cried all night. He'd lost count of how many times he'd climbed out of bed and reheated the water in the water bottle. Even the ticking of the alarm clock failed to soothe Zorro, and the pup clearly wanted others to share his pain.

Kade's eyes felt gritty. What really sounded good was pulling the shades and going back to sleep, but he'd be late for church if he didn't get moving. Skipping altogether seemed an attractive option, but he knew he couldn't do that. He was the morning's worship leader, plus he'd promised to take over Mike Farrell's Sunday school class while Mike visited family in Boston. He had to get up.

He tossed back the covers and swung his legs over the edge of the bed. Zorro heard him stirring and promptly began to whine and cry in his box by the outside door. Kade sighed and shuffled out of his bedroom to check on the puppy. Why was he doing this? Lauri had promised to care for the puppy herself, yet last night she'd wheedled him into taking over that job yet again while she went to a slumber party at a friend's house.

When she came home today, Kade intended to remind her that Zorro was *her* dog. No more shirking of her motherly duties. If she didn't want to care for the puppy herself, he would take the dog back to the pound, though the thought pained him. Still, he had to be firm. Lauri needed to grow up and face her responsibilities. He'd give it a few more days.

Kade picked up Zorro and grimaced at the mess in the box. He started to clean it up then stopped. No, this was a job Lauri needed to do. He took the puppy outside and tried to get him to potty, but Zorro hadn't figured out what to do yet. He attached a long rope to the puppy's collar and left him outside. There was no snow forecast for today, though the air was nippy. Still, the pup's coat was thick, and he'd be fine.

⸎

Kade's fatigue dropped away once he was among his church family. He kept watching for Lauri—she was supposed to bring her friend to church today—but by the time service was over, she still hadn't shown up. His initial anger escalated when he got home; she wasn't there either.

He fed the puppy then stalked to his truck and took off toward town. Lauri's friend Tracie Mitchell lived in a house on the outskirts of Rock Harbor. Kade pulled up in front. He stared at the house but saw no movement. The siding used to be red, but the color had worn away in most places. Most of the shutters had blown off, and the ones still attached tilted at an angle as they clung to the sides of the windows with only one screw. An assortment of tricycles and toys littered the porch, which was missing a few boards.

He got out of the truck and strode to the steps. Careful to avoid the missing tread, he went to the front door and knocked. There was no answer, so he pounded harder.

"I'm coming. I'm coming. Keep your pants on." The irritated voice coming through the door sounded female.

The door swung open, and Kade faced a woman with wispy blond hair scraped back from her forehead into a clip at the back of her head. She shuffled the baby on her hip and stared at him.

Her pale blue eyes regarded him with suspicion. "Mrs. Mitchell? I'm Lauri's brother, Kade. I wonder if I might have a word with my sister?"

"She ain't here. I ain't seen her since Tracie moved in with her dad in Marquette a month ago."

Kade digested the news in silence. His anger grew, but he managed to keep his voice calm. "I need to find my sister. Do you have any idea where I could look?" Whatever Lauri had been up to, it wasn't good.

Mrs. Mitchell gnawed on her bottom lip. "I 'spect you could check their hangout by the river. You go past Wilson's barn and turn at that dirt track that leads back to Rock River. Park at the river and take the path to the right. Go 'bout a mile, and you'll come to a fork in the path. Turn left, and it will take you to a lean-to by the river the kids all use." A child behind her began to whine, and she slammed the door in Kade's face.

He stood on the porch for a moment then gave a heavy sigh and went to his truck. He made a mental note to call the pastor's wife and suggest that some women call on Mrs. Mitchell and offer the church's help with the house. Then he started the truck and pulled away. It would be like Lauri to assume Kade would wait for her to show up. But Lauri was in for a big surprise. He was done giving her the benefit of the doubt. He should have cracked down harder, sooner. His stomach churned at the thought of what she'd been doing all night. And with whom.

He drove through town to the other side, past Wilson's barn. He almost missed the dirt track. No wonder he'd never noticed it before; it was nearly overgrown with brambles. Kade heard the thorns screech over the paint on his truck as he squeezed down the lane.

After a short time the track widened a bit, though heavy vegetation and tall trees nearly blotted out the sun. Potholes made the going slow, and once he almost hit a tree stump poking up through the fallen leaves. Rounding a curve, he nearly hit a woman in a heavy navy sweater. She wore an old leather fedora on her head and looked vaguely familiar. Kade had a feeling he should know her, but he couldn't make the connection. He assumed he'd seen her around town a time or two.

Her eyes startled and went wide. For a moment she looked as though she might run, then she straightened her shoulders and watched him pass before turning toward town again. He wondered briefly what she was doing back here. He'd seen no houses or anything that hinted of permanent residences.

He finally reached the river and parked. The river was barely more than a stream after the dry summer they'd just had, though he knew in the spring it would boast some beautiful waterfalls. He got out of the truck and took the path Mrs. Mitchell had told him about. Walking along the narrow dirt walkway, he found plenty of evidence that teenagers frequented this area: gum wrappers, soda cans, the remains of a Snickers candy bar, and the ubiquitous cigarette butts. Looking closely, he noticed some of those butts had been hand-rolled.

His lips tightened. Lauri had better not be dabbling in drugs. He'd send her away to military school or something if he had to. He walked as quickly as he dared along the uneven path and finally came to the fork Tracie's mother had mentioned. He turned left and minutes later heard the sound of young voices.

The scent of wood smoke drifted to his nostrils, and he quickened his steps. Pushing his way through a brier patch, he saw a group of four teenagers seated around an open fire. His gaze went to his sister. She sat on a blanket on the ground, leaning back against the legs of a boy who was sitting on a log. She was smoking like the rest, but he was relieved to see it wasn't marijuana.

"Hey, what time is it?" The red-headed girl tossed another log on the fire as she asked. Kade recognized her as Mindy Sturgeon, the high-school principal's daughter.

"Two o'clock," the boy behind Lauri said.

"Holy cow," Lauri said. "I'd better get going. I've missed church, and Kade will be spitting bullets." She started to her feet, but the boy grabbed her by the ponytail and pulled her back against him.

"Relax. He'll get over it. We've got all day yet."

Kade stepped out from the trees. "Wrong," he said. "Party's over."

Lauri screeched and jumped to her feet. The rest of the kids stood hastily and tossed away their cigarettes. Shock rippled over his sister's face, but Kade could see the anger underneath the way he could see a rock at the bottom of a riverbed.

"What are you doing here?" she demanded.

"I might ask the same question of you," he said dryly. "I understood you to be at Tracie Mitchell's, but her mother tells me she hasn't seen you in weeks. Weeks, Lauri." He pressed his lips together. The rest could wait until they were at home. "Get your things."

"Hey, man, we weren't doing anything wrong—" the boy began.

"Stow it," Kade said. Obviously ill at ease, the rest of the kids stood with their hands thrust in their pockets. "Do your parents know where you are?" he asked.

The boy glared at him defiantly while the other two looked at the ground. This kid was bad news waiting to make the front page. "I didn't think so," Kade said. "What are your names? And don't try to lie your way out of this."

"Chip Elliott," one of the boys said. His brown hair was tousled, and he wouldn't meet Kade's gaze.

Mindy opened her mouth, but Kade cut her off. "I recognized you, Mindy." He turned his glare to the boy. "Who's Mr. Smartmouth?"

The boy's defiance was only a veneer. Kade saw panic flicker in his eyes. The teenager mumbled something.

"What was that? Speak up," Kade said sharply.

"Brian Parker," the boy said a little louder.

Brian Parker. Kade's gaze narrowed. "You Max Parker's boy?" Max would have a coronary. The town doctor was proud of his social standing and kept his family in order.

Brian's brave front dissolved. "You're not going to tell my dad, are you?"

"I haven't decided yet," Kade said. He didn't like meddling in other people's business, and it wasn't his job to police Rock Harbor's teenage population. Maybe he'd better stick to his own responsibilities. But he'd let the kids sweat it out a bit. Maybe next time they'd think twice about being so foolish.

He saw Lauri hadn't moved. "Get your things," he told her. "Unless you want your friends to hear what I have to say."

Lauri dropped her gaze. He waited while she went to the lean-to. The silence was long and uncomfortable for the kids, who shuffled their feet and looked everywhere except at Kade.

When she reappeared with a backpack over her shoulder, he addressed the group. "I suggest you all head for home as well. It might be good to confess before I find time to talk to your parents myself."

The kids scattered, and Kade took Lauri's stiff arm. Lauri jerked out of his grasp. "I don't need your help," she snarled. They walked back to the truck in tense silence. He knew she wouldn't hold her anger for long.

Lauri threw herself into the seat and slammed the door. His mouth tight, Kade slid beneath the steering wheel and jabbed the key into the ignition. The engine roared when he floored the accelerator, and it felt almost as satisfying as if he had been able to let loose the roar of rage building in his own chest.

The tires spun in the soft dirt, then the truck moved away from the river. Kade eased his foot off the pedal. The sandy track was too treacherous to go fast, much as he might want to expel his frustration by driving recklessly. He glanced at his sister. She stared out the window, her jaw tight. Then rage burst from her in a flood of bitterness.

"You've ruined my life; I hope you know that!" The gaze she turned on him would have burned him if his own anger hadn't been just as hot.

"Let's not discuss this until we get home," he said tightly.

"Everything always has to be your way, doesn't it? Well, not today.

Let me out of this truck." She struggled with the truck door and managed to open it.

Kade hit the brakes as Lauri hurled herself out of the truck. He threw the transmission into park and jumped out, leaving his door open. Lauri had landed in a patch of raspberry brambles. The harder she tried to extricate herself, the more deeply the thorns pierced her.

"Oh, ow!" She began to cry. Blood marred her forehead, and droplets appeared on her arms.

"Stop thrashing. Let me help you." Kade took out his pocketknife to cut her loose. Laurie kept still, her only movement coming from her chest as she sobbed.

"You don't care about me," she wailed. "I'm just a nuisance to you and everyone else. I wish I'd died with Mom. I hate my life. I hate this town, and I hate you!" Freed from the briers, she sat up and buried her face in her hands.

Her words stung. Could she really hate him? Kade knelt beside her. "That's not true, Lauri. You're the most important thing in my life. You're the reason I'm here in Rock Harbor. I want to do what's best for you." He swallowed and dabbed at the blood on her forehead. She stood.

"You don't even know me anymore, so how can you know what's best?" Spent from her rampage, she let her hands fall to her sides. "Just leave me alone." She brushed past him and got back in the truck.

Kade wished he knew the magic words to reach his sister. She was getting sucked away from him in a whirlpool of rebellion that would ruin her life. He couldn't let that happen. Somehow, there had to be a way to reach her.

17

$\mathcal{A}$t six o'clock, darkness still cloaked Rock Harbor. Snow had finally come to the U.P. Nearly six inches of it blanketed the ground this early Monday morning. Naomi had thrown a coat over her exercise shorts and T-shirt and stood shaking with cold on the lighthouse porch. She rang the doorbell then waited to hear the patter of Samson's feet and his soft woof before letting herself in. Bree had lit every candle in the place, and their apple-cinnamon fragrance welcomed Naomi.

She shut the door behind her and rubbed Samson's head. He whined and wiggled all over with pleasure. "Where's Bree, boy?"

He woofed softly again and turned to look up the stairs. Shrugging out of her coat, Naomi tossed it over the mourner's bench in the entry then went up the steps.

"Bree?" she called. She followed the sound of a rhythmic thudding down the hall to the door on the left. Through the open door, she saw Bree running on the treadmill in her exercise room. She wore a headset, and her face was a mask of concentration.

Her jerk of surprise was almost comical, and Naomi grinned. Bree slipped the headset down to her neck and turned off the machine.

"Is it that time already?" She grabbed a small towel and mopped her face. "Get the aerobics video ready while I get some water."

"You trying to show me up? I'd have rubber legs if I tried to run before aerobics." Naomi took the Denise Austin aerobics disc out of its case and popped it in the DVD player. She knew Bree trained hard. They both had to in order to manage the grueling ordeal of tramping over rough terrain on searches.

Bree went to the small refrigerator in the corner and took out a bottle of water. "Want some?"

"Not yet."

Bree took a long swig, and Naomi studied her friend's face. Had she been crying again, or was the redness merely from exercise?

Bree saw her staring. "I'm fine, so don't fuss."

"You've been crying."

Bree took another swallow of water. "It snowed last night."

"I know." Naomi knew Bree was obsessed with the snow and cold. She wished Bree could understand her son wasn't beneath that cold blanket of snow. But it did no good to harp on it. Maybe she'd feel the same way if it were her son lying out there somewhere, his bones naked and uncovered. This world seemed so real, sometimes it was hard even for her to imagine what heaven must be like.

"Let's work up a sweat. I'm not ready for this cold yet. And turn on the sauna," Naomi added.

"I already did," Bree said. She picked up the remote and pressed the play button.

It was better not to talk about some things. They did their aerobics routine then went to the sauna. Naomi stretched out on the slatted cedar bench closest to the ceiling where the air was hottest. She had a book with her but laid it aside. Bree lay on the high bench along the other wall.

Bree rolled over on her stomach. "You haven't told me about your date." Her tone was mildly reproachful.

"It wasn't a date. The kids were there."

"Then why are you blushing?"

"I'm not blushing! It's the heat." Naomi couldn't help the stupid grin that took control of her face.

"It's a sad state of affairs when I have to hear about my best friend's love life through town scuttlebutt." Bree rolled back over and crossed her arms under her head.

"I don't really have a love life, so there's not much to tell." Naomi didn't know why she was so reluctant to talk about it. Maybe she was afraid talking about it would break the special connection that seemed to be developing between her and Donovan.

Bree sat up and stared at her. "Is this serious or something? We've always talked about your men friends, but right now you look the way Samson does when he's rolled in something dead: defensive and ashamed all at the same time. Give me the scoop, or I'll have to treat you like Samson and send you outside."

Naomi managed to laugh at Bree's feeble attempt at humor. "I don't know how he feels yet. I'm afraid to know."

"You know how you feel so soon?"

"It's not soon. I've always liked Donovan," Naomi protested. "And now that he's free . . ."

"You don't intend to let him get away again, is that it?"

Bree said the words mildly, but they stung. "Is that so wrong?" Naomi whispered.

"No, sweetie. I just don't want to see you get hurt. A man in Donovan's position might grab hold of the first available female. I want you to be loved for yourself, not because the guy needs a caretaker for his kids. You're too special to settle for that."

Naomi squeezed her eyes shut. "I'm thirty-two, Bree. I want a home, a family," she said huskily. She didn't want to face Bree's doubts—the same ones that kept her tossing in bed at night. Donovan *did* seem desperate. Who wouldn't be? But in spite of that, she clung to the hope he could love her for herself.

"There are worse things than being unmarried," Bree said.

Naomi knew that was true, but being with Donovan and his children felt right. She felt like a puzzle piece that fit perfectly into an empty spot. She'd prayed and prayed about it, and she really believed the Lord approved of this match.

The women left the hot, cedar-lined room and jumped under the cold shower spray before going back to the sauna. Questions roiled through Naomi's mind. What if this didn't happen for her? What if Donovan was merely using her because he needed someone for the kids? She wished Bree hadn't brought it up.

"You still haven't said what you did Saturday," Bree said.

"We went shopping for school clothes for the kids. Emily had outgrown all her jeans, and Timmy needed new shoes. Then we all went to lunch at the Suomi." Naomi smiled at the memory of their day.

"How did that go?" Bree asked as she led the way back to the sauna.

"Emily is still on her guard with me. She wants you to marry her dad." Naomi attempted a smile. Bree frowned.

"Is that why you didn't want to tell me about it? I told you I wasn't interested in Donovan."

"I know she's just a child." Naomi chuckled, but it had a hollow quality to it. She yawned. "This heat is making me sleepy. I suppose it's about time to get out."

"I have some breakfast burritos in the freezer. You want to stay for breakfast?" Bree stood and clicked off the sauna heater.

"No thanks. I need to get home. But you and I are supposed to go to Anu's for supper tonight. She's fixing spinach lasagna." Naomi followed Bree to the cold shower spray for the final time. "I'll drive tonight. Pick you up about five-thirty, eh?"

"Now that's an offer I can't refuse," Bree said with a smile. "Hey, don't forget your book."

Naomi shook her head. "I lose more books." She took it and followed Bree out of the sauna. Naomi could see the worry in Bree's eyes and wanted to reassure her, but how could she now that the same worry had rooted in her own heart? She might be setting herself up for a world of hurt. If she wasn't willing to take a risk though, she might as well be dead. Without risk, she had no hope of gain. She pushed away the doubts and decided to concentrate on her day. They had supper with Anu to look forward to. She just had to deal with a million details at the bed-and-breakfast first.

Anu greeted them at the door with a hug then put them to work chopping vegetables for salad. The aroma of the lasagna, pungent with garlic and spices, filled the house. Bree loved Anu's house. Furnished with clean-lined Finnish furniture in a light wood, it was homey and welcoming. The three women had often gathered in the kitchen for heart-to-heart talks. Arabia china in a warm yellow color accented the blue-and-white decor.

"Sit down, girls." Swathed in a bright blue apron, Anu came into the dining room with the lasagna. "Supper's ready."

When they were seated, Anu said grace and Bree found herself listening to the words. Was Anu really thankful for every morsel of food she ate, every blessing God brought to her?

Anu lifted her head and began to ladle the food onto their plates. "Bree, what are you finding out about poor Fay?"

"Not much," Bree admitted. She was getting tired of that question. Everyone seemed to think she had an inside track on the investigation just because she'd found Fay's body. There were no answers in sight. Fay's murder seemed just as random and senseless today as it had the night Samson and Charley discovered her body.

"Mason seems overwhelmed by it all," Naomi said.

"Fay's old boyfriend is back in town," Anu interjected.

"He's been here since the funeral," Naomi said. "I think Mason considers him a suspect."

"Yes." Anu nodded. "I told Mason to look at him."

"Do you know him?" Bree asked in surprise.

"He used to be my gardener. Hot-tempered, though a fine worker. One day he threw the pickax through the shed door when it got stuck shut. Two weeks later, he ripped out my prize roses when his sleeve got tangled in the thorns. I had to ask him to leave."

"Wow," Bree said. "I had no idea. What did he do? Did he leave?"

"He pounded on the door and smeared mud on the windows." Anu raised her eyebrows for effect. "Mason had to come. This was before Eric went to prison."

"So Eric's temper is nothing new to Mason," Bree said.

"Oh no. But you must stay away from him, *kulta*. He is a dangerous man. I can see from your expression you want to know more, but you cannot get involved with that man."

"I read that psalm you told me to read," Bree said. She paused to study their expressions. "You should see your faces. Don't look so surprised!"

Anu collected herself. "And what did you see there? Did it help you?"

"It made me wonder about Rob," she admitted.

Anu's hand stopped partway to her mouth with a forkful of lasagna. "What about Rob?"

Though she'd been steeling herself to bring up this subject with Anu, her courage nearly failed. "He claimed to be a Christian, yet he did things that were wrong."

"I won't ask you what sins my son committed, as I'm sure they were many and varied," Anu said. "No one is perfect, my Bree, only forgiven in Christ. I must confess to my own besetting sins of pride and jealousy. God helps us to overcome our sins, but we often slip and fall. What part of the psalm made you think of Rob?"

"The part about a righteous man being remembered forever. People still talk about him and mention things he did."

Joy radiated from Anu's face. "How lovely to hear that, *kulta*. Did you find anything else in the Scripture?"

"I saw you in there," she said.

"Me?"

"'Blessed is the man who fears the LORD, who finds great delight in his commands,'" Bree quoted.

Color flooded Anu's face.

"I think I can rule out Kade as a suspect too, now that I've gotten to know him better," Bree said. "That psalm says a righteous man will never be shaken. Kade is like a rock. And he's fearless. You should have seen him dangling from the tower."

"'His heart is secure, he will have no fear,'" Anu recited.

"I didn't know you suspected him!" Naomi said. "He would never do something like that."

"Well, he was at the scene just before we found Fay, remember? And he *is* Eric's cousin, so for a while I wondered if he helped Eric get rid of her—if Eric killed her, of course."

"You have too much time on your hands," Naomi said. "It's caused your imagination to run wild."

"So who do you still suspect?" Anu said.

Bree wanted to tell her what Hilary had said the night of the party but kept her mouth shut. There were just some things a mother didn't need to know. "Steve, Eric, and Lawrence," she said. "I want to talk to Eric. He spent a lot of time with Fay, if we believe town gossip. Maybe he saw the woman in the hat. I don't know where he's staying though."

"Sheba McDonald might know where he is," Anu said. "Mason should ask her. But let Mason handle this, *kulta*."

Bree didn't ask how Sheba would know. Sheba knew everything. She didn't say anything more. Mason would know where Eric was, and Bree didn't want Anu to know she was going to poke around.

Anu carried the leftover lasagna to the kitchen, and Bree and Naomi collected the supper dishes.

"Have you told your mother about Donovan?" Bree asked Naomi as they worked.

Naomi shook her head. "I'm not sure how to approach it. If she's in favor of the idea, I'll have to suffer through her advice and meddling. If she's against it, she'll likely snub Donovan on the street and begin to question my every movement."

"She'll be livid if she finds out from someone else." Bree understood what it was to fear a parent, but Naomi had no real reason to be afraid of Martha.

Naomi sighed. "I know. I'll do it soon."

Bree suspected that if Naomi would just once take charge of her life, Martha would back off. But she knew it wasn't in her friend's nature to be aggressive. Naomi was one of those dear souls who watched to see what she could do for others, someone who would rather serve in silence.

Whoever got Naomi for a wife would be a lucky man, though Rob's opinion had been different. He'd always said a wife like Naomi would bore a man silly. But then Rob's tastes had run to bungee jumping and skydiving.

Bree wondered about the other woman in his life, Lanna March. How had he met her? How long had he been seeing her? She would probably never know, and maybe that was best.

While Anu was starting the dishwasher, Bree slipped into the living room and made a quick call to Mason. He told her Eric was at a deer camp near Big Piney Creek, but he cautioned her not to go alone. He would go with her as soon as he took care of other business. Bree didn't answer. She hung up and asked Naomi if she would mind going with her. "If you're sure you can take the time away from Donovan," she added with a grin.

"Of course," Naomi said. "You shouldn't go alone."

"I don't want to wait for Mason. He can't go for a couple of days. If we go at midmorning, we won't disturb the hunting."

"Give me a call when you're ready to go."

18

$\mathcal{M}$ ore snow fell Monday night. Tuesday morning, Bree figured there was close to eight inches of snow on the ground. She was running late and rushed to shower. Toweling off, she heard the trill of her cell phone. As she wrapped the towel around herself, she quickly checked the display and saw Kade's name on the caller ID.

She finished dressing before calling him back. "What's up, Kade?"

"Some fool hunter has gotten himself lost in the woods." Kade's voice was rough and gravelly, as though he hadn't slept. "Can you grab Naomi and get out here? The guy's been missing since yesterday at three."

"They just now reported it?" Bree was already beginning to gather her things.

Kade gave a weary sigh. "They were too drunk to notice, I guess. And the guy left his coat behind. All he's wearing is a flannel shirt with a vest. It got down below twenty last night." He told her how to get to the location.

"You call Naomi while I finish getting ready." She clicked off the phone. "We've got a search, Samson," she told her dog.

By the time she picked up Naomi and made it out to the scene, nearly an hour had passed. The sun felt good on her face, and she hoped the missing hunter was someplace where the sun could warm him. But the North Woods were so thick that in some places the sun never hit the ground.

The command center was still being set up when she arrived at

Loon Falls, about two miles off Beaver Road. A truck was backing the familiar trailer into position in the snowy clearing. Kade saw Bree and Naomi and waved from the tree line. Bree parked, then she and Naomi let the dogs out and went to meet him.

His tired eyes blinked above dark circles that almost looked like bruises. Bree had a hunch that something more than the missing hunter had robbed him of sleep. Something in his eyes—pain?—made her want to fix whatever it was. Maybe she would have a chance to talk with him about it later. The realization that she was glad to see him unsettled her.

"What've we got?" she asked him.

"Bubba Martin, age twenty-three. His friends are still very unconcerned." Kade shook his head. "If they're the best he can do, he's hurting."

"I don't know him," Bree said. Even the name Martin didn't sound familiar.

"He's from down around Ironwood. His mother is on her way."

"We have any articles of clothing?" Bree turned and stared into the woods. With that much time elapsed, the young man could be anywhere. It didn't sound like his circle of friends was the type to have any real wilderness survival savvy. He probably didn't even know enough to stay put and wait for the searchers.

Kade moved closer and held out a paper bag with something white inside. "He wore this T-shirt yesterday."

"I'll give the dogs the scent," Naomi said, taking the bag. The dogs each thrust a nose into the bag then began to strain at their leashes.

Bree and Kade both turned and began to walk toward the woods. Bree knew she needed to keep things on a professional level with Kade, but being near him was like standing on the lighthouse tower during a storm—scary and exhilarating at the same time. She hadn't reacted to any man like this since Rob. The feelings were unfamiliar and terrifying.

She wanted to step closer, to nestle her head against his shoulder, to turn her cares and worries over to someone bigger and stronger than herself. It was a feeling she needed to guard against. No one could solve her problems.

"How's Zorro?" she asked. Better to keep things distant.

He sighed. "Chewing everything. And Lauri's no help. She's gone more than she's home."

She glanced at him. "I could come over for another lesson." As soon as the words were past her lips, she wanted to snatch them back. The last thing she needed was to be around him more. He likely felt nothing for her but friendship anyway. But all the rationalizing in the world didn't change her longing to get to know him better.

"That would be great! When can you come?"

His eagerness heartened her. "Maybe this evening, if it's not too late by the time we find our missing hunter." She was committed now. His gaze caught and held hers. The awareness in his eyes dried her mouth, and she finally looked away.

They reached the edge of the woods. "Want me to let the dogs go?" Naomi had a leash around each wrist, and the dogs practically dragged her forward in their eagerness.

Bree grabbed Samson's leash. She took his head between her hands. "You ready, boy?" The dog panted with excitement and whined. She unclipped his leash and let him go. "Search, Samson. Go find him."

The dog raced off into the woods with Charley close on his tail. Naomi, Bree, and Kade ran after them. A sense of déjà vu came over Bree. Their search for the O'Reilly children seemed eons ago. So much had happened in the two weeks since.

Funny how life could twist on you like an unfamiliar road until you weren't sure which way you were pointed anymore. That was just how Bree felt. She'd started out to find Rob and Davy, yet how long had it been since she'd really searched for them? Little by little, life was beginning to creep back in. She didn't know if she was happy or sad. Maybe she'd turned a corner.

The dogs were on a hot trail. Their posture told Bree the hunter couldn't be far.

Sure enough, thirty minutes later the dogs began to bark, then Samson came bounding to her with a stick in his mouth.

"Show me, Samson," Bree commanded. The dog led her over fallen trees dusted with white snow then around a stand of pine to a small clearing. A young man huddled against the side of a jack pine.

"Bubba Martin?" she asked.

He blinked slowly, and she realized he was suffering from hypothermia. She opened her ready-pack and pulled out a blanket. "Pour him some hot coffee from the thermos," she called over her shoulder to Kade and Naomi. Naomi moved first.

Bubba shivered. "So cold," he whispered.

"We'll get you warmed up," she promised. Naomi handed the coffee to Bree, and she lifted it to Bubba's lips. A sense of accomplishment washed over her in a warm tide. Another successful search. But her euphoria quickly collapsed. What did it all matter if the most important search of her life ended in failure?

When they got back to the command center, Bubba's mother was there, a bleached blond in her early forties with angry brown eyes. She rushed to her son and began to harangue him in a voice that caught Bree's attention. Frowning, she stood and listened. She'd heard that voice before.

Then it came to her. Lanna March.

Bree approached the pair. Bubba's head was down as his mother berated him.

"Yes?" she snapped when she realized Bree was staring at her.

"I think the paramedics need to check Bubba. He's suffering from exposure and hypothermia."

"Who are you?" the woman growled. Her scowl deepened.

Bree called herself a fool for thinking Rob would have anything to do with a woman like this. "I'm Bree Nicholls."

The woman's face sagged, and she backed away. Her gaze darted away from Bree's. "Fine, you take him to the ambulance. I'll meet him at the hospital."

"Wait, you never told me your name," Bree called.

The woman ran to her car, a mid-eighties Ford with rust eating the wheel wells. She slammed the car door and sped away.

Bree had always possessed a knack for voice recognition, and she was sure that woman was the one who had called her, the one who wanted her to let Rob go. But why would she be afraid of Bree? Shaking with the revelation, she stumbled back to the trailer and filled out the necessary paperwork, then she and Naomi drove to the deer camp where Eric Matthews was supposed to be holed up.

Big Piney Creek was only five miles away. After Bree parked the Jeep, they got out with the dogs and began to walk back to where Mason said the deer camp was located.

Naomi was uncharacteristically quiet. She kept stealing glances at Bree, and it was making Bree uncomfortable. "Spit it out, girlfriend. What's on your mind?"

Naomi bit her lip. "You really like Kade, don't you?" she said finally.

Bree gulped, and heat rushed to her cheeks. "Is it that obvious?"

"Only to me. Weren't you just yelling at me about not telling you everything?" Naomi said in a teasing tone.

"I just recognized it myself," Bree said. "I didn't realize it until he walked toward me this morning. Isn't that stupid? It's like there's this connection between us. I can't explain it."

"I know just what you mean. Like you can almost tell what he's thinking by looking at him."

Bree nodded. "I don't know where it will lead, if anywhere. I'm not sure I want it to lead anywhere. My life is such a mess, and I don't want to involve Kade in the fallout."

"Kade's a Christian, you know," Naomi said softly.

The comment came like a slap of cold water in Bree's face. A real wake-up call. It was something she didn't want to deal with. All the more reason to keep him at a distance.

"Rob was a Christian, but—" She broke off.

"But what? So he let you down or hurt you in some way. Are you sure you're not just angry with him for dying, for leaving you here?"

"I wish it were that simple." She'd held her guilt so close for the past year, she didn't know if she could reveal it even to Naomi. But the more she had tried to hide it, the more fearful she'd become of opening herself up to the future.

"Then what is it? I've seen you change this year, Bree. You never used to have all this insecurity. Tell me."

"Rob was having an affair!" Bree waited for Naomi's reaction.

Naomi put her hands to her face then lowered them and stared at Bree. "Not Rob. Are you sure?" She brushed the snow from a log then lowered herself onto it. "Sit down. I have to chew on this a minute."

Bree sat beside Naomi and laced her fingers together in her lap. The snow muffled the sounds of the forest, and she listened to the silence. "A woman called the day his plane went down. She said they were in love and if I wanted him to be happy, I'd let him go."

"Did she identify herself?"

Bree nodded. "Lanna March. Her number was unlisted. I called Rob on his cell phone. He denied it, but his anger was so out of proportion, I knew it was true. That was just minutes before he got in the plane to fly home. Don't you see, Naomi? I killed him and Davy! If I had waited, discussed it calmly when he got home, my family would still be alive."

"So that's why you're afraid to speak your mind anymore," Naomi said.

"What if I hurt someone like that again and never have the chance to make it right? I wanted him to feel the same hurt I did. Rob was a good pilot. I wrecked his concentration."

"You can't know that, Bree. There could have been something wrong with the plane, a wind shear; any number of things could have caused the crash. It wasn't you though, and you can't change who you are because of some misplaced sense of guilt."

"That woman at the search, Bubba's mother. Her voice reminded me of Lanna's. For a minute I thought—" Bree broke off in thought, then she set her jaw. She knew she was right. She never forgot a voice. "In fact, I'm just sure it was her voice. But she's much older than Rob." She ran a hand through her hair. "Oh, nothing makes any sense."

"If you're sure she's the one who called you, we should check her out," Naomi said thoughtfully.

Bree didn't want to think about Lanna anymore. She glanced at Naomi. "What do you think of Rob's Christianity now?" Bree asked.

"I'm disappointed in him, but he was human, Bree. Being a Christian doesn't change the human nature we all still deal with. God doesn't recognize degrees of sin. Rob's sin was no worse than telling a little white lie or gossiping or losing your temper. God forgives it all. His love is unconditional."

Unconditional love. Bree had never thought of it that way before. Her heart longed for that kind of acceptance. Anu accepted her in that way, but Bree worried how her mother-in-law would react if she knew Bree's heart fully. For the first time, she understood the appeal of accepting God's love. The God of Bree's experience was a mischievous cat who played with his creation like a ball of twine until it was a hopeless mess. But God hadn't stepped in to save her family—didn't that prove his disinterest? She wished she could believe in this unconditional love idea.

The women let the dogs roam a bit before starting off for the creek. Bree rehearsed what she would say to Eric. Tramping through the woods, they made plenty of noise to alert any hunters to their presence.

Their bright orange gear should show through the foliage, but just to be sure, they sang for a while then talked loudly and shouted to the dogs.

Bree hated deer season. Michigan had allowed a short extra gun season this year, and as she and Naomi walked through the pristine winter wonderland, Bree saw the evidence of the hunts: Hunters' tree stands, spent shells, broken arrows, and patches of blood littered the white snow. Though she understood the need to keep the deer population under control, she hated the violence of the method.

It was nearly three o'clock by the time they arrived at the camp. Bree stepped over a line of beer cans that encircled the site like an aluminum fortress. Four men lay snoring on top of their sleeping bags while a fifth lay on the hood of a battered green Ford pickup. The fire in the center of the camp had gone out, but the men were either too drunk or too tired to care.

Bree glanced at each face. She recognized a few, but she didn't see Eric.

"There are eight sleeping bags," Naomi pointed out. "Three men are gone. Let's look around. We'll find them quicker if we split up. You check the creek, and I'll wander through the woods a bit."

"Don't forget to make noise," Bree warned her.

Naomi nodded and took Charley with her. Bree whistled for Samson, and they went down a rocky path to the creek bed. The snow had made the slick rocks treacherous. Standing on a boulder, Bree glanced across the Big Piney. Only a trickle of water passed over the rocky surface of the creek.

Singing "Jailhouse Rock" at the top of her lungs, Bree wandered along the edge of the creek for several minutes then turned to go back. Samson pricked his ears and whined. "What is it, boy?" She paused and listened. The faint echo of voices reached her ears.

She pushed through a thicket of brush and found three men sitting along the bank of the creek. They stopped talking when they saw her. The Larson brothers and Eric Matthews.

Blue eyes as cold as a glacier looked her over. "You're that dog woman," he said. "Fay's friend. I suppose the cops got you following me too? What'd I tell you, Mitch? That idiot husband of Fay's has turned the whole town against me."

"You seem to have done that on your own," Bree said. A low growl escaped Samson's throat, so she kept a hand on his head.

"What's that supposed to mean? I had nothing to do with Fay's death," Eric said.

"I didn't say you did." She moved closer and stared into his face. There was a coiled tension in him that made her wary.

"No, but you and everyone else looks at me like they think I'm the Boston strangler."

"Calm down, Eric." Mitchell Larson, a heavyset man of about forty, leaned over and handed Eric a beer. "Let's see what the lady wants."

Eric took the beer and popped the top. Taking a big swig, he wiped his mouth on his sleeve. "Okay, dog lady, what do you want? It can't be an accident you're here."

Bree had to tread warily with Eric's temper already on edge. "No, I was looking for you. I hear you're out in the woods a lot, and you spent some time with Fay. I'm looking for a cabin Fay said she came across. A woman lives there. She wears an old leather fedora. Have you seen a place like that?"

Eric frowned. "What makes you think I'd tell you, even if I did, eh?"

"What harm could there be in telling the truth?"

"You want the truth? How about this—I didn't kill Fay. Why isn't the sheriff checking out her husband? He's the one with something to gain. The fine, upstanding bank manager needed the insurance to avoid bankruptcy."

Bree had seen the letter at the house threatening legal action if Steve didn't pay a bill of two hundred fifty thousand dollars. How much more did Steve owe? "How do you know this?"

"Fay told me."

"You went to jail for hurting her."

His face darkened, and he got up. Bree took an involuntary step back, and Samson lunged at Eric. She grabbed his collar when Eric pointed a gun at the dog's head.

"Get out of here, you and that mangy mutt of yours. I loved Fay. This town is bent on making sure I never forget what I did. That was a long time ago, and I was young. I loved Fay." His face contorted. "She forgave me, even if no one else did."

Against her will, Bree found herself believing him. "She was a married woman with a baby on the way."

"That marriage was a mistake, and she knew it." He waved his gun in the air. "Steve doesn't want to believe it, but that was my baby."

"How do you know?"

Misery filled his face. "I just know. She would have gone away with me."

"Even if you had to force her?" Bree knew she was skating near the edge of his temper, but she had to goad him once more.

He pointed the gun at her head. Samson snarled and struggled to free himself from Bree's grip. "I should shoot you now, you and that dog," Eric snarled. "You do-gooders are all alike. You think you know what's best for the world, and the rest of us just need to shut up and follow your rules. No rules would have kept Fay and me apart. She knew it, and I knew it." He gestured with the gun. "Now get out of here before I live up to everyone's expectations."

Bree knew she'd reached his limit, so she turned to go. Samson didn't want to leave. He kept growling and lunging toward Eric.

"Hey, Eric, that dog would make good target practice. We could say we thought he was a deer." Marvin Larson jeered and threw a rock.

It hit Samson on the rear, and the dog whirled with a snarl. It was all Bree could do to hang on. Tugging at his collar, she managed to drag him away. It wasn't until she found Naomi and made it back to the Jeep that she realized she was shaking. That could have gotten ugly. She should have had a man with her. Someone strong like Kade.

She told Naomi about the encounter as they drove back to town.

"Do you believe him?" Naomi asked.

"I didn't want to," Bree admitted. "But I think he might be telling the truth. I saw some papers at Steve's house that indicated he was in financial trouble. I have to tell Mason."

No clear plan came to either of them. They stopped at Mason's office and told him what Bree had found and what Eric had said. He growled at her for not waiting for him then promised to look into it. After letting Naomi out at the Blue Bonnet, Bree turned back up Houghton Street and drove out toward Kade's cabin. Her palms felt sweaty where they gripped the steering wheel. Telling herself she was a mature woman of twenty-nine instead of a giddy teenager on her first date did not help them dry out.

Kade's truck was parked outside the cabin when she stopped. He was in the yard with Zorro and Lauri. Lauri waved an excited greeting. "I've been working on what you told me," she said proudly as Bree climbed out of the Jeep. Zorro ran to Samson. The older dog sniffed the puppy then pointedly ignored him.

"See how Samson is treating him? That's because he's the alpha dog," Bree pointed out. "That's what you have to do with Zorro. I'm not paying any attention to him yet either. You wait until he's not begging for attention, then call him so he knows to come on your terms, not his."

"It seems so mean," Lauri said. "He's just a baby."

"He's a canine baby. He'll be more secure once he knows what to expect." After the puppy wandered off a bit, Bree snapped her fingers. "Zorro, come."

At the sound of his name, the puppy raised his head. Bree knelt and patted the ground. "Come, Zorro."

The puppy raced toward her, his black ears laid back with his efforts to move quickly on short legs. "Good Zorro," Bree said, scratching his ears. "Now you call him, Lauri."

While Lauri practiced the tips, Bree found her gaze straying to Kade. Was that admiration in his eyes? Her chest felt tight.

"Want to see what I do here?" he asked.

"What do you mean? You live here, right?" She walked toward him.

He grinned and took her arm. "Among other things. I'll show you the important stuff." He took her out back to a series of pens.

The gentle touch of his hand on her arm sent a warm glow through her. What was wrong with her? She wanted to stop right here in the middle of the path and burrow into his arms, which was stupid because she didn't want to get involved, especially with a Christian.

The sight of the animals made a good excuse to pull away. "Oh, you have deer!" She reached out to grab a handful of corn in a box near the pens.

"Orphaned wildlife," he corrected. "I'll let them go once hunting season is past." He pointed out a raccoon and a porcupine as well. "Sometimes I have birds—you've met Mazzy—as well as a bear cub or two. I just released two small black bears last summer."

"Kade Matthews, modern-day Dr. Doolittle," Bree said, smiling.

He grinned. "I wish I could talk to them too. It might make my job easier."

"How did you get started doing this?" She tossed a handful of corn to the deer and laughed when the smallest one came right up to her and ate out of her hand.

"When I was ten, my dad brought home a baby raccoon whose mother had been killed by dogs. I named him Mask—not very original, but I sure loved him. Dad insisted I release him when he could fend for himself, and I was devastated. But as I grew older and helped return other animals to the wild, I realized how wise Dad was. It's my way of tending the garden."

Bree frowned, not sure what he meant, and he saw her puzzlement.

"As in tending the garden like God assigned Adam to do. In Genesis, God told Adam to name the creatures and tend the garden. I take that to mean we should care for his creatures and not deplete the resources. The earth is ours to use but not to squander. I try to do my small part."

How rare, Bree thought—a middle-of-the-road approach to environmentalism. A small raccoon reached out to Kade with tiny hands, and he picked it up. It patted his face then crawled to his shoulder and perched there comfortably. Bree laughed and decided she was glad she'd taken the chance to learn more about Kade.

Anu was right. Scriptures did reveal things about a man. Kade was one of the gracious, compassionate, and righteous ones. She'd thought she could rule him out of the murder, but now she was certain.

19

Rachel kissed the sleeping boy on the forehead as she tucked the covers around his chin. She loaded the wood stove with as much fuel as she dared then damped it down so it would burn long and slow. The cabin might not be as warm as it could be, but the fire would last longer this way. No amount of wood would make it last two days though.

She stood on the threshold of the cabin and glanced back toward Sam. She wished she didn't have to leave him alone, but she had no other option. Sam would be fine as long as he stayed inside and under the covers.

Sighing, she shouldered her backpack and eased the door shut behind her. When she heard the latch click into place, she turned and made her way across the clearing, dimly lit by the first rays of sunrise.

Her breath plumed in front of her as she walked toward Ontonagon. There was no bus or taxi service from Rock Harbor, and she had no money for a ride to Ontonagon even if one had been available.

It was nearly 9:30 by the time she reached the bus station. She jostled her way aboard amid a crowd of passengers and found a seat at the back. She'd barely slept the past two nights for worrying about Sam; now she fell asleep before the bus had finished loading.

She awakened as the bus neared Chicago nearly thirteen hours later. When the bus finally stopped, she disembarked and stood in the middle of the crush of passengers as they pushed and shoved their way to the next bus. What should she do now, and where should she go? The cold wind off Lake Michigan sliced down her back, and she zipped her jacket to her chin, jammed her hat down low on her head, and pulled on her gloves.

She turned and plodded through the crowd. Once clear of the masses, she glanced around at the Chicago skyline, twinkling with light from the skyscrapers. Rachel had forgotten what it was like to be in a big city. She felt more alone here than in her little cabin in the woods.

She had one shot at not having to stay out in the cold all night. She made her way to a phone booth and perched her backpack on the cold steel ledge near the phone. Fumbling in the pack, she found a slip of paper with a number written on it. There was no guarantee the number was still good. It had been nearly ten years since she'd last spoken to her brother.

Her hands shook as she dropped two quarters into the pay phone. Once the phone began ringing, she almost hung up. What would she say to him after what she'd done? But the thought of huddling in the cold all night was a strong goad.

"Hello."

The voice was gruff but familiar. She wet her lips. "Frank? It's Rachel."

The pause was long, then Frank finally responded, "What do you want? I figured you was dead by now."

"I need a place to stay tonight. Just for one night. I leave tomorrow." Hating the pleading tone in her voice, she drummed her fingers on the cold metal shelf in the booth.

"Don't you think you've done enough to me and my family?"

"Please, Frank. I have nowhere else to go. I'll just sleep on the floor and be gone tomorrow."

Frank snorted. "I guess you can't do any more damage. Where are you?"

Relief as sweet as a summer rain washed over Rachel. She gave him her location and hung up. What had swayed Frank to allow her to stay? He still sounded just as bitter. She found a spot in a doorway sheltered from the wind and settled down to wait. The nervousness she felt made her jittery, and she wished she had a cigarette. She hadn't had any money for smokes in over a year though.

About half an hour later she saw a car cruising slowly down the street. Maybe that was Frank. She stepped out of the doorway and into the beam of a streetlight so he could see her. The car pulled to the curb. The window went down and she stepped to the door, her heart in her mouth.

"I don't have all day. Get in if you're coming," Frank said.

She got in the car. The blast of warm air from the vents made her eyes water, but the heat felt heavenly. After fastening her seat belt, she turned to look at her brother. He was staring at her through bushy gray eyebrows.

"You ain't changed much," he said. "Hair's grayer, like mine." He snorted a laugh as he pulled back onto the road, but his eyes were still suspicious. "What you doing here?"

"Job interview," she said. "You don't look different either."

He patted his stomach. "Hannah's fattened me up some."

"It looks good on you. You were always too thin."

He grunted. "Don't think you can get around me with flattery. I still hate your guts. You burned down my house!"

Rachel gulped. "I was just trying to help, Frank. I thought if you had the insurance money, you could keep Paulie out of jail."

"And instead, you nearly put me in there with him! You always were stupid, Rachel."

"Then why'd you come get me?" she snapped, annoyed with him for bringing up all the old baggage. But then what had she expected? All her life she'd heard she didn't have any common sense, and while what she'd done to his house might prove that to some people, Rachel had known it was the only way to save her nephew. Was it her fault the plan had taken such a bad turn?

"Because of you my daughter has never married. What man would have her with all those burn scars on her face?" Frank slammed the steering wheel with his hands.

Rachel hunched over against the door. "I didn't know Hannah was still in the house," she said. "You know that, Frank. I never would have done anything to hurt her."

Frank's antipathy was so strong that Rachel struggled to breathe. This had been a mistake. There was no forgiveness in the man. Several miles later, Frank sighed and his animosity seemed to leak away. "Yeah, well, you never did have no sense, Rachel. But you always had a good heart." He stopped at a small, one-story house. Built in the forties, it couldn't be more than eight hundred square feet. "Here we are. Hannah's working tonight."

"What's she do?"

Frank snorted. "She's a nurse like you."

Frank parked then slid his bulk out of the car and plodded up the walkway. He twisted the key in the lock and opened the door. "Home sweet home," he said.

The air smelled of stale cigarettes and beer, just like the house she'd burned down. Rachel followed him inside.

"Leftover casserole's in the fridge if you want some," he told her.

By the time she finished eating, Rachel and Frank had settled back into their old relationship. He was as hungry for companionship as she, hungry enough to grudgingly forgive her. By the time she left the next morning, he had agreed to let her and Sam move in until they found a place of their own.

Life in Chicago suddenly became more attractive. She and Sam could move right away, even if she didn't get this job. If she lived in the city, she could find employment in no time.

In a way, the whole scene felt familiar. She slipped back into city life as if slipping into a comfortable sweater she hadn't worn in years. The sights, sounds, and smells of the city gave her a sense of place, something she'd missed in the woods.

Frank dropped her off for her interview the next morning. Dressed in wool slacks and a nice sweater left over from her days as a nurse, she felt like her old self, confident and put together.

When she walked out an hour later, she had a job. Her heart sang as she changed her clothes and headed for the bus station. She and Sam would be so happy here.

⁂

The fire had gone out hours ago. Sam huddled under the blankets, but he still wasn't warm. When would she be back? He hated to be alone. When he was alone like this, too many thoughts whirled in his head. Sometimes strange memories tried to poke their way through. Sometimes he could almost catch them.

Some of them were good. He remembered his mommy, his daddy, his dog. Whenever he tried to talk about these thoughts to *her*, her mouth pinched up like she'd eaten a lemon. She told him not to think about them. Sometimes he remembered his daddy yelling. Then the plane crashing in the trees. He hurt all over and he'd tried to wake Daddy up, but he wouldn't wake up.

If he thought hard enough, he remembered that he had another name once, but he couldn't think what it was. Every day it got harder for him to catch the memories—as hard as it was for him to catch the chipmunks. They didn't like his new hair color any better than the old one.

Sam clasped his arms around himself. Maybe he could light the fire. She had said not to try, but she'd been gone a long time. She was gone when he woke yesterday, and then the fire had gone out when it got dark. He'd shivered all through the night, and he was still cold.

It would be even colder soon. The sun was going down, and the wind had started to blow hard.

The wind blew snow under the door and around the windows. Biting his lip, he slipped out of bed. He already had on his slippers, but even they hadn't helped his feet stay warm. He dragged a blanket with him and wrapped it around his shoulders. First he should use the privy. She had left a potty inside, but it was smelly and nasty. Sam's lip curled. He'd go outside.

Opening the back door, he stepped into the yard. The snow came nearly to his knees, and he struggled to get to the little shed behind the house. Sam moved quickly. He left the privy door open a little so he wouldn't be in the dark.

It was spooky to be out here alone. She always came with him and talked to him outside the door. What if a bear came and ate him? Or wolves. He'd heard the wolves howling last night, and he'd cried. She would be disappointed in him. Only babies cried, she said.

He finished and hurried back to the house. He breathed more easily when the door was shut and latched. He rewrapped the blanket around his shoulders then walked toward the stove. If he could use the privy by himself, he could do something as easy as lighting a fire.

He touched the stove. It was cold, as cold as he was, maybe colder. The lever turned easily in his hand, and he looked inside. The ashes were white, and wind whistled over him with the stove open.

He glanced at the pipe thing. What had she called it? He stood on his tiptoes and managed to turn the thing straight up and down, as she had shown him. He'd watched her start a fire a hundred times. He couldn't count to a hundred yet, but he knew it was a lot. The kindling was in a box by the door. Trailing the blanket behind him, he took a handful of the kindling with his free hand and tossed the pieces into the stove.

No, wait, that wasn't right. He had to put newspaper under it. He pulled out the kindling, piece by piece, and laid it on the floor in front of the stove. There was a box of newspaper by the bed. He took a piece, wadded it up the way she always did, and laid it in the stove. Then he piled the kindling on it. Taking a deep breath, he picked up the box of matches beside the stove.

She said never to play with matches, but this wasn't playing. If he didn't do something, he would freeze like the dead fox he'd seen last winter. He bit his lip while he opened the box of matches and took one out. Holding the box as he'd seen her do, he ran the match across that rough strip on the box. The match burst into flames, and it startled him so much he dropped it. It fell to the stone in front of the wood stove and quickly went out.

Sam took out another match. He held the box and the match at arm's length and squinted his eyes. Striking the match, he barely flinched this time when it flared. He held it to the paper in the stove. The paper flamed, and Sam grinned. He'd soon be warm, and she would be so proud of him. Crouching in front of the stove, he basked in the bit of heat radiating from the burning paper.

The dry kindling caught and began to crackle. Sam watched for a few minutes, mesmerized by the dancing flames. He held his hands in front of the fire to warm them. The fire popped and snapped, a wonderful sound to Sam. He longed for the fire to really start heating up the room.

Slowly, he fed the flames with more kindling. As long as he stayed right in front of the stove with the blanket wrapped around him, he felt warm. He knew he needed to throw some of the larger logs on the fire, but he was afraid. What if he put them in wrong and they rolled out again? All his work would be wasted.

Soon the kindling box was almost empty. Sam took the last handful and put it on the fire. He might as well try to do something now. The fire would soon be out anyway. Struggling with the weight of it, he picked up a split log. He leaned into the stove and pushed the log onto the flames with all his might.

The log seemed to turn in his hands before it hit right in the middle of the fire. The kindling scattered, and several pieces flew out the stove door. One landed on Sam's blanket. It smoldered then flared into flame. Sam screamed and turned to run.

20

$\mathcal{B}$ree curled up on the sofa and sipped her tea. Warm and content, she almost didn't answer the door when the bell rang. Samson padded to the door and waited expectantly. The bell rang again. She tossed the fleece throw off her legs and reluctantly went to the entry.

Hilary stood on the porch, huddled in a sheepskin coat. "It's freezing out here." She brushed past Bree and came inside, stomping the snow from her boots. "Mason is working late tonight, and I was bored. Want to order a pizza?"

"I just warmed up some leftover chicken enchilada casserole Martha sent over. There's plenty left. You want some?" Bree took Hilary's coat and hung it in the closet under the stairs. She ordered Samson into the living room. No sense in riling Hilary with his presence.

"Sounds good. I wouldn't turn down a cup of hot coffee either." Hilary followed her into the kitchen.

As Bree heated Hilary's meal, she wondered how she could bring up Hilary's outburst at the party. Her suspicions would nag her until she laid them to rest.

Hilary sat at the small dinette in the corner. "Mother wants to know if you'll bring some of your cranberry salad and the sweet potato casserole to Thanksgiving this year."

"I think I've still got the recipes here someplace," Bree said. Had Hilary really come by because she was bored? Under normal circumstances, Hilary would have just called to ask about Thanksgiving arrangements. Bree set the casserole in front of her sister-in-law along with a cup of coffee then sat across the table from her.

"Smells good." Hilary chased several forkfuls of food around the plate before she set her fork aside. "Mother told me you're giving up the search," she said.

Ah, the real reason for the visit. Bree steeled herself for Hilary's cajoling. "I'll search until the first of the year, then I'm going to get busy with a training school. I've found a couple of possible sites." Hilary was blinking rapidly, and Bree looked away. Tears might make her lose her resolve.

"I just came by to tell you I agree with your decision," Hilary said.

Bree wasn't sure she'd heard correctly. Wide-eyed, she stared at Hilary. "You . . . you agree?"

"Mother told me I was being selfish, and I guess I was. I've been pretty hard on you this past year. I know we've had our differences, but you'll always be my little sister."

This was a softer, more vulnerable Hilary than Bree had ever seen. "I've only ever wanted your approval," Bree said in a low voice.

"You've driven yourself to find Rob's plane, and I haven't been very appreciative. I'm sorry." Hilary smiled ruefully. "I'm not easy to live with; just ask Mason. I blow my top and say things I don't mean when I should keep my mouth shut."

The perfect opening. "Don't we all. Just like what you said about Fay the night of the party. I knew you didn't mean it."

Hilary frowned. "What did I say about Fay?"

"That you hated her, and her baby should have been yours."

Hilary waved a hand. "I was just upset about the doctor's news. You never really forget your first love, but Steve and I would have been divorced before a year was out. I need someone stable and patient like Mason. I wouldn't trade him for a dozen Steves." Her eyes darkened with pain and she looked at her casserole. "We're doing what we can to get Mason's sperm count up. We haven't given up hope yet. For a while I'd forgotten God is in control."

Bree wanted to know this Hilary better. She thought of Psalm 112. There was something in there about a righteous man being steadfast and trusting in the Lord. Hilary hadn't killed Fay. Relief washed over Bree until she felt almost giddy.

By the time Hilary left, Bree sensed a new friendship building between her and her sister-in-law, a new understanding. This family would survive the tragedy and go on. It was time to put the past away.

Davy was gone. The first step to accepting that fact would be hard. She looked toward the stairway. There was no time like the present. Leaning forward, she caressed Samson's ears. "I think maybe it's time, boy. You want to help me?"

The dog whined and got up. Stretching, he nosed her hand.

"Let's do it," she told him. Together they walked up the steps. Bree stopped at the closet at the top of the stairs and took out the empty boxes stacked inside. Her heart began to slam against her ribs. It had to be done, she told herself.

Tears pooled in her eyes, and through a blur she walked to Davy's room and pushed open the door. She would start with the toys. Kneeling beside the toy box, she packed the blocks first. Davy had loved his blocks. Together they would build towers, then he would chortle with glee and knock the blocks in all directions. She had bought him a box of Lincoln Logs for his third birthday, and he was fascinated with the various ways he could make them fit together.

Sobs spilled from her throat as the memories washed over her. She hugged a teddy bear to her chest and rocked back and forth. She couldn't do this. Maybe she should ask Naomi to do it for her. The bear still smelled faintly of baby powder and bubble-gum toothpaste.

She slowly pulled the stuffed animal away from her chest and placed it to one side. Davy's favorite stuffed animal, a koala bear he'd called Pooky, had gone down with him in the plane. She would keep this one instead. She drew in a deep breath, then another. The rest of Davy's stuffed animals went into the box. She forced herself to move forward.

Step by step, she could get this done. She opened the closet and began to pack Davy's clothing. The little suit he'd worn to Hilary's first campaign party, the sweats that matched his daddy's, the bib overalls he'd worn when they'd made mud pies.

She allowed herself to dwell on each memory. The process would be a cauterization of sorts. If she could get through this, she could get through the rest of her life.

The dresser was next. His small underclothes, socks, and T-shirts went into the box. She pulled out his Barney swim trunks and remembered the way he turned as brown as a squirrel over the course of the summer. Shouting with laughter, he would scream, "Watch me, Mommy," then plunge into the icy waves that splashed Superior's shoreline.

The cold water never seemed to bother him. Even when his lips would turn blue, he would beg to stay in the lake. Rob had called him their baby salmon, all slippery and glistening from the water. Shaking, she sat in the rocker until she could go on. The memories crashed over her with the force of a Lake Superior nor'easter. For a few moments she thought she might sink beneath those crushing waves just as the *Edmund Fitzgerald* had done.

She left the chair and went to the bed. Davy's Superman bedspread, sheets, and curtains were as he had left them. Four quick flips and the bedspread was folded and in the box. Then she stripped the sheets and tossed them into the box as well. She dragged the toy chest under the window and closed the lid. Standing on top of it, she could just reach the curtain rods. The hooks didn't want to let go any more than she did, but she finally managed to release them, and the curtains dropped to the floor.

Four boxes. Davy's young life had been reduced to four boxes. Bree stood and looked around the stripped room. Her heart felt equally stripped, and raw as well. She would ask Kade to help her move the bed to the attic. Maybe she could find a queen-size bed at the second-hand furniture shop. The room was large enough for one, and then her cousin and his wife could have a decent night's sleep when they came to visit, though that wouldn't be for some time. They were working in Saudi Arabia for the next two years.

Somehow, taking the boxes of Davy's things to the attic seemed wrong. One by one, she carried them downstairs to the kitchen. She wished she'd thought of it sooner, but she knew what to do now. She would just have to work harder to accomplish it. Her Carhartt overalls hung on a peg by the back door. She started to put them on then realized it was too dark to pick the right spot. Tomorrow she would dress warmly and dig a hole under the apple tree that held Davy's tree house. There she would bury Davy's things.

She would finally have a grave site of sorts where she could place flowers and remember her son—something better than an empty grave at the cemetery. The search was over. She would let it go now. Life wouldn't be the same without her boy, but she couldn't live in the past anymore. The future beckoned, and she was ready to face it. She would help Steve find who killed Fay. If that led to the woman in the cabin, fine. But if it didn't, she was okay with that too.

⁂

The snow slowed her progress. Rachel plodded through the drifts with the sun shining weakly through the trees. Sam would be so glad to see her, and even more glad when he heard the news. No more cold cabins for them. By this time next week, they'd be far away from here, somewhere no one could trace them. Somewhere no one could separate them.

She stopped to catch her breath and checked her watch. Nearly two o'clock. Her inner compulsion to see Sam, to make sure he was all right, drove her on. He was such a little boy, and she knew she should not have left him home alone for two days. It had turned colder than she'd expected while she was gone. Ten inches of snow covered the ground, and she wished she had her snowshoes.

Frank would declare her predicament more evidence of her poor judgment, but then he had never given her credit for anything. Necessity was a hard taskmaster. He had just intended to let Paulie go to prison. Even when she'd provided the way out, Frank still hadn't intervened for Paulie. Her nephew deserved better from his own father. Maybe when Paulie got out of prison, he would come to visit her. Surely he knew what she'd done for him.

She would even let him stay with her, once she and Sam got their own place. Or maybe they'd get a place big enough for the whole family. Smiling, she started off toward the cabin again. She made it the rest of the way in just over fifteen minutes, and the sight of the cabin warmed her. A light shone through the window, and she frowned. Sam shouldn't be wasting the kerosene that way. But maybe the lad was frightened.

She sometimes forgot just how young Sam was. He often seemed so much older than four. Those eyes of his had seen horrors no child should witness. He never spoke of his dead father, but she saw his memory in the boy's eyes. As she pushed the lever to raise the inside latch, the scent of smoke, strong and acrid, burned her nose, and her heart raced.

"Sam?" Alarm made her speak louder than she'd intended. A charred blanket lay by the wood stove. The stove door stood open and wind whistled through the cabin like through a wind tunnel.

Frantic now, she rushed forward. She heard a groan. "Sam?"

"It hurts." Sam raised his head from where he lay on the floor near the back door.

Soot covered his face and hands, and his pajamas were black with it. One sleeve had been burned, and even from here, she could see the blisters on his arm.

She rushed to kneel at his side. "Sam, what happened?" His body was chilled. She examined his arm. Second-degree burns, nothing worse. And only in one small area. There seemed to be no other damage.

She scooped him into her arms, carried him to the bed and bundled him beneath the covers, then rushed to build a fire. The kindling box was empty. Confusion churned her mind. This was the second time he'd disobeyed her in the past few days. What had happened to her sweet, obedient son? His disobedience had hurt him. She pushed away the guilt she felt for leaving him alone. He would have been fine if only he'd obeyed her. Necessity was a hard taskmaster.

She grabbed the ax by the door and quickly shaved some kindling from a split log. Within minutes she had a fire blazing, and its pleasant warmth began to creep into the room. Ignoring his pain-filled eyes on her, she washed his burns and applied a salve.

"This is what happens when you don't mind your mother," she told him.

"I tried to do it like you showed me," he murmured.

"Don't try to blame me for your misbehavior," she said. "I told you to leave the fire alone."

"I was so cold."

Rachel bristled. He didn't know what cold was. She was the one who had traipsed through the cold Chicago wind all night, and for what? To give a nice home to an ungrateful child. She trembled with the urge to punish him then reminded herself he'd already reaped the consequence of his disobedience.

"The fire jumped on me. Mommy always said to 'drop and roll,' so that's what I did."

His mommy. He hadn't mentioned her in months. "I'm your mother now," Rachel said sharply. She tossed the water out the back door then busied herself with cleaning up the mess. She could not pack with the cabin in this mess. They would be on the bus for Chicago in two days. Frank had promised to pick them up at the station.

She would give him a stern lecture about obedience tomorrow. Frank would toss them out if she couldn't keep the boy under control. If Sam didn't do what he was told, she didn't know what she would do. He had severely disappointed her. She would have to make him understand that.

When Rachel finished cleaning, she pulled on a flannel nightgown and crawled beneath the covers next to her sleeping son. There was so much to do over the next couple of days. But she would breathe easier once they were gone from this place. No one would ever find her and Sam once they reached Chicago.

❧

A distant hum woke her. From the brilliance of the morning light, she knew it had snowed overnight. She ran to the window and surveyed the blinding landscape. There was at least eighteen inches of snow on the ground. The racket increased, and she caught a glimpse of a snowmobile moving fast through the trees. The rider must be an idiot to travel so fast over this terrain, especially under such conditions.

The sound trailed away in the direction of the old copper mine. Rachel frowned. Could that have been the man she'd seen carrying the woman's body? What was he doing snooping around here? Sam was still in a deep sleep. She quietly pulled on her clothes then let herself out of the cabin.

Her snowshoes hung on a nail outside the door, along with her binoculars. She slipped the binoculars over her head then put on her snowshoes and started toward the mine. She loved the woods after a deep snow. The peace and serenity soothed her. All she could hear was the sound of her own breath whistling through her teeth as she tramped through the winter wonderland.

The sound of the snowmobile died suddenly, and she guessed from the sound that it had stopped at the mine. Hurrying as fast as she dared, she struggled through the snow until she came to the edge of a clearing. The old Copper Queen, its wooden shaft and outbuildings weathered and dilapidated, sat at the far end of the clearing. The snow had stopped falling, except for the occasional flake, and she had a good view from where she crouched.

Over the past fifty years, the forest had reclaimed much of the area, but the Copper Queen still stood tall and proud. Last summer Rachel had come here and poked around, hoping to find some relic of the grand old lady's heyday. But all she had ever picked up were old bottles and a few quartz rocks.

The rider had parked the snowmobile near the entrance of the main offices. She didn't dare leave the cover of the trees. He had to come out sooner or later. She scanned the surrounding area and detected nothing that concerned her.

Crouching on her haunches, she settled back to wait, though she knew she would have to head back if he didn't come out soon. Her stomach growled with hunger, and Sam would want breakfast when he awakened.

Rachel took a deep breath. She loved the air's sharp, cold freshness. She would miss this in Chicago. But the cabin would always be here. Maybe she and Sam could come up for an occasional visit. No, that wouldn't be a good idea. Once they were gone from here, they needed to stay gone. She and Sam would have to disappear—without a trace.

A movement caught her eye. She tried to bring the binoculars to her eyes, but the brim of her leather fedora blocked her view. She took it off and laid it beside her then focused the binoculars. A man carrying a duffle bag came out of the building. His face was turned away, and Rachel cursed.

"Turn this way," she whispered.

As if he heard her soft words, the man turned fully toward her. Through the binoculars, Rachel saw his face clearly. It was the same man, just as she had suspected. His cheeks were red with cold, and the concentration lining his face told her that whatever he carried was important. He secured the bag onto the back of the snowmobile and hopped onto the seat. The roar of the engine cut through the cold air. Then he pointed the snowmobile directly at Rachel.

Panicked, Rachel scuttled back farther into the brush. She didn't come out until the sound of the engine faded, then she scrambled to her feet and rushed toward home. She'd had no business even coming out here other than to satisfy her curiosity. It was stupid to put herself in danger like that. If he'd seen her, he might have killed her just like he killed that woman.

Hurrying into the cabin, she latched the door behind her with a relieved sigh. The sooner they were gone from here the better.

"I'm hungry." Sam's plaintive voice broke into her thoughts. "It's cold in here."

He was right. The fire had gone out while she was gone, and the chilly wind had quickly stolen the remaining warmth.

"I'll have it going again in a jiffy," she said cheerfully.

"Are you still mad at me?" Sam's woebegone face peeked over the edge of the covers.

"I'm not angry, but I'm very disappointed in you, Sam." When his face crumpled in tears, she softened her tone. "You must learn to always obey me, son. Always. I only want what's best for you."

He began to sob, and Rachel went to take him in her arms. "There, there," she soothed. "We're going to leave here in a few days, Sammy. You'll have other children to play with, and a nice house with heat that comes out of registers instead of a stove. You won't ever again have to worry about being cold."

"Never?" He hiccuped and rubbed his nose on the back of his pajama sleeve.

"Never. I promise. Won't that be fun? We'll be in a big city with lots of other people."

"What about my squirrel?"

"Well, we'll have to leave Marcus here. He wouldn't like it in the city. He wouldn't have as many trees to play in, and it would be hard for him to find nuts."

Sam screwed up his face as he thought about it, then he nodded. "Can I come back to see him sometimes?"

"We'll see if we can find you a new squirrel in Chicago. And we can walk along the lakeshore and feed the ducks. That will be fun." She kissed him on the forehead. "Now let's take a look at your burns this morning. How are you feeling?"

"My arm stings. Can I have Captain Crunch?"

"We're all out of Captain Crunch, but I have Cheerios." She ran her finger over Sam's burns, and he flinched. Pressing her lips together, she went to fix his breakfast.

After breakfast she tackled the laundry. She heated water on the stove and dumped it in the washtub. She propped up the washboard in the tub and rubbed the clothes against it vigorously. As she worked, Rachel imagined the life they would have in Chicago. Never again would she be alone; she would always have Sam, and he would always love her. No one had ever really loved her, not even Frank. But someday Sam would thank her for saving his life, for putting him through school. He would show his gratitude by taking care of her when she got too old to take care of herself.

School. She would have to get a forged birth certificate and immunization records. Then she could get Sam to a doctor for the shots he needed to go to kindergarten. It would all work out.

Draping the wet clothes on a retractable line across the cabin, she finished the laundry as quickly as possible. They needed more wood. She went to the door and took down her coat. Where was her hat? Her heart dipped. She'd lost it, probably at the mine. She had to have her hat.

She got Sam dressed. "How would you like to play a game, Sammy?"

His head bobbed up and down. "What kind of game?"

"A spy game."

"What's a spy?" His tongue poked out as he worked at tying his shoes.

"Someone who watches what is going on and reports back to headquarters. You be the spy, and you can report to me."

"That sounds fun!" He jumped to his feet.

"Get your snowshoes on," she told him.

He stopped at the door. "I don't like the snowshoes. I want to play in the snow without them."

More disobedience? This was getting to be a habit, and one she intended to break. "Don't argue with me. Get your snowshoes on."

Sam's lower lip thrust out, and he shook his head. "I don't want to."

Rage boiled over, and Rachel grabbed him roughly by the arm. Too late she realized it was his injured arm, and he cried out. "It's your own fault," she said. "Now get outside and get your snowshoes on like I told you."

Sobbing and holding his arm, Sam did as she said. She didn't know what had gotten into him. If he kept causing her this much trouble, what would she do? This must be what all the magazines meant when they talked about children becoming rebellious. What would it take to break Sam of that streak?

Sam slowly strapped on his snowshoes then stood and waited while she put hers on.

"Let's go," she said curtly.

It was slow going with Sam. Rachel was beginning to wish she'd left him home, but she needed him to keep watch for her. They finally reached the mine. She paused and listened but heard nothing.

"Follow me," she told Sam. She led the way across the clearing to the building where she'd seen the man. "I want you to stand guard here. Your job as a spy is to listen for any people or snowmobiles," she said. "If you hear anything, just yell for me, okay?"

He nodded. "Okay. But hurry. I'm scared."

He was always scared. When she got him to Chicago, she'd have a doctor look at him. She patted him on the head, turned on her flashlight, and went down into the shaft building. An hour later she was dirty and tired but no wiser. It was going to take someone smarter than she was to figure out what that man had been doing there.

When she exited the mine, she saw a man standing with Sam. The boy was crying and trying to get away from him. Did Sam know him? There seemed to be a frightened recognition on his face. She looked around for a weapon and grabbed a chair leg from a pile of rubble. Creeping forward, the snow crunched beneath Rachel's boots and the man turned to face her. The breath left her lungs when she saw the gun in his hand.

"I'd put that down if I were you," he said casually. A sock hat covered his hair, and the rest of his form was buried in a thick coat. He held up her fedora. "You were here before, weren't you? What did you see?"

She let the chair leg drop from her fingers. "Nothing. You with a duffel bag, that's all. Let go of my boy." She hadn't heard his snowmobile.

"I want you to keep your mouth shut about what you saw."

"I don't know who you are anyway."

"You could point me out. But now that I've seen the boy, I know you don't want to draw attention to yourself."

"What do you mean? Please, let go of my son," she whispered.

The man grinned and released Sam. "Go to your *mother*, boy."

He knew she wasn't Sam's mother. Her fear ratcheted up a notch. Sam limped toward her, and she grabbed his good arm and dragged him close to her side. "I'm not saying anything." Sam clung to her tightly.

"Good. Because I know someone who would be very interested in finding the boy. Someone who has been looking for him. You obviously know where the plane is. You're going to take me there. Let's get going."

She balked. She had to come up with a plan. "It's too far in the snow."

"My snowmobile is over there." He motioned to a dip in the terrain in a stand of aspen. "Move."

"The boy is tired," she protested. "Come tomorrow, and we can go while he's having his nap."

"I've been looking for it for a year. I don't intend to wait."

She had no choice but to follow him across the snowy ground. He got on the snowmobile and motioned for her and Sam to get on behind him. There would be room for the three of them; the man was slim and Sam was small. Sam began to whimper.

"Hush," Rachel said sternly. She had to think.

The man turned the key to start the snowmobile, but all it did was click. He muttered an oath under his breath and tried again, but the engine still refused to start.

"Get off," he growled. "I'll have to walk back. I'll be over to see you tomorrow. You'd better be there, or you'll be sorry."

Her tongue wanted to form words of defiance, but all Rachel managed to do was nod. She wished she had his gun. She wouldn't hesitate to use it. No one was going to take her boy. It was only after she was home again that she realized her fedora was still at the mine.

This time it could stay there.

21

$\mathcal{B}$ree checked her watch. Nearly one. The heavy snow prevented her from burying Davy's belongings, and she had nothing else pressing to do today. She had been meaning to get out to the mine, and there was no time like the present. With her snowshoes, the snow cover was no problem. She put Samson in his search vest then gathered her ready-pack. She stuffed Fay's diary into the backpack and headed out. Though she'd been reading the diary carefully from back to front, Fay's minuscule writing made for slow reading, and so far she'd found nothing but Fay's selfish musings about her empty life. Steve wanted it back today.

Bree drove up Houghton Street and saw Naomi walking down the street with Charley. Bree stopped the Jeep and rolled down the window. "Hey, I'm heading out to take a look at that old mine. You want to come?" Charley barked, and Bree grinned. "I think he answered for you. You're not busy, are you?"

"Not unless you count avoiding my mother's questions," Naomi said. She put Charley in the back with Samson and climbed in.

Bree stopped at the bank and grabbed the diary out of her backpack. "I'll be right back," she told Naomi. She walked back to Steve's office and handed it to him. "I'd like to look at it again as soon as possible, Steve."

He nodded. "I'll glance through it as quick as I can. I just have to protect myself. I hope you understand."

She nodded. "I'd better go. Naomi and I are going out to check the mine."

His head jerked up. "I might join you after I finish here."

"I can use all the help I can get." It was about time Steve started taking a more active role. She left him and hurried outside.

"What's your mom have to say about you seeing Donovan?" Bree asked Naomi when she got back into the Jeep.

"I may have to move out." Naomi grinned to show she wasn't serious.

"That bad?"

"Terrible. I never should have told her I was interested in Donovan." Naomi put her head in her hands and rocked it from side to side in a mock expression of pain then leaned her head back against the seat. "She wants to invite Donovan and the kids over for supper. Now I ask you, Bree, doesn't she get it that things haven't gone that far? We're just friends exploring where it might lead."

"Has Donovan said that?"

"Well, sort of. He asked me if I'd ever wondered what might have happened if we'd dated in high school."

"You deserve someone really wonderful, Naomi. I hope Donovan is the one." And though she didn't say it, Bree hoped Naomi's marriage—if it got that far—would turn out better than Bree's own. But that wasn't fair. The early days had been happy, and maybe they would have been again. She would never know.

"What are you thinking about? You have a strange look on your face," Naomi said. "You've been different lately. Even Mom remarked on it."

"Different how?"

"I don't know exactly. Maybe more at peace with yourself—or maybe it's just resignation. I can't tell."

At peace with herself. That sounded good if she could make it a reality. "I'm trying, Naomi. I think one day soon I'll be able to go forward and not be stuck in the reruns of my life. The memories will still be there, but they won't consume me like they used to." She gave a self-conscious laugh. "I packed up Davy's things last night. I thought I'd make a guest room."

"Oh, Bree, that's wonderful!"

Bree blinked and glanced at her friend before turning her attention back to the road. "You approve? I thought you'd be horrified and wonder what kind of mother I am."

"I've worried about you turning Davy's room into a shrine. You'll always love Davy. We both know you'll always mourn him. But it's time, Bree."

Bree parked the Jeep by the highway. The road back to the mine was too snow-covered to see the dangerous potholes and tree stumps, so it would be safest to walk in.

"What are we looking for?" Naomi asked as they got out and allowed the dogs to race on ahead. They could wander until it was time to go home.

"I'm not really sure. A lot of details about Fay's death seem to lead back to this mine. Maybe it's coincidence, but I want to be sure."

"You mean you wonder if someone killed her for money?"

"It's possible." Bree ticked the suspects off on her glove-covered fingers. "Her uncle wanted her to sell to the New York conglomerate so he could get more money than what Palmer was willing to pay. He might have killed her to stop the sale. Of course, Steve nixed that idea, but Lawrence couldn't have known that ahead of time."

Naomi wrinkled her nose. "This is getting too scary for me, Bree. You need to let Mason handle it. New York conglomerates, big insurance policies, huge debts, and a boyfriend just out of jail. It's all too horrible."

They reached the mine, and Bree pointed to the ground. "Looks like someone's been here recently. I wonder if it's all related to the sale?"

Numerous footprints had tamped down the snow all across the clearing. Bree walked toward the main building. "Let's check the main shaft."

"Talk about stumbling around in the dark," Naomi grumbled. "We have no idea what we're looking for."

"Something worth killing for," Bree said. Darkness yawned through the mine shaft building's open door, which was attached by only one rusted hinge.

Bree didn't really want to go in, but she was done with fear. Fear had kept her silent when she should have talked to Rob about where their marriage was headed from the moment he grew distant; fear kept her from speaking her mind and being herself; fear of the future trapped her in the past. In all the ways that really mattered, she'd been a coward, and it shamed her. But no more.

She fumbled in her backpack for glow sticks and handed one to Naomi. Together they broke the sticks, and an eerie green light forced back the blanket of darkness. Bree immediately felt better. Naomi followed as they pushed deeper into the shaft building.

A giant steam hoist rose in front of them like some ravenous prehistoric beast. Bree had heard the hoist could lift eight tons of copper ore. Naomi uttered a tiny scream then gave a shaky laugh. "It looks like it wants to eat someone," she said in a hushed whisper.

"We could offer it Eric Matthews," Bree said. When they both laughed, she felt better. This wasn't so bad. She could do this.

Stepping over paper, discarded crates, and piles of rock, they walked farther into the shaft. They came to a split in the hall. Bree looked down each branch as far as she could see.

"You go left, and I'll go right," she told Naomi.

"I think we should stay together," Naomi said. "What if part of this old mine falls on one of us?"

"It seems sturdy enough. It will take us forever to search if we don't split up." The sooner they finished this job, the sooner they could get out of this dank place. The stale air in here made her think of tombs and graveyards, a macabre thought that brought a surge of panic. She swallowed her fear and turned to the right.

"I don't like this," Naomi called as she headed down the other hall.

It might not be the smartest thing to go alone without the dogs, but it would take too long to round them up. Besides, the walkway only went down. A damp chill radiated from the yawning hole, and she didn't want to enter it, but Bree forced herself to go on. She would never find the answer to Fay's murder if she didn't find some courage.

Down, down she went, the dim light of the glow stick lighting the way. The darkness seemed a living thing that teased her beyond the reach of her stick's feeble light. When she couldn't stand it anymore, she grabbed her flashlight and flipped it on. The bright white light pushed back the shadows, and she caught her breath again.

Several kerosene lanterns lined the shelves along the way. Maybe there was fuel in one of them. She looked closer and saw they were all full of kerosene. Evidently the fuel wasn't worth hauling out of here— lucky for her. Fumbling in her pack, she pulled out a box of matches and lit one of the lanterns. Holding the lantern high, she resumed her descent.

She came to a split. So much for there being no way to get lost. She'd just have to remember which way she chose. Chewing her lip, Bree saw a track running along the ground to the left. She'd follow it. If she didn't find anything in fifteen minutes, she would go back. She set the stopwatch function on her watch. She walked for what seemed like forever, but when she checked the time, only five minutes had passed. She looked up. A barrier stood in her way, and she stopped. It was a huge door that stood partway open to a room carved out of stone. Maybe it was an office or something.

She walked inside and stumbled over the rock that held the door open. The rock shifted, and the door slammed shut. With a cry, she flew to the door and grabbed at the handle. It wouldn't budge. Placing the lantern on the floor, she twisted the knob with both hands, but it didn't turn at all. She began pounding on the door.

Bree shouted until she was hoarse then looked at her watch just as the fifteen-minute alarm went off. Full-blown panic loomed at the edge of her mind, but she fought it. She reminded herself she was a professional. The key was not to panic. Naomi would get the dogs, and Samson would find her.

The darkness pressed in on her, and she grabbed the lantern and held it high. The room seemed to be a makeshift office of some kind. An old desk sat in one corner, its metal drawer rusting from the damp. Several equally rusty filing cabinets stood against the other wall. Several filthy blankets were heaped on the floor in one corner, evidently the haven of some homeless person in the dim past.

The touches of humanity in the room calmed Bree's rising terror. Sucking in several deep breaths, she found her cell phone and tried to dial. No signal. She put it away slowly. All she could do was be calm and wait. Easier said than done.

Setting the lamp on the desk, she pulled out the office chair and grabbed an old rag to wipe it down. After examining it for bugs and spiders, she eased into it. Though her heart still throbbed with trepidation, she no longer felt as though she might begin to scream uncontrollably. What could she do to keep her mind off her predicament?

The desk beside her held six drawers. The metal shrieked when she opened the first. She poked gingerly at the contents: rusty paper clips, pencils, a chalkboard eraser, an assortment of yellowed labels. The next drawer held papers, and she pulled them into the light. The crabbed handwriting was hard to read, but Bree soon got the hang of it.

Ledger sheets documented measurements of ore and sales to smelting companies. A letter dated May 1965 to a person named Wilson Cutter in Detroit caught her eye. According to the letter, a new vein of ore had been discovered at the Copper Queen. Gold. But the mine closed in July of 1965. Bree frowned. Had it been a false alarm, or had this letter never been sent? Maybe someone had found out about the gold in the mine.

Another paper, folded in half, fluttered to the floor. She grabbed it, but before she could open it, a clank sounded outside the door. Stuffing the paper into her pocket, she sprang forward and began pounding. "I'm in here!" she shouted.

Moments later she heard Samson's whine. He began to bark, then the deeper tones of a man's voice reverberated through the door.

"We're here, Bree; I'll get you out," Kade shouted through the door. "The door's locked, but I have a crowbar. Naomi, over here! I've found her."

Metal screeched against metal as Kade pried the hinges loose. "Stand back," he called.

Bree stood away from the door, and it crashed inward. Dust flew into her face, and she coughed as she stumbled into Kade's arms. Samson barked joyously then leaped onto her leg. She patted his head then leaned against Kade's chest.

He hugged her tightly, and she burrowed into his strong embrace, just as she'd longed to do before. It was just as she'd imagined. With his arms tight around her, she felt safe and protected.

He spoke into her hair. "What were you thinking, prowling around down here all alone?"

She finally pulled away and slanted a grin into his face. "A good investigator goes where the clues are."

He grinned back. "A good investigator doesn't get lost."

"Bree!" Naomi's shout echoed down the cavernous hall, and the dim glow of her light stick grew brighter. Charley raced ahead of his owner and jumped on Bree in an ecstatic show of relief. Moments later Naomi rushed out of the darkness and grabbed Bree in a tight clutch.

Both women burst into tears.

Kade looked at Samson and sighed. "Don't try to understand it, boy."

The women giggled and wiped their tears before trooping out of the dark mine into the clearing. Bree stepped into the open air and stretched her arms to the sky. "I wasn't sure I'd ever see the sun again." It had started snowing, and the fresh cold air smelled wonderful after the staleness of the mine.

Kade rubbed Samson's curly coat. "With this dog, I don't think you'd ever have to worry about being lost. He would always find you."

Bree knelt and threw her arms around Samson's neck. "And I never even thanked you, Samson." He whined eagerly and licked her on the chin. She buried her face in his fur and hugged him again, then stood. Laughing, they struggled through the snow and toward their vehicles. Samson moseyed off into the woods. After a few minutes, he began to bark.

"What is it, boy?" Bree called. She left Kade's side and hurried to where the dog stood in a stand of white pine. Samson poked his head out of a thicket. He had something in his mouth. Bree bent over and took it from him.

"Find anything?" Naomi called.

Bree turned and held up something brown. "It's a hat," she said.

Naomi frowned. "Let me see." She joined Bree and took the hat. "A floppy brown leather hat," she murmured.

"What's so special about that?" Kade asked.

"Remember the O'Reilly kids and their witch? They said she wore a floppy brown leather hat. And Mason said the same thing."

Kade slapped his head. "I've been so caught up with the way Lauri—I forgot until just now! I saw her!"

"Where?" Bree grabbed his arm.

"Out by Rock River on Sunday."

"Let's see what Samson can find out." She held the hat under Samson's nose. "Samson, search!"

The dog sniffed the hat then turned and ran off into the woods. Naomi had Charley sniff it as well and sent him out. The threesome followed, but it became clear after a few minutes that the dogs didn't have a scent. Bree and Naomi called them back and headed toward the car with Kade. Bree managed to hide her disappointment. She didn't want Kade to feel worse than he already did.

"Are we done here?" he asked.

"I guess so. Hey, you never told me what you were doing here."

"I was answering a call about a deer hit by a car out this way and saw your Jeep," he said. "I thought I'd see what was going on. When I got to the mine, I heard Naomi shouting your name, and I knew something was wrong. We called the dogs and started looking for you. I was afraid you'd gotten stuck somewhere—or worse."

She turned to check on the dogs and found Samson at the edge of the forest. He was whining and his tail was tucked between his legs. "What's wrong, boy?" She walked over to where he sat. Kade followed.

The dog seemed distressed, his brown eyes almost speaking to them in misery. Kade patted his head. "What's wrong with him?"

"He's acting like he does when he gets a death scent," Bree said. She glanced around. "I don't see anything though."

The wind had blown the snow off a pile of rocks nearby, and Kade caught a flash of red-black. "What's that?" He knelt and brushed more snow away. A reddish stain covered one of the rocks, and spatters of the same substance dotted several others. "It looks like blood."

"Blood?"

"You tell me. Would Samson give a death alert on an animal's blood?"

Bree shook her head and stared at him. "What if it's Fay's blood?"

"That can't be right," Naomi said. "Unless . . ."

"Unless she was killed here and moved to the other site. He got her out of the car by the road, laid her on the ground for a minute, then hauled her to the cliff bottom," Bree said.

"Let's get Mason," Naomi said.

Bree called Mason on her cell phone. "He's on his way," she told them. Bree and Naomi let the dogs continue to search while they waited for the sheriff.

❧

Mason and Deputy Montgomery finally showed up and had barely had time to take samples of the bloodstains when they got a call about a hunting accident. Mason promised to call when he had news.

"Let's go to your place," Naomi said when the sheriff pulled away. "The snow is really coming down, and we don't want to get stuck out here."

Bree drove slowly back to town, with Kade following in his truck. The wind blew the snow in gusts across the road, and she strained to see through the whiteout. When they got to her lighthouse, she made some coffee then paced the kitchen, wishing Mason would call.

"Quit pacing," Kade ordered. "Let's think of something to do to keep us occupied."

All three were silent for a moment.

"We could get that light going in the tower," Kade offered.

"She's been working on it," Naomi said. "She won't ask for help."

"What needs to be done? I'm pretty handy with a hammer." He flexed his muscles and the women laughed.

"A Fresnel lens needs to be installed. It's bulky and heavy though. Rob sent the original one out for repair. It came back about a week before he died and has been in the garage ever since."

"What are we waiting for? I'm going to get it." Naomi headed for the back door.

Bree found the expression on Kade's face unsettling. A softness eased around his mouth and eyes that made her mouth go dry. "Do I have dirt on my nose?" she asked him.

"Sorry. I was staring, wasn't I?" He stood. "Let's get that light installed."

Bree took Kade to the garage and pointed out the Fresnel lens tucked in the corner under the wooden worktable. He dragged it out.

"Don't you need permission to light these towers over the harbor?" he asked as the three of them maneuvered it into the house.

"Rob applied for a permit as soon as the lens arrived," Bree explained. "It's been sitting on my desk for months."

Kade nodded. They paused in the kitchen for a rest.

"I hope you're planning to feed us after this," he said, wiping his forehead. He eyed the stairs warily.

"Um, you don't know what you're asking," Naomi said, laughing. "Unless you like frozen pizza or popcorn."

"I've eaten my share of frozen pizza," Kade said.

Bree's cheeks grew hot. "I can cook more than frozen pizza." She grinned weakly. "But I think that might be all that's in the freezer." She really had to do something about eating better.

"I knew it," Naomi said, gloating.

"Now let's hook this baby up." Kade patted the lens.

They had to stop and rest several times, but they finally managed to get the lens to the light tower. The women left Kade to do his job and went to the living room.

Naomi dug her book out of her backpack. "I think I'll read awhile and unwind. I'm at a really exciting part."

Naomi's comment reminded Bree of the paper she'd found at the mine office. She stuck her hand into her pocket and pulled it out. Unfolding it, she read the top: "'The Hound of Heaven,' by Francis Thompson." Mathilda had said something about a hound of heaven the day they'd been at the animal shelter. Curious, Bree began to read.

The language was hard to follow at first, but then the literature studies she'd done in college kicked in and she read on more smoothly. As the poem talked about the "Hound of Heaven" stripping away all to leave nothing but God, something tugged at Bree's heart. Was that what he'd been doing to her?

"Look at this, Naomi," she said, holding out the yellowed paper.

"What is it?" Naomi took the paper. "Where did you get this?"

"At the mine."

Naomi frowned. "How strange. Of course it *is* a poem from the eighteen hundreds. Maybe someone else felt God's pursuit."

"You sound like you believe he does that—pursue. Did you understand the poem?" Bree looked down at the words again.

"It's an allegory about how God pursues us to bring us to himself. He is who you need, Bree. Can't you see how he's been chasing you, caring for you? Samson and Charley are driven to find lost hunters and kids; God is driven to pursue you. He saved you from the fall from the tower. Kade *just happened* to be out by the mine today, and I never could have gotten that door open without him."

"A coincidence," Bree said, turning away, though a part of her longed to know it as something else.

Naomi gently persisted. "Anu says coincidence is a nonbeliever's way of explaining God's hand at work. Can't you see God's providential hand in your life?"

God's hand in your life. The words penetrated Bree's heart, and she saw the truth. *I am He Whom thou seekest,* the poem said. It was God she needed. A heavenly Father who truly loved her and cared for her soul.

She put her hands to her cheeks. "You're right, Naomi. I'm tired of running. I want what you have, what Anu has."

Naomi prayed with her, and when Bree raised her head, the colors of the world had shifted as though she'd stepped out of a black-and-white TV into a cinematic event. There were no clanging bells, no singing birds, but she felt the whisper of another presence. Her Hound of Heaven had found her, and she was his. "Thank you, God," she whispered. "Thank you."

22

*T*he next morning Bree hummed as she rummaged through the cabinets for something edible. Even the sight of Davy's boxes failed to dampen her spirits. There would be time enough to bury them. She felt certain she would see Davy again someday, and that joy eased her sadness.

Too excited to eat cold cereal for breakfast, she decided to go to Nicholls's for coffee and cinnamon rolls. She wanted to see Anu's face when she heard the good news. Kade had been overjoyed last night and had insisted on making a fancy dinner to celebrate her decision. He'd gone to the store and brought back enough supplies to feed an army. He'd made beef stroganoff fit for a king.

She grabbed her coat and the book Naomi had left behind. She could drop the book off on her way home from the store. Though it was only seven, she knew Anu would be there by now. Bree and Samson trudged down Negaunee and onto Houghton Street through the snowdrifts. She used her key to let herself in. The aroma of yeast and cinnamon was enticing.

"I hope you have enough for me," she called out as she walked toward the back of the store.

"Bree, I wasn't expecting you. You're up early." Anu hugged her, leaving a smudge of flour on Bree's jeans. "Oh, dear, I'm sorry."

Bree brushed at the flour. "It's coming off, don't worry. Those smell wonderful. Can I have one?"

"Of course. Coffee is on too." Anu's gaze was sharp as she took in the smile on Bree's face. "You look different this morning, *kulta*. Has something happened? You've found a place for your new business perhaps?"

"Better." Bree poured a cup of coffee and took a cinnamon bun from the pan. Licking the icing, the grin spread on her face, and she giggled.

"You look positively giddy," Anu said. "What is it?"

"I'm a Christian," Bree said simply. "I'll see Davy again, and Rob." The burden of her pain and disillusionment over Rob's betrayal was gone now too, she realized. It no longer crushed the life from her.

Anu cried out and rushed to hug her. Bree set her breakfast on the table and embraced her mother-in-law. Anu held her at arm's length. "Now you are truly my daughter in all ways," she said. "Remember this moment, *kulta*, this first love for God. Holding to it will see you through the storms life brings."

"There are more?" Bree asked with a smile.

Anu wanted to hear all about Bree's journey toward God, so they sat at the table and drank their coffee while Bree explained the events of the past few weeks.

"Have you talked to Mason or Hilary?" Bree asked finally. "Did you hear what I found at the mine yesterday?"

Anu shook her head. "I had a church meeting last night, so I didn't get home until after ten."

Bree told her about the blood.

"The mine is so familiar." Anu pursed her lips. "So familiar. My husband Abe worked at the mine the year before it closed down. As the accountant, he was good friends with Matthew Kukkan, Fay's grandfather. There was some talk of looking for gold at the mine. Silly, eh? My Abe told them even if there was gold, it would be too expensive to extract from the copper ore."

Bree gave a frustrated sigh. "But we still don't know if the murder had anything to do with the mine or if Fay was killed in a jealous rage by one of the three men."

"And what of the woman who might know where my Rob's plane crashed? Any news of her?"

"We found her hat out by the mine yesterday, but the dogs couldn't pick up her scent." Bree was still thinking of the gold. "I wonder if it would be more feasible to extract the gold now?"

"You must ask Mason. Not that it matters now," Anu said. "I don't know why I even mentioned they'd thought to look. Nothing ever came of it."

"I think I'll stop by his office now." Bree rose and bent to kiss Anu's cheek. "Thank you for being such a good example for me to follow," she whispered.

Anu touched her cheek. "Now you must carry the light, my Bree. Remember the psalm: 'Even in darkness, light dawns for the upright.' That is you now. Let your light shine here in Rock Harbor."

"I'll try." Buoyant, Bree called Samson, and they went out into the snow again. Mason wasn't at the office, but Montgomery said he'd be back around 8:30. She had time to drop off Naomi's book.

Bree rang the doorbell at the Blue Bonnet then tried the door. Martha or Naomi had already unlocked it, so she stepped inside. "It's just me," she called.

Martha bustled down the hall, a voluminous chef's apron tied around her rose-colored dress. "Bree, dear, you're just in time for breakfast."

"That's what I was hoping for," she said. "I had a *pulla* and coffee with Anu, but I'm still hungry."

Martha laughed, and her cheeks turned pink. "You can join Naomi in the dining room. We don't have any guests until tomorrow, so it's just us."

"Even better." Bree went through the parlor to the dining room. "Hey, girlfriend, you left your book at my house last night. Again."

"I knew I did when I tried to find it last night." Naomi took the book with a shamefaced laugh.

"You need to carry your books on a string around your neck." Bree smiled and sat beside her friend.

Martha wanted to hear all about Bree's newfound faith. When they were done, Bree went to call Mason, but the phone rang before she could dial.

"I'll get it," she called. "Blue Bonnet," she answered.

"Naomi?" a deep voice asked.

Bree recognized Donovan. "Hello, Donovan. This is Bree."

"I wonder if you could ask Naomi to come over right away?" Donovan sounded distraught.

"What's wrong?" she asked sharply.

"A contractor has a bad water leak and needs supplies right away. I need to hurry in and open the store. I was hoping Naomi could watch the kids for a few minutes until the bus comes."

"We'll be right there," she assured him. She rushed to the kitchen to get Naomi.

Five minutes later they were running up the walk to the O'Reilly house. Donovan met them at the door. He thanked them quickly as he ran out. Just as Bree and Naomi went to find the kids, a wail came from the end of the hallway.

"Timmy's locked in the bathroom!" Emily threw herself into Naomi's arms. Bree was glad to see a bond seemed to be developing there.

"We'll get him out quickly," Naomi said, running a hand over Emily's hair. "Does your daddy have a screwdriver somewhere?"

She nodded and ran to get one.

Bree took the screwdriver and stuck it in the lock. "Call Kade in case I can't get this open," she told Naomi.

Naomi carried Emily with her and went to the living room, where Bree heard her call Kade and ask him to come over. Bree spoke soothingly to Timmy on the other side of the door as she worked on the lock. Jiggling and twisting the screwdriver, she finally heard a click.

"I think I've got it!" She turned the knob, and the door opened. Timmy fell into her arms. She picked him up, and he wrapped his legs around her. The feel of his small body brought a lump to her throat.

She and Naomi soothed the children then began to help them get ready for school. Ten minutes later the front door banged, and Kade's voice called from the entryway, "Everything okay?"

Still carrying Timmy, Bree went to join Kade. "Got him. He's okay, just shook up." She smoothed the hair back from his face and pressed her lips to his forehead. "Ready to get down?"

He nodded, and she put him down. "I want Pooky," he said.

Bree froze. Her chest felt so tight she could barely breathe. "Pooky?" she finally choked out.

Timmy went to the couch and rummaged under a blanket. He turned triumphantly and held out a small, brown koala bear. "Pooky," he said.

Time rolled backward like a riptide. Bree swallowed hard.

"Timmy, *no!*" Emily said. "You're not supposed to tell. The witch of the woods will come back and hurt us. Remember how mad she got at Sam?"

The witch of the woods again, but who was Sam? Bree held out her hand. "Can . . . can I see Pooky a minute?" she asked. She was dimly aware of Naomi joining them in the living room. Keeping her eyes on the bear, she managed to walk forward on legs that felt no stronger than spaghetti. Davy's bear was like a part of him. She'd longed to find it.

Her hands shook as she reached out to take the stuffed animal. There must be hundreds of these little bears around, she told herself. But a tingle went up her arm when she touched the bear and saw the Barney swim trunks it wore. There was a raspberry stain on the right leg over Barney's face from when Davy had helped her pick enough berries to make a cobbler. Closing her eyes, she clutched Pooky to her chest.

"Oh, dear God, help us," Naomi prayed in a hoarse whisper. "I've been here several times and never seen it."

"We hided it," Emily whispered. "We didn't want her to get mad."

Slowly, so slowly, Bree eased down onto the couch. She heard her voice as if from a great distance. "Timmy, where did you get this?"

"Sam gave it to me."

"Who's Sam?"

"We told you!" Emily said impatiently. "He belongs to the witch of the woods. He's her little boy. He gave it to Timmy when he was sick, but then Timmy dropped it. When Sam visited us last week, he said he'd found it and still wanted Timmy to have it. We weren't supposed to tell anyone."

Bree was trembling as if she were weak from the flu. She was afraid to breathe, afraid she would wake up. A little boy in the woods with a woman who seemed bent on avoiding people. And now Davy's favorite toy. What did it all mean? Logic said the woman had found the plane and given Davy's things to her little boy, which was what she'd assumed about the glove. But what if it was more than that? Was it possible? She was afraid to breathe, afraid to really look at it clearly.

She pulled Emily to her. "This is very important, Emily. What did he look like?"

"Don't jump to conclusions, Bree," Naomi said. "The woman gave it to her son."

"What's going on?" Kade asked.

Bree blinked and stared up at him. "This belonged to Davy," she whispered. "It's his favorite toy. I'm sure he had it with him when the plane went down."

Kade's eyes widened. He knelt beside the children. "We need to find this witch of the woods, kids. Can you remember anything about where her cabin was?"

The urgency got through to the kids, for they grew sober with eyes as round as sand dollars. Emily looked as though she might cry. "It was dark, and we were lost," she said.

"I know; I know," Kade said, patting her on the shoulder.

Bree suddenly remembered the hat. "Kade, would you get my ready-pack out of the Jeep?"

Recognition at what she wanted with the pack came into his eyes, and he nodded as he went quickly to the door. He returned moments later with the pack in his hand. Bree took the pack and unzipped it. She pulled out the hat.

"Hey, that's her hat!" Timmy said.

So the witch and the woman Fay saw were one and the same. "What did Sam look like?" she whispered.

"He was little like Timmy," Emily said. "And he had dark brown hair."

Brown hair. Her stomach plummeted. Davy's was red like hers.

"What about his eyes?" Naomi asked.

"Green!" Timmy announced triumphantly. "Like my marble."

"Like Bree's?" Naomi asked.

Emily tipped her head to one side and stared at Bree. "Yes, just like yours," she said. "And he had freckles like yours too."

"And he limped," Emily added.

Bree stared at Naomi. "Is it possible?" she whispered.

"I'm afraid to hope," Naomi said quietly.

He couldn't be alive, could he? This was surely just some other child who'd been given things from the wreckage of the plane. Bree's heart warmed from the tiny hope that flickered there.

"We're going to be late for school," Emily said in a small voice. "We missed the bus."

"Show me where you saw the woman," Bree said to Kade, jumping to her feet. "We'll drop the kids off at school then go out to where you saw the woman." She wasn't sure she could drive, she was shaking so hard. "Can you drive?" she asked Naomi. She nodded and took the keys.

Naomi got the kids into their coats. On wobbly legs, Bree walked to the Jeep and got in on the passenger side. Naomi buckled the children into the backseat then got behind the wheel. Kade put the dogs in the rear compartment before he climbed into the backseat.

"Pray hard," Naomi said, slipping the Jeep into gear.

Bree nodded. She'd started pleading with God as soon as she realized this might not be a dream. Thankfulness welled up in her. The sense of God's presence was a comfort she'd never expected.

The discard pile by the door had grown larger. Rachel knew she could only take what she and Sam could carry. She had no time or money to make another trip out here. They would buy what they needed in Chicago once she started earning some money. They had to get out of here before that man came back. He frightened her, and Sam had cried for hours when they'd gotten back to the cabin. He'd clearly recognized the man.

The pitiful stack of things they would take lay on the bare mattress. "You ready to get packed up, Sammy?"

He nodded. "Why can't I take my books?"

"They're too heavy, son. You've read them all anyway. I'll buy new ones you haven't read yet when we get to our new home."

"Can I take *The Little Engine That Could*? It's not heavy."

He'd read that book so many times the copy was dog-eared and grimy. But he was right; it was light. "I suppose. If there's room."

"There's room." He scampered to the bed and began to pack his small backpack.

He owned little. Just the bare necessities she'd managed to buy.

Three pairs of pants and shirts, four sets of underwear and socks, and the coat he would wear out of here. Rachel resolved once again to do better by him once they were in Chicago. She joined him at the bed and packed her own meager possessions.

She was frantic to get away. The cabin seemed almost claustrophobic to her today. What if the man came back before they were gone? What did he want with Sam's plane? Outside, the sun shone brightly on the snow and nearly blinded her. Inside, it was dark and confining. They would leave this place behind and never look back.

The past was just that—the past. The future beckoned as brightly as the snow. Maybe she should change her name. And once she got some money stashed away, they could leave Chicago and go where there was no chance of ever running into that man.

She and Sam would be new creatures, born this day into a world of possibilities. The dreams she held for Sam were grand; she knew that. But possible. Anything was possible today. They just had to get out of here.

Sam finished packing his backpack. "I'm ready," he said. "Are we going to eat first?"

"Are you hungry already? It's only nine o'clock."

"A little." He looked shamefaced.

"How about some beef jerky to gnaw on?"

He nodded eagerly.

She got him some jerky. "Think you can eat it while we walk? It will take several hours to walk to Ontonagon."

Sam nodded. "I can walk."

"Okay." She opened the door and grabbed their snowshoes from the hook outside. "Let's get these on."

Once they were ready, she shut the door behind them and left it unlocked. Let some other needy person find a haven here as she and Sam had done. It had served them well, but it was time to move on.

"Wait, I forgot my yo-yo!" Sam struggled through the snow back to the house and disappeared inside. He reappeared moments later with his yo-yo clutched in his hand. "Emily gave it to me."

"Well, put it in your pocket, and let's get going. Say good-bye, Sam. We're off to a new life."

"Bye, Marcus," Sam called to his squirrel. Marcus chattered from his tree and watched as they walked across the clearing.

Rachel turned for one last look. It was done. No one would ever find them now.

23

$\mathcal{B}$ree's chest was tight with a mixture of hope and disbelief as they neared town. Her goal was so close. Naomi turned off on Summit and stopped in front of the school. Kade helped Emily and Timmy out of the Jeep and walked them through the school doors. The preschool teacher took charge of Timmy, and Emily went on to her class. When Kade returned, they drove down Houghton Street, intent on getting to the forest. As they passed the bank, a figure stepped into the snow-covered street to flag them down. Steve's face was red with the cold, but he wore an excited grin. He waved Fay's diary in his hand. Naomi stopped, the Jeep's back end fishtailing a bit. Steve ran to Bree's door, and she lowered her window.

"You won't believe it!" he panted. He flipped open the diary. "Look." He pushed the open diary under Bree's nose.

Impatient with the delay, she glanced at the words: *The assayer says there's gold in the mine. Gold. I can hardly believe it. Does he know? This changes everything.* "Who's 'he'?" Bree asked.

"I don't know. But this has to have something to do with her death. We need to talk. Where are you headed?" Steve asked.

"We might have a lead to my family," Bree said. She didn't want to take the time to explain it.

Steve's eyes widened. "I'll come with you. We'll talk on the way." He didn't wait for an answer but got in the backseat with Kade.

"I carry an extra pair of snowshoes; you can use those," Bree said. "But you're going to get cold in those pants." Steve was dressed for the office, not for hiking through heavy snow. The temperature today hovered near zero, and a cold wind blew out of the north. Steve didn't seem to care.

Naomi drove out along the access road to Lake Superior. The waves tossed foam onto the beach, and the wind whistled through the Jeep's grille.

"I'm having a hard time staying on the road," she muttered. Her knuckles were white as she fought with the wheel.

"Want me to take over?" Kade asked.

Naomi nodded and pulled over, then she and Kade exchanged places. The delay made Bree want to scream with frustration. Half an hour later they stopped at the track where Kade had seen the woman.

"This is it," Kade said. "There's too much snow to risk taking the Jeep in. We'll have to go on foot."

Bree let the dogs out. Then she pulled out Pooky, the hat, and the paper bag with Davy's shirt she'd been using as a scent article. She pushed back her hair impatiently as the wind teased it from under her parka hood and blew the curls into her eyes. She knelt beside her dog.

Samson whined as though to ask what was wrong. She put her arms around him. "I'm depending on you, boy. I can't do this alone. Please, please, find them." Samson whined and licked her face. Tears leaked from her eyes and soaked the fur at his neck. Holding the stuffed bear and the hat under his nose, she let Samson sniff them. Then she had him sniff Davy's scent article. His tail began to wag when he smelled Davy's scent.

"Find Davy, Samson." Bree let go of Samson and started after him with her heart in her throat as he bounded away. "Please, God, let it be Davy," she whispered. The cold wind stung her face, but she barely noticed. Intent on keeping up with Samson, she plodded over the snow-covered ground in her snowshoes, not caring whether the rest of the team was managing to keep up. The dogs seemed to know right where they were going. Samson bounded over and through snowdrifts with his nose high in the air. His tail waved grandly, and exhilaration seemed to pour off him in waves.

Bree had never seen Samson so excited. But no, she was setting herself up for a crushing disappointment. At the end of this search, all she was likely to find were dead bodies, not her Davy alive and well. Naomi was probably right: The woman had found the wreckage and had taken Davy's things home to her own child.

But wasn't the wreckage exactly what she'd spent the past year looking for—her husband's and son's dead bodies? With that goal finally in sight, it seemed a poor trophy. Their souls were what mattered. And for the first time in her life, she was at peace knowing they really weren't out there under this thick blanket of snow. Heaven was where they were residing. And as she'd told Anu, she would see them again.

They came to an old road that crisscrossed through the forest, and Bree paused to rest. Steve panted beside her as he hurried to keep up. "This borders Asters land," he gasped, out of breath. His dress slacks were wet with snow. "Another old mine is down that way. That one was abandoned back in the eighteen hundreds and has never been the producer the Copper Queen was."

Kade sat on a stump poking up through the snow and pushed his hat back from his forehead. "I think they've lost the scent."

The dogs nosed around the clearing for several minutes, but it was clear Kade was right. The rising frustration in Bree's heart brought tears to her eyes. They'd been so close.

"Did you see anything else in the diary?" she asked Steve. She'd only briefly skimmed it, but Fay's handwriting was hard to read. It was the only lead they had.

"Truthfully, I just started looking at it this morning. I was almost afraid of what Fay might say about the baby." Steve pulled it out of his jacket. He brushed the snow from a downed tree then settled down on it. Bree pulled out a handful of pistachios. Kade took a few, but Steve, and of course Naomi, refused them. Bree sat beside Steve as he flipped through the pages, skimming quickly. He was used to Fay's poor penmanship and seemed to have no trouble reading it.

About five pages from the end, Steve made a sound. Bree leaned over to see.

Steve read it aloud. "'The most peculiar thing happened today. I was hiking in the woods and ran across a cabin near Big White Rock. I knocked on the door, and a woman I'd met earlier came to the door. I hadn't realized there were any cabins in that area. She seemed scared when I showed up and asked for a glass of water. It might be my imagination, but I thought that old seat in the ravine beside the cabin looked like an airplane seat. I think I might investigate a little more and find out who she is." Bree jumped to her feet. "Big White Rock. You know where that is? It doesn't ring a bell with me."

"I know it!" Naomi put in excitedly. "We're in the wrong spot. It would be quicker to drive to Lake Richmond and go from there. Come on!"

"I know it too," Steve said. "It's near some of my land."

They raced back to the car. Since she knew where they were going, Naomi drove. They headed along snow-covered dirt and gravel roads to Lake Richmond, a small haven for loons deep in the North Woods. Naomi drove the narrow road until it petered out near a stand of jack pine.

"Big White Rock is about two miles west of here," she said.

"Fay didn't say which direction from the rock," Bree said.

"The dogs will know," Kade said. He opened the back hatch and let the dogs out, and they all put on their gear again.

Bree had the dogs sniff the items again, and within seconds Samson had the scent. He raced off with his tail held high. Her heart surged, and she hurried after him, the sound of her snowshoes *whoosh-whooshing* in the cold air. Samson ran as though he knew right where to go. He kept pausing and looking back impatiently as if to ask why she couldn't keep up.

All Bree could do was focus on putting one foot in front of the other. Over wind-swept hills and valleys filled with snowdrifts, they followed the dogs. The minutes ticked by as the sun rose higher in the sky.

They finally reached a creek bed and crossed it, their boots crunching through the top layer of ice to the cold water trickling beneath it. Chilled through and through, Bree willed herself to the crest of the hill on the far side.

Below them in a clearing sat a small log cabin.

"That's got to be it!" Steve shouted.

Excitement ran through Bree like an electric current, and she saw the same thrill on her friends' faces. Bree ran full tilt down the hill to the front door of the cabin. She knocked on the door. "Hello!"

When no one answered, she cautiously pushed the door open and peered inside. Her stomach twisted when she saw the single empty room inside. She saw a box of old clothes beside the door. Samson raced past her and grabbed a toy fire engine in his mouth. His tail beat a furious dance in the air as he licked the toy and whined.

A child had been here, but was it her child? Bree could only watch Samson's reaction and thrill to the possibility. "Where is he, Samson? Search!"

The dog barked then dashed from the room. He dropped the fire engine as he ran toward the backyard and vanished into the woods.

"Wait for me!" Bree ran after him, plunging into the deep shadows of the forest.

Bree could sense Samson's excitement, and it fueled her own. They had to be very close. Kade, Steve, and Naomi thrashed through the brush behind her, but she didn't wait on them. She could conceive of nothing beyond this moment of pushing past brambles, struggling over rough terrain on her snowshoes, and keeping her gaze on her dog. Samson paused at the top of a hill and began to bark excitedly. He disappeared, and Bree struggled on to the top of the slope.

Below her in a clearing sat a woman on a log. Beside her was a small figure. The woman rose and put her hands out as if to ward off the dog's attack, but Samson paid no attention to her. He ran straight to the small figure. Even from here, Bree could see the little boy's fearlessness. He jumped up and ran toward the dog.

"Sam!" the woman cried.

"Sam!" the little boy shouted. He threw his arms around Samson's neck, and the dog licked his face in a frenzied display of joy.

Bree knew her legs were moving, but the scene seemed to freeze as a still life, the air around her a vacuum. Laboring against the atmosphere that kept her from the child, she pushed on, and finally the little boy's face grew closer. He was laughing, and she'd seen that dimpled grin thousands of times. Her gaze traced the contours of his cheeks, his pointed chin, the wide forehead so like her own.

The hair beneath the knit cap was darker than Davy's, but nothing could hide the fact that her son stood before her, alive and well. He looked up, and his green eyes widened. His arms fell away from Samson's neck, and the dog stood still as if he sensed this was Bree's turn.

Bree had almost reached him. "Davy?" she whispered. She wanted to touch him, but what if he disappeared as he always did in her dreams? His face blurred as tears stung her eyes.

"Mommy?" he asked.

The strength drained from her legs and she collapsed to her knees in front of him, her fall cushioned by the snow. His small fingers touched her face with a tentative touch as though he was as unsure of her as she was of him. Bree folded him in an embrace, and he snuggled against her as if there was no place he'd rather be. "Davy, Davy," was all she could say. His hair smelled of wood smoke and little boy. She buried her face in his neck and breathed in the scent of him, an aroma better than any *pulla* or *panukakkua*.

He wrapped his arms around her and burrowed closer. If it was a dream, she wanted never to awaken. He felt whole, but was he really all right? She ran her hands over his back and legs as he clung to her and refused to let go. He didn't wince at her probing fingers but sighed in contentment to be in her care.

Davy finally pulled away. He cupped her face in both his hands, a mannerism she'd almost forgotten. "Where were you, Mommy? I couldn't find you."

"I've been looking and looking for you, sweetheart. Samson and I have never stopped looking for you." Bree was sobbing so hard she could barely get the words out. She'd almost given up, she realized with a sense of shame. How good God was that he had brought this incredible blessing to her.

"I knew you'd find me," he said. "You and Sam." He reached out and caressed the dog. Samson wiggled all over with pleasure and pushed his nose between Davy and Bree. Bree threw an arm around the dog and drew him into the circle. Her family. The three of them.

Kade, Steve, and Naomi reached them. Naomi was sobbing and clinging to Kade's arm for support. Steve stumbled along with a dazed look on his face.

There were tears in Kade's eyes as well, and Bree's heart was touched by his compassion and empathy.

"This must be Davy," he said.

Bree was so full of emotion, she could barely whisper, "Davy, this is Kade Matthews. He's been helping me look for you. Naomi and Steve too."

Naomi knelt in front of them and held out her arms. "Remember Aunt Naomi?"

Davy nodded and limped over for a hug. His forehead wrinkled as he thought. "Where's Charley?" He released her then went back to Bree's arms.

"He's out looking for you. His nose isn't quite as good as Samson's," Naomi said.

There was a bark from the top of the hill, then a reddish shape came streaking toward them, and soon Charley was all over Davy in a dance of joy.

Gradually, Bree became aware of the woman standing at the edge of the group. Her arms hung slackly at her sides, and her face was a mask of misery. Bree stood with Davy in her arms. She faced the woman and wondered what she could say. At least the woman had kept him alive. But why hadn't she brought him to town and reunited him with his family the minute he was found?

"Who's your friend, Davy?"

Her son's small face grew solemn. "Her name is Mother. She takes care of me," he said.

From his short explanation, Bree gleaned a wealth of information. No one else had ever taken her place with Davy. He had never accepted this woman in Bree's place. Her heart was too full to speak. She tried, but nothing came out.

Swallowing, she tried again. "Who are you?" she whispered.

The woman raised pale blue eyes shadowed with sorrow. "Rachel Marks, ma'am."

"I want to know everything," Bree said. "How you found him and why you kept him and where the plane is."

Rachel nodded. "I know."

"Let's take you home, little guy," Kade said.

The woman's gaze darted left then right as though she might bolt, then she slowly reached out a hand and grasped Bree's. "I'm sorry," she said. "I loved him so much, you see." Tears slid down her windburned cheeks. She dropped Bree's hand and followed them up the hill.

Bree carried Davy slowly while the rest of the group hurried ahead.

This was her time with him. She would remember the feel of his small arms clinging to her neck forever. His breath warmed her cheek as she recited everyone who would be glad to see him. "Grammy Anu, Aunt Hilary, Uncle Mason—they've all missed you so much. And remember the twins, Paige and Penelope? You won't believe how much they've grown."

Davy made a little sound of contentment. "Is Daddy coming too?"

Bree caught her breath. She wondered how much he remembered of that terrible day of the crash. "You and Daddy went fishing," she said. "Wasn't it fun for just you and Daddy to go fishing—just the boys?"

"I didn't like it when Daddy yelled."

"Daddy yelled?" Bree asked. Rob had been a loving and caring father. He'd rarely raised his voice to Davy. "Why did he yell at you?"

Davy stiffened, and his voice came out offended. "No, Mommy! At Uncle Palmer."

Confusion made her pause to catch her breath. "Uncle Palmer went fishing with you?"

"I guess so." Then he shook his head. "No, I 'member. He came to visit us at the lake."

"Why would Daddy yell at Uncle Palmer? We don't yell at friends, remember?"

"I know. But Daddy didn't want Uncle Palmer to do some things. Like hurt people. We don't hurt people."

"Who did Uncle Palmer want to hurt?" Bree was growing more confused. Palmer had never mentioned he'd seen Rob and Davy. In fact, he'd mourned the fact he hadn't been able to check Rob's plane before the crash.

"I guess Daddy, 'cause he hit him."

"Uncle Palmer hit Daddy? Where?"

"In the nose. There was blood, and I cried." He said the words matter-of-factly.

"Do you know why he hit Daddy?"

"I don't know," Davy whispered. "But Uncle Palmer found gold."

Gold. The only place he could have found gold would have been at Fay's mine. And Fay was dead. *And so was Rob.* In her diary Fay had written that she wondered if "he" knew. Could the "he" she referred to be Palmer? Bree's mouth was dry with an unnamed dread. Palmer wouldn't hurt anyone. Would he?

Another thought slipped through her mind like a Windigo wraith. *Palmer worked on airplanes in the military.* Bree didn't want to entertain such a thought, but the suspicions were multiplying.

Davy put his palms against her cheeks and pulled her face in front of his. "Don't look scared, Mommy. We got away from Uncle Palmer."

Bree didn't know what he meant, but she decided not to ask him any more questions now. She didn't want him to see her agitation, and he'd been through enough. There would be time to sort it all out later.

"Put your head against my shoulder and take a nap," she told him. "Everything is fine, sweetheart. You're with Mommy now, and we're going to be okay." But even as her son's breathing deepened and his weight sagged in her arms, her thoughts tumbled over one another like rabbits running from hunters. She couldn't believe it, could she? There had to be some other explanation.

"The plane is just over there." Rachel's soft voice startled her so near to her right side.

Bree looked to where Rachel pointed. A deep ravine ran along here. Bree swallowed hard. Rob's body lay there under a blanket of snow.

Naomi came up beside her. "Let me take Davy," she said softly. "Go on. This is what you've been searching for."

In a daze, Bree carefully handed her sleeping son to Naomi. Steve and Kade flanked her as Rachel led the way to the ravine.

"I hope you don't mind, but I didn't want the animals to get the man, er, your husband, so I buried him."

Relief flooded her. "Thank you," Bree whispered. She stood on the edge of the ravine and looked down at the plane. The Bonanza Beechcraft was level with the top of the ravine, and the wind had swept it clear of snow. One wing was shattered and bent, the windshield was missing, and most of the top appeared to have been sheared off.

Bree closed her eyes. She'd searched eleven months for this moment. The crushed plane was mute evidence of the horror Davy had gone through, of Rob's last moments on this earth. Why had it gone down? He and Palmer had kept it in perfect shape. Palmer. Could Palmer have actually hurt Rob? She was afraid to think it through.

She'd come this far. Opening her eyes, she gripped Kade's hand, thankful for his steadiness and concern, then she slid down the ravine to the plane. Steve followed while Rachel turned away and rejoined Naomi and Davy. Bree fumbled at the door, but it refused to open. Kade wrenched it open for her. Though it was hard, she needed to do this—see if there was anything in the plane's cabin that might reveal the truth about what had happened.

She'd expected bloodstains, but the brown seats and effects of the weather hid most traces. Many of the gauges were shattered. Davy's blanket was in the back. It had brown stains on it, which probably accounted for Rachel's decision to leave it behind.

"What are we looking for?" Steve's face was pinched with cold.

"Davy said something strange. He told me Palmer fought with Rob, that he'd found gold, and was planning to hurt someone."

Steve took half a step back. "Are you saying you think *Palmer* might have killed Fay?"

All Bree's doubts coalesced into deep suspicion. "More than that. I think he might have had something to do with the crash. He's an airplane mechanic. He never told me he stopped to see Rob and Davy at the fishing cabin. All he's ever said is how much he regretted being gone so he couldn't check out the plane for Rob. He blamed himself. What if he really is guilty?"

They all fell silent. Bree's gaze met Kade's, and she saw the anguish in his eyes, pain for her. It gave her strength to know his soul was so tuned to hers.

"I'll help you," he said. "Any idea where to begin?" He entered the plane and stooped to look around.

"No. We need to see if we can figure out what caused it to crash." It seemed a hopeless task amid the jumble of debris. "Not that I know a thing about the mechanics of this plane."

Kade knelt and began to go through the rubble. Rob's tool chest lay upended against the rear seats. Tools were scattered beside it. At a loss, Bree knelt and began to pick up the tools with her gloved hand and put them back in the toolbox.

She remembered when Rob had bought these tools. He'd bought a complete set of Stanley screwdrivers because he liked the black-and-white handles. Seeing them here on the floor of the crashed plane pained her. Maybe Davy would like to have them someday.

"Hey, come out here!" Steve called.

Bree scrambled over the wreckage, and Kade followed her. They found Steve crouched under a wing.

"Look."

The jumble of wires he showed them meant nothing to Bree. "What's wrong?"

"Someone has shorted out this fuel transmitter. See this wire? It's been jumpered across the contacts."

"What does that mean?" Bree asked.

Steve sighed. "It would make the gauge read full when it wasn't."

Bree leaned in closer to look and saw something glint back inside the wing. She reached in and touched it. A screwdriver. She pulled it out. It was red, blue, and clear, not white and black.

"Something wrong?" Kade asked.

"This isn't Rob's. He always bought Stanley. This is a Craftsman." She turned it over and caught her breath.

"What is it?" Kade moved closer.

She held it out. The letters PLC were engraved on the handle. "Palmer's initials. He always marks his tools like this."

"Maybe Rob borrowed it," Kade said.

"Palmer never loans his tools."

The silence was almost palpable. "I like Palmer," Steve said. "I always have. Why would he kill Rob? Fay I can understand, if she found out about the gold and wasn't going to go through with the sale. The diary makes it sound like she'd hired an assayer to look at things."

"That might be why she wouldn't let me join her the morning she died," Bree said. "I assumed she was meeting—" She broke off with an apologetic look at Steve.

"You assumed she was meeting Eric," he finished. "It's okay."

"So Palmer must have met her at the mine," Bree continued, "killed her there, and taken her to the cliff to make it look like an accident."

"Maybe," Steve said. "But how do we prove it?"

"We need to get Mason out here for fingerprints," Kade said. "The National Transportation Safety Board too, to investigate the cause."

"Are you guys about done?" Naomi spoke from the top of the embankment. "I'm freezing, and Davy has grown since the last time I lugged him around."

The discovery of Palmer's screwdriver had left Bree shell-shocked. This couldn't be happening. An incident about tools tickled the edge of her memory, but she couldn't seem to grasp it, no matter how hard she tried. It did no good to try to force it.

"We're coming," Bree finally called back.

A few minutes later, they gained the shelter of the cabin. They shucked their snowshoes at the door, then Naomi went to the stove and began to build a fire while Kade went out to split more wood.

Davy opened his eyes when Bree laid him on a cot. She took his coat off and ran her hands over his arms and legs. He winced when she touched his arms. Frowning, she eased him out of his shirt. There were red marks on his arms that looked like burns. She bit her lip. He needed to be seen by a doctor. Continuing her examination, she noticed his leg was still a bit crooked, obviously from a break. But at least he was alive.

He lay quietly under her gentle touch, his eyes drooping as he became warmer. She started to stand.

"Don't go, Mommy," he murmured.

Leaning down to kiss him, Bree caressed his hair. "I'll never leave you," she whispered against his ear. He gave a contented sigh and closed his eyes again. She kissed his forehead and backed away.

Kade came in with an armload of wood. He dropped it by the stove then went to Bree. He touched her shoulder and whispered, "Steve and I have been talking. My cell phone is dead. I'm not sure if the battery needs to be charged or if the service is down, so we can't call for help. Why don't we go for a couple of snowmobiles? It would be easier on Davy if he didn't have to walk, and it's a long way for you to carry him. I'd be glad to carry him, but he doesn't know me. A snow-mobile would have you all out of here in no time."

"That's a great idea," Bree said. "Rachel seems harmless. Naomi and I will find out what we can from her while you're gone."

Kade nodded. "I feel sorry for her. She obviously loved Davy very much." He paused to regroup his thoughts. "We'll be back in an hour or so. There's plenty of wood for the fire." He put his palm against her cheek and smiled down into her eyes. "God gave us an incredible mir-acle, didn't he?"

The touch of his hand added to the crazy sensations swirling inside her. "I can't believe it's real and not a dream."

"Believe it. You've got a little boy to take care of again."

Steve closed the door to the stove and joined them. "Louis Farmer has snowmobiles, and he's only five miles away. We'll get to the Jeep and be back in no time."

Bree nodded. "Just hurry. I can't wait to see Anu's and Hilary's faces."

Kade let the dogs out, then he and Steve left. Naomi followed them out to make sure the dogs didn't trail after them.

Bree's gaze found Rachel standing awkwardly in the corner as if she wanted to escape notice. "Have a seat, Rachel."

Rachel regarded her silently before going to the rocker by the window. She looked out anxiously before easing down into the seat. They sat in silence for a long time.

"Tell me how you found Davy," Bree finally began. "Why didn't you bring him to town to find me?" She struggled to keep the anger from her voice. "Didn't you realize he had a family who mourned him? I thought he was dead."

Tears overflowed as Rachel squeezed her eyes shut. "I—I didn't mean to do anybody any harm. I moved out here to have some peace and quiet." She gulped. "M—my picture had been in the papers for weeks, and I was tired of it. Everyone thought I was responsible when some of my patients died in the nursing home where I worked, and even after the jury said I was innocent, reporters camped outside my house and called at all hours. Everyone saw the accusations, but no one seemed to care when the truth came out." She pressed her lips together.

"What about Davy?"

Her lips trembled. "When the plane went down near my cabin, I rushed to see if I could help. The man was dead, but the little boy was still alive. He kept muttering, 'Sam, Sam.' So I just started calling him that." She looked out the window again.

"He's always called our dog Sam," Bree murmured.

Rachel nodded. "Anyway, he was real bad off. Both legs were broken, and he had a concussion. I didn't dare leave him, and besides, I'm a nurse. No one could take better care of him than me." Tears trickled down both cheeks.

"What about the burns?" Bree wanted to know.

Rachel dropped her gaze. "He tried to start a fire when I wasn't around."

Horror moved in a freezing wave over Bree. "He could have been killed!"

"But he wasn't," Rachel said with a touch of defiance.

Bree thought there was more to the story than the woman was telling, but she'd find it all out later. At least they were minor burns. She would call the doctor right away. "Go on with the rest of the story," she told Rachel.

Rachel nodded. "By the time he was well enough for me to take him into town, I couldn't do it. I never had any kids of my own, you see. Sam—Davy, I mean—he and I took to one another right off."

"Did he ever ask for me?" Bree asked. Jealousy scalded her with red-hot fury. Davy was *her* son. Though she should just be thankful this woman cared for him, she couldn't help the burning resentment.

Rachel nodded again. "In the beginning. As time went on, he seemed content here." She clutched her hands together in her lap. "You have to understand . . . I loved him so much."

Rachel's obvious sincerity softened Bree's anger.

"When the man said people were looking for him, I knew I had to get away."

"What man?" Bree asked.

"I don't know his name, but he's buying the old mine." She nervously looked out the window again, as if searching for something. "He killed the bank manager's wife, and I knew he'd kill me too. I saw him put her body in his trunk."

So it was all true. But why had Palmer killed Rob? Could Rob have threatened to blow the whistle on his plans? Could that have been his motive? She had to find out the truth.

"He knew you had Davy?" That hurt too. Palmer had witnessed her grief all these months, and for the last few weeks, he'd known Davy was alive.

Rachel nodded. "He said if I didn't tell what I saw, then he wouldn't tell that I had Davy."

Bree heard Samson's welcoming bark and went to the door. Before she could open it, Mason burst in with Naomi on his tail. His gaze centered on Bree's face, and he went to her and enveloped her in a huge hug.

"Kade called me on his way to get the snowmobiles. He said his cell phone must have been in a dead spot because he got a signal once he was on the road. Where's Davy?" He spotted the little boy lying on the bed. Tears came to his eyes. "Wait until Hilary and Anu hear. I haven't called them yet. I thought you'd want to surprise them."

"I do," she said, a smile curving her lips at the thought of their wonder. "But there's more, Mason." She quickly filled him in on what she suspected about Palmer.

Rachel stood and turned to the window. Bree watched her as she spoke to Mason. She was wringing her hands.

Mason seemed to absorb it all quietly. "We've got Rachel to testify that she saw him carrying Fay's body, but we need proof he killed Rob."

The distant whine of a snowmobile reached Bree's ears. "Are they back already?" she said, glancing at her watch. "It's too soon."

"It's him," Rachel cried, clearly agitated. "He told me I had to take him to the plane today. I was hoping we'd be gone before he got back. You have to get away; he'll kill you!"

Naomi and Mason stared at her, but Bree ran to Davy and scooped him up. He awoke and smiled sleepily at her. She popped him into his coat. "I've got an idea," she said. She handed Davy to Naomi. "Go with Aunt Naomi, sweetheart. She'll take you out to play with Samson and Charley."

Davy frowned and reached for his mother. It hurt Bree not to be able to take him in her arms.

"What are you going to do?" Naomi asked.

The roar of the snowmobile grew louder. "Mason, grab our snow-shoes from out front. And the dogs—get them in here." Bree snatched up some of the discarded clothes by the door and hurried to the bed. She stuffed them under the blanket to make it look like Davy's small body still lay there.

"Rachel, act like nothing is wrong. Take him to the plane. Mason and I will be hiding nearby. We'll surprise him, see if we can get him to confess. Naomi, keep Davy out of harm's way."

"I don't like this," Naomi said, putting on her snowshoes. The dogs whimpered, sensing something was wrong.

"I don't either," Mason said. "But it's the best shot we've got." He and Bree put on their snowshoes as well.

The whine of the snowmobile stopped abruptly by the front door. "Go, go," Bree hissed. She hurried to the back door and shooed Naomi through with Davy and the dogs, then she and Mason followed. She could only hope and pray Rachel would be able to carry off her part of the plan.

She sent Naomi, Davy, and the dogs off to the west while she and Mason headed east to the plane. "Let's get inside," she told Mason. He nodded, and they climbed inside and crouched down out of sight.

The minutes ticked by as the cold seeped into Bree's bones. Then she heard voices approach.

"Down there," Rachel said.

"At last." Palmer's voice was exultant.

Bree's stomach flipped, and she clutched his screwdriver in her hand.

"I think you should let me confront him," Mason whispered.

"You're backup," she whispered. "He'll think he can overpower me. He won't know you're here, and he'll reveal more to me." Mason sighed, and she knew she'd won.

"Wait here," Palmer told Rachel. "I need to retrieve something from the plane, then I'll be out of your life." The *whoosh* of his snow-shoes came closer.

Bree's chest hurt with tension. Glancing at the screwdriver in her hand, she remembered the incident she'd been trying to think of. When she'd eaten dinner with the Chambers family, Lily had mentioned a tiff they'd had when Palmer couldn't find a missing screwdriver. Evidently, he'd figured out where it was.

Bree rose from her hiding place and held up the screwdriver. "Looking for this, Palmer?"

He stopped in his tracks. Shock slackened his mouth, then his eyes went flat and hard as he recognized the screwdriver in her hand.

"You were our friend, Palmer. How could you kill Rob? Was it because he was going to stop you from getting your hands on that mine?"

"We were buddies," Palmer said. "He should have been excited to be a part of it."

"You never counted on his faith interfering, did you? He told you it was wrong, and you couldn't let him tell Fay about the gold."

"Looks like you've got it all figured out."

"Enough to know you killed my husband. Why don't you tell me the rest?"

Palmer gave her the smile she'd once found charming. "I wanted him as a partner for the new venture. We could have extracted the gold with new technology and made a fortune. He thought we should tell Fay and Steve about the gold and let them decide whether to sell with full disclosure. I couldn't believe it! He wanted to turn down a chance to make millions. Millions! What kind of man would do that?"

"A righteous one," Bree said. This sounded more like the Rob she knew.

Palmer made a face. "I knew he would blab everything when he got back."

"My call didn't help his distraction," Bree murmured.

Palmer grinned. "I thought you'd tell everyone about that."

For a minute what he said failed to register. Then her eyes widened, and she wanted to hit him. "*You* had someone call. There was no other woman, was there? Rob was never unfaithful," she whispered.

"People would think he downed the plane out of guilt."

Bree just managed to keep her shock in check. "Her real name is Lanna Martin, not March, isn't it?"

"You figured that out too, huh? You're smarter than I gave you credit for."

Bree struggled to reconcile this cold stranger with the man who'd been such a good friend. "I met her," she said. The familiarity of the woman's voice hadn't been her imagination. "You went to the lake to make sure Rob hadn't told anyone about the gold."

"I went to try one more time to convince him. I didn't want to kill him, but the creditors were hounding me. I would have lost everything."

"But he still wouldn't listen, so you sabotaged the plane and made sure he wouldn't spoil your plans. You didn't care about killing Davy with him." It was almost too much to take in. "And Fay found out about the gold anyway, so you had to kill her too. I would imagine you called her on her cell phone and had her meet you at the mine."

Palmer shrugged. "Very good."

"The assayer had told her about the gold, and she was going to cancel the sale. So you killed her and put her body at the foot of the cliff." She moved from the plane cabin to the ground and approached him, even though Mason had warned her to keep her distance. She wanted to look in the eyes of the man who'd befriended her, the man she'd turned to when she grieved. Bree wanted to strike him, to put her hands around his neck and choke the life out of him. She stared at this man she'd known and loved as a brother.

In one smooth movement, Palmer's hand dipped into his jacket and came out with a gun. "You wanted to find Rob. Now I'll just have to send you where he is." He cocked the hammer on the gun.

Bree stared into the barrel of the gun. She couldn't let Davy be orphaned. Why hadn't she listened to Mason's warning? At all costs she had to stay out of Mason's line of fire. He would know how to handle Palmer.

Mason popped up with a gun aimed at Palmer. "Throw down your gun," he ordered.

Palmer didn't even blink. His arm snaked out and pulled Bree against him. He pressed the gun against her head. "Drop it, Mason," he ordered.

"You drop it," Mason said.

Bree trembled, but it was more from anger than from fear. Palmer couldn't be allowed to get away with it. "Don't listen to him, Mason," she said.

"You have no choice, Sheriff," Palmer said. "Shoot me, and my gun goes off."

For a long moment, Bree thought Mason would refuse to drop his gun, then a hiss of frustration came from his throat, and he tossed the gun to the ground, where it disappeared into the snow.

"Come along, Sheriff. It's cold out here. I think we can conclude our business back at the cabin." Holding Bree in front of him, he marched his prisoners back up the hill. They met Rachel at the top, too terrified to have considered running for help, Bree imagined.

If only Samson were here. If only she had a weapon. Palmer meant to kill them; she could see it in his darkened eyes, blank as a reptile's.

Inside the cabin, he grabbed a rope hanging on a nail by the door and tossed it to Rachel. "Tie them up. Be quick about it."

Rachel slowly took the rope and tied Mason to a chair, then tied Bree's hands behind her back.

"Make it tight," Palmer said.

Rachel cinched the rope. The rough hemp bit into Bree's wrists, and she winced.

"Now tie her to the chair by the bed." Palmer moved closer and watched as Rachel pushed Bree into the chair and looped the rope around the back.

Bree flexed her muscles, thankful she'd been working out and had muscles to flex. Maybe she could create enough slack to work her way free. She prayed for God to send help. Her mind raced for a way out. The gun pointed straight at her heart. If she could keep Palmer talking until Kade and Steve got back, maybe they could overpower him.

Her heart leaped when she heard a familiar sound at the door. Samson. His low growl told her he knew something was wrong. "How much does Lily know?" she asked, desperate to distract him.

"None of it. She would have talked to Fay. She's way too honest. We always said we balanced each other out." He laughed uproariously at his joke. He motioned with his gun toward Rachel. "Sit down." When she obeyed, he lashed her to the rocker.

Bree had to keep him talking. "So why move Fay to the cliff? Mason would likely have assumed she fell and hit her head at the mine."

"Authorities investigating her death might have found something. I couldn't run the risk. She was already dressed for climbing, and I thought no one would be the wiser."

This was like something out of *Invasion of the Body Snatchers*. The Palmer she thought she knew would recoil at the thought of murder. Who was this man?

"Enough chatter. I'm afraid the time has come to say good-bye, and I have to admit it makes me sad. Lily will be devastated, and I so hate to make her unhappy." His eyes held a sheen of moisture as though he really did regret what he had to do.

"What are you going to do with us?" Rachel asked in a small voice.

"I thought about locking you in the mine and caving it in, but your bodies would eventually be found. I should shoot you, but it needs to look like an accident." His gaze wandered to the stove. "A fire. There will be no evidence left to determine cause of death."

"Our skeletons will be lashed to chairs," Bree said desperately. "And you think that won't look like foul play?" Think, think. What could she use as a weapon?

"I'll have to take that chance," Palmer said. "With a little luck, the rope will burn up too."

How long had it been since Kade and Steve left, maybe an hour? They should be back by now.

Palmer approached the stove and picked up the packet of matches lying there. Samson was growling and whining even louder outside the door. Bree had one chance. She shrieked at the top of her lungs. "Samson, help!"

Palmer brought the gun around in alarm as seventy pounds of brown, black, and white fury crashed through the window. Glass shattered inward with a shower of shards. Snarling, Samson leaped onto Palmer and seized his hand in his jaws. Both man and dog crashed to the floor, Palmer kicking and shouting as Samson pinned him down with his teeth on his arm.

Wriggling her arms in the ropes, Bree felt the strands loosen.

Screaming in anger, Palmer tried to bring the gun up to shoot Samson, but the dog whipped his head back and forth, and the gun flew from Palmer's fingers. With his front paws on Palmer's chest, Samson pushed his muzzle against Palmer's throat.

At the feel of the dog's teeth, Palmer screamed and thrashed. "Get him off me!"

"Lie still, Palmer, or he'll tear your throat out," Bree warned.

Bree finally felt the rope give. Twisting her wrists, she managed to get one free, then the other. She jumped to her feet and dived for the gun.

Bree pointed the pistol at Palmer and moved to untie Mason. "Samson, release," she commanded.

With a final growl, the dog stepped back, his eyes still following Palmer's every move. Palmer shook himself and got slowly to his feet. His wide-eyed stare fastened on the gun in Bree's hand.

"You know you won't use that," he said easily. He started toward her, but Samson immediately moved to block him. The dog's low growl stopped Palmer in his tracks.

"I will shoot you if I have to," Bree said. "I won't let you hurt anyone else." She'd never shot a gun, but she'd empty every bullet in this gun into Palmer if he forced her.

"Sit in that chair," she ordered.

Palmer must have seen the intent in her face, for his smile faded and he moved slowly to the chair. Keeping an eye on him, Bree finally got Mason free and gave him the gun. She picked up the rope and tied Palmer to the chair.

An ironic smile touched the corners of his mouth. "You've surprised me, Bree. I didn't know you could be so ruthless. Have you thought about what this will do to Lily and the girls? You could just let me go. I'll get Lily and the twins and leave town."

"You killed two people, Palmer," Mason said. "Even if she wanted to, I couldn't let you go."

Bree called Samson to her. She saw the bloody tracks he left on the floor. "You're hurt," she said softly. She knelt to check on the dog's wounds. Once she made sure the blood was from superficial cuts, she put her arms around him and buried her face in his fur. He'd risked his life for her. "Thanks, Samson," she whispered as he licked her face. Then she rose to go to her son.

24

Kade and Steve parked the snowmobiles outside Louis Farmer's barn and thanked him. Bree carried her son through the snow to the Jeep. She knew she could put him down and let him walk, but she couldn't bear to let go of him. If God hadn't sent Samson at the right time, they would all be dead. There was no doubt in her mind that once Palmer realized Davy was missing, he would have tracked down Davy and Naomi and killed them too.

Steve and Kade both offered to carry Davy for her, but she refused. She wanted to get him home and pore over every inch of him to make sure he was all right. His good arm clung tightly to her neck, and she breathed in his little boy scent with a joy so overpowering she thought her heart would burst.

He was several pounds heavier and a bit taller; otherwise, he hadn't really changed in the year they'd been separated. But Bree knew he had undergone psychological changes after the ordeal he'd been through. She would ask the pastor at Rock Harbor Community Church if he could recommend a good counselor.

She couldn't seem to shut off the tap of tears. The rest of the family would be overjoyed. Bree could only imagine Anu's and Hilary's reactions. The whole town had mourned with her; now they would all share her joy. Her happiness was tinged with sorrow for what Rob and Fay had gone through. And what Lily and the girls would go through in the years to come.

They reached the Jeep, and she buckled Davy in with the seat belt beside her in the back. Kade drove, with Naomi in the passenger seat and Rachel in the back with Bree and Davy. Steve had offered to help Mason transport Palmer.

Davy leaned his head against Bree and fell asleep before they reached the main access road. Bree curled her arm around him and pulled him close. She'd nearly lost him a second time. Anu and Naomi said coincidence was how a nonbeliever explained God's hand in the world. Now she knew there was no such thing as coincidence. God moved in the world as he saw fit.

They reached the edge of town, and Bree asked Kade to drive straight to Anu's store. Hilary should be there today too. "Lay on the horn and drive slow," she told him.

Kade grinned and obliged. Bree felt like a queen as they rode toward Nicholls's. She lowered the window and shouted into the air, "He's alive! He's alive!" The horn blared in cadence to her shouts.

Davy woke up at the commotion, and she pulled him onto her lap. "Wave, Davy, wave," she whispered.

Folks came to their doors to see what the disturbance was about. "Davy's alive!" she yelled again.

Davy peeked over the side of the window and waved. "Do I know them?" he asked.

"They know you," she assured him. Some ran after the car when they recognized Davy, and by the time the Jeep reached the store, the crowd had grown to the status of a parade.

The Jeep rolled to a stop outside Nicholls's Finnish Imports. Bree threw open the door and scrambled out with Davy in her arms as Anu and Hilary came to the door.

"What is going on?" Anu said.

"I've found him. It's Davy! He's alive!" Bree said through sobs.

Disbelief and shock rippled over Anu's face. Tears began to stream over her cheeks as her expression registered recognition. "Davy?" She closed her eyes then opened them again.

Hilary dropped the white vase she held, and it shattered on the sidewalk. She put her hands to her cheeks and began to weep. Stumbling over the broken pottery, she and Anu ran toward the Jeep.

Bree rushed to meet them. "Remember Grammy, sweetheart? And Aunt Hilary?"

Shyly, Davy nodded. "Grammy gave me Pooky," he said.

The color washed out of Anu's cheeks until she was as pale as the pieces of pottery littering the sidewalk. "It is my Davy," she whispered. She held out her arms, and her grandson looked at Bree then stepped into them.

Anu hugged him for several long moments before she gently passed him to Hilary. Around them, the townspeople murmured, and Bree saw many wiping tears from their cheeks.

Hilary kissed Davy. "Remember me and Uncle Mason?" she asked.

Davy regarded her for several seconds then nodded. "You have a train in the garage," he said. "I saw Uncle Mason. He arrested Uncle Palmer."

Hilary gasped and looked to Bree. Bree nodded and made a shushing motion.

"That's right," Hilary said. "You and Uncle Mason put the train together."

Davy twisted in Hilary's arms, and he looked through the crowd until his gaze found his mother. "Mommy," he called.

Bree knew she would never tire of hearing that word. She went to him, and he reached for her. She pulled him close, and he wrapped his legs around her and put his head on her shoulder.

"I'm tired, Mommy," he said.

"We'll go home soon," she promised. Home. Their lighthouse would be a real home again. The thought brought tears flooding back to Bree's eyes. Though she hated to let go of Davy, she passed him to Naomi and asked her to take him into the store to see if he needed to potty. Quickly she told Hilary and Anu how she'd found Davy.

"Mason has taken Palmer into custody. He killed Fay." She paused. "And Rob."

Hilary gasped and put her hand to her mouth. Her wide eyes filled with horror. "What are you saying?" she whispered. Beside her, Anu swayed, and Hilary put an arm around her mother.

"Palmer found gold in the mine." Bree quickly explained Palmer's schemes.

"Poor Lily," Anu murmured.

The women fell silent. The past months of wrestling with Rob's infidelity had given Bree a taste of what Lily would go through, except Bree had been fortunate to discover her husband really was the honorable man she'd married. Lily would have no such comfort.

Naomi brought Davy back outside, and the family and towns-people milled around, talking and rejoicing with them.

The crowd finally began to disperse, and Bree was ready to head back to the house when Mason showed up. He got out of the vehicle the grimness around his mouth easing when he saw Bree with Davy in her arms. "This makes everything worthwhile." He took Davy in his arms, and the little boy patted his face. Mason's eyes welled up with tears.

"What about Palmer?"

Mason handed Davy back to Bree. "In jail and in shock. I hate to have to tell Lily," he said in a low voice. "I need to find out what this woman knows," he nodded toward Rachel.

"I was just heading home. You can question her there."

While the happy reunions were going on, Rachel Marks had sat motionless in the backseat of the Jeep. Her stony face stared straight ahead, but Bree was sure the woman wasn't as stoic as she seemed. She'd seen the emotion in Rachel's face when she proclaimed her love for Davy.

Kade moved to Bree's side. "Davy's tired, and you're exhausted," he said. "Let's get you home."

"Come with me?" she whispered. He nodded and pressed her hand. She felt the promise in it. The future seemed as bright as the sun bouncing off Lake Superior.

Naomi kissed Bree on the cheek. "Just drop me by my place. I want to tell Mother and then call Donovan and the kids. Emily and Timmy will be so excited to know they can play with Davy anytime."

They piled into the Jeep, and Mason followed in his SUV. Bree dropped Naomi off at the Blue Bonnet then parked in front of the lighthouse. Exhausted from the day, Davy had fallen asleep again, so Bree carried him, eagerly guarded by Samson, up the stairs to his room.

"I'm making coffee," Kade called up after her.

She was so glad he'd come with her. She needed him here, and he'd sensed it. Standing at the door to Davy's room, she realized the room was stripped of his possessions, so she carried him to her bed. She would restore his room before he awakened.

Rachel and Mason were in the parlor when she went downstairs. Rachel stood against one wall with her hands behind her. She pressed herself against the plaster as though she wished she could sink right into it, and Bree felt a twinge of pity for the woman.

"The coffee will be ready in a few minutes," Kade said. He came to stand behind her and put his arms around her waist. She leaned back against him, thankful for his strength.

"Do you want to press charges?" Mason asked Bree.

What could Bree say to that? While she hated that the woman had kept her son from her, Bree was grateful she had saved Davy's life.

Mason waited, and fear replaced the stoicism on Rachel's face.

Bree shook her head. "I'm not going to press charges, Mason. Davy is alive. I can thank her for that. God must have sent her to him."

Tears welled in Rachel's eyes, and she dropped her head. "Thank you," she whispered.

Mason nodded then questioned the woman about what she'd seen, scribbling notes. "I'm going to need an address where I can reach you when Palmer's case comes to trial."

Rachel gave him her brother's address in Chicago. "Can I go now?" she asked.

Mason nodded. She walked to the foyer and looked longingly up the steps. "Could I see Sa—Davy, one more time?"

Bree hesitated and turned to look up into Kade's eyes. "What could it hurt?" he said softly.

Davy was sleeping anyway. She reluctantly left the warmth of Kade's arms to lead the way to her bedroom. Samson lay on the floor beside the bed, and Bree knew it would be many days before the dog let the little boy out of his sight.

Davy lay on her Ohio star quilt with one arm flung out to the side. It was a pose he'd adopted as an infant, and tears clogged Bree's throat to see it again.

Rachel clutched the doorjamb as she watched the sleeping child for a few moments. "Thank you, ma'am," she said. "If he ever asks about me, would you tell him I love him very much? I wouldn't want him to think I deserted him."

Bree nodded. She touched Rachel's arm. "Before you go—I want to thank you for burying my husband." Her grieving for him would begin again, as it must. He hadn't betrayed her, after all. It was going to be hard to forgive herself for the way she'd screamed at him, the accusations she'd flung.

"I knew the boy would want his father buried."

"Thank you then from both of us," Bree said. "And thank you for caring for my son."

"You won't forget to tell him what I said?" Rachel's faded blue eyes swam with tears and a resignation that tugged at Bree's sympathy.

"I'll tell him," Bree said. She escorted Rachel down the steps. "Mason, could you run her to the bus stop? It's a long walk to Ontonagon."

Mason nodded. "Let me get my coat." He motioned for Bree to follow him to the living room.

Bree followed him. "What's wrong?"

"You sure that was wise?" Mason asked.

"I couldn't put the woman who saved Davy's life in jail," she said softly. "And I feel so bad for Lily and the girls. They'll be devastated. I need to go to her."

He pressed her arm. "You've got a little boy to enjoy right now. Give Lily a chance to absorb the blow. She might blame you at first."

He rejoined Rachel in the entryway, and they left.

"It's been quite a day," Kade said. "Ready for some coffee?"

Bree followed him to the kitchen. The coffee aroma made her stomach rumble. "We haven't eaten all day," she said.

"I thought I'd whip us up something. You're all done in." He handed her a cup of coffee. She took a gulp, and the hot liquid began to warm the places that were still chilled.

"First, I need to make up Davy's bed," she said. "Unpack his things. I'd packed them all away."

"I'll help you," Kade said. He carried the boxes to Davy's room.

Bree took great joy in making Davy's bed and putting away his toys while Kade hung the curtains back on the windows.

"I have something else I want to do," Kade said. "Come with me." He led her up the stairs to the light tower. The Fresnel lens glittered in the bright moonlight. "I came by with my electrical kit this morning, but you'd already left. The door was unlocked, so I went ahead and hooked up the electricity to the light." He reached over and flipped a switch.

Light flooded the tower then began to strobe out over the water. Bree let out a cry of delight. She turned to Kade and stepped into his arms.

"You light up everything around you just like this tower," he whispered into her hair. "I'm thankful God brought you into my life." His lips brushed hers in a feathery kiss full of promise.

Then his cell phone trilled.

He sighed and dug it out. "Hello." He listened without interruption. "I'll be right there," he said. He clicked off the cell phone. "It's Lauri. Her car died over by the high school. I'd better go get her."

"Come by in the morning for breakfast."

He smiled and brushed the back of his hand across her cheek. "You're really something, Bree Nicholls."

"So are you, Ranger Matthews." She pressed her cheek against his hand. "See you tomorrow."

"I'll let myself out. The rest of the family will be descending any minute, so take advantage of your time with Davy." He hugged her and quickly walked toward the steps. She followed him as far as the second-floor landing, then waved as he went on down to the front door.

Back in Davy's room, Bree had just placed the last of his books on a shelf when she heard the patter of his feet down the hall. The click of Samson's nails on the hardwood floor accompanied him.

"Mommy?" He stood in the doorway, rubbing his eyes. As his gaze wandered around the room, his eyes widened. "I forgot about my room."

She held out her arms, and he ran to her. "I kind of forgot you too, Mommy. Why did I forget?"

"You'd been hurt, sweetie." She smoothed the hair back from his forehead. "We have lots of time for you to remember everything."

"I'm glad to be home, Mommy." His small face sobered. "Can we go get Daddy and bring him home too?"

Bree's exhilaration faded. "Do you remember the crash, sweetheart? The plane crash."

Davy's eyes grew wide, and he nodded slowly. His green eyes filled with tears. "The plane hit the trees. Daddy yelled."

Bree struggled with the tears that burned in her eyes. "Daddy was hurt really bad. He can't be with us anymore. He would if he could."

Davy buried his head in her lap and wept. "I miss Daddy. She said he was in heaven. Can we go to heaven to see him?"

The floodgates of Bree's tears opened, and she wrapped her arms around her son. Their tears mingled as she cried for her lost husband in a way she'd never been able to before. Her stomach knotted with pain as she wept for the years they could have spent together watching Davy grow up, and for the male role model Davy would never have. Soon she would bring Rob home too, to rest in the Rock Harbor Cemetery with his grandparents.

Davy's tears finally stopped, and Bree's as well. She gathered him into her arms. "We'll see Daddy again someday, but not for a long time. Daddy wants you to grow up to be a fine man, one with integrity and the same kind of strength and honor he had. Someday I'll tell you all about what kind of man your daddy was. All that matters now is that God brought you home, where you belong. Let's thank him for that."

"We have to thank Sam too." Davy reached out and patted the dog. Samson's tail swished eagerly at the attention.

Bree petted the dog. Her own personal "hound" had followed a bit of heavenly intervention and found Davy. He would always be her earthly reminder of how God had searched for her and found her, even as she wandered in her own wilderness.